About the author

Born in Baghdad, Iraq, Siobháin is one of six children born to her Irish mother and Iraqi father. She was educated at Kylemore Abbey, Connemara, and then graduated from the College of Marketing & Design in Dublin. She and husband Ross live in Malahide, County Dublin, with their three children.

Acknowledgements

This book, despite its considerable life cycle, has passed through very few hands, but each touch has had a profound impact on its progress and for that I have to say a few thank yous:

To Nadia and Lara for their positive feedback on a dreadful first draft! Thanks for telling me it was great.

To Emma Walsh, for a first professional view on a raw manuscript.

To Mary in Village Books, Malahide, for her advice and guidance at a time when I faced a wall and found it hard to get over.

To Susan Feldstein for her astute and constructive critique that helped me move this book to the next level.

To Fiona Barron for her legal expertise and contributions.

To the team at Poolbeg, in particular Paula Campbell: Thanks for reading and re-reading the various drafts of *Dark Mirrors*, for your suggestions and direction. Thanks for taking a risk and trusting me to deliver the finished manuscript. Thanks for saying yes and making me smile wider than I've done in years. And to Gaye Shortland, thanks for putting manners on my writing, for your razor-sharp instinct, attention to detail and expertise in turning this rock into a shining diamond.

Apart from those mentioned above, I owe a huge debt of gratitude to a number of people who have advised, guided and supported me in a multitude of ways throughout this entire process:

To Vanessa O'Loughlin at Inkwell for her recommendations: a fantastic resource for writers.

Thanks to authors Michelle Jackson and Conor Bowman for giving me the advice I needed to avoid making a huge publishing error: glad I listened.

To my past colleagues at Eason, who joined me on the last leg of this journey, in particular Maria Dickenson for her good counsel, Stephen Boylan for his patience in listening to me babble, and Alan Johnson for sharing his knowledge and expertise. For Cormac, Wilf, Brian and Rita, who became enthusiastic sounding boards and made this final stretch a whole lot of fun. Their goodwill and genuine faith in my abilities gave me the final push that was needed to get this book finished. Thanks also to Ruth, Lynn, Kevin, Derek, Eamonn, Sandra, Anthony, Niall, Patricia, Claire, Caoilfhionn, and the two Davids, O'R and O'C. It's been emotional!

To my good friend Andrina, for her unwavering positivity and personal strength, always giving, always generous, always there. She's just fabulous!

And Melanie, thanks for listening when I needed an ear, thanks for the advice and the laughs. Just what the doctor ordered.

A special thanks to my parents, Nael and Anne, and my siblings, Nadia, Layth, Lara, Layla and Lydia who have been there for me throughout. A special mention, though, needs to go to Lara for her constant and persistent nagging – yes, nagging. She is one of the reasons why this piece of work was never far from my mind. So Lara, I'm delighted to say, the story is . . . it's done. And as for my brother Layth, well, thanks a bunch, bro – you're the best.

To my husband Ross: thanks for your enduring patience and encouragement and for being there when it mattered. Thanks for your creative spark that helped shape and name this book.

And to my incredible children, Daniel, Lara and Lulu: you are the guys that make me smile every day without fail. Thanks for not minding on those days and evenings when I was busy typing away instead of hanging out with you. When you're old enough to read this, I hope it will make you as proud of me as I am of you.

For my husband and best friend Ross, and the greatest kids a mum could ask for, Daniel, Lara & Lulu, not forgetting Baby James

Chapter 1

Her eyes opened as the weight of his body depressed their mattress. The smell of perfume and alcohol drifted into her slumber while a shaft of cold air chilled the warmth beneath the duvet. She did her best to keep her breathing steady, and inhaled deeply to catch that scent again. It was a sweet smell, slightly musky with essence of heather. Or was it lavender? She wasn't quite sure. A sickly smell. Not his aftershave and certainly not her own perfume.

Well, she silently acknowledged, at least he's come home this time. And, closing her eyes, she let the familiar pictures form of her apparent rival. She assumed, despite his consistent denials, that it was another woman keeping him away from home. It seemed logical and though, as a rule, she hated to generalise, wasn't that what normally happened when a man hit forty? Usually she would challenge him about his whereabouts, but tonight was different. Tonight she felt different. It was comical really, almost like he wanted her to catch him. Had he stopped hiding from her or had he just become sloppy? Careless even. Because she never followed through on her threats. She didn't have the guts. Until now. The clichéd assumptions were always there: they could work through their differences, make it through the "rough patch". And Esmée stayed with him on that basis. It never occurred to her – never, not even for a single moment – that perhaps she'd got it wrong. Lying there beside him, listening to his breathing settle into a steady rhythm, she accepted for the millionth time that she just couldn't help herself. In spite of him, and all the shit that came with him, she did, in truth, love him. But even so, it had to stop. And it was that knowledge that made her different. Lying there beside him now, if only for a brief moment, she felt an enormous sense of relief. It was over.

And, when at last she became drowsy and her eyes heavy, sleep eventually conquered.

She woke what felt like seconds later to the sound of the shower running in the en suite. Her eyeballs felt like they were on fire inside sockets that were a size too small. She swallowed hard to quench the thirst that parched her mouth and, turning towards the closed bathroom door, considered the day that faced her.

He would, she assumed, expect her to say something about his late return. He was probably in there, right now, concocting his alibi. But this morning she had no intention of asking him for an excuse. Resigned and exhausted she threw back the covers, swung her legs to the floor and steered her toes into fluffy pink slippers. Opening the window to welcome the morning sun, she stole a breath of freshness as it rushed past to fill the room. Sensitive to the suddenly silent shower, she warily anticipated his re-entry into the room, bracing herself for what would be the first deliberate task of the day: to behave as though nothing had happened. She was petrified by the fear of failure and at the same time exhilarated by the thought of possible success. Intoxicated by this blend of emotions, Esmée navigated the room blindly, collecting Philip's carelessly discarded clothes while rejecting the urge to bring his shirt to her nose.

Pushing her frustrations aside, for the last time she reached overhead to haul down the silver hard-shell suitcase that sat on top of the wardrobe. Placing it with a heavy bounce on the bed she turned to the various drawers, cupboards and closets to extract, bit by bit, the pieces of his travel wardrobe. She was the expert, having done this so many times before. Suits first, shirts then with matching ties and, of course, underwear, socks and comfortable shoes. When Philip emerged finally from the bathroom she was matching a tie to his striped shirt and, despite her best attempts to ignore him, couldn't help but steal a quick glance in his direction. Even at forty, eight years her elder, he looked fantastic. Regular workouts at the gym took care of that and he was neither shy nor ashamed to admit he indulged in all sorts of body-pampering. Would she miss that body? Perhaps. Before, definitely before, she would have answered yes. But this morning she just wanted to be rid of it, his body nothing more today than a sore reminder of an intimate relationship long since gone. And missed.

"What are you doing, Esmée?"

His question, yanking her back to reality, was laced with impatient disdain and that condescending tone he knew she hated.

"What does it bloody look like I'm doing?" she snapped, unable to hold back the caustic sting while continuing to place his shirts with deliberate care into the case. "I'm packing your case!"

This chore, packing his bags, was one of the many housewifely duties she had accepted over the years. Without fail she laundered his clothes in readiness for his next trip. And recently he seemed to be travelling more often than not, at least twice a month for a week, sometimes two, and as she had stopped asking about the purpose of the trips, he had stopped trying to lie about them. Why she bothered packing for him she wasn't entirely sure. In a way, she supposed, it was a therapeutic exercise, laying item after item carefully into the case, pressing the air out of each new layer, making way for the next. But today her actions were that little bit slower and more deliberate than usual – so conscious of her soon-to-be-estranged husband looming over her, watching her every move with his own level of emotional suspension.

"For God's sake, Esmée!" His whinge was more irritating than usual. "Do you have to make such a meal of it? My flight's not till twelve. What's the story? Have you nothing better to do?"

"Exactly!" She tossed the tie that was in her hand over her shoulder and into the case as she turned away from the packing, pausing as she passed him to give him 'the look'. "To be honest I've plenty to do, so maybe you should finish packing your own bloody case, shouldn't you?"

And with a raised eyebrow she turned on her pink fluffy heels to take her turn in the bathroom. Firmly, but careful not to bang it, she shut the door after her and locked it. Then she took hold of the basin, gripping its white porcelain edge till her knuckles blanched.

"Asshole." The word was muttered aloud, as if she wanted him to hear. Lifting her head she looked at the mess that was her own reflection. "How," she quizzed rhetorically, "can a round mirror hang lopsidedly?" And with a sideways cock of her head she took in all that was wrong around her: the crooked shelf, the wobbly seat, the tilting roll-holder . . . When no answers came from the face that stared back, she turned the critical inspection on herself. "And when do laughter lines become wrinkles?"

Tracing the fine lines around her blue eyes, she followed their short geography that radiated, almost symmetrically, to her cheeks and circled under her eyes. Was she imagining it or were they multiplying right there before her? Resigned to their undeniable existence, she pulled back the thick chestnut tresses that fell chaotically about her shoulders and secured them with a black velvet bobbin. As a child she had hated her hair, puzzled by the envy that the wild locks generated amongst her many girlfriends. A half smile, warmed by the ridiculous memory, helped soften the tired face that watched so analytically. Studying her cheeks, one side, then the other, she sadly conceded that she had stopped noticing or even caring about herself and wondered if it was too late to do anything about it. She rarely wore make-up any more, wore jeans instead of short skirts, and floppy T-shirts instead of tight tops – because now they were more comfortable not to mention practical.

"That's the problem," she chastised her mirror image. "I've become satisfied with being just ordinary."

And with less than half-hearted enthusiasm she set about her every-other-day, apparently completely pointless, cleansing routine.

Although never a beauty, ugly wasn't a word to describe Esmée Myers either. Her zest for life gave her a spark, a spirit, that seemed to make her more attractive than most. It gave her skin a warm glow and her laugh an infectious edge. But there was little sign of that spirit now in the exhausted expression that looked back at her from the lopsided mirror.

The silence on the far side of the door made her a little uneasy. She checked the handle slowly to make sure it was locked – not that Philip would come in after her, but she just wanted to be sure.

What the hell was he doing?

Sitting down on the closed toilet seat, she rested her elbows on her knees and wondered just how long she should stay there in order to achieve maximum effect. Not that he really cared one way or another, she reminded herself, as the smell of fresh coffee reliably informed her he was already downstairs.

"Asshole," she said again, the word slipping out far too easily. She couldn't help it, and anyway he deserved it.

Opening the door to sneak a safe peep out, she spied there on the bed the half-empty case, untouched, just as she had left it. Yep. He deserved it all right, and plenty more besides. Refusing the responsible urge to finish what she had started, she walked past the bed and out of visual range of the chore. Out of sight, she reckoned, out of guilt's range. Instead she chose a much nicer task and went to wake the children.

Her beauties were still fast asleep with the look of encapsulated, if somewhat accidental, angels all snuggled up in their cosy beds. Her pride and joy. She could quite easily watch them sleep for hours, their faces pictures of innocence. Looking about their relatively large room, she conceded, not for the first time, that no matter how often she tidied it would always be nothing more than a tangled mess and fighting the inevitable chaos was futile. Turning off the nightlight, she dragged aside the heavily patterned curtains and pushed open the window, hoping that a bit of fresh air might chase away the musty smell of stale bread, a slice of which was definitely lurking in some dark recess of the room.

All about them were pure white walls, except for one that was festooned with a larger-than-lifesize *Jungle Book* mural. It was their favourite movie; Amy loved Baloo, the big lolloping bear, while Matthew preferred King Louie with his long orange orang-utan arms that swung left and right. When Matthew was four and Amy two, Esmée had focused her once-active artistic talent on this project. For weeks the children watched fascinated as with each new layer of paint their fairytale unfolded magically before their very eyes. The story seemed to tell itself as each day of her personal three-week commission passed and the images began to melt onto the oversized canvas. But for Esmée, her favourite part of this illustrated masterpiece was the dusky blue sky with candyfloss clouds painted overhead. She and the children would often lie on the floor and imagine they were on a deserted country hillside with a big old oak tree at its summit, its broad arms protecting them from the beating sun. And as they lay flat on the 'pretend' soft green grass, if they stared up long enough and concentrated hard enough, they could see the emulsion shapes glide gracefully across their dizzy sky.

In amongst the mess she bent to pick up poor Buzz Lightyear who had lost his wing somewhere in the melange of toys strewn randomly about the floor, accidentally pressing the big red button on his chest.

"To infinity and beyond!" he called.

Appropriate words, she thought, while optimistically seeking out his missing appendage.

Disturbed by the call, Amy stirred in the bottom bunk only actually waking to the whining whinge of Philip's voice.

"Jesus, Esmée! What the hell do you do all day?" His face was contorted with exaggerated disgust as he scanned the room from the doorway. "This place is a disaster – do you not think you should tidy it up?" His comment was thick with intended sarcasm. Without waiting for an answer or responding to his daughter's sleepy call for her father he turned, fresh coffee in hand, and closed himself into his study next door.

Esmée glanced at the figurine in her hand and then to the closed door and was tempted to follow him through it and place the plastic cartoon character where infinity actually had an end. Wisely deciding against it she put the toy in its basket, forcing herself to think of the children.

As always Philip spent the rest of the Saturday morning engaged in his den, doing whatever it was he always did behind that closed door. Esmée, on the other side, tended gently to their offspring and two hours later they all piled into the car. To an ignorant bystander they presented a possible picture of a perfectly happy family.

* * *

As such they drove to the airport: Esmée the dedicated homemaker and he the handsome breadwinner sitting slightly agitated in the passenger seat with the children chirping happily in the back. But as she parked, a little haphazardly much to Philip's continued irritation, in the busy drop-off zone outside the departures terminal she knew different.

He joined her at the rear of the car where she extracted his bag from the boot, eager now to have him gone so she could get on with the next phase of her scheme.

"Here . . ." He handed her a filled-out cheque, his neat scroll presented beautifully, as always, in perfect blue ink. "Your allowance." He pushed the offensive item towards her, frustrated by her momentary reluctance to take it.

Should she?

"And I'd like you to account for it all this time," he said, translating his irritation into an ungracious and nasty action.

She lifted her eyes from the valuable slip of paper to her husband's face and saw, not for the first time, a distance from which she now accepted they could never recover. Taking the cheque from him, she retreated with reluctant acceptance, knowing that to turn it down just wasn't an option. A multitude of stinging retorts queued on the tip of her tongue, itching to be released, but she was tired. Scrapping with him there on the tarmac of the busy airport was pointless. Instead she took a controlled breath and placed the cheque into the breast pocket of her sloppy red fleece. Throughout the entire transaction she held

8

his stare, stubborn, bitter, seething. She so wanted to slap his nasty little face. Could feel the sting in her throat, and his cheek on her hand. But she was helpless, restrained, and once again he had the upper hand. Her inner voice, the voice of command and reason, held her back and reminded her that this would be the last time he could humiliate her. Or so she thought.

"Be good for Mum," he warned the children through the open window, his pointed finger loaded with menacing caution, "or I'll bring you nothing back."

They were used to his abrupt tone. He hadn't always been like that but it seemed that as Matthew and Amy got older, old enough to be more than playthings that could be handed back to their mother, he cared for them and understood them less. This emotional detachment manifested itself as retail substitution and where tenderness and affection failed, gifts delivered. So he bought them whatever they wanted: new DVDs, kitchen sets, footballs, basketballs, rugby balls, new dollies; all they had to do was ask. It drove Esmée nuts because what he so obviously failed to realise was that five minutes of his undivided attention would probably have satisfied them more. Time to stop and play with them and all their fancy toys. But he was always too busy, even to give just a single hour of his precious time. Something always got in the way of his empty promises, something always more important or distractingly significant.

Looking at him now as he threatened their children through the window, those damned butterflies erupted in her tummy. This was a moment, a milestone moment that she would never forget: they were together for the last time as a family unit.

"Goodbye, Philip," she whispered as she watched him go. Sliding back into the driver's seat, she put the car in gear and drove away, glancing only briefly in her rear-view mirror to watch him disappear from view as he entered the terminal building.

Chapter 2

The bell didn't have a chance to finish its cheerful chime before Esmée had whipped open the door to greet her tardy friend.

"Fionnuala Higginbotham," she said in mock reprimand, using the full version of her friend's name purposely, "where have you been? You were supposed to be here an hour ago!"

"Relax, Es," replied her crimson-lipped friend. "I just got a little side-tracked, that's all – but not to worry – I'm here now!" and she raised her arms overhead with regal aplomb, just for effect, before pointing to the large cardboard boxes that sat beside her feet on the doorstep. "Here, help me with these," she directed, bending down to pick the nearest up and thrust it forward for assistance. "And there's a heap more in the car." She indicated over her shoulder with a quick flick of her head towards 'Daisy' parked half-off half-on the kerb at the end of Esmée's short cobblelocked drive.

"Auntie Finyyyyyyy!" came the collective screech of delight as Matthew and Amy, sliding in stocking feet on the timber floor, came to an abrupt halt at the knees of their adored guest.

"Hey there, guys!" Fionnuala cried with equal enthusiasm. "And how are my two favourite buddies today then?" She collapsed to the floor beside them, preparing to wrestle regardless of her skinny jeans and strappy stilettos, and wrapped both of them in her bare arms to plant firm kisses on each of their cheeks.

As always Matthew recoiled, escaping efficiently from her grasp, shrieking wildly. At six years of age, kissing girls, no matter how old, just wasn't cool. He pulled a disgusted face and wiped his cheek with the back of his hand, dragging the bright red lipstick all over his grimacing features – it was all part of a well-rehearsed game.

Fionnuala Higginbotham, or Fin, as she was known to her friends, was Esmée's best and only remaining friend from her Fine Art college days and like a snowfall in summer she, the only daughter of the late Lord and Lady Higginbotham, was extraordinary and totally unexpected. An accomplished honours student, Fin if she so chose would never have had to work a day in her gifted life, but despite this she focused her enormous talent on painting abstract and wholly modern explosions of colour – because she could. This, coupled with her parents' heritage and high profile, meant that she was the golden child of the elite social circle, with her commissions taking pride of place in the homes, offices, restaurants and galleries of the Irish rich, influential and famous. But the thing that Esmée loved most about Fin was that there were very few things she took too seriously, not even herself or her craft, and often she wondered about the sanity of her many customers who paid extortionate amounts of money for a unique signed 'F Higginbotham'. These painted forms, she explained flamboyantly to her many admirers and begrudging critics, came easy to her. Her work, she expanded, was about "the balance of shape, colour and a little bit of madness". But despite her laudatory claims, incredible rise to fame and superfluous earnings, Fin remained a good friend and confidante to Esmée. Her down-to-earth attitude and never-failing ability to always find an alternative outside-the-box perspective was like a magnet for Esmée. She couldn't help but be drawn to Fin's infectious and deliciously spontaneous nature.

Philip, on the other hand, disliked Fin intensely and although he would never openly admit it he resented this single reminder of his wife's wild, blithe and irresponsible days as an art student. With not a good word to say either about Fin or to her, he habitually infuriated Esmée with his persistently offhand and, more often than not, just plain rude comments about her best friend. His attitude was so obvious that to try and conceal it was pointless and the more Esmée pleaded with him to at least try and be civil, the more obnoxious he became until eventually she, with Fin's consent and understanding, simply stopped pleading. But her artistic friend gave as good as she got without ever going so far as to cause further grief for Esmée, refusing – much to Philip's disappointment – to let his nasty jibes get to her. Once again knowledge reigned supreme as Fin quickly and wisely recognised that he feared her because she was a constant threat and a dangerous reminder of what Esmée could have been and still had potential to be.

"What ya doing, Fin?" little Amy enquired with great curiosity as she watched her adopted aunt pull box after box from Daisy's boot.

"Helping your mummy, pet," Fin replied, throwing a knowing glance at Esmée.

With her curiosity unfulfilled, Amy turned instead to her mother. "Mummy, what's Auntie Fin doing with all those big boxes?" she asked, picking up the largest of the lot, almost twice her tiny size. "This can be my house," she declared decisively as it swallowed her up from her teeny head to weenie toes, only for her to trip over the threshold, propelling the box across the hall and her face onto the step, whacking her nose on it.

With the small blood-spill from her nose mopped up and the novelty of Fin's arrival, along with the mystery of the curious pile of empty boxes well and truly dissipated, the children quietly retreated to the den where the prospect of watching Scooby Doo seemed far more interesting than listening to Fin and their mother chat about adult stuff.

Esmée cast a final motherly glance at the now captivated children, gently closed the adjoining doors to the kitchen and leaned against them to breathe deep and then release the captive volume of air slowly through her pouted lips.

"So tell me," she enquired, pushing herself away from the doors to cross the tiled floor and collect two mugs from the cupboard while Fin filled the kettle, "what could possibly have 'sidetracked' you on today of all days?"

And so began yet another tale of Fin's great nocturnal adventures that Esmée, as always, lapped up and enjoyed. For over half an hour Fin recounted her saga while Esmée listened and laughed at what was, as always, a drama. And when the performance was over and her tale finally told, Fin let the laughter die out fully before broaching the subject of what was this day's production.

"So. Are you ready for this?"

The comment thrust Esmée back into her own sense of reality with a reluctant thud.

"I think so," came her sober response.

"And how's your head?"

"Fine. I think." Esmée paused for a moment, looking up to the

14

ceiling, contemplating the lie she had just told before changing her mind. "Actually, I'm scared witless, terrified in fact." Putting her mug down carefully on the table, she stood and moved to look through the windows of the timber doors that led to her small back garden: the little green space that she had tended and planted with brightly blooming flowers and shrubs, her own personal therapy. The garden that after years of attention looked mature and all grown-up, a bit like herself really, she thought ironically.

"Deep down, here," she said, placing her hand over her breast, her breath clouding the glass, "I know I'm doing the right thing, for me anyway. But it's not only me, is it?" She turned back to look for a possible answer, not really expecting or indeed wanting one. "What about Matthew and Amy? Am I doing the right thing for them?" Her heart through her eyes interrogated her friend. "The thing is, it's not just the affairs, Fin, and Christ I could kill him for each of them!" Her head moved from side to side with an air of certainty. "It's what has happened to me. I don't like who or what I have become." Taking a sustained breath, her eyes vacantly scanned the space in front of her. This wasn't the first time she'd had this realisation but having yet to find a satisfying answer she, like an unsettled spirit, kept coming back to haunt it. "I have spent the recent years of my life with a man I promised to love, honour and respect, but he's taken a selfish view of those oaths, expecting me to love him without him loving me back, to honour him while he disrespects me – when all I have ever asked of him is affection and trust and he can't even give me that."

Her words were quiet, considered and controlled as she attempted to reaffirm the reasons why and so answer all her questions and satisfy the part of her that hated anything other than the 'safe' option.

The atmosphere in the comfortable kitchen changed in a mere few sentences from playful to desperate. Sitting back into her chair at the table, Esmée took her head in her hands and, gripping it firmly as if it would explode if she let go, spat out, "Ahhh fuck!"

And Fin simply listened, patiently, affording her friend the opportunity to reason and, hopefully, realise the answers for herself. This was not the first time they had sat and talked like this, or rather that she had listened and Esmée talked. Fin was Esmée's sounding-board and was careful not to influence her decisions, despite her own bad feelings about Philip. She had supported Esmée at every juncture and critical moment throughout her uniquely individual decision-making process. Fin was glad to be there for her friend, proud to be helping, satisfied that she was making a difference.

"Look at me!" Esmée's hands motioned to herself from her head to her feet, to the room around her. "I'm only thirty-two for Christ's sake and already I'm on my own!"

The absolute desperation in her voice scared Fin a little, touching her very core, and taking Esmée's hands in her own she let her friend cry without interruption. They sat motionless, in the kitchen, waiting for the tears to stop. When they eventually did, Fin bent down and picked up her oversized bag and rummaged for a while before eventually extracting a set of keys and, placing them on the table, pushed them towards Esmée.

"It's ready," she said.

Esmée fingered the bunch lightly without picking them up, knowing that to do so was in a way a final commitment to see her plan through.

"Christ, Fin, I don't know . . ." A sense of last-minute panic took over, tears forgotten as she wiped their remnants with her sleeve. "He's a swine, but he's still their father."

"Look, Esmée, I can't really help you here," Fin said firmly, circling the table to kneel by her friend. "You have to believe in yourself and know that you're making the right move. And, believe me, I will support you no matter what decision you make." Massaging the trembling hands she squeezed them tight, her voice filled with such intense emotion that it shook. "What I will say is that when I first met you over twelve years ago you were a wonderful, bright, sparky and passionate girl but for the past four years, probably since before Amy was born I suppose, your spirit has broken. Your spark has gone, your passion is missing. Your belief in yourself as an individual has somehow been beaten from you and, for the first time in ages, I have seen a whisper of that same amazing woman trying to escape from this mundane world that Philip has pushed you into. You have come so far, don't turn back now."

The door from the den opened slowly and Matthew's innocent little face peeped through to the kitchen, calling a halt to Fin's impassioned monologue.

"Are you okay, Mom? Why are you crying?"

His sad eyes peered round at her, protecting himself with the door, afraid of what he might hear or see. He hated when his mummy cried and she was doing it a lot lately. He could hear her at night after she tucked him in and kissed him goodnight. She always smiled at him, ruffled his hair and kissed his crown but he knew different. He would wait for her to go downstairs and then listen hard. He was happy when, by the time he drifted off to sleep, there were no more sounds of his mummy's tears. Daddy was never home when she cried. He liked when Daddy came home because then Mummy wouldn't cry.

The two women looked at each other, the impact of the boy's questions enormous.

"It's my fault," Fin answered quickly, getting to her feet. "I just told Mummy a sad story, that's all."

Esmée went to her son and pulled him from behind the safety of the door into a smothering hug.

17

"Look!" she said, holding his face tenderly close to her own, putting on the biggest and most sincere smile she could muster. "Mummy's not sad, just a little silly, that's all."

Matthew returned his mother's stare and she watched as his own equally unconvincing smile built, cementing itself firmly on his little flushed face.

"Now! How about you get your sister and put your shoes on. Fin . . ." she took on the tone of a thrilling movie trailer, "is taking you on an adventure!" She threw a glance over her shoulder at Fin to signal that things were back on track.

Acknowledging this next step, Fin picked up the keys from the table and threw them to Esmée who, like a baseball catcher, instinctively raised her hand overhead and caught them firmly in her fist.

Chapter 3

Esmée was leaving. She had two days in which to pack and move on. By the time Philip returned from Paris she and the children would be gone. With her resolve firmly back in place, there was no turning back. Not now.

She waved the children and Fin off on their day trip, leaving her a good few hours to get started. She hadn't yet quite decided how to tell him, but that would come. She considered leaving him a note – lying, perhaps, on the kitchen table? She also thought about just calling him on his mobile and telling him over the phone before he arrived home.

Originally, she had thought it best not to say anything at all, to just let him come home, see they had left and punish him that way. But even she knew that that was nothing short of sadistic and discounted it as an option. She accepted that it was based on an unrealistic wish for him to frantically seek her out and beg her forgiveness like a repentant love-crazed fiend, sorry for his misdemeanours. In this particular fantasy he would promise never to hurt her again, to be faithful and to love her till his dying day – a flight of her active imagination for sure and not very likely. She wondered, as she picked up two of the empty boxes and climbed the stairs with a heavy heart but renewed sense of determination, how long it would actually take him to notice they were gone. Surveying the children's room with the empty boxes at her feet, she parked that question.

"One thing at a time, Esmée," she reminded herself aloud and began to sort through and collect the toys and books that she would take for the kids, resisting the urge to reminisce as she went.

After half an hour, both boxes were full. She was careful to pack only the things that she knew they would miss – their favourite teddies, the sleepy story books, jigsaws, games – she sifted through them all, taking some and leaving others. They would, after all, still have to come back here – at weekends probably, she thought, as she closed over the boxes – he was still their father after all. He'll probably see more of them once we're separated, she thought, the ironic realisation driving a searing stake of guilt through her heart, rocking her conscience to its core. And with little else to do except stop or keep pushing forward, she took the first box downstairs to close and seal it. The first was the worst, she mentally rambled, doing her level best to distract herself. The milestone. And after this one the rest should be a doddle. She re-climbed the stairs to get the others. Every other weekend, that's when he could see them, and Wednesday afternoons, she supposed – wasn't that the norm with separated parents?

Bullshit! She kicked back, refusing to give in, defiantly challenging her morbid torturous mood. As it stood, with all his travel they were lucky to spend a full day with him anyway, never mind a whole weekend. Well, he'd have to sort that out for starters. With more than a hint of frustrated malice, she closed over the second box with a firm slap.

Three hours later and the hall was full. The more she packed the more she thought. The more she thought, the angrier she became so that, by the time the boxes and black bags were bursting with clothes, toys and books, she was consumed with furious fathoms of rage, enough to drive the much-needed determination that would carry her further forward. Piling as much as she could into the boot and back seat of her car, while leaving just enough room for herself, she turned the ignition and with one final push on the throttle reversed out of the driveway and turned her back on the house that had for so long been their settled, comfortable suburban home.

Ten minutes and four long miles later through the bustling village she pulled up and parked outside a whole new world.

How is it, she asked herself as she stared at the quaint two-up, two-down terraced cottage with its canary-yellow door, how is it that bricks and mortar can mean so much and make such a difference?

Pushing the key into the latch of Number 6, Brook Lane, she entered their new home. The smell of fresh paint hit her hard as she walked into the living room.

Wow, she thought, casting a glance around her new surroundings. Walking slowly, taking everything in, she toured the open-plan living space and ventured cautiously into the compact but more than adequate kitchen.

The place had, at her cautious request, been freshly decorated and furnished. Although expecting to see a difference she wasn't prepared for how good it felt. An overwhelming sense of achievement and pride filled her as she wandered from room to room. The hard negotiating, to-ing and fro-ing, as she searched for a house to rent, had been worth every secret minute of it. She felt the weight of the whole ordeal lift – and it had been just that, an ordeal. She had never had to parley in her life, well, not seriously anyway, and it had taken every ounce of steel she had within her to stand her ground. With no one beside her supporting and driving her, Esmée had no way of measuring if she had gone too far or if there was more rope to pull. And this was the result. All thoughts of whether or not she'd done the right thing, got the best place, secured the best deal, were abandoned as she turned on the spot, breathing deep the penetrating turpentine whiff, as if it were the scent of a fresh summer's day. It had seemed so much smaller the last time she had stood here but now, freshly painted, it appeared brighter and certainly bigger than she remembered. Finished exactly as she'd asked, with white walls with just a hint of honey mixed in to bring a subtle warmth and highlight the shadows of the simple cornice overhead. She stood in the middle and turned to take in the original features of her new habitat: the cast-iron fireplace with burgundy-and-yellow floral inset tiles, the granite black grate just itching to be lit, tempted by the small turf pile laid out in its hearth. And what about the deep-pile burgundy rug on the polished pine floor or the rotund lamps that sat like two fat ladies topped with wide-brimmed cream hats on either side of the chimneybreast, each casting a warm golden hue into the old room? She could go on and on – about the heavy golden curtains framing the sash windows or the FH painting that hung over the mantel . . . now there was a surprise! A little too much perhaps? Definitely not. It was perfect. And as if to contradict the rooms' humble origins, in the furthest corner sat a flat-screen television complete with DVD and video player.

The kids will love this, she thought, as she sat into the first couch, sinking comfortably into the soft cushions to study and enjoy her new surroundings. It was without doubt a truly wonderful feeling and she let the indecision and stress of the past few weeks lift effortlessly, like bubbles of hot air, from her shoulders. It felt right and she couldn't have stopped the contented smile of self-satisfaction from embracing her whole face even if she had wanted to. Taking the remote control, she switched on the telly.

What a picture, she marvelled as the wide screen immediately filled with a picture-perfect, crystal-clear, high-definition image. Bloody wonderful!

Curiosity finally got the better of her – there was so much to see in this, her tiny haven – and pushing herself out of the comfort of the chair she went to explore the rest of the house with a juvenile sense of anticipation. Like an inquisitive child she opened the new cupboards, fridge, oven, microwave and dishwasher with a combined feeling of bewilderment and delight. And upstairs was no different: the entire house from the ground floor up to the main bedroom had undergone a complete transformation from being an ordinary, tired interior into a warm, bijoux home.

Esmée did her best to contain the excitement that was simmering inside her. She couldn't wait to get unpacked and settled. Hurriedly she unloaded the stuffed car and carted in the multitude of boxes and bags one by one.

Anxious to get the rest of her belongings, she wasted no time in securing the door behind her to take the opposite route of that morning's journey.

She wanted to share this moment with someone. But the mantle of concealment she had created around her left no one but Fin and she was at the movies with the kids. She could have done with the company of either of her sisters, Lizzie or Penny, right now. Loneliness overwhelmed her. She'd just have to wait.

By the time Fin and the kids returned from their escapade, Esmée had packed and stacked the rest of her things and had created a short line of boxes, waist-high, shrouded with the anticipation of new beginnings. Surprisingly there wasn't that much stuff really, much less than she had first thought. But, she found as she treaded the floors, wandering from room to room, there was very little she actually wanted, only what was rightfully hers: clothes, cosmetics, her CDs, a few ornaments and a couple of framed pictures. Philip could have the rest; she knew he would fight her for it anyway. His argument would undoubtedly be that he had paid for it so she could sing for it. And she wasn't that bothered, neither caring for nor wanting any of it and anyway there was no room at the cottage.

Fin was amazed at Esmée's apparent transformation from an uncertain minion to a determined chief. Esmée had been so uncertain, a bag of nerves, but had consistently insisted that this was something she had to do for herself.

"It's time I stood on my own two feet," she had said, turning down the offer of help.

And seeing her now and experiencing the tremendous sense of achievement alongside her, Fin was glad of the refusal, at the same time a little guilty for giving her friend less credit than she was obviously due. Well done, Esmée.

And the effect of her small win was incredible. Esmée's smile radiated joy and corrected, to a degree, her imbalance of self-esteem. She felt fantastic, the best she'd felt in a very long time, with the day's excitement pushing her horrors to one side for a while. She was sorely tempted to keep packing, impatience being one of her failings, wanting to get everything in place instantly. But reason and common sense, for once, prevailed. She couldn't be sure exactly how in the end she managed to control her impulsiveness and she probably never would. Perhaps it was her absolute determination to get this right, not only for herself but for Matthew and Amy too – the last thing she wanted to do was freak them out. A mature decision, she concluded, applauding her own level of self-control. And she felt so much the better for it so that when she settled in for the monumental 'last night', cross-legged and alone on the sitting-room floor, she felt surprisingly alive and a little bit dangerous.

Surrounded by old photographs, letters and general junk from her school and college days, she sipped slowly on a glass of wine while sifting through her life gone by, memories that had lain dormant in a plain brown box under the stairs, unnoticed and forgotten, for almost a decade. Letters, postcards and trinkets. It was odd to sit and relive their moments of glory: an old badge from her first rag week, a train ticket from that summer 'hippie trip' across Europe, flyers from gigs, beer mats with quirky messages written in bleeding ink. An old forgotten life with missed emotions, camaraderie, friendship, mischief, ambition and fun. Lots of fun! All stirred up now to muddy the already cloudy waters with charms and snapshots. A journey through time, an omen maybe: taking back ownership of her life before Philip? She felt odd, a little bitter perhaps, resentful of what she knew she had missed out on. But how could she possibly regret the last ten years? Because without them there would be no Matthew and no Amy and life without them was simply unimaginable. The old faces looked back at her as she sipped on her lonely drink, passing photograph after photograph through her hands and wondering what they were all doing now – they all looked so young – mind you, so did she! All hips and bones! Carefree and beautiful. Fin still saw some of them out and about every now and then. They used to ask after her, but that had stopped ages ago and she wondered if they would remember her now? They were so different: they with their varying degrees of success, not a child between them, living up the single life, late nights and later mornings. Would they even recognise her? She wasn't a patch on the old Esmée . . . Realising she was beginning to wallow, she swallowed the last bitter drop before sweeping everything back into its box. Taping it shut, she added it to the top of the heap in the hall.

Too much melancholy, she told herself before turning out the lights and climbing the stairs to her bed.

Chapter 4

She drove like a novice, deliberate and slow, taking her time down the tree-lined avenue and through the village, with Matthew in the back seat. Feeling exceptionally uneasy she manoeuvred the car through the busy streets, slicing through the elongated shadows cast by the afternoon sun as its rays percolated dramatically through the gaps in the trees. Fin, accompanied by Amy, tailed them with the remaining boxes and bags jammed into her boot.

"Where's this, Mum?" Matthew asked as eventually they came to a slow stop outside the cottage.

"Wait and see," she replied quietly, with more trepidation than excitement. "Wait and see."

"Who lives here?" he persisted.

Esmée took off her seatbelt and turned to look at her son.

"This," she told him calmly, "is our new house, our new home – it's where we're coming to live."

Pausing, she gave him a moment, letting it sink into his six-year-old brain, unsure of what kind of a reaction she should expect. But he said nothing, his eyes, in response, darting frantically between the brightly painted door and his mother and again out the window of the car to further examine the pebbledash walls and pretty flowers in baskets that swung gently in the morning breeze. Esmée could only imagine the thoughts that flitted through his tender mind and tried to encourage him with a smile.

"So what do you think?" she asked.

His response was simple and understandable. "But why, Mummy? What's wrong with our own house?"

"Nothing, honey, nothing's the matter with it – but this house is for us only."

"What do you mean?"

His sudden feeling of anxiety was palpable. She wasn't dealing with this very well – she'd done it all wrong.

"I mean it's for you, Amy and me. Just us."

She should have warned him beforehand, broken it to him with a little more sensitivity.

He stayed quiet for a while, just looking. Esmée knew better than to say anything more, not yet anyway. She could almost hear his mind ticking over, almost see the cogs turn as piece by piece the bits fell into place and the final assumption was gleaned although not necessarily understood. But he said no more, just peered out the window at the two-storey building with the number 6 on its front.

Esmée got out of the car and walked around to open his door. Amy and Fin were already waiting and together they went inside. Esmée and Fin stood back and let the two children wander one after the other through the house. Esmée knew that Amy was too young to even begin to understand the implications of this move, but Matthew, well, he was a smart and sensitive six-year-old and that made her nervous.

"This could go either way," she commented through gritted teeth to Fin as she watched him stroll nervously through the small living space, eventually climbing the stairs behind his decisively more inquisitive sister.

"It's not as big as our own house," he challenged when he returned to stand before her with his hands firmly lodged in his pockets, his furrowed brow exposing his worries as he stood glancing furtively around him, poking at the carpet with his toe. His eyes were wide, his cheeks faintly flushed and his mouth turned slightly downward.

And finally! The question Esmée had been dreading crossed his lips.

"Isn't Daddy coming too?"

There! It was out and the world hadn't caved in around them!

She knelt so that their eyes were level and stroked his face gently. Her voice was soft and bursting with emotion as she tried to answer him as best and honestly as she could without totally freaking him out.

"No, pet, Daddy's going to stay at the other house. But he'll come and visit you and I promise you can visit him whenever you want." She brought her hand to her chest to seal the pledge.

"But won't he miss us?" he asked sadly, mixed up and confused as tears defied the brave tone in his little voice.

"He won't have a chance to miss you," she replied honestly, seizing him into her grasp. "He'll see you more than ever before," she reassured him, holding him tight as if squeezing him might expel the sadness from his tiny, precious body.

"What about my other toys?"

"Well, your favourite toys are right here, in the box beside your bed." She pointed to the ceiling to indicate their presence in the room upstairs. "And if you want to bring anything else just tell me and we can go and collect it."

He thought about this for a while, like an adult taking mental stock of his situation, but it was obviously a little too much and his bottom lip began to quiver.

"But, Mummy," he sobbed, "my friends – they won't know where I live – how will they find me?"

He cried quietly at first, until the swell of emotion brought a wave of tears from a child who hadn't the energy to pretend any more that he was grown up.

As Amy watched curiously Esmée held him close, her heart spiking with the pain she was inflicting on them.

"Don't be silly!" she said, battling with her own failing composure and the hard lump that was threatening in her throat. "Sure we can always show them where we live, can't we?" She lifted his chin with her finger so she could look into his eyes. "Why don't we have Simon, Eamonn and Shane over to play tomorrow after school? How does that sound?"

He nodded gently, liking the sound of the promise, and Esmée could feel his heartbeat settle somewhat but his body still heaved as he held on tightly to her.

"I like it, Mummy," whispered Amy, tugging at her sleeve, obviously feeling left out of the moment.

"That's just fantastic!" Esmée laughed, pulling her little angel into the family embrace. "Now. Why don't we go and have a look at your new room? We'll unpack your toys and you can show me where we should put everything."

"And just look at the lovely telly," she gushed as they passed through the sitting room. "You can watch all your DVDs here. Isn't it great?"

Both children agreed eagerly as they led her to the stairs and up to their new room, leaving Fin downstairs to order the pizza.

That night, with both children fast asleep, Esmée took a framed picture of their father out of one of the still-to-be unpacked boxes and placed it on the bedside locker between them. While they were worried that their dad would miss them, she knew that it would be they who would miss him more. Inexplicably she had an uneasy feeling – she couldn't quite put her finger on it, but something didn't feel right. Putting it down to stress and emotional uncertainty, she closed the door gently behind her, leaving it slightly ajar just in case. She crept downstairs to join Fin, collapsing into her new couch and letting the stress and anguish of the day's events drain from her body in a long heartfelt sigh.

Accepting a much-needed and well-deserved glass of wine, Esmée raised it in a toast to her friend. "Here's to you, Fin! Thank you for everything."

"Here's to you, missus!" Fin toasted in return. "I'm so very proud of you!"

"I'm proud of myself, too," said Esmée, smiling. "I feel weird but nice." She chose not to mention her earlier feeling of disquiet, adopting instead a positive mood. "Excited, I suppose, in a perverse kind of way," she elaborated. "Thanks for all your help, Fin – I couldn't have done it without you, you know."

"I know," came Fin's smug reply, "but hey, isn't that what friends are for?"

They drank their wine in silence and watched the flames that flickered and danced in the fireplace, throwing hypnotic shadows across the walls and onto the ceiling, each mesmerised and preoccupied with her own thoughts.

"When is he due in?" asked Fin finally, voicing what she knew was on Esmée's mind.

"Tomorrow evening, about seven, I think. I'll have to check. I'm debating whether or not to pick him up and tell him face to face."

"He'll run a mile if he sees you sitting there waiting for him! He'll know something's up!" Fin laughed.

"Well, I don't really want to sit in the house waiting for him and I think I have to face him." She took another sip of the anaesthetising ruby-red liquid. "I'll decide in the morning," she concluded, tired of thinking.

"What about your mum and the girls?"

"Yeah . . ." Esmée was vacant, drifting in her response as she considered how her family might react. They knew nothing of her problems with Philip. As far as they were concerned, she and Philip had the perfect marriage. Boy, were they in for a shock! "I was going to call in to Mum in the morning after I drop the kids off. She'll pass the word. I don't know if I could face the girls, not just yet anyway."

She loved her sisters and they were great fun on their own but dynamite when together. Esmée could imagine their reaction and that in itself was reason enough to make her break out in a cold anxious sweat. But whatever they might do, however they might react, for her there was no going back. The girls, along with her mother and brother would just have to deal with it. With self-appointed bravery she raised her glass defiantly.

"The future!" she toasted.

But as she put the delicate glass to her lips, for a second time that evening she was flooded by the troubled feeling that something – something on the fringes of her perception – was badly amiss.

Chapter 5

Esmée pulled into the driveway of her mother's dormer bungalow and parked beneath the sprawling yellow canopy of the laburnum tree. The short pebble path led her to the front door and, using her own key to let herself in, she closed the door firmly behind her.

"Mum!" she called into the hushed silence of her old home.

Putting her bag and keys down onto the ancient mahogany sideboard that had guarded the front door for what felt like centuries, she leaned without thinking towards the gilt-framed mirror to inspect her reflection.

Fixing one of the many loose strands back into the tussle of her hair, she called out once more. "Mum, where are you?"

With their father dead, she and her sisters tried to visit their mum as often as possible. It had been a sudden and utterly unfair end to her dad's rich and still vigorous life. A decorated and dedicated garda, Frank Gill was shot down in cold blood during a bank raid that had gone horribly wrong, and his death had devastated her mother.

"I feel like this," she had said, referencing a single sock she caressed with her fragile fingers, refusing to let it go, its match lost somewhere in the vortex of the hot-press. "I'm useless without him." And refusing to discard anything that still had his smell, kept the sock and everything else in the closet in Penny's old room.

It took a few years before she really began to cope and eventually move on with her life. There were bridge clubs and book clubs and gardening clubs and pensioners' days out almost every other week, but even so the girls kept a close eye on her and tried as much as possible to occupy even a small space within the impossible and very apparent void.

Frank and Sylvia Gill adored each other through all the years of their marriage and, as Esmée's father had regularly boasted, it had been love at first sight. Her heart swelled as she remembered the affectionate looks her parents shared on the night of their last anniversary dinner. Had it really been just three weeks later that they were gathered as a family again to mourn him? If Esmée had not witnessed their kind of love, their kind of true love, she would never have believed it possible. Their intense but tender affection and compassion for each other, even after all those years, spilled over onto their children to whom they had promised that no matter where they would end up in the world, this house, their house, would always be their home. So much was this notion actively impressed on them that in the early stage of Esmée's planning she actually considered moving herself and the kids back to this, her home. It would only have been for a short while, a stopgap of sorts, but in the end she decided against it. Mainly because she knew that her mum would not approve of her plan and would do her damnedest to change her daughter's fragile mind. She predicted that her mother would be bound by her instinct and experience to brand it "a madcap ridiculous idea in the extreme". And after her mother's many years of wedded bliss, how else could Esmée imagine her mother would behave? Was it reasonable to expect her to understand?

Esmée's difficulties were a secret. In the beginning she had confided in her brother Tom who lived in London, had sought his advice, but not recently – recently she had distanced herself from him, for very pertinent and painful reasons. But she hadn't told her mother and sisters anything; she was sure that, for them, a failed marriage constituted a failed wife. As far as they were concerned, she was happily married, living in a nice house with her nice, successful and handsome husband with their two nice and beautiful children. It was all very nice. How much more "nice" could she ask for? And sure why would it or should it be any other way?

Resigned and nervous, she walked down the hall of her family home in search of her mum, instinctively inhaling the smell of the house: vanilla and sweet tobacco. It was a wonderful, welcoming and comforting smell that she had so often tried to replicate with posh candles and scented potpourri, but it was never the same. Eventually she realised that the lifetime of happy memories captured in an aromatic atmosphere was impossible to replicate no matter how hard she tried.

In the kitchen a warm mug of coffee sat half full on the countertop, telling her that her mother wasn't far away, and from the window above the sink she spied her kneeling, tending to the flowerbed at the far end of the garden. These late spring days, it seemed, were spent nurturing the responsive shrubs with beautiful results. She truly did possess the proverbial green fingers and everything she touched really did flourish with a minimum amount of effort. It was innate; she was a plant whisperer, the patience for which Esmée just did not inherit. The only thing her mum wouldn't do was mow the grass – that had always been her dad's job and now that responsibility was sorrowfully fulfilled by young John Sullivan from down the road who for a student's ransom of eighty euro a month tended the front and back lawn once a week.

Esmée put on the kettle and went out onto the deck. Hearing the French doors slide open, her mother turned and looked up.

"Ahh, Esmée, sweetheart!" she exclaimed, a genuine smile lighting up her face. Sitting back onto her heels while resting the trowel and mucky gloved hand on her knee, she shielded her eyes from the sun with the other and smiled up at her daughter. "I didn't hear the car – did you walk?"

Her mother lived only half a mile away and on sunny days, just like this one, Esmée would often drop in, having walked the kids to school.

"No, Mum, not today," she replied, stepping off the deck and onto the uneven, slightly parched lawn to walk towards the gleaming woman.

Bending low, Esmée planted a kiss on her mother's soft plump cheek that smelt, as always, of perfume and powder.

"Give me a hand up, love."

Esmée took the extended hand and gently hoisted her mother upright.

"What's up, Mum?" she asked, noticing the insufficiently discreet wince as her mother used her bent knee to support and push herself up.

"Oh, it's nothing!" came the flippant reply. "I'm just getting old, that's all!" She laughed with forced gaiety as she took hold of Esmée's arm and steered her through the garden, pointing out the progress of her prized gladioli as a distraction.

But even as they inched forwards, Esmée could feel her

mother's weight pressing on her arm and made a mental note to mention it to her youngest sister Penny, a nurse at one of Dublin's general hospitals. Tightening her arm muscles to bestow a little extra support, Esmée helped her mother complete the short amble towards the house.

"How are the kids today?" Sylvia asked. "I missed you at the weekend. Penny and Conor were here yesterday for dinner. We did call but there was no answer at the house. Did you not get the messages?"

"Ehh, no, we were out most of the day," Esmée lied flatly, not sure what else to say to this unexpected question. She hated lying to her mum and was very much aware that the purpose of her visit today was to break the inevitably unwelcome news.

Together they passed into the kitchen through the garden doors, leaving them open in order to enjoy the temperate breeze that nudged and moved the reluctant air inside.

The kettle was just boiling. Perfect timing.

"Let's have a cuppa," her mother announced, conclusively diverting her daughter's uncomfortable attention.

Esmée, not unlike the cornered criminal with no option but to confess, wandered restlessly around the familiar dining space of the kitchen, dragging her fingers across the thick pine table and matching honey-coloured dresser as she passed them by. Undecided as to whether she should sit or stand, she could feel her mother watching curiously as Esmée fidgeted and toyed with the tiny china figurines, collected over years and huddled together on the dresser shelves, their delicate, colourful shapes polished and proud.

This is a bloody nightmare, Esmée's inner voice shrieked, putting one ornament down only to swap it for another. How the hell am I going to do this?

The pain was obvious on her face as her eyes moved

desperately about the room, looking for something else to focus on, settling eventually on one of the many-framed pictures that hung in the informal family gallery on the tired and once delicately patterned wall. She saw herself, her brother and two sisters captured in a smiling instant. She must have been about fifteen when the picture was taken – that would have made Tom seventeen, Lizzie twelve and Penny ten. Looking at the grinning group, she cast her mind back to remember that moment, a snapshot in time. Held by the slightly faded smiling faces, she wondered how they, her siblings, would react to her situation. Despite their differences – with sisters being sisters there had been a few – and the girls were very close. She saw them at least twice a week and spoke to each of them almost every other day and, while every now and then they would squabble and bicker, it was never for very long – no sooner was it started than it was over.

But with Tom it was a little different. They, Esmée and her brother, had a pretty big falling-out when he left his wife for another woman, and things had been strained ever since. If he hadn't left of his own free will Rachel probably would have kicked him out anyway, having caught him in a compromising embrace with a young lady friend at least half his age. At the time Esmée had been so disappointed in him. How long was it now, she asked herself – six, maybe seven months? Close enough that she could easily recall her feeling of absolute disgust. Selfish really, she knew, but she just couldn't believe that he had turned out to be just the same as Philip. She felt betrayed and a little humiliated by the very person, the only person, she had trusted to talk through her fears about Philip's adultery. He was her big brother who had always protected her and she, in return, looked up to him, respected and admired him. Together they had spent hours talking, discussing her suspicions about Philip and what she should or shouldn't do. He talked her through the worst moments and helped her cope. He had comforted her and jeered at her husband when all along he was doing the same thing to his own wife. He had, she decided, betrayed her too. He had let her down. He had let himself down. Adding insult to the already salted wound, his young lady friend disappeared after a matter of weeks. He had let everything go, lost it all, and for what? A quick shag with a slapper called Jacinta, if memory served her right. The outcome of their final confrontation was mutual silence: phone calls, spontaneous visits, casual texts, they all came to an abrupt and concrete end. She refused to listen to what she thought were childish, clichéd excuses. Her instinct at the time was to call Rachel, to console and advise her. But she never did call. Why? Because despite her big brother's poor and reprehensible behaviour she couldn't be disloyal to him like that, and so she chose instead to punish him by distancing herself from him and, in doing so, she served only to punish herself more. She missed him so much, now more than ever, and it hurt.

She wondered how long it would take for her mum to call and tell him what she had done? The spiteful little girl inside her hoped he would feel guilty. She hoped that when he saw the devastation of their, his and Philip's, combined infidelity, by the natural laws of cause and effect he would be sorry for his own as well as Philip's actions. Maybe now he would understand why she couldn't be around him, why she had to separate herself from him.

"Esmée?"

She didn't immediately register her mother's voice nor did she immediately understand the stunned and anxious expression etched on her face. Confused and distracted by her mute rant, it took her a few moments to realise that the cause of her mother's apparent horror was the tears that were flowing freely down each side of her face. She was crying, there in the kitchen, in front of her mother. She was crying. And it was freaking her mother out.

"Esmée? Whatever's the matter?" Embarrassed, not really knowing what to say or what was best to do next, Sylvia moved intuitively to embrace her weeping daughter. Esmée never cried. She was the strength of the family, always had been, keeping an eye on the girls, fixing things, making things right. It was just what Esmée did. She never cried – well, if she did no one ever saw it. Especially not her mum! After Frank's death her eldest daughter had been the tough one, holding everyone and everything together, reversing the roles and mothering both her and her two sisters. So this discovery was alarming, to the point where Sylvia instantly knew that whatever it was, it had to be significant. Taking her daughter by the shoulders she turned her to face her, eager to comfort and anxious to understand.

"Esmée dear, whatever's happened? Please tell me."

Despite herself, Esmée couldn't help the deep sob that erupted like a stifled belch from between her trembling lips. She instinctively moved into the comforting circle of her mother's arms, unfettering the emotion that she had sworn she wouldn't, shouldn't expose.

"Oh Mum, it's such a mess!" Esmée's head found the curve of her mother's shoulder as the dam that had thus far restrained the tears so efficiently finally gave way. It had been a long time since she had been held like this, had her back rubbed and consolatory words whispered gently in her ear. She was twelve all over again and it felt good to be mothered. She too recognised the reluctant reversal of roles, knowing that normally it was she who gave the hugs and platitudes and reckoned that it was only right now for her to be on the receiving end of such a familiar embrace. Memories of her childhood sparked in her mind: that comforting touch, those safe, warm arms, her mother's fresh smell, the transfer of emotion from child to parent, willing the bad things to disappear forever, to make it all right. Yes! It felt good and she didn't want to let go.

Reluctantly her mother extracted herself from the embrace and taking a tissue from what, when they were kids, seemed like a never-ending store compactly concealed up her sleeve, she handed it to Esmée.

"Esmée, please talk to me, tell me what's wrong," she implored.

"I'm sorry, Mum," Esmée sniffed, wiping her eyes. "I didn't mean for this to happen."

"What? Didn't mean for what to happen? Come on sit down, love. Talk to me!" Sylvia moved her towards the table and, pulling out one of the heavy timber chairs, steered Esmée into it. Setting a second in front of the first, she sat down opposite her daughter.

"Now!" she begged, firmly taking hold of her daughter's knees, and to a certain degree, control of the situation.

Sniffing and regaining her breath, Esmée looked at her mother and considered for a moment exactly what she should say and how she should say it. But the words refused to come out, choosing instead to rush around inside her head, like rampant stormtroopers on an international exercise, forming silent statements, none of which made any sense at all. Closing her eyes, she took a deep breath, steeling herself for her mother's predictable reaction, willing herself to be calm as she looked into the beautiful grey eyes in an intensely worried face.

"Mum . . ." She paused, regaining some of her composure. "Mum, I've left him." There! It was out! As simple as that. It felt surprisingly good. Four words forming a remarkable yet basic statement. Taking courage from those first and surprisingly painless words, she scuttled on, pushing the words out before her pluck gave way. "The children and I have moved out. I've left him, Mum."

She felt her mother flinch and visibly recoil, a confused look crossing her face.

"Jesus, Esmée, what do you mean? Left who?" The question

was obviously rhetorical as she continued to interrogate. "Moved out! Where? Why?"

Words failed Esmée. She simply didn't have the vocabulary to explain it properly, the answers being far more complex than their corresponding simply presented questions. It was just too hard, probably impossible, to find a concise way of telling her mother that she had just had enough. And was that reason enough? Could she communicate this to her mother efficiently without it sounding childish, trivial or naïve – or, worse, all three? All she could do was shake her head slowly, lowering it to look at the thinning hands that covered her own, observing the translucency of the ever-loosening skin and avoiding the obvious disappointment and grief that glazed her mother's face.

"My God, Esmée, I knew things weren't good between you and Philip but I never imagined for one minute they were this bad."

"How did you know?" Esmée shot back, astonished by her mother's perceptive comment, forgetting for a moment the drama of her position.

"I'm your mother, Esmée, and I know these things."

Esmée once again found herself in a closed and emotional embrace and, joined together across their knees, they sat in silence for some time letting the information stew and thicken and, for now, there were no more tears.

The clock ticked on the wall and time slowly drifted by, tick after tock, until ultimately it was her mother who withdrew first.

"Ahh look, the tea's cold now. Let me make a fresh pot." Sylvia's words were solid and safe as she stood up with great conviction to once again go about creating the age-old medicinal brew.

Esmée rested her elbows on the table, held her face in her hands and wiped the moisture from her cheeks while watching her mother go through the ritual. Scalding the pot first before pouring the steaming water on top of generous heaped spoons of fresh breakfast tea leaves, she then laid the table with full-fat milk, white sugar, a plate full of Jersey creams, a china cup and a large blue mug. Esmée found her mother's activity soothing and felt her pulse slow down in rhythm to the precise and deliberate movements, and the need to weep temporarily passed. Neither woman spoke, each lost in her own thoughts, as the silver strainer was placed over the mug and the amber liquid poured through its pores. Adding milk and two spoons of sugar, Sylvia handed it to Esmée with a warm smile and a biscuit. That was the wonderful thing about her mum, Esmée thought while taking the first sip of her sweet tea – her mum always knew exactly what to do, seeming to understand almost immediately that Esmée needed time to calm down, to gather her thoughts and straighten things out in her own head before attempting to vocalise them. And Esmée knew that, although they never really discussed it, for her mother the sanctity of marriage was all-encompassing and she too was using this moment of silence to absorb the devastating and morally controversial news.

With her own delicate china cup supported protectively between both hands, Sylvia sat down opposite her daughter.

Esmée was immediately struck by the intense look of worry, cloaked by the encouraging smile, in the depths of her mother's piercing but sympathetic grey eyes. A look so profound that, no matter how well suppressed, it still managed to work its way through the shine of concern and affection.

"Why didn't you come to me before this? Has he hit you?"

"No, Mum, it's not like that. It's hard to explain."

"Well, try . . . what has he done?" She was gingerly seeking an explanation of whatever monstrous act that resulted in this exceptional outcome. And it had better be good.

Esmée tried to ignore the poorly veiled disappointment in her mother's tone and, unable to hold her stare, looked up uneasily at the light that hung over the table. Watching it gently swing in the light breeze from the open door, with its woven wicker shade stained by the years of vaporous flavours from many home-cooked meals, deepened in colour to a rich tan, Esmée considered the best way to answer this simple question. She thought about the first time she had figured out what Philip was up to. Amy was three months old and cutting her first tooth. She vividly remembered the argument, the controlled accusations of insanity and the convincing denials.

"He's been unfaithful to me, Mum," she declared bluntly, laying her palms flat on the table. "Not once or even twice. I'm not exactly sure how many times. For all I know, for the past four years, and maybe before that, Philip has been shagging every woman in Dublin except me." Her head dropped low in shame, waiting for her mum to react, and when she didn't she added: "We don't talk, we don't laugh, we just exist, and I, well, I can't do it any more."

"Are you sure?"

"Sure about what?"

"Well, sure that he's being . . ." But she couldn't bring herself to say the word, "you know . . ." indicating through the movement of her eyes and brows the meaning of 'you know'.

"What? Sure about the affairs?" With targeted childishness, Esmée purposefully placed emphasis on the last word. "As sure as I know that pigs don't fly."

"Have you talked to him about it?"

"Of course I have, Mum – you don't think I've just packed up house and home without trying to sort this out, do you?" She was beginning to lose both her patience and temper, trying hard to remember that her mum was only asking, that she knew no different and was checking to see that her impetuous daughter had, unlike during her many previous crises, checked all bases before reacting.

As if to justify her actions and, she supposed, to help her mother understand, Esmée went through the sequence of events that led to her departure: the discussions, the arguments, the failed counselling and ultimately the icy wall of silence.

"Each time he was so persuasive, Mum. He promised me time and time again that nothing was going on. He swore on Amy's life, for God's sake! And I believed him. I convinced myself that I was just being paranoid, told myself that it was all in my head. But little things just kept happening, little things that nagged at me – they just didn't feel right: receipts for presents I never got, late nights at work, phone calls on his mobile in the evenings, his unexplained absences from work . . ." Esmée laughed bitterly while the words tripped forth.

"And then, then one night he actually called me 'Karen' and I believed him when he apologised, telling me she was this new girl at work. I swallowed it, justifying it to myself by remembering how we used to call you 'Teacher' when we were kids! Remember? What a complete idiot!"

As she spoke, recalling it and so reliving it, her mother sat and listened to the tale, taking it all in, trying to make rhyme and reason out of Philip's actions.

"It all sounds so obvious now, so clichéd . . . anyway . . ." Esmée continued in her matter-of-fact tone, lost in the narrative of the last four years of her ridiculous union to Philip, unaware of the pools that had once again built up in her sad blue eyes, "eventually we stopped making love – there wasn't even sex any more, but I didn't stop trying. I tried to encourage him, to instigate it. I made nice dinners, tried to dress nicely. I even overhauled my underwear drawer thinking I could bring him back, thinking if I made myself look good he'd notice me again, that he'd want me again." Unconsciously she smeared her tears across her cheek and into her hair. Her voice shook and her chest heaved as the depth and reality of the story once again took a hold over her.

"But I stopped in the end because it just wasn't working and his constant rejection was killing me. You know," she confessed quietly, "we haven't had sex in almost two years."

If she was trying to shock her mother with this blatant statement of fact she failed miserably. Sylvia didn't so much as flinch, being at a point way beyond shock. She thought her daughter's marriage was solid – troubled but solid. A bit like hers and Frank's. They'd had their good years and their bad years but they were rock-solid. And in sympathy all she wanted to do was reach out to her daughter, to make it better. She also wanted to castrate Philip. But on the other hand, she wasn't convinced. He just wasn't the type. But then, she thought, is there a type? Swallowing the concrete lump in her throat she held back, knowing that Esmée had to finish this without her and as she did, as any good mother would, she collected her thoughts and composed her reaction and advice.

"And I miss it so much, Mum, I really do. I'm only thirty-two for God's sake. I'm human and I need intimate contact."

Her mother blushed at the notion of her daughter's sexual desires that, if she were honest, she really didn't want to know about.

"Sometimes I just to want to reach out to him, for him to hold me. I'm not after mad raging sex any more, I can live without that, but I can't live without intimacy and companionship."

Sylvia watched and listened in complete dismay as Esmée poured out her heart and, when desperation and the tragic reality of her daughter's circumstances became apparent, she went to her, knelt beside her and cried with her.

"Oh Esmée," she whispered with the love only a mother can possibly give and, placing a gentle kiss on her forehead while wiping away the tears she could catch, repeated her name softly, over and over. "Esmée, Esmée, Esmée, you should have come to me, I'm here for you. We're all here. You might not believe me but I do understand what you are going through. Really I do."

Here she paused. She had her own story. Was now the time to tell it? This was a parenting moment for which there were no instructions, no rulebook. Painful as it was to acknowledge, Sylvia accepted that there were some secrets which, ultimately, were meant to be revealed and that they, in controlled circumstances, could be fashioned to help, perhaps to avoid a repetition of errors or maybe to illustrate simply life's big picture.

What do I do, Frank? she silently asked the spirit that had never left her.

Do I tell her? Can I tell her? But she didn't really need to ask his permission. She could feel him, sense him there with her. He was a presence that passed through her, a pulse of electricity that tickled every nerve-ending on the back of the hand that gently swept the face of their weeping child. He gave his approval and taking a deep breath she knew that the confession wasn't a betrayal but a means to an end. Now more than ever she needed to support her daughter, no matter how painful or humiliating.

"Esmée, your father and I . . ."

Esmée looked upon her mother kneeling at her feet, unable to explain the charge that at that moment connected them so intensely.

"You know there were times when we drove each other mad," Sylvia went on. "Times when we hated, even despised each other . . . it wasn't always a bed of roses." There was melancholy laughter in her voice as she iterated further, needing to put her daughter's plight in context and help her see sense. "We had our fair share of problems."

Sylvia's face coloured strongly and, keeping her eyes low, she stood up with a wince and set about clearing the table. Esmée's gaze followed her with curiosity.

"Do you remember those bunk beds?" It was a loaded question thrown over her shoulder while walking to the sink with the half-empty cups.

"Yes," Esmée answered with a cautious nod, sensing a revelation in the offing, her interest aroused.

"Well, we bought those to make a spare room for your father. We didn't sleep together for the best part of a year, you know."

This was news to Esmée. Her memory of that particular family event was one of excitement and anticipation. She remembered the power of her assignment to the top bunk and Lizzie's relegation to the bottom. She remembered the fun and games that those beds brought, transformed with draped blankets and torches into caves and treasure troves. The move into her little sister's room was made without argument – so releasing the fourth bedroom on the half landing for her dad's new 'study'.

"Christ. Mum, I never realised." She was amazed as slowly the links connected and the revelation finally dawned.

As if proving a point, her mother nodded purposefully. "I know. We made sure that none of you found out." Gripping the dishcloth harder, she continued. "You know, I thought he was having an affair too."

"Dad wouldn't do that!" Esmée leapt up, almost choking on her own breath as she pushed out the objection, shocked that her mother could even think like that.

"Why not?"

"Because he just wouldn't – because he loved you, he loved us!"

"Yes, he did, there's no doubting that, but like you I knew things weren't right. I never asked him and he never told me."

Steam billowed from the tap as she spoke to the water that filled the sink to wash the few dishes.

"Even when he was . . . just before he . . ." the same magnetic charge tickled her skin as she felt his essence brush by, "before he passed away, I thought about asking him but I didn't have the nerve. What would I have achieved if he said yes? Why would I ruin what we had? Why end our time together by looking to the worst of so many beautiful wonderful years?" She passed her hand across her chest and smiled pensively, quietly lost in the memory. "In hindsight," she eventually continued, "I doubt it was true, but if he had done I'd understand why."

"Mum! You're kidding – aren't you?" Esmée found the conversation almost too hard to take. It was certainly taking a turn that she hadn't anticipated. She actually felt nauseous as her mother stated her case.

"We were in a bad place, he and I," Sylvia went on, "and people do funny things when they're depressed."

Esmée's head was reeling, having always thought, never doubted, that her parents had the perfect life, the perfect marriage. Depressed, who was depressed? Her father? Why?

"But we got through it," Sylvia continued as she rinsed the soapy cups under the hot tap. "We kept at it, not only for ourselves but also for you, your brother and sisters."

In that moment Esmée saw her mother in a very different light. She didn't know if she felt respect or pity.

"I don't know what to say, Mum."

"There is nothing to say really," her mother consoled her almost cheerfully. "In those days you didn't go to counselling – you just got up and got on with it."

She came back to the table, drying her hands on a tea towel before throwing it over her shoulder and sitting back down. "I knew my place, and that was to be by your father's side, through thick and thin, to support and care for him. I was his 'other half'! I pushed him when he needed a shove and held him back when he needed to take time out. I listened to the stories from his day when he got home in the evenings and advised him when he needed help. Those stories in the evening over dinner completed my day." She stopped to allow memories that she had blocked out for a long time now to come flooding back. "I used to host the most wonderful dinner parties for his work people, you know." A vacant misty look came over her as she proudly remembered – as they both remembered – those magnificent nights.

Esmée recalled how her mother would rush upstairs to get ready in the late afternoon just before her dad would arrive home, how she wore those brightly patterned maxi skirts and garish ruffled shirts with eye shadow and lipstick to match, and how she always looked and smelled divine. She remembered the way the crystal on the set table would sparkle in the candlelight, refracting through the delicate grooves on the expensive and finely crafted glass, saved for special occasions such as these. Gifts of fresh-cut flowers, boxes of chocolates tied with red ribbon and the embarrassment when she and her siblings were paraded proudly, like good children, in front of Mr and Mrs Whoever! Collectively they would smile sweetly in their best pyjamas, dressing gowns and rosy faces, before being marched up the stairs to bed like the essence of innocence, angelic children that they were! And whilst the guests enjoyed their meal there would invariably be a "mission" to the kitchen to retrieve and retreat with pickings of the sumptuous feast that would have taken the whole day to prepare: filled vol-au-vents, salads, succulent beef, crispy roasties dipped in thick gravy, chocolate gateaux, fruit salad, trifle with whipped cream and the ultimate prize – After Eights! What a coup! To creep back upstairs having successfully scored a couple of those wonderful wafer-thin minty chocolate squares was trophy indeed!

"Your father always said his career in the Force was down to those dinner parties!" her mother said, her adult memories very different to Esmée's. "And despite it all, the ups and downs, we were a great team!" Her tone was upbeat and ceremonious.

They sat for a while, each momentarily lost in their disparate memories of their former years, Esmèe reflecting that her father hadn't in fact advanced much in his career before he was killed. Reluctantly her mother spoke again, breaking the nostalgia of the moment.

"These days promotions happen over a round of golf while in my day it was over a good home-cooked meal surrounded by your happy family. Family values – that's what counted." Her tone was firm and authoritative.

"Mum?" Esmée asked nervously. "Why are you telling me this?"

"I'm not sure. Up until now I've never really spoken about this to anyone – I haven't needed to." She paused, raising her eyebrows in recognition of the extraordinary place in which she now found herself. "I suppose what I'm trying to say is that maybe you need to try and understand why he's behaving like this. Talk to him. Tell him how you feel. You can't give up on your marriage."

"Did you say that to Tom when he walked out on Rachel?" The question, oozing with sharp bitterness, escaped unchecked.

Her mother's face reddened as she hastily replied. "Your brother's situation is different."

"How so?"

"You'll have to ask him that."

Esmée asserted there and then that she had made the right decision in not telling her mother of her plans in advance of their implementation. Either Esmée was totally blinkered or her mother genuinely didn't understand and, while deep down she appreciated the enormity of her mother's shocking confession and was rocked by the possibility of her father's indiscretions, she genuinely doubted her dad had ever cheated on her mother. But one thing was pretty clear: Esmée knew why her mother had made the humiliating confession: she wanted her to stay with Philip, because that's what a good wife does.

Confused, hurt and disappointed, she couldn't wait to get out of the house but she reluctantly stayed with her mother for a little while longer, to answer her questions about where she was now living, how the children were and how she actually planned to survive financially.

"It won't last forever, you know, and what will you do then?" Sylvia remarked. She was referring to the money Esmée's father had left her in his will and which Esmée had put aside for a rainy day – a rainy day that had now clearly arrived.

This final point acted as a full stop to the conversation. It was all a little too much a little too soon for Esmée and, diplomatically, using the need to shop as an excuse, she got up to leave, promising to call her sisters that afternoon.

"They'll be very upset you haven't spoken to them about this before now, so be prepared," her mother warned gently as they walked together to the front door and out to the car.

Esmée rolled down the window to bid her final farewell as her mother bent down to look in at her.

"Esmée, I'm sorry. I don't think I've been much help to you. I know it's very different for you, but please think very seriously about what you're doing."

Esmée smiled reluctantly up at her, doing her best to make the smile real.

"I will, Mum, I promise."

"And no matter what you do, I'm with you, all the way."

With that, she leaned in the window and planted a soft kiss on Esmée's cheek.

"Drive safely, pet!" she called, withdrawing to safety as Esmée reversed out of the driveway.

Chapter 6

Half an hour later and Esmée was wandering vacantly around the supermarket, struggling with a dodgy-wheeled trolley that appeared to mimic her gradually faltering confidence. She felt she was floating, disconnected from reality. Like Big Brother watching his specimens' every move through a lens, she watched herself wander from aisle to aisle, placing apparently essential groceries into the wonky trolley, item by item. Would she even need all this stuff? Would she be back in that house by this time tomorrow? Questions! Questions! Too many questions that, for the moment anyway, were impossible to answer for sure.

As she stood in the queue for the checkout her mobile rang and, digging it from the depths of her bag, she recognised her sister Penny's number.

"That didn't take long!" she commented smartly and without so much as a second thought pressed the reject button, its vibrations a moment later telling her that her sister had left a message, which she also ignored. The morning's conversation with her mum had confused and drained her and she just wasn't willing to go through that again.

It rang again as she packed the shopping into the boot of her car, only this time it was Lizzie.

Well, what did you expect? she asked herself as she again diverted the call, threw the phone onto the passenger seat and drove the short distance from the supermarket to the cottage.

Unpacking the shopping and deciding as she went along where things should go was pleasantly uplifting and magically therapeutic. The house had a delightful warmth and charm that seemed to massage her aching soul and ease all her stresses elsewhere. She glanced at the clock on the microwave and gave herself two hours before she had to collect the kids and with that in mind, sauntered into the lounge, kicked off her shoes and sank into the luxury of the couch. Balancing her freshly brewed mug of coffee on her knee, she let her head tilt onto the soft cushioned back, closed her eyes and rolled her disjointed thoughts round and round, trying to make out the rights and wrongs of it all.

Her mum's words echoed annoyingly in her head. Family values! "Family values, my backside!" she said aloud. It was family values that had helped her put up with Philip for this long but even they had a limit. She didn't want to put Matthew and Amy through this turmoil but, she asked herself: Doesn't there come a point where enough is enough?

She thought about her dad and what he might or might not have done. It was so hard, impossible in fact, to get the earlier revelation out of her mind. She didn't believe it for a single moment – her normally intellectually astute mother must have made a mistake. But what would he want her to do now? She pondered as she sipped her coffee. She was sure that he wouldn't have wanted her to be unhappy, but in her heart of hearts she knew that he would have agreed with his wife. He might have instigated a quiet man-to-man chat with Philip, warned him probably, but his overall advice would probably have been quite pragmatic: put up and shut up. Looking at the chair opposite, she imagined him sitting there, in his woolly cardigan with the brown cross-hatch buttons, his legs crossed, while rhythmically he puffed on his pipe, pausing every now and then to let a billow of smoke escape to the ceiling and catch his breath, ready for more. Scrutinising her, calculating, through the slits of his lids, squinted to avoid the sweet-smelling haze, he would give her his opinion.

"Now you listen here to me, Esmée Jane Gill," she could hear him say.

For a third time that day her phone rang, disturbing the intimacy of her fictitious moment and as her father's image melted away she answered it without saying hello.

His deeply resonant tone sounded in her ear after a short pinched silence.

"Esmée? It's Tom."

"I know," she replied curtly. "I recognised your number."

"How are you doing?" he asked, the sympathy in his tone telling her he knew her situation.

"I take it you've spoken to Mum?"

"Yep."

"Mad, isn't it?" Esmée mocked pitifully, expecting no compassion from her estranged brother.

"Yep."

"Is that all you have to say? 'Yep'?" she quizzed, sitting out the silence before his monosyllabic response echoed.

"Yep."

She couldn't help laughing, genuinely this time, feeling the tension dissipate a little.

"I've booked a flight home," he said. "I'm coming in on the six o'clock flight on Friday. We should talk."

"Okay," she replied, taking the extended olive branch offered, surprised by his sense of urgency but pleased that he thought enough of her to come home. "I'll pick you up. Text me before you take off."

"See you then, and Esmée . . ."

"Yeah?"

"Hang in there."

Despite herself a warm feeling of appreciation came over her as she put down the phone. Her brother was an asshole but he was still her brother. She'd deal with him face to face. Finishing the last of her coffee, she wondered what her state in life would be on Friday: alone, single, or forever married?

Once again, her phone rang. It was Penny, again, and as before she rejected it.

She took her mug into the kitchen, rinsed it and left it on the polished stainless-steel drainer. Then, resting her bum against the counter top, she moved her thumbs with great speed and dexterity around the small key pad to compose a text to her obviously and understandably concerned sisters: **Sorry for silence. Man trouble. Don't want to explain twice. Call to 6 Brook Lane this evening at 6. Es**

It took all of thirty seconds for each to respond with a simple **OK.**

* * *

That afternoon after school, as promised, Matthew's buddies came over to play havoc in the new house. Esmée had told their mothers that morning outside the classroom that she would pick them up after school and drop them home to their respective houses at

56

about five. Each offered to collect her son but Esmée insisted that she would deliver them home, not wanting to have to explain to them, of all people, why she was living in a different house. They'd hear all the details in good time: the schoolyard was alive with busy gossips expertly masquerading as bored housewives eager to share the latest titbits of information. It was there that she found out about the apparently romantic meal Philip had shared with a woman who was definitely not his wife. Susan Morecombe had delighted in complimenting his companion's sleek dark hair and tall slender figure, but Esmée, anxious not to be made a fool of, reversed the role to inform her informer that Philip's so-called date was, in fact, his sister home from Arizona. The memory of Susan's face, a long bony face framed with limp hair, complicated by a mouth full of forwardly aligned teeth that only a horse could be proud of, remained with her still. God knows what Susan saw Philip do with his 'sister' that night to make her cheeks turn red so visibly! If Philip was going to play off-side he could at least have the decency to be discreet.

The boys had great fun that afternoon and she actually heard Matthew boast about his new house. They watched *Shrek*, ate pizza and hunted for bugs in the teeny-tiny back yard. It was a reassuring start.

Amy, on the other hand, was particularly clingy. Usually she'd be in the thick of it with the boys, but not today – today she became Esmée's shadow, following her everywhere, sticking to her side like glue. Together they put bedclothes and towels in the hot press, folded and put away the clothes, found places for toys and finally had tea and juice together at the small kitchen table. And, despite her little lady's odd behaviour, Esmée classed the afternoon's exercise as a complete success.

She took the giddy troupe of boys home at five – they were in great form and eager to come again to play.

Back at the house, promptly at six she heard Lizzie's car pull up outside and moments later the chime of the doorbell. She was calm, composed, ready and standing on the far side of the timber door, hand on the latch, preparing herself to face the girls. She stood for a moment longer, smiling to herself, listening to the almost audible terse whispers of the two on the other side. They had obviously come prepared, having no doubt discussed their combined strategy en route. Lizzie most likely would have taken the lead and purposely collected Penny from the train to brief her. In a way she felt sorry for them because they really had no idea how to deal with the situation, each advising the other quietly as to the best course of action. Their hushed bickering stopped abruptly as Esmée swung the door open and they stood facing her. Armed with a bunch of flowers and two bottles of wine they looked like they had been caught with their hands in the biscuit tin. And for a brief moment they just stood there looking at their elder sister, all fingers and thumbs, not knowing what to say before finally, without consulting each other, they stepped forward in tandem to hold and squeeze her tight.

Esmée broke the ice with a grand but quick tour of the house and while they seemed suitably satisfied with her new environment, they couldn't disguise their concern about the cost.

"How much is it setting you back?"

"It's not bad really," Esmée replied vaguely, not really wanting to reveal the amount, and using her mother's expert diversion tactics pointed out the brilliance of the flatscreen TV with its record and playback facility.

The children, already dressed for bed, were sprawled across both of the two-seater couches watching a Disney DVD, exhausted after the day's events and still a little disorientated. There had been no mention of their father – they were, after all, used to going long periods without seeing him – but Esmée was anticipating a possible bombardment of questions at some point soon. The girls kissed and cuddled their niece and nephew with extra enthusiasm before retreating to the kitchen where Penny rooted for a corkscrew with which to open the wine.

Esmée brought out three glasses and placed them on the table.

"None for me," she instructed as Penny poured. "I have to go out for a couple of hours. Are you okay to hang here till I get back and we can talk properly then?"

Getting them here under false pretences, kind of, was an unfair ploy she knew, but a necessary one. Anyway, she'd be back in no time and would have plenty of time to fill them in.

"Where are you going?" they asked, surprised by her declaration, looking at each other in disbelief.

"I'm collecting Philip from the airport." Esmée tried to make it sound like she was in control and placed the gift of freshly arranged freesias, her favourite, in the centre of the kitchen table while she calmly spoke.

Both sisters stopped and stared.

"What!" they harmonised.

"I'm collecting him from the airport and I'm going to tell him that the kids and I have moved out," she explained coolly.

"You mean he doesn't know?"

"No."

"You've got to be joking!" Lizzie was shocked.

"Fucksake, Esmée! Have you completely lost it?" Penny demanded.

Annoyed by her sisters' outburst, she turned to them. "Maybe I have, I'm not sure. But don't give me that condescending tone – at least wait until you know the full story!"

"I'm sorry, Esmée, I'm just . . ." Lizzie paused, searching for the right word, "surprised, I suppose."

"Apology accepted. Just don't rush to judge me, all right? Look, let me get this over with – I'll come back and we'll talk properly then." She glanced up at the clock and picked her bag off the back of the chair. "His flight is due to land at seven." She paused for dramatic effect. "So if I'm not back by ten, send out a search party." She laughed at the unsmiling stony faces of her sisters, waiting in vain for the gag to sink in. "It was a joke," she prompted dryly.

"Ohhh!" they sang, nodding in unison, not even remotely amused.

Leaving her stunned sisters alone in the kitchen, she snuck past the drowsy kids and left the house to embark on the next stage of her journey. It was just after half six. It took her exactly twenty minutes to get to the airport and another ten to find a parking space.

As she drove round and around the car park she practised her opening lines. Fin was right – Philip would be surprised to see her. She never collected him – he always took a cab and he would ask her why she was there: to which she would reply that they needed to talk. *'We need to talk.'* No doubt he'd say something dismissive like: *'Not now'* or *'Can't it wait?'* And then he'd probably lay on a lame excuse like he was tired or something. But she would have the advantage because he couldn't escape or walk out like he usually did. She would have him belted into the seat beside her and would tell him straight out that she and the children had left the house and therefore him. *'We've left, Phil. The children and I have moved out.'*

It sounded reasonable enough on her own in the car as she drove the marked concrete course. She would take the long way home and that would probably give her thirty minutes with him, thirty-five tops, depending on traffic.

She didn't want to hang around, didn't want to listen to his bullshit excuses and certainly didn't want to go into the house.

'Don't go. Please, Esmée! Don't leave me.'

60

Then she would drop him and go. Simple as that! The less time she spent with him the less time he had to tell her she was mad, paranoid or useless.

The final walk into arrivals enervated her confidence, making her suddenly very apprehensive. Her heart raced and her stomach churned. This was it and she was early. Walking over to the monitors suspended overhead, she checked the aircraft's progress:

EI268 Paris, Charles De Gaul expected 19:05

She checked the on-screen clock in the corner: five to. She had plenty of time. Selecting a chair with a good vantage point she sat down and waited and as she waited she watched.

They came out in groups, the travellers, and as they emerged through the glass doors most turned first left then right, uncertainly, seeking out friends or family, aware that all eyes were on them as they faltered in their tracks. Many eventually broke into relieved smiles as they recognised a familiar face. But her heart went out to those whose welcoming committee either hadn't turned up or were just late. The anticipation of walking through those formidable doors was for nothing as they wandered crestfallen and sometimes angry to the seated area beyond the barrier. But it was those who marched through without stopping that she was most curious about: the voyagers who walked emphatically to the exit without hesitation. Where were they going? Home, perhaps? Business people, experienced travellers, just like Philip, who regularly came out through those doors expecting no one and seeing no one? She looked up at the monitor again: seven o'clock – the plane had just landed. It was early. Shifting in the hard acrylic seat she sat up, honed and alert. She would have to look out for him because he certainly wouldn't be looking for her.

Five minutes, ten minutes . . . he should be coming out any time now. Fifteen . . . twenty . . .

She stood up and walked to the central barrier directly in front of the doors, straining to see if she could tell by the tags on people's luggage or the writing on the duty-free bags where they had come from. They were exiting now in greater numbers and she scanned the faces of each and every one of them mentally checking them off one by one: No! No! No! No!

She thought she recognised his form approaching through the opaque glass only to be let down in the final seconds as the man rounded the opening left by the sliding doors. It wasn't him.

The crowd petered out in waves with still no sign of Philip. Anxiously she moved closer to the barriers, pacing a little but without taking her eyes off those doors.

Shit! I've missed him!

For an excruciating twenty more minutes she scrutinised a further few hundred faces, letting the panic rise unchecked in her gut. She checked her watch once more and only then considered the possibility that he wasn't coming through those mesmerising doors. Keeping a wary eye on them, she went to the information desk flicking her head around each time the doors opened: No! Not him.

"Excuse me!" she called to the ground hostess behind the oversized counter "I'm waiting for a passenger from the Paris flight, but he doesn't seem to have come through."

The manicured woman checked the screen in front of her, tap-tapping intermittently on the keyboard until eventually looking up from the display to confirm what Esmée in her heart already knew.

"They should be all through by now," she said, the sympathetic puppy-dog look in her eyes nothing more than an unsuccessful attempt to placate her, "but I'd wait a while longer if I were you – there are always a few stragglers."

"Right. Thanks," said Esmée, and patting her hand on the

counter she turned away, not quite sure what to do next.

Pulling her notebook from her bag, she checked to make sure she had got the details right. Maybe he'd missed the flight? Then, checking the monitors again she quickly established that there were no other flights due from Paris that evening. Gathering her thoughts she waited, just watching, until finally after an unproductive hour she walked reluctantly and with an air of uncertainty back to her car, with no option now but to go back to the house and wait. She certainly didn't want to call his mobile – she didn't want to lose the advantage of surprise.

It was well after eight by the time she got back to the house. Philip's car was in the driveway just where she had parked it. It hadn't moved. The curtains were still open and no light shone from the inside. Her previous abode was empty. She pulled up to the kerb, turned off the engine and snuck up to the window, like some kind of prowler, to peer cautiously inside.

"Where the hell is he?" she cried aloud and, pushing her key into the door, entered only to be met by an oppressive silence. The house felt stuffy and empty, missing the laughter and games of its recent occupants. She stood in the hall for a while, feeling like an intruder, unsure where she should go before eventually deciding on the kitchen. Putting on the kettle, she made herself some tea then sat at the breakfast bar and began the agonising wait for her husband's return. Where was he? He had to have missed the flight! Getting up, she marched to the phone in the hall and checked the answering machine just in case he had called. No messages from him. It just didn't make sense; she was sure he had said he was in Paris and returning on that flight. Certain, in fact. And even if she had missed him at the airport he should definitely be home by now. Perhaps they'd lost his luggage? Airlines were always doing that to him. She should have waited longer. Should she have paged him? Round and round her thoughts went, confused and erratic, ultimately imagining all sorts of disastrous scenarios. Maybe he'd been knocked down on the way to the airport or maybe . . . My God! Maybe he wasn't coming back at all. He'd left *her*. First.

And as she sat there in the darkness, minding the clock, watching the big hand and eventually the little hand move around its big white face, she couldn't help but think about what her mother had said that morning. Perhaps she was being unreasonable, selfish even. Could she have handled him differently? Was she doing the right thing?

In her mind she finally settled on the notion that Philip's reaction to her newsflash would dictate her next course of action. She was losing her bottle, the wait unnerving her and her resolve wavering. Maybe if she got him to promise to go to counselling again, if he promised to see it through this time, maybe she should stay. Maybe this was the shock that he needed. Maybe he would see the error of his ways? If he came home at all.

She had just called Lizzie on the mobile, to make sure that they didn't take her literally and come looking for her, when she heard a car door slam outside. It was a quarter past ten.

Sitting at the counter now, in her mind's eye she tracked his movements to the door. The knot in her stomach tightened and she could feel the blood throbbing through her veins, its effects concentrated in the edges of her temples. She needed to pee. She needed a drink. She was going to be sick. Quelling the nauseous feeling in the pit of her stomach, she prepared to face him, the last part in her plan, so far.

The front door slammed. Silence. She heard the heavy thump of his case as it hit the timber floor. No movement – obviously assessing the silence around him. Hearing the shuffle of fabric she visualised him taking off his jacket and hanging it on the banister at the bottom of the stairs.

Here we go, she thought, sitting up as his footsteps headed in her direction.

He entered the kitchen and stood in the doorway

"What are you doing sitting here in the dark?" he asked, pressing the light switch on the wall beside him.

Her eyes flinched as they adjusted to the new brightness in the room. She actually hadn't noticed how dark it was. Her throat was dry.

"Where were you?" she asked

"Jesus! What is this, sixty questions?" he retorted.

"No, just the one. I'm just curious to know where you've come from, that's all."

"Well, seeing as I just flew in from Paris one could assume I came from the airport."

His sarcastic reply washed over her as her mind raced forwards, trying to keep one step ahead of him.

"You landed on time then?" she asked innocently.

He looked at her, sensing a trap but not quite sure exactly what.

"No," he said, opening the fridge to extract a beer. "We were delayed an hour."

"Really?" she said, the distrust evident in her tone. "Well, that's funny because I went to the airport to collect you and your flight actually landed five minutes early." She had no idea where this was headed, winging it completely as the plan deviated so far from its original course, his blatant lie ringing a fresh set of alarm bells. "Where were you, Philip?"

"What, are you checking up on me now?"

She heard the defensive anger in the acid tone of his response.

"No, Philip, I actually stopped checking up on you months ago." She had the control and he was cornered.

"What the hell are you up to, Esmée?"

He was obviously totally unprepared for her careless approach.

She knew she must seem different: stronger, intimidating, aggressive even, which was not her style.

"What am *I* up to?" she said, throwing his question back to him, emphasising the "I", pushing back on the guilt because this time, for once, it was she who was 'up to something', something that he would never have suspected. "Well, Philip . . ."

She stood up and rounded the counter to stand tall in front of him.

He had completely ruined her perfectly timed plan and she had now no option but to go for this totally un-rehearsed, un-prepared plan B where, for once, she had the upper hand and was quite enjoying the experience.

"I wanted to collect you from the airport to prepare you for what you would find here when you got back."

"And?" he asked throwing his arms up, swinging them around, splashing beer onto the floor. "What have I found apart from my lunatic wife sitting here in the pitch black?"

"Only because you lied about your flight, otherwise I wouldn't be here at all and, to be honest, I actually don't care where you were or for that matter where you're going, because wherever it is I'm not going with you." She was calm and controlled. Her voice wasn't raised but her diction was clear and her pitch perfect.

His eyebrows furrowed in confusion as she continued evenly.

"What I wanted to tell you was that when you came in that door . . ." she gestured towards the front door, "you would find an empty house because the children and I have moved out."

She hadn't expected to be so abrupt and was surprised by her own forthright offensive. Moving back a pace she raised a hand to her heaving chest. There! It was done.

Philip stepped toward her, towering tall; a menacing blackness crossed his face. For a mad minute she thought he was going to hit her. Gauging the distance she retreated a step back, the sound of her own heartbeat booming in her ears, resounding like she'd run a three-minute mile. She held his stare, his intense, ominous and spiteful stare – she could feel his eyes boring deep into her, feel them clutch her soul and wring it until all remaining feelings she had for him were strangled. She had played her trump card and he had nothing to better it. He had lied to her once too often and this, conclusively, was the final straw.

He took a slow measured stride forward and placed his beer bottle carefully on the counter, then leering down he spat at her through clenched teeth and biting jaws. "Well, what are you waiting for?"

Esmée did a double take. "I beg your pardon?"

"I said, what are you waiting for?" he snarled, his volume rising and colour intensifying, the pressure in the room building as, pointing to the door, he looked down at her and bellowed: "Go on! Fuck off so! Get the fuck out of here and don't bother to come crawling back when you run out of money!"

"What?"

"Are you deaf or something?" he screamed, leaning dangerously close, so close she could smell his alcohol-laden breath.

Without warning he took hold of her hair, gripping it tight at the back of her head, pulling her back till her neck felt it might snap. He walked her backwards then pushed her against the island – she grabbed it to keep her balance. She saw his hand rise from the corner of her eye but hadn't the time to move before it connected hard against her brow.

She swivelled with the force of the blow and fell onto the edge of the island.

"Shall I draw you a pretty picture? Shall I spell it out for you?" he mocked menacingly, following her as she grappled to stay upright, his eyes wild and his face wearing a saccharine smile. He poked his index finger hard into the soft part of her shoulder. "Well? Shall I?" he sneered, pushing her with his finger.

Even her arms wrapped over her head couldn't protect her. She took the second blow to the underside of her cheek. But she didn't fall. Her upper body pivoted from her hips while her hair swung round to stick to the blood that was seeping down her cheek. But she didn't fall.

Picking up her coat and bag, he grabbed her by the shoulder and shoved her towards the door. She winced as his fingers dug in to propel her forward so forcefully that she stumbled, putting her hand to the wall to regain her balance. He pushed her again out into the hall – this time she tripped over his case and fell, hitting her head on the hallstand. Grabbing her by the back of her T-shirt he pulled her up, its neckline cutting into her throat. Her hands grappled at her neck as she tried to release the pressure.

Opening the front door of the house he shoved her through it and out into the balmy evening darkness, throwing her bag and coat after her. She landed hard, face down on the short gravel driveway. The front door slammed behind her.

She pushed herself up, her hand going instinctively to her head. She felt a short sharp pain as she touched the wide gash across her forehead. Stunned and gasping for air she gathered up her coat and bag, struggling to keep her balance as she stumbled towards the car. Fumbling in her pockets she prayed that she had put the car keys in one of them. Her fingers, trembling with fear and shock, finally clutched the familiar shape. Pressing the unlock button on the fob she climbed into the car, locking the doors after her.

Curtains twitched as her old neighbours watched her drive away and, as she exited the quiet up-market estate, her body bruised and cut, shaking with the trauma of the abuse inflicted upon it, she cried from her heart and vowed never, ever, to darken the door of that house again. But it was not a promise she could keep.

* * *

In the darkness of the tall oak trees the man watched the silver Volvo speed jarringly away from Number 12 Woodland Drive. Protected by the deep shadows of the broad foliage, he leaned against the tall tree-trunk and drew deep on the end of his cigarette, its fiery glow highlighting his stern angular features before it was casually flicked into the undergrowth. Pushing himself nonchalantly off the trunk he emerged from the trees, flipping open his mobile as he walked. As he lifted it to his ear he glanced around calmly, ensuring that the previously flapping curtains were once again still.

"He's back," he reported into the handset, facetiously adding, "Seems to be havin' a spot o' trouble with the missus."

He listened as instructions were issued. There were no goodbyes before he flicked the phone closed and walked undisturbed past the neatly parked cars and carefully manicured gardens. Pausing at Number 12 he looked up and down the street once more before approaching the front door, fixing the leather collar of his knee-length coat as he went. He stood still for a short moment in front of that door, priming himself, stretching his neck muscles, until eventually he extended his arm to its full length and rang the doorbell.

A long black shadow bled over the driveway as his broad bulk blocked the bright yellow light that filtered through the glass of door. It was opened sharply to him.

An acid smile stretched across the visitor's face as he spoke.

"How yeh, Philly, man? Are yeh not gonna invite me in?"

Pushing his host roughly back into the house, he stepped forward and closed the door firmly behind him.

Chapter 7

It had been a long night and Esmée, waking slowly, hoped and prayed that she had experienced nothing more than a horrible, horrible nightmare. The excruciating pain that pierced her brow when she turned on her pillow told her otherwise. She had no idea what time it was, her watch having fallen victim to the previous evening's events, a cruel irony considering it was Philip's gift to her on their wedding day. Taking it from her wrist, its sad face crushed and ruined, she cast it onto the bedside table, listening as she did to the empty silence of the cottage. Not a sound.

She wondered who had taken the children to school, knowing full well that one of her sisters would have done so. They had taken over swiftly last night, sweeping into action as soon as she walked through the door. She tried to remember the detail but it was nothing more than a hazy blur. The only thing that was vividly lucid in her memory was the look in her husband's

Neanderthal eyes before he came at her. And as she lay there, her eyes still closed, she focused hard on piecing together the chronicle of the previous night's events.

She remembered stalling the car as she tried to steer it out of the estate, trying to stop her legs from shaking and at the same time co-ordinate the pedals while wiping blood from around her eye. She remembered Lizzie's shocked yelp as she collapsed in the door of the cottage and the explicit profanities that escaped Penny's normally virtuous mouth while tending to the cuts on her face, hands and knees. And she would never forget the chill of the bathroom floor-tiles where she sat and the persistent whirl of the fan as it extracted the smell of antiseptic to the air outside. She recalled her miserable pointless protests at Lizzie's stubborn insistence on calling the police and the somewhat familiar face of the investigating officer who had sat before her, coaxing, encouraging her to answer his probing questions: Who? Where? When? Why? But she couldn't speak. Her head was spinning. She didn't want to speak – his questions were like needles pricking at her brain, making her head hurt more. And was she hallucinating or did Conor, Penny's doctor fiancé, turn up too? It was too much. There were too many of them, she couldn't concentrate and her head was stinging like mad. After that . . . nothing.

Esmée had no idea when or how she got to bed; all she knew was that was where she ended up and where she now awoke. Her body ached and her head hurt. She felt hungover.

Turning slowly out of respect for the throb in the core of her skull, she buried her face in the soft pillow. A mixture of confusion, guilt and humiliation forced its way through the disorder of her thoughts. How stupid was she? She'd thought she was so smart, so in control.

"Esmée, you eejit! You complete and utter spanner," she muttered into her pillow as she remembered with embarrassment how she had challenged him, goaded him, and pushed him to his now apparent limit. Why couldn't she have just kept her mouth shut? If only she'd left well enough alone. If only she'd gone with her first plan of saying nothing. If only she'd stayed put. If only she'd listened to her mother. If only . . . Too late now. Now it was all screwed up and, she believed, it was all her own doing.

She must have fallen back to sleep because when she next opened her eyes Penny was sitting on the side of the bed, stroking her hand.

"Hi ya!" Her vocation was obvious as she adopted her genuinely concerned bedside manner.

"Hi," came Esmée's hoarse reply, her mouth dry and gritty.

"Here, drink this," Penny persuaded soothingly, taking the glass of ice-cold water from the bedside locker and handing it to her, making sure there was grip in her hands before letting go of it.

"What time is it?" Esmée whispered.

"Ten after two."

"Shit!" She tried to hoist herself up without spilling the water. "It hurts like hell . . ." Instinctively she raised her free hand to her forehead. "Who's got the kids?"

"Don't worry. Fin's got them."

"Oh God, I forgot to ring Fin!"

"No offence, sis, but that's the least of your worries! Right now you need to relax. Anyway, we called her for you – once we got you sorted I gave her a shout." She was smoothing out the duvet as she spoke. "Lizzie took the kids to school this morning and Fin's taking them to hers this afternoon. She'll drop them off later on."

With no energy left with which to object, Esmée could do nothing but obediently finish her water under the watchful supervision of Nurse Penny. Her eyelids felt like they had weights attached and she had no strength in her neck.

73

"Conor gave you a sedative last night," Penny explained, busying herself about the room, unable to look Esmée directly in the eye. "So you'll need to take things gently for today anyway. You're going to feel a bit groggy for a while."

"Conor?"

So! She hadn't imagined him. She lay back on the bed, holding her hands over her face in utter mortification.

"So Conor saw me last night," she whimpered, embarrassed and ashamed.

"Esmée, I didn't know who else to call," Penny said, raising her shoulders and pleading forgiveness with her hands. "You wouldn't go to the hospital and that cut on you head is quite deep. You needed him. To be honest, I needed him."

She paused before tentatively pointing out the obvious. "You've taken a bit of a battering. I didn't know what else to do."

"Is it bad?" Esmée asked, spreading her fingers so as to peer through them, then tentatively feeling around the edge of the bandage that covered one of her cheeks and half of her eyebrow.

"Rough enough, but you look worse than it actually is, I suppose."

"Show me."

Taking the small make-up mirror from the wall Penny carried it timidly over to her elder sister.

Esmée looked at the offending item for a moment as if deciding whether or not she really wanted to see. Sitting up, she took it in her hand and, bracing herself, held it up to her face. To a background of Penny's objections, Esmée slowly peeled back the bandage.

"I need to see it," Esmée challenged firmly. The pain as the plaster pulled at her already sensitive skin made her wince. "Ooooh, shit!" While not as bad as she had imagined, it was bad enough. A forlorn sigh said it all as she examined the damage to her face. Her left eye was a complex collection of blues, purples and crimsons. Above her eyebrow, beneath the tidy clinical dressing, a raw gash about an inch long stood out, swollen and raw, against her pale complexion. Broken veins seeped blood under the puffed skin of her left cheek, which had been scratched and grazed by the gravel as she fell. And around her neck a thick red welt formed a perfect choker. And together they looked as sore as they felt.

"Well, that's just great. What am I supposed to do?" Feeling each injury one by one, she looked up at Penny and desperately declared, "I can't let the kids see me like this."

Panic rose in her voice along with the realisation that any attempt at a superficial cover-up was pointless. She felt the hairs rise on the back of her neck and the cold spill of trepidation chase its way down her spine all the way to the extremities of her fingers and toes. Unable to stop herself, she began to shiver, casting the mirror on to the bed.

"What the hell have I done?" she asked herself aloud. "And what am I supposed to do now?"

Bringing her legs up towards her under the duvet and clasping her hands about her knees, she sank her head onto them.

"You haven't done anything wrong," Penny insisted, moving forward to console her, knowing that the words sounded flat and clichéd but she didn't know what else to say right then. There was plenty she wanted to say, but wisely accepted that this was not the right moment.

Esmée felt utterly sorry for herself as well as foolish, not to mention ridiculous, but there were no tears. Just shame and a deep foreboding that whatever change she had instigated last night had reached a level far beyond her original expectations.

"I need a shower," she said finally into the duvet.

She was determined not to be the little bird with the broken wing and, ignoring the discomfort of her movements, unrolled and extracted herself from the tempting refuge beneath the covers. When she stood, her head felt like it might float off without the rest of her body, which weighed an approximate ton. Penny steadied her, holding on until the head-rush passed.

"Do you need some help in there?" Penny asked.

"No, I'll be fine, I think."

"Sure?"

"Yeah, I'll yell if I need you."

"Okay . . . ehhh . . ."

Esmée faltered at the door, casting an uncertain bruised eye back at her sister, who seemed very uneasy, without apparent reason, and extremely reluctant to leave.

"What is it?"

"Nothing."

"No, seriously, what?"

"Okay. Look, the Guards are downstairs – they want to try and talk to you again."

"You're kidding me! Right?" Esmée cried out painfully, throwing an incredulous accusing stare at her sister.

"I didn't call them!" Penny defended herself, holding her hands up and shaking her head. "Lizzie did it last night but you weren't in a fit state to talk, so they've come back today to speak to you, that's all." The words rushed forth, a weak attempt to exonerate herself and allocate the blame elsewhere.

"Are you crazy? Why on earth would I speak to them?"

"Esmée!" Penny implored, a little bit shocked by her sister's attitude.

"No way, Penny, I'm sorry. I know you all mean really well, but no way!"

Using the wall as support before her trembling knees yielded to the pressure of her body, she steadied herself and felt her way into the bathroom.

Then Penny heard the bang of the door and click of the lock. Running her hands through her hair, she followed in her sister's tracks in disbelief. Standing at the door, she knocked gently, waiting hands on hips for a reply from the far side. When none was forthcoming she spoke firmly but quietly through its timber, conscious of the two officers sitting only feet from the bottom of the stairs.

"Esmée! You have to talk to them. You can't let Philip get away with this. It's not right."

The door opened with a sharp yank and Esmée motioned frantically for her to enter. Closing it after Penny, she whispered doggedly, "My God, Penny, what do you want me to say to them?" Her finger pointed through the floor to the room below. "Yes, Officer," she said sarcastically, folding her arms in front of her, wagging her head as she spoke, "I'm the thick housewife with the madcap plan of the century for the great escape – it didn't go quite as planned and now I'm screwed!"

"How about telling them what happened?" Penny persisted. "Tell them how you got those!" She was getting cross now and speared her index finger towards the cuts on Esmée's face. Her frequent exposure to women just like this allowed her to see immediately that she was getting nowhere so, shifting approach and keeping her tone sympathetic but firm, she tried to penetrate the classic blank wall of resistance that her sister was fast constructing. "Esmée, for God's sake, I see this every bloody day in work: women whose husbands go too far but who never do anything about it." Pausing, she hoped that the weight of her professional knowledge and experience would sink in. "They don't want to say anything either but most of them end up right back in casualty in a worse state than the last time. This can't be you, Esmée. You have to tell them. I can't see you like this again."

"Penny. Let's be clear about this." Esmée was doing all she

could to keep her cool. "There is a huge difference, because I'm not going back. Am I?"

But Penny stood firm, unconvinced, eyeballing her sister and shaking her head in incredulity.

"Look," Esmée pleaded, exasperated by her persistence, "this is between Philip and me." Sitting down on the edge of the bath, hoping not to faint, she tried to explain her point of view. "What he did was wrong. It was scary and, yes, it was vicious. Yes, I feel like shit and I have no intention of letting him get away with it." Gripping the white sides of the bath to steady herself, she wished Penny would understand and just back off. "But I'll deal with this in my own time and in my own way." She held on and focused into a stubborn stare. "I told him I was leaving him, taking his kids away for heaven's sake. Is it any wonder he went berserk?"

Casting professionalism aside, Penny snapped back. "That's no bloody excuse, Esmée Myers, and you know it! But if that's what you really think, well, you tell that to them because I don't buy it." And, throwing one last stinging glare, she swung the door open and slammed it after her.

Esmée understood that Penny was upset, almost on the verge of tears. She'd be the same, worse even, if she were in Penny's shoes – but she didn't think she could face the humiliation of talking about what had happened. In a mere few hours she had been robbed of her dignity, her pride had been crushed and she felt disgraced and mortified. And now, dealing with all that, she was expected to stand in front of strangers and expose herself? And for what? What was the goal? More humiliation? Public acknowledgement that she had failed her husband, herself, her marriage, her family, her children? Penny must be delusional.

Throwing off her pyjamas she stepped into the shower and turned the dial to maximum. Facing the hot spray she let the hard drops rain down on her. It really did sting like hell but she didn't care. She stood there for an age, not caring about her two unwanted visitors waiting below, and let the water spill over her, breathing in the steam, feeling it tighten in her chest. Despite her long sedated sleep she was emotionally weary and physically drained. She tried to halt the relentless whys that continued to rush through her head.

Why did it spin out of control like that? Why didn't she listen to her mother?

Why did she have to challenge him like that? Maybe if she'd approached it differently it wouldn't have ended the way it did. Why did he have to hit her? She knew he'd be pissed off, but why this?

Why? Was it love that drove him to it? Or was it that he cared nothing for her at all, that he wasn't remotely concerned about the certain repercussions. Turning, she let the spray pelt her tense shoulders, dropping her head till her chin touched her chest.

He had never been aggressive to either her or the children before, so why now?

What had changed?

Was it always there? Hidden deep beneath the charming façade in some veiled abyss of his soul?

Was she responsible for unleashing it?

Or perhaps it was something else?

If so – what?

And what of her two visitors downstairs, no doubt waiting impatiently, Penny probably reluctant to let them leave despite any protestations? Maybe they were occupying themselves by deviously probing her over-eager little sister, their casual questions cloaked in innocence in an attempt to get as much out of her as possible.

What the hell was she supposed to do next? There was too much noise in her head and she just couldn't think, couldn't hear for all the static. It had to stop. She could feel her pulse increase and temperature rise. Immediately the lightness of her head intensified. With no way out of this ridiculous situation she was trapped, lost in a vast bleak corridor of locked doors with a useless fist of keys and a choice: one chance – pick the right one, or else. Confused, angry and caged in this beautiful waterproof cell, the once therapeutic vapours now suffocating her, she needed to get out. Fumbling, she felt for the shower controls and flung open the doors to gasp violently at the cold air outside. Dropping to the wet floor, she breathed deep and allowed her beating heart to settle back to an even pace. She had no idea how long she lay there. She was sure her delay would be seen as avoidance by her visitors. But she didn't care. Picking herself up and wrapping the towel around her, she knew she was cornered. Armed with nothing more than a rolling mental sequence of questions she had no option but to get dressed, go downstairs and face the music.

Chapter 8

Composed and dressed simply in dark-blue fitted jeans, loose white shirt and mixed blue scarf tied protectively around her neck Esmée descended the stairs quietly. She paused for a minute on the last step to see if she could decipher the whispers coming from Penny and the two plainclothes police officers, a man and a woman, who sat waiting for her to appear.

As she rounded the newel post of the stairs all three stood to immediate attention, like schoolchildren greeting the headmistress, mugs in hand, feet firmly together.

Penny, wearing that same guilty expression that always gave her away when they were kids, made the polite introductions: "Detective Sergeant Maloney. Garda Burke."

Esmée nodded as she took each invited hand firmly in her grasp, recognising Detective Sergeant Maloney as the Garda who had turned up the previous night. The mental mist was beginning to clear.

"How are you this morning, Mrs Myers?" The detective sergeant's query seemed genuine enough.

"Esmée, please," she insisted before sitting on the edge of the sofa opposite them. "I'm fine, thank you."

Penny took up a position on the sofa arm beside her and laid a protective hand on her shoulder.

God, he's ugly, Esmée thought maliciously, but he probably thinks he's gorgeous. He's the kind of geek that kisses his own reflection and prances around naked, admiring himself in the mirror – just like in those really cheesy movies. A Mel Gibson wannabe, but not the cute, modern Mel Gibson, but Mel as he was in the days of the first Lethal Weapon. He was utterly naff, with his highlighted blond hair and that aged brown-leather bomber jacket with the rolled-up sleeves and, oh my God, were they cowboy boots under the legs of those jeans? Ughhhh!

"We've met before," she realised as she sized him up. "Before last night, that is."

"You're right," he affirmed with a knowing smile, apparently fully aware that she was giving him the once-over. "I called to your house a couple of weeks ago. You thought you'd had a break-in."

"Ahh, that's right!" Esmée recalled, raising her head slightly, recollecting their previous, fairly nondescript, encounter. How hadn't she noticed those boots back then?

"I met your husband that night too, although he didn't seem too happy to see me and my partner."

Esmée nodded in reply, remembering the inexplicable uproar Philip had caused having found the police in the house when he'd got home that evening.

"Would you like to tell us what happened last night?" he went on. "You didn't seem up to talking when we called." He looked to his partner for silent confirmation.

Esmée's response was polite, practised and above all cautious.

"My husband and I are having some difficulties."

It felt strange to use the word husband in the context of this obviously guarded conversation in which she was participating only to appease her sisters, reluctant to explain to these strangers the mess she had created.

"My sisters shouldn't have bothered you," she apologised, casting a reproachful glance at Penny. "Really, it's nothing. It got out of hand. We argued. That's all." She felt Penny's grip shift and tighten on her shoulder.

"It doesn't look like nothing to me," Maloney responded, eyeing the fresh dressing on her forehead.

Aware of his stare, she raised her hand instinctively to her head, unable to control the red hue that seeped into her cheeks. "I realise it must look awful but I just tripped on my way to the car, that's all. I stormed out, you see." It seemed a plausible answer.

"Really? And your neck?" he questioned, his sceptical tone telling her he wasn't convinced.

Her eyes jerked up to meet his. Either she was being completely paranoid or he was actually mocking her. Who the hell did he think he was?

"I saw it last night, Esmée. Looked pretty sore to me."

Shifting uncomfortably on the edge of the sofa, unconsciously rubbing the base of her neck, she felt the tender ridge beneath the soft fabric of her shirt.

"We called to your house after we left here last night," he continued, not waiting for her to answer. "We found these outside." He extracted from his pocket her mobile phone and purse. "You must have dropped them when you, eh, fell."

She leant forward to retrieve them – she hadn't even noticed them missing. Well, why would she? He gripped them moments longer than was necessary, catching her eyes as he did so, willing her to be aware that he knew she wasn't being honest.

"You must have been in quite a hurry?"

She really didn't like him and she found herself getting angry at his accusatory tone. Time to take control.

"Like I've already told you I stormed out – an angry wife's prerogative, Detective Sergeant," she retorted defiantly, noticing his left hand's naked ring finger. "Now, really, you're wasting your time. This is a personal, private issue between Philip and me. An issue which we will deal with, together, as a married couple. Now, if you please . . ." She stood up, indicating their exit path with her hand. "I have things to do. My children need collecting and I have shopping to get in."

Maloney shrugged and got to his feet, the other detective taking the lead from him.

Esmée followed them to the front door.

Probably used to always getting in the last word, Maloney turned before releasing the latch.

"In case you're wondering, we didn't get to speak to him – your husband that is. He wasn't home. Or . . ." he stopped and turned to look at her before continuing, "if he was he wasn't answering."

Garda Burke, who up until now had remained silent through all of this, exited the house behind Maloney but, before moving further towards their thankfully unmarked car, she turned and handed Esmée a plain white printed card.

"My number's on that," she said gently. "Call me if you change your mind."

Esmée stood at the door and watched them go.

* * *

Detective Sergeant Gregory Maloney heard the hard slam of her front door over the din of the idle engine. It had been a long shift and he was looking forward to getting home. He should have gone home that morning but this was one he wanted to follow up. He hadn't liked Philip Myers the first time he met him and he liked him even less now.

"What do you make of it?" Garda Sarah Burke asked as she got in.

"I'm not sure."

"She's an awful eejit, sticking up for him like that. Some women are nuts."

He looked at her. "Do you think? Have you not considered that maybe she's more embarrassed than anything?"

"Snotty, more like. I just don't understand women like her. I'd want to lynch him, not make out it was all my fault."

"You'll learn," he predicted.

Back at the station, he felt truly exhausted. Hopefully he'd be able to sleep when he got home. Greg hated the night shift. He could never sleep during the day, his dreams were too vivid. He thought about her while he drove home and was still thinking about her when he sat drained in front of the television, his boots strewn on the floor beside him. She was hot and wasted on that gobshite. He didn't think she was stupid – misguided perhaps, but not stupid. High maintenance definitely, the feisty ones always were. That's why he'd stayed single. Didn't have the patience for it.

He was curious about what had gone on there, not only last night but before then. Her sister, the previous night, had given him a short debrief, describing what sounded like a good reason for a scrap – but for him to slap her round like that? That wasn't on.

He recalled their last encounter. It was only some weeks back. He was on lates that evening too and she had returned home thinking the house had been burgled. Burglaries weren't normally his thing but there had been very little action that night so he had no problem answering the call.

Something had definitely gone down in that house, of that he was sure, not only because of the suggested physical evidence at the scene but mainly because when the husband turned into the driveway he went ballistic with both her and them. The first memorable thing Philip did was to charge straight into the house and up the stairs and when he came down he was calmer, like the panic was over. He had something to worry about and, whatever it was, it appeared to be still safe. Greg remembered Philip's defensive but almost cocky reaction when he tried to get further into the house and the disparaging arrogant reprimand he gave his wife for calling them in the first place.

"For God's sake, Esmée, you never listen, do you? I told you I'd be home as quick as I could. What did you call the police for? They'll only make shite of the place!"

He also recalled the embarrassed blush on her pale cheeks and the quick but apologetic look his partner Dougie gave her. Which was unusual in itself because Dougie "The Bulldog" Masterson usually didn't give a crap.

Philip had shown no concern for their kids or for the potential danger they could have faced had the intruder still been in the house when they arrived home, nor would he allow Greg and his team in to investigate further or take any prints. Now what could a man like Philip Myers have to hide?

At the time her reaction to his bizarre behaviour was blasé: she was obviously used to it. So to see her now, out of the house, was satisfying.

He liked her. A lot. But she was sharp, had an edge to be reckoned with and sharp wasn't his type, although that didn't stop him fantasising about how she might look in his arms, how she might taste, might feel or the methods she might use to keep him on his toes. Hmmmm . . . He usually went for a more submissive type, the smaller delicate flowers, the kind that needed protecting which, of course, he was good at, and at that his reputation preceded him.

In his heyday he was dark and dangerous: dark, drunk and dangerous. Back then, against regulations, he supplemented his meagre wages by part-time work as a bouncer in a not-so-salubrious pub on the other side of the city, far enough away for him not to be recognised. He'd stand tall, proud and powerful at the door and depending on the mood he was in he might, or might not, let you in. His boss turned a blind eye to the nixer and the hangover – everyone was at it until they got caught and he was caught rapid. The pub was raided on his last Saturday night there, for class A drugs. He had to think on his feet but he didn't run. To his credit he never knew what was going on, being too distracted by the varying degrees of 'skirt' that flirted and offered him endless delectable pleasures.

But his boss liked him, knew his father, was there the day he was shot by a rogue bullet fired by one of his own. A sad day.

"Clean up your act, boy," was the advice. "Your father would turn in his grave."

And he did clean it up. The episode had scared him shitless. He ditched the job, the booze and the coke, but kept the girls; they were his only vice, to which he still felt entitled.

And despite her edge, he was curious about Esmée. There was something vulnerable about her, something fragile that he felt he should preserve. Yep. He'd keep his eye on this one, he thought. As for the husband . . . at the time of the break-in he'd made a mental note to do a few follow-up checks: there was something not quite right. But he never did, obviously distracted by something else that came along. Now, however, he was going to make it his business to find out what was up.

Chapter 9

"**P**once!" Esmée hissed venomously at the door as it slammed after them.

"Who the hell does he think he is, coming in here with that stupid haircut and those ridiculous boots?"

Forgetting herself she sank forcibly into the couch, grimacing with the pain that juddered through her head like a chainsaw as she landed.

Penny, still seated on the sofa's edge with her mouth agape, appalled by her sister's behaviour, shook her head in disgust and then stood to look down on her with obvious disdain.

"You must be nuts! They wanted to help you and you behaved – well, words fail me!"

"You sound just like Mum!" Esmée retorted defiantly. "And just so you know it, I don't want their help."

Choosing to ignore her sister's childish response, Penny closed her eyes to mentally push the words, firmly rejected, over her head and stood with her hands on her hips, looking as well as sounding like her mother.

"And what happens if Philip turns up at the door to have another go at you? What then, smart-ass? Didn't think of that, did you?"

Furiously taking the last word, she turned and marched out of the room.

Esmée remained on the couch, rebellious, defiant and unfazed.

"He doesn't know where we live now, does he?" she whispered churlishly, leaning forward to pick up her mobile from the table. It appeared to have escaped its ordeal unscathed. Pressing the power button at its base, she waited for the screen to light up. She keyed in her PIN and listened to the familiar tone as it connected to her network. Returning it to the coffee table, without taking her eyes from it, she leaned back into the couch and waited, silently counting: one, two, three . . . By the time she'd reached fifty and it still hadn't vibrated she knew there were no messages. He hadn't called. Maybe he had but just didn't leave a message? Had it been damaged in the fall? Standing up she picked up her phone, walked to the telephone by the window, dialled her number and then waited patiently for the long seconds to pass before it rang in her hand.

In an instant Penny rushed from the kitchen, panic in her face, looking around to see where her sister had got too, anxious about the potential caller.

"Relax! It's only me," Esmée said, slightly amused, replacing the phone into its cradle. "I just wanted to see if it was still working."

"No message then?"

"Nope," she replied, trying hard to conceal the disappointment in her voice, embarrassed at being caught checking her own messages.

Penny retreated to the kitchen and this time Esmée followed. This was ridiculous. She sat down at the table and watched as Penny filled a glass with water from the tap and placed it in front of her, along with two painkillers.

"You should take these now," she instructed, the compassion displayed earlier missing from her tone.

"Jesus, Penny, don't be cross," Esmée pleaded, looking up at her.

Words threatened in Penny's returning stare: there were so many words she wanted to say but couldn't. Irresponsible. Stubborn. Rude. Childish. But, she realised, they would have been valuable words wasted. So instead she let them be and responded instead with a disapproving sigh and a simple "I just don't understand you."

Esmée grimaced in response and Penny instinctively bent to her sister and wrapped her tightly in her arms. The anger was soon gone, replaced then with love and empathy for her elder, in year's only, sibling.

"How do you feel?" Penny asked, finally letting go.

"Battered!"

"Be serious, Esmée!"

"Fine really. My head is throbbing a little and I do feel bruised but I'm fine."

"Then these will do the trick. Take them." She gestured towards the pills.

Taking them in her hand, Esmée threw them back one by one with swift gulps of water.

Rubbing her sister's back, Penny joined her at the table.

"You want to talk?"

"Not really. I wouldn't know where to start," she shrugged.

Penny waited a while before asking, "What are you going to do?" There was a vulnerable tenderness in her voice.

"I haven't a clue, I've never done this before, you know." Esmée was unable to contain the sarcasm.

"You never told us how all this came about," Penny prompted gently.

"I thought Mum would have."

"Only a little – she wasn't very clear on the detail."

Given everything that had happened in the last twelve hours it made sense to recount the tale, to put it in context, and Esmée, knowing that her sister wasn't going to let it go, told her story in broad strokes. Its delivery was, this time, different. She no longer had to justify her thoughts and feelings and, in fact, telling it this time round seemed to release some of her guilt. Philip, through his actions, had justified hers, had proven himself to be a complete shit and she was the resultant casualty. She felt oddly detached, like it had happened to someone else, a third party, anyone else, just not her.

"Has he ever hit you before?"

"Isn't that weird? Mum asked me the same question yesterday. She asked if that was why I was leaving." A natural question, she supposed. "But no. He never lifted a finger to me, to any of us. That's what's so odd about all this. He just isn't like that. It doesn't make sense, does it?"

"Do you think he's on drugs?" Penny asked seriously.

Esmée had just gulped some more water and now it spurted out, together with a hysterical burst of laughter.

"I'm serious, sis," said Penny. "His behaviour is really odd and maybe, well, there's every chance that he could be taking something."

But Esmée couldn't hear her through her giggles.

"Well, if it's not drugs then it's something else," Penny continued, a little hurt by the reaction to her perfectly plausible explanation, "because this is not rational behaviour. Something else has happened to him. How is his job? Everything okay there?"

"Yes, yes, it's fine," Esmée replied, doing her best to hold back the laughter so as not to offend Penny any more and wiping the tears from her eyes. "He's got his new car, he's making more money than ever and they're putting him forward for promotion, or so he says."

"Then maybe it's too much pressure? He's travelling a good bit – maybe he can't cope?"

"Cope, my arse. He's just a dickhead. What are you doing excusing him anyway?"

"I'm not, really I'm not. It's just, well, it's not making sense."

"Tell me about it."

Silence passed between them, the throb in Esmée's head refusing to shift.

The shrill ring of the doorbell sliced through the sanctuary of the afternoon like a hot knife through butter. Both women jumped, looking from one to the other as they cautiously pushed back their seats and tiptoed through the living room towards the door. The fear was infectious. Esmée's heart thumped in her ears as she peeped through the safety of timber blinds. But it was relief that swept through her as she spied Fin on the far side accompanied by Matthew and Amy. Was it that late already?

"It's only Fin and the kids!" she announced to her sister and pulled open the door to greet them.

"Hey there, guys!"

Her welcome was reciprocated by Amy who ran at her to hug her legs and then, throwing her bag to the corner, continued her flight to gleefully embrace her aunt.

"Auntie Penny, you're still here!" she cried happily.

Matthew followed after and Esmée, forgetting her injuries, bent down to kiss him, stopping only as she saw his horrified reaction to her face.

"Mummy, what happened to your face?" he cried, reaching out

his hand to gently touch the bandage and plasters.

"I fell when I was out jogging." Where that came from she'd never know, but it was the first thing to enter her head.

"But you don't go jogging, Mummy," he responded, confused and unconvinced.

"Now you know why!" she replied stupidly, kissing him on the crown and turning abruptly away.

Following her round, refusing to let it go, he fought to get a closer look and recognising defeat she knelt in front of him and invited him to look closer.

"I shouldn't have been running so fast, eh?" She laughed as he inspected the bruising inquisitively.

"Can I touch it? Is it sore?" he enquired ever so gently, concerned for his mum, but itching to feel the swollen and blotchy skin as only a six-year-old can be.

"Go ahead," she said, and followed with the lie, "It's not sore."

Slowly he reached out and tentatively touched her face, his own wincing in sympathy.

"Wow, Mum!" he exclaimed, distracted by the oddity before him. "You really shouldn't go jogging again!"

Laughing at her son's innocence, she stood up to face Fin who with sorrow in her eyes took in the bandage, bruises and scratches just as Matthew had. Esmée stood self-conscious and awkward, allowing herself be scrutinised like an animal at auction.

"Oh God, Esmée," Fin whispered as she hugged her, "are you okay?" She held on to Esmée's shoulders while leaning back to examine her further.

For the third time that day Esmée replied, "I'm fine. Really!" and, tired with it, changed the focus. "Come on!" she called out to her children, summoning all the energy and good nature she could muster. "Let's get some supper!"

Fin stopped her as she was about to move away.

"Nope, we're going to Granny's, aren't we?" Looking at the kids, now jumping with excitement, she sought their affirmation.

"Yeah!" they yelled in unison. This was a real treat, going to Granny's on a school night!

"She's got Guinness stew, mashed potatoes and trifle for tea!" encouraged Fin, licking her lips and rubbing her hands theatrically like something on children's TV.

Esmée couldn't help smiling as she recognised her favourites. If her mum, as she suspected, was making a comfort meal for her eldest daughter it would without doubt include her homemade tomato soup and brown soda bread for starters. Esmée deduced from the menu that her mother knew about last evening's adventure and wondered who had told her.

"We just came to get you," Fin finished off.

Matthew took hold of his mother's hand. "Are you coming?" he asked.

"Absolutely!"

"Come on then!"

Here goes, thought Esmée with enormous trepidation as she grabbed her coat, turned on the alarm and followed the others to the car, concerned about how her mother would react.

The short journey didn't take long. Lizzie stood at the open door to welcome them. Ever discreet, she shooed the children to wash their hands before wrapping her arms around Esmée. Holding her tight, she didn't need to utter a single word to communicate the intensity of her feelings and by the time the kids returned from the bathroom, it was business as usual with a cheery "Let's go eat."

In no time they were sitting around the table, napkins on their laps, eyes closed with hands joined in prayer for the grace before meals.

Esmée observed her family as they reverently listened to

Matthew recite the words of the blessing with great accuracy and enormous concentration. Her heart filled with pride and, feeling her throat tighten with the onset of threatening tears, she pinched herself hard, focusing on the pain. No sooner had Matthew uttered the last Amen than a tearful Penny, manhandling him into a tight bear hug, planted a kiss on the top of his head.

"You're the best, Matthew Myers, do you know that?" she cried as he tried to escape her grip.

Feeling eyes on her, Esmée instinctively looked around to find her mum staring at her, smiling weakly, her own eyes brimming.

"I'm okay," she mouthed silently to her.

Appeased, but not convinced, her mother averted her assessing gaze, swiftly transforming her expression, with impeccable efficiency, to a beaming smile.

"Amen is right!" she sang out, splaying her palms towards her family, "Now! Let's enjoy this!"

It was an instruction they all followed with great fervour.

"Smells great, Mum!" Lizzie announced as she caught the aroma of the creamy tomato soup before putting the spoonful to her lips.

They were entertained throughout the delicious meal by the eager tales from Matthew and Amy about their day at school. The innocence of volcanoes made out of mash, with the thick gravy oozing from the manmade hollow, helped to create a feeling of normality as its architect told his grandmother about his mother's nasty accident.

Glances filled with a concoction of veiled amusement and unease darted from adult to adult as they listened and commented on his matter-of-fact delivery.

"Well," his grandmother concluded, "we're all going to make sure Mummy doesn't fall again, aren't we?" She looked at each of them, allowing her final gaze to rest on her eldest daughter, the undertone of her words apparent to the adults around the table: together they would make sure that Philip would not harm Esmée again. Reassurance for the young boy and unequivocal support and love for his mother was communicated from the head of the table by the matriarch.

Conor arrived just in time for dessert.

"Sorry I'm late," he apologised, nodding to Esmée.

She acknowledged his contact with a tight embarrassed smile before diverting her concentration to the trifle that sat before her which, if she wasn't mistaken, had an extra layer of custard, just the way she liked it.

"Coffee anyone?"

"I'll make it, Sylvia," Fin offered. "You sit down, you've done enough. Come on, guys! Help me do the dishes." Obediently the kids each took their plate to the sink and under Fin's expert direction, piece by piece, cleared the table. Without the diversion of the children, a tense blanket of silence settled over the adults at the table. Esmée, knowing what was on their minds, chose to deal with it head on.

"You can all stop looking at me like that," she appealed quietly. "I'm fine. I swear."

Conor looked at her and asked about her wellbeing.

As he slipped into his efficient doctor mode, she could easily imagine him in his white coat and stethoscope, smiling down at his patients while on rounds. They'd love him, she was sure, who wouldn't? He was tall, good-looking, nice tan, good teeth . . .

"No dizziness? Lightheadedness has passed? No nausea?"

No! She was fine.

"Has he been in touch, love?" asked her mum seriously.

"No," Esmée said, unable to completely conceal the disappointment in her voice.

Sylvia didn't offer a reply, just shook her head slowly and

lowered her eyes. She was very fond of Philip and his behaviour had hurt her more than even Esmée could have imagined. Their in-law relationship had been a strong one, built up solidly over the years and now Sylvia, along with her daughter, felt a great loss. No matter what happened next it would never be the same again.

"Can we talk about something else, please?" begged Esmée.

Lizzie, picking up the baton, stepped up to the mark.

"Tom was on today," she informed the group as she stirred the coffee that Fin had poured. "He's home this Friday."

They discussed his impending arrival in great detail and agreed that the opportunity for a reconciliation was too good to miss and Esmée should collect him.

By eight the children and some of the adults were tired, cranky and ready to go to bed.

As the children and Fin piled back into the car, Esmée lingered at the door with her mum. Reluctantly Sylvia let her go, feeling helpless and guilty for questioning her daughter's decision to leave her husband while Esmée, reassured and comforted by her mother's change of heart, gladly agreed to call her the next day for a nice chat. Penny left with Conor, promising to call the next day, while Lizzie invited herself to dinner the following evening. Obviously heeding their mother's veiled warning to watch over her, they intended to stick to her like glue.

Esmée was as tired as the kids and couldn't wait to get home, looking forward to only herself and the telly for company. She ached all over and needed to be on her own if only to empty her head.

Fin offered to stay but didn't argue when the offer was thanked but declined.

"Let's meet for breakfast in the village then," she suggested.

"Breakfast sounds good but can we have it here?" Esmée asked with more than a hint of panic in her voice.

Fin, her eyes flicking quickly to the bruising intensifying on Esmée's face, agreed without hesitation. "See you about ten so," she said before getting into the car. "And I'll bring the bagels!" she shouted out the open window before driving away, leaving nothing but a plume of acrid blue smoke in her wake.

Esmée smiled affectionately and watched her round the corner before going back into the house.

Finally! she thought.

With the children tucked in and fast asleep, Esmée took two more painkillers and made herself a cup of hot chocolate. Not the stuff out of a sachet, but the real thing. With full-fat milk! She deserved it! Taking it into the sitting room she snuggled into the couch to enjoy the silence and solitude and let the day drain from her body, savouring the rich, sweet liquid before finally allowing herself do what she'd been dying to do all evening.

Picking up her mobile she again checked her messages. Nothing. Without needing to think, having decided much earlier what she would do next, she dialled Philip's number, her heart beating madly. It rang three times before diverting to his familiar voice.

"Philip here. Can't take your call but I'll get back to you as soon as."

She rang off without leaving a message.

Assuming he had recognised her number and didn't want to talk to her, she waited ten minutes, finishing but not really tasting the dregs of her chocolate, watching the empty fireplace and feeling every second tick silently by. Turning off her number-sending she tried again, but this time it didn't even ring, diverting immediately to the same stupid message. She tried again ten minutes later and again twenty after that with the same result each time. What to do, she asked herself. What to do? Should she leave a message? Maybe keep trying? Why wasn't he answering? She held the phone tight in her hands, squeezing it hard.

"Shit!" she said aloud. "What is he playing at? He should be trying to call me, not the other way round!"

She should be the one diverting his calls, not chasing him like an idiot. She stood up, pacing circuits around the small room, dodging furniture while trying hard to dissipate the anguish and anger and panic that was slowly rising. She had needed to speak to him. Had to understand why. If it weren't for the kids she'd be in that car and driving to him right now, banging on his door, making him apologise, making him say he was sorry and forcing him to tell her, explain to her why. Why? Why? Why?

"Shit!" she called out, only louder this time.

She just wanted to see how he felt. Maybe he was mortified, scared even and too afraid to call her? Maybe . . .

Maybe you should stop second-guessing him, she reprimanded herself.

"Shit. Shit. Shit!" She retraced the circular track of her steps around the room, irritated and annoyed.

The more she thought about him, about her, about why he wouldn't speak to her, the angrier she got until ultimately she felt she would burst. She had more questions than answers, more problems than solutions, with absolutely no way to solve either, no way to sort out the mess, not on her own anyway. She was powerless. This was pointless and not how it was supposed to be. In a final and blinding moment of burning frustration she took the phone in her hand and, giving the screen just a single second's consideration, grimaced and swore at it before heaving it across the room, watching it fly and spin through the air before it smashed against the unforgiving wall at the opposite side.

"Fuck you!" she roared into the silence with the symbol of her anger in pieces at her feet.

Clutching her head, she exhaled, forcing every bit of air from her lungs and feeling every ounce of it leave her body. She held still, not breathing for as long as she could, before inhaling again to refill the empty cavity.

Sapped of her energy, she was tired and sore.

She knelt to collect the scattered pieces of the phone and put it back together. It would be just her luck, she thought, if the stupid thing was damaged.

"Fuck it," she said, mourning the permanent fracture across the screen. Probably, unlike her, the phone was not beyond repair. Humiliated and ashamed by her childish outburst, she couldn't decide whether to laugh or cry.

Feeling sorry for herself she locked up the house, activated the alarm, turned off the lights and trudged heavily upstairs to bed, the safest place in her whole world.

Chapter 10

For the rest of the week Esmée found herself to be the unwitting owner of numerous shadows in the form of her mother, sisters and friend Fin. She almost regretted that her phone was still in working order, since they rang her at all times of the day, and called round at the drop of a hat to see she was still alive and probably to make sure Philip hadn't come round and bludgeoned her to death. Obviously that wasn't the excuse they gave, but Esmée knew that they were petrified, more so than she. But they needn't have worried: Philip made no contact whatsoever and since the evening she had thrown the phone at the wall Esmée hadn't tried to call him again.

Much as she'd hate to admit it, she was actually enjoying the frequent company of Fin and her family. It was reassuring, and in part endearing, to see them making such an effort and, although in the beginning Esmée wanted time to think, now in the aftermath of her outburst she wanted just the opposite. Now she didn't want to think at all because, no matter how hard she tried, it just didn't make any sense and only served to piss her off to the point of fury.

They had stopped asking questions and conversation seemed to revert peacefully back to the mundane and the ordinary. Every now and then though something, some spontaneous observation or maverick comment, would cross their minds and slip out unguarded. At first Esmée was embarrassed by their slip-ups but as the week progressed she didn't know what she enjoyed more: seeing them cringe or listening to their clumsy attempts at covering their words.

By Friday Esmée was bored of the safe confines of the blind cottage walls and agreed to meet Fin in a small coffee shop in the village for brunch. The bruising on her face had matured to a jaundiced shade of yellow and she no longer wore the bandage on her forehead. And, although not an hour went by without thinking about Philip, she was actually beginning to feel a sense of normality.

She was enjoying her new home, her feelings of security, self-control and responsibility. There was little doubt that she was hurting and found it hard to understand how he hadn't, at the very least, called to see how the kids were. They hadn't yet asked about him but as Friday, and the weekend, arrived she knew their questions were inevitable and wouldn't be long coming.

The sun, like a failing geriatric, shone weakly on that early April morning as she walked with her skipping children to school, their faces bright and rosy from the mischievous wind that chased their tails and gently coloured their glowing cheeks. Holding their hands, with both schoolbags on her back, Esmée chatted happily with them about the plans for the weekend. Distracted by the prospect of seeing Uncle Tom again, they didn't think about their father and answering their questions about the possibility of gifts and maybe, if they were lucky, sweets, was a doddle. She promised they could go with her to collect him that evening – with no school the following day a late night wouldn't hurt them one little bit. And if she was honest she too was feeling a little giddy at the chance of clearing the air and making friends, once more, with her big brother.

Having handed her offspring over to the care of their respective teachers, she retraced her steps home, stopping off en route in the local shop for a notepad and pen. Earlier that morning in bed while waiting patiently for the alarm to bleat, she told herself it was time: time to stop parking the things that needed sorting and deal with them head on. A list, she therefore decided, was the most appropriate course of action.

It was almost ten by the time she eventually sat down at the kitchen table with her favourite CD playing on the stereo and pen at the ready. As the mellow, soothing vibes of Air filled the room she focused on the blank sheet of white, lined notepaper on the table before her. This list, she knew, would not only serve to "out" her tasks but would also placate her family who still worried about her constantly. She appreciated that they were concerned about her, nervous even that she had no idea what she was doing and so as much for them as herself she knew that this list was essential.

The first item on her list had got to be rent.

She wrote:

1. Rent

With all that had happened she hadn't really sat down and done the real maths. She knew how much the house cost per month but hadn't really considered it in the grand scheme of things. Her bravado had so far stretched only to the terms of the lease and now the prospect of actually having to look after the cost of putting a roof over their heads, something that up until now had been the sole responsibility of her husband, loomed before her like the Grim Reaper.

Then there were her other finances. She really needed to see how much money she had. Again, while she had a good idea, it was a little too vague so the second item on the list was the bank.

2. Bank

She would check her balance after she had met with Fin and see exactly how much she had left of her father's inheritance. He had bequeathed to her and her siblings thirty thousand euro each. And even though she certainly had dipped into it, they were small amounts – treats for the kids but not expensive ones – and now the deposit and three months' rent in advance on the cottage – so she expected a balance of close enough to the original amount.

When she first began plotting her scheme, she worked out a rough idea of her costs so she knew approximately how long it would last, but now she needed to be precise.

On top of that, she thought as she studied the two words on her list, Philip's silence probably meant that she couldn't rely on any income from him, not even maintenance for the children, not immediately anyway.

Knowing that her cache wouldn't last forever, she was in no doubt that her next task on the list should be to think about getting a job.

3. Job

She had to laugh. The notion of getting a job after eight years of being a housewife, and a damn good one at that, was daunting and she considered this prospect with huge scepticism, immediately feeling the optimism slip ever so slightly out of her purpose. It took all she had not to dwell on it.

Just because it's on the list, she told herself calmly, doesn't mean I have to sort it immediately.

Esmée knew all too well that her training as a fine artist wouldn't cater for the needs of her dependant family and in the absence of any great ideas as to what she might do, could do, she quite rightly paid respect to the foreboding vision of her future. The prospect of going back to college titillated her and, although not an easy or indeed financially sound notion, she decided to include it as a potentially positive possibility worth investigating, and jotted it down as the next item on her list.

4. University Prospects

"What's next?"

She was on a roll – it wasn't as hard as she had thought. The fear that had prevented her from starting this list in the first place seemed utterly unfounded. Encouraged, she read through the numbered challenges aloud. "Rent, Bank, Job, Uni . . ."

"What else do I need to do?"

It seemed obvious. He had to be the next item on the list. He should have been at the top of it. She recalled the quiet conversation that she had inadvertently overheard the night before between Lizzie and her mum. She considered her sister's whispered and covert opinion, which, with the benefit of a few hours' sleep, she was forced to admit was, in fact, right. Dismissing the annoyance she had felt at the time as she slipped away discreetly to avoid any unnecessary confrontation, Esmée admitted that she wouldn't be able to handle Philip on her own. She imagined the next item and the consequences of committing it to paper. Reluctantly she withdrew the pen from between her clenched teeth and, putting its nib to the sheet, carefully scribed the single word that would, without doubt, take her relationship with Philip to the next, albeit descending, level:

5. Solicitor

The more she looked at that single word on the page the more it seemed to dance contemptuously across it, the last but possibly most influential item on her inventory of tasks. And despite her resolve it still seemed a bit premature. Originally, when she began plotting her departure, she had thought that given time she and Philip could be adult about the situation and agree terms of their separation before involving a solicitor.

Philip. Where the hell was he? The guilt in her own belief that this mess was of her own making had begun, over the course of the last few days, to migrate more towards anger. His actions and her focused thoughts now compounded that feeling.

While Esmée was smart enough to know that she wasn't entirely blameless in the generation of the current scenario she sure as hell didn't deserve what she got, nor did she deserve the torment of his silence. And what about the children? Was she really willing to put them through such an emotional battle? Not really. If she could avoid it she would, but did she have a choice? It was her job as their mother to protect them even if it was from herself, not to mention their father. Surely between them they, she and Philip, could sort this out properly? Be adult about it. Mature, for the children. What a cliché! One she never thought she would ever need to use. Well. He could be as pig-headed as he wanted, she would not play his ridiculous games.

Once again working herself into an emotional panicked frenzy, she cast the notepad on the table.

"That's it!" she declared, stomping across the room to pick up her phone.

She dialled the number – not surprised when, like all the other times, it connected direct to his voicemail – only this time she did leave a message.

"Philip," she stated firmly into the handset, "it's Esmée here. Can you please call me? Your children would like to see you and I think it's time that you and I had a talk." There wasn't a tremor in her voice. Fixed and steady, she continued, "I suggest you call me on my mobile, as soon as you find time in your obviously busy schedule." Unable to avoid the sarcasm, she was almost sorry as soon as it was said. Pausing briefly, running out of words, she finished the call. "We can arrange a time then."

Without saying goodbye she hung up, infuriated by the absence of a face to slap.

"Fucking asshole!" she spat at the phone that sat silently, as if mocking her in its cradle, her voice filled with an intensity that stunned her. He had pushed her to the edge and she was feeling every ounce of nasty hatred ooze from her body, like a weeping septic wound, waiting impatiently to find itself inflicted painfully on her husband. Her emotions were getting the better of her, a constant pressure pulsating in the back of her head, a cumbersome load bearing down unrelentingly on her small shoulders.

The sound of the phone broke through her trance. Jumping from the floor she leapt at it, sure it was Philip finally returning her calls.

"Where are you?" the voice on the other end said.

"What?"

It took a few seconds to register the female voice.

"Es, are you there? It's me," came Fin's slightly startled voice.

Gathering herself, Esmée snapped back to reality. "Shit, Fin, I'm sorry, I must have dozed off," she lied convincingly.

"Not to worry!" Fin chirped. "I'll order you a cappuccino. Now wake yourself up and get your ass down here!" Then she was gone.

In spite of herself, Esmée smiled. She was her own worst enemy and Fin as always was there for her, sometimes by design, sometimes by accident, to help.

Taking Fin's instruction seriously, she washed her face and skimmed a comb through her hair, pulling it back with a grip. Grabbing her coat and bag, she paused at the door as she remembered her list.

After all that, she thought ironically, turning back to snatch it from the table.

* * *

A posh name for an everyday caff, Crème was a small unassuming but cosy coffee shop on the village main street. It took a moment for Esmée's eyes to adjust to the dim light that swallowed her as she entered, quickly seeking out Fin who, seated by the misted window nursing her frothy cappuccino, waved to her.

"That didn't take long," she commented, welcoming her friend with a hug. She handed her the menu. "Brunch is on me!" she announced while poring over the delicious bill of fare.

Esmée listened while her friend called out the tasty culinary possibilities, considering whether or not to tell her of her earlier frustrated 'moment' and the peevish message left on Philip's voicemail, eventually deciding against it, classifying it as a personal clandestine moment to which she was entitled. Enjoy this, she told herself, forcing the angst and frustration out of her mind. "Hmmm . . ." she mused, finally deciding to treat herself to a greasy Full Irish, hash browns and all.

Once they had ordered, Esmée took her well-considered list from her bag.

"Here," she said, placing it proudly on the tablemat in front of Fin. "Read that." Crossing her arms she leaned back into her chair to await the verdict. She watched Fin pick it up and smile with curious eyes before reading through the short inventory.

"Who's been a busy little bee then?" she quipped, rereading it. "I'm impressed and particularly interested in item number five." She pointed at the word *Solicitor*, throwing a challenging stare across the table.

"I knew you would be," Esmée stated calmly, folding her masterpiece in halves and then quarters. "I know you all are. That's why it's there!" Placing the list back in her bag, she faced

Fin's challenge with a grin, happy that it had achieved its desired effect.

Their meal, filled with caffeine and conversation, passed all too quickly.

"Are you coming round for dinner tonight?" Esmée asked as together they strolled back to her car.

"What's the occasion?" Fin asked.

"Have you forgotten? Tom is flying in tonight. And I promised the kids we'd order in pizza."

With no plans, for once, on a Friday evening, Fin happily accepted the invitation, glad that Esmée, despite her circumstances, seemed to be getting on with things. They arranged for her to call round at about eight, and with Lizzie and Penny both having said they would be over to greet their brother it was guaranteed to be a full, if somewhat squashed, house and Esmée was looking forward to it immensely.

That afternoon, after collecting Amy from the schoolyard, politely side-stepping the other eager-to-chat mums, Esmée made her way back into the village. First she stopped at the bank, which she left mere minutes later, armed with a statement showing her balance. Then she and her young daughter returned to the café, this time for ice-cream, where she scanned the statement while waiting the remaining half hour before collecting Matthew. Satisfied not only that there was enough there to survive for some time to come, it was also one item on her list that was proudly in hand.

Heading home with the children she decided to ask Tom to help her with the sums; he was great at that sort of thing. Lizzie was the one to ask about the solicitor, hoping she could recommend one of her colleagues, someone with experience in the area. Someone separate from her family unit. All in all it looked like it might all come together nicely.

111

* * *

Promptly at seven she turned into the airport car park. Déjà vu. The welling nauseous sensation in the pit of her stomach reminded her, with mortifying discomfort, about the last time she was there. Was it less than a week ago? she asked herself as together her little family made their way into the arrivals hall. It felt so much longer than that.

When his London flight landed and Tom finally emerged through those awful opaque security doors, she didn't have to point him out – the children recognised him immediately as he walked to the end of the barrier. She, forgetting they weren't talking, hugged him with every ounce of her body, really glad to see him. Holding her at arm's length, he scrutinised the fading marks on her face.

"Christ, Esmée!" he exclaimed in disbelief, half under his breath.

Matthew and Amy stood back until, encouraged, they greeted him shyly. They hadn't spent much time with him, and so for them he was as good as new!

"Come on!" Esmée turned, breaking up the reunion and, pulling him by the hand towards the exit, avoided the look of pity in his eyes while, mesmerised, the kids walked beside him, looking up in awe at their tall, handsome Uncle Tom.

"How long can you stay?" she asked as they made their way to the car.

"As long as I need to," he replied, unable to stop looking at her face "That's the beauty of being a software developer." Then he sang with a cheesy showman grin: "*Any time, any place, anywhere!*"

There were welcome diversions in the form of hugs and kisses from her awaiting sisters when they got back to the house. She was glad not to be the centre of attention for once and let them chat and play in the lounge while she ordered the pizzas, pottering around the kitchen gathering plates and glasses. The sound of excited and boisterous chitchat made her feel the happiest she had in a long time. They would eat in the lounge by the fire, she decided. It was cosy and informal and this was, after all, supposed to be a treat. She placed a bottle of red wine along with a corkscrew beside Tom, inviting him to do the honours. He caught her eye and smiled up at her from his cross-legged position on the floor where he was showing Matthew how to fix his Lego Stormtrooper carrier.

"There!" he announced, raising the now fully working model up for his nephew to examine.

"Wow!" was all Matthew could say as quickly, seizing the moment, he dashed upstairs to fetch an armful of toys that needed the same attention.

Watching the interaction with interest Esmée noticed that Matthew didn't know what to say to his smart uncle who had just opened up a whole new world of promise to him. His father had never sat with him like that, to play, exploring the endless possibilities and new beginnings for a multitude of broken Lego models. They hadn't shared even a moment's closeness like that, asking simple tasks of each other – should they put it back together or make something new entirely? Rather than fix it and, by the looks of it, it wasn't that hard, Philip would have just replaced it. Opening the box was about as creative as he ever got and it was heartbreaking to watch Matthew discover this for himself. She wondered if he knew exactly what he was missing out on? Was he even aware of the void that only his father could truly fill? Would he grow up to be as emotionally ignorant, inept and unattached as Philip? Thankfully, at that moment Fin and pizza arrived together so they gathered round the small coffee table to devour the contents of the oil and tomato-stained boxes.

Esmée forgot her poignant thoughts as the cottage filled with laughter in the swaddling golden light and the rest of the evening slowly slipped by. The animosity between Esmée and her brother was forgotten, as the warmth, solidarity and energy of the group lifted her spirits.

It was after eleven before the children gave in to exhaustion and agreed to go to bed.

She was reading them a bedtime story when she heard the doorbell ring.

"I'll get it," Lizzie whispered from the bedroom door where she had been standing, listening to the story.

Satisfied that they were both asleep anyway, Esmée crept out of their room and, placing the unfinished book on the shelf by the door, tiptoed nimbly down the stairs after Lizzie while cursing the instigator of the shrill ring. She rounded the corner of the last stair only to come face to face, for the second time that week, with the two familiar figures of the local constabulary, cowboy boots and all.

Chapter 11

He knew he'd see her again, but he hadn't banked on it being for this reason. If he'd had to guess the next step, it wouldn't have been this. Something kicked as he saw her face visibly turn when she came down the stairs. Sometimes he really hated his job.

She certainly didn't conceal her annoyance.

"Detective Sergeant Maloney! It's a little bit late to be calling, don't you think?" she said, glaring at him. "And I have guests."

"Apologies, Mrs Myers, this won't take long," he said politely.

Casting her eyes impatiently towards heaven, she nodded and stepped aside to let her unwanted visitors make their way into the living room. They murmured greetings to the others, nodding in recognition to Penny and Lizzie.

Someone turned up the lights in the room, changing the atmosphere instantly; even the flames of the fire seemed subjugated and dull.

"Mrs Myers," Maloney began formally, his tone different from the way Esmée remembered from earlier, uncomfortable almost.

He seemed unquestionably stiff and inhibited as he shifted his weight from one brown boot to the other whereas his token sidekick, Garda Burke, like before, remained quiet, letting her superior do the talking.

Taking his hands out of his pockets he gestured to the sofas. "Do you mind if we sit down?"

"Actually I do! It's late!" she needlessly pointed out for a second time, not quite sure why she was being so brusque.

"Esmée," he continued awkwardly, "this is fairly important and I think you should sit down."

She didn't like his tone, it made her uneasy, and she liked even less the familiar use of her name even though she had asked that he use it during his last visit.

"Please, may we have a word in private?" He looked suggestively left and right at her family.

Esmée watched in disgust as Lizzie and Penny bounded out of their seats like their butts were on fire and immediately set about clearing the empty boxes and wineglasses from the floor and table before scuttling off to the kitchen. Traitors!

Fin, shrugging her shoulders, stood up from her cross-legged position on the floor beside the fire and, gathering the remaining debris, she too left the room. Tom, however, stayed put.

Nodding to the police officers to take a seat, Esmée again registered the absence of the cocky attitude Maloney had displayed earlier in the week. They each sat on the edge, literally, of their seats, leaning towards her as Esmée once again sat opposite. Déjà vu.

"Now . . ." she invited impatiently, prompting them to speak.

Maloney eyed Tom with distrust.

"This is my brother, Tom," she offered, noting his glance.

116

"Whatever this is about you can speak freely in front of him."

Maloney cleared his throat and, focusing once again on Esmée, hesitated briefly before saying quietly, "Esmée, it's about Philip."

"Look," she interjected impatiently, "I told you on Tuesday I had nothing to say to you about him – it is a private matter and I –"

"I'm sorry, Esmée, but this isn't about that," he interrupted.

Instinctively Esmée knew something was very wrong.

Garda Burke lowered her head to study her clasped hands while her colleague, clearing his throat, spoke.

"Esmée, we found his car parked at Cliff Walk this evening."

Her stomach turned and her heart began to beat a little faster. She looked Maloney in the eye, concentrating on his words, trying to plot them in her head as he continued.

"Whose car?" she asked, knowing full well exactly who he meant.

"Philip's car. We were called to the scene by a passing hill walker."

"The scene?" she echoed, baffled by his terminology. What the hell was he talking about? A contorted look of confusion crossed her face as she looked from one police officer to the other, with Burke giving away her novice status by refusing to even look at her.

"The car appears to have been abandoned. There is no sign of him."

"Stolen!" Esmée exclaimed. "Jesus, thank God for that!" The relief was audible in her voice as smiling she placed a reassuring hand over her own heart. "I thought you were going to tell me something dreadful had happened!" She felt Tom's hand rest on her shoulder as he, on impulse, moved closer into the circle of the group.

"No, Esmée, you see, that's it," said Maloney. "We don't actually think it was stolen."

"What then?" she asked, irritated by her stirring panic and annoyed by their refusal to just spit out whatever it was they were on about.

Again, Maloney cleared his throat and putting all his experience into action leaned closer towards her, with compassion and sympathy in his eyes.

"We found this on the dashboard."

He took a small blue-tinted envelope from his inside breast pocket and handed it to her.

Esmée: her name was scrawled untidily across its front.

Looking at him while shaking her head in bewilderment, she took it slowly from his outstretched hand.

Pushing up the fold at the back of the envelope she extracted a single sheet of matching blue-lined writing paper, the kind she hadn't seen in years and was surprised that they still made it – not the kind she would have guessed Philip to possess. It was folded sharply once across its middle. She opened it out, doubling back on the crease. Her hand covered her mouth while, drawing her eyes together in absolute confusion, she read, reread and tried to understand the words written in Philip's familiar scrawl:

Esmée, I love you so much. I never meant to hurt you. I did it for us, for Matthew and my lovely Amy. Please remember that and forgive me. Philip.

She read it and reread it, wishing it to make some kind of sense. Looking first at Maloney, then Burke, then finally at her brother she sought some kind of mental assistance in understanding what exactly it was she was reading. Her head felt heavy, too heavy for her shoulders, with little black spots forming in front of her eyes, rotating faster and faster, randomly darting, blurring her vision, a snowstorm of confused thoughts, getting thicker and thicker, bouncing off her retina. Questions she couldn't answer filled her consciousness.

Did it really mean what she thought it meant? The words pierced the backs of her eyes while the paper on which they were written scorched her hands, sweat formed under her arms, beading on her brow . . . and what was that smell? The blinds came down and then there was black.

Chapter 12

They took her to the car, parked just as they described, in the car park at the beginning of Cliff Walk, where she and Philip had walked many times before. The sky was almost cloudless and the moon almost full, shining bright over the bay, providing a light glow over the night which was unusually cold for the time of year. A bitter wind chased through the exposed area to tussle with the small crowd that had gathered, like moths, attracted by the bright flashing lights of police cars. She wished she'd worn a jacket and fought hard to keep her hair in check.

The audience watched the unexpected side show with curiosity, as the exit of this pale and stunned woman through the rear door of the police car opened the next scene in the real-time drama. Usually these people came after dark for the spectacle of Dublin Bay's dazzling illuminations. Some would kiss and cuddle, others just sit on the low wall to watch the amber lights of the city reflect and glisten against the pitch-black sea in the bay. A few of them now stared as the rumours and mumblings of a suicide filtered through, while others offered their opinion to anyone who would listen: urban myths belonging to the area accompanied by tales of bodies never found, the regularity of "this sort of thing" and the last poor soul to "go".

Do what? Go where? What on earth were they talking about? What was Philip doing here anyway? Esmée asked herself, doing her best to ignore the intrusive, inquisitive spectators. There must be, had to be, some reasonable, logical, explanation. Things like this didn't happen to normal people, normal people like her. A corridor of whispers formed in front of her, parting like the Red Sea to allow her to pass through to the end, a destination that loomed at the finish of the unofficial guard of honour. Her field of vision focused in on the car, gleaming, polished bright and silver. In the surrounding darkness the surreal spotlit vision intensified as she approached. The door was opened for her by some insignificant other. Pausing to swallow, she peered inside with Maloney by her side while Tom stood back, watching, hands clenched in the pockets of his suede jacket, willing his sister to be strong.

On the floor beneath the steering wheel and in front of the pedals Philip's shoes lay perfectly positioned, side by side, with the artificial light from a reflected torch echoing back off their perfectly polished black leather. They looked as good as new but she knew they weren't. As with his every other possession he always took great care of his shoes, polishing them before every use. And tucked neatly inside the left shoe were his black-and-grey Pringle socks. That meant, she deduced absurdly, as she looked around the pristine interior, that he must have been wearing either his black or grey woollen Ted Baker trousers. He was quite predictable that way, always coordinated: certain shoes with certain socks with certain trousers with certain shirts. He hated not "matching" and had often thrown tantrums when the right piece of his ensemble wasn't fit for wearing. Esmée knew every item of his wardrobe and from these small clues could picture vividly how he might have looked as he had parked, exited and locked the car.

In the middle compartment of the walnut-veneered dashboard sat his wallet and keys. Esmée turned to Maloney who nodded, indicating it was okay to pick them up. She sat into the charcoal-grey leather seat, and picking up the wallet flicked the catch and opened it out. On the left side were his credit cards – Visa, American Express and MasterCard, they were all there. His bankcard was there too and inside the slim black pouch was stuffed a bundle, probably about three hundred euro-worth, of crisp, new, fresh-out-of-the-bank notes.

The keys were as they should be, on his personalised BMW key chain. She plucked each, one by one: the car key, the two front-door keys, the key to his study, the back-door key and one other she didn't recognise – smaller than the rest it was more like the key to a bicycle lock or a petty-cash box. Reflectively she toyed with them, soothed by their jingle while she scanned the car's interior.

"Where was the letter?" she asked, handing up both the full wallet and the keys to Maloney.

"It was sitting on the dashboard, just there." He indicated with his finger to a point behind the steering wheel. Her eyes followed the trajectory and stared at the spot where she assumed it had sat and thought about what he had written. "I love you so much," he had said but there was no goodbye.

"What do we do now?" she asked solemnly, extracting herself from the 'scene', finally ready to co-operate. "What happens next?"

Together they turned and walked back to the police car, blanking the news-hungry audience. She got into the back seat, supported by Tom who took hold of her hand and returned her weak grin with a concerned but encouraging smile.

Maloney sat into the front passenger seat and swivelling around to her asked, "You okay?" to which Esmée simply nodded. "We'll take the car back to the station a little later on," he told her as they pulled away past the small crowd and down the hill.

"What about Philip?" Esmée asked quietly, feeling Tom's grip tighten around her hand.

"We're not sure yet. It's too dark for the full team to start out now, but we've put the coastguard on notice so they'll head out first thing for the sea search – but the Search and Rescue helicopter will go out now and scan the cliffs, just in case . . ."

She nodded vacantly, assembling in her head the notion of what a sea and cliff-side search might involve. The idea of Philip out there, somewhere, cold, wet, alive or dead brought tears to her eyes and pierced her heart with an intensity that words couldn't describe. And if, as everyone was suggesting and appeared to be obvious, he had taken his own life and committed his body, eternally, to the waves, he didn't want to be found alive. Did he? But that wasn't Philip's style, she denied, refusing to accept the vision in her head as a possible reality.

"You've got this all wrong," she announced as they reached the end of the hill, "This isn't Philip. It's not his way, he wouldn't do this." Urgently she turned to Tom, seeking some level of endorsement and when none came she laughed feebly. "You know he's probably at home right now with his feet up watching the telly."

"We checked, Esmée," Maloney said. "He's not there." He watched her face in the rear-view, feeling her pain.

"Then we have to check again," she insisted looking at both him and her brother, imploring them to have faith. If they believed then it might be true.

"You think he's dead, don't you?" she accused.

And because they did, neither answered, but Maloney wanted to help, wanted to stop the hurt, and nodding to the driver instructed with a pointed jerk of his head. "Let's go to his house." She needed to see for herself.

Their driver took the left instead of the right and headed to 12 Woodland Drive.

Appeased but fearful, Esmée sat back and held onto the handle above her head. "This is all my fault," she whispered, hardly noticing the tears that spilled down her face as the darkness sped by outside the clear window.

It took just under fifteen minutes to get to the house which, just as Maloney had described, appeared dark and unoccupied. Their unmarked police car came to a halt at the edge of the kerb. Maloney turned and looked at her expectantly.

Reaching into her bag she hunted for her old house keys.

"I've left them!" she cried, frantically ransacking her bag.

"It's okay," Maloney soothed. "Look, I'll use these." He extracted Philip's from his pocket.

"I'm not going in," she declared suddenly. "I can't." She was afraid of the emptiness she might find.

Nodding patiently, he got out and for the second time that evening walked the short distance to the front door. Out of courtesy to the possible occupant he rang the bell and stood there waiting for what seemed to Esmée like an age. She sat in the car, counting the seconds, willing Philip to appear alive and well. When he didn't Maloney turned briefly towards the car before inserting the key in the lock to enter the house. Tom got out and went in after him. She saw the lights go on in the sitting room and the familiar environment come to life. She could see them standing in the doorway and looking around the obviously empty room and moments later they turned and the room once again fell into darkness. She couldn't watch any more. Through closed eyes she could sense them investigate, imagined them going from room to room through the house, opening door after door, until eventually in almost perfect time she lifted her lids to see Maloney and Tom exit the house and lock the door behind them.

"Here," Maloney said, getting into the car and handing her Philip's keys, minus the car key. "You can hang on to these."

She took them from him and held them in her hand, massaging the smallest unconsciously, staring out the window vacantly while making the short journey to the station. Her thoughts were completely empty but her heart was full of shame.

When they got there she and Tom were led through the quiet public office into a sparsely furnished garish-yellow interview room. It smelt old and dank with tattered posters on the wall promoting everything from cyclist safety to confidential crime lines. The fluorescent lights above their heads flickered while they waited patiently, reading the cheeky graffiti scratched onto the tabletop before them.

Garda Burke came into the room after a short while with two mugs of steaming milky tea on a tray, accompanied by chocolate-covered HobNobs. Before she left the room, Esmée asked what was going to happen next. Taking her hand from the door, Burke turned back into the room and sitting down she told Esmée that they would need to take a statement from her about the last time she saw Philip, about his behaviour and his general movements. She explained how they'd examine the car.

"Just routine procedure," she assured her, saying that the rest depended on the results from the search. "Detective Sergeant Maloney will go through it all with you." With that she rose and left the room, closing the door gently after her.

Esmée was tired and emotionally drained.

"I can't believe it, Tom. It just – it just feels like it shouldn't be happening – it doesn't feel real."

She tried to catalogue her thoughts, tried to measure the enormity of what that parked car, the empty house and, above all, the note meant.

"I've no idea how I should take this. What do I do next?"

At a total loss, the guilt once again setting in, she thought about what might have provoked Philip to . . . She couldn't finish her own sentence, because truly no one knew what he had done.

"Maybe he just went for a walk," she said, "you know, changed his shoes before he got out of the car."

"What do you think? What is your instinct telling you?" Tom asked.

"I don't know what to think," she answered truthfully, flustered and stressed, running both hands through her hair. "I was so busy concentrating on myself I never thought to look at him." Her chest hurt as the anguish of such a huge oversight struck her. "It never dawned on me that he might be unhappy too."

Putting her head in her hands, she admonished herself. "How could I have been so blind?"

"What was going on in his life, Esmée?" Tom asked, rubbing her back.

"That's the terrible thing, Tom – I have no idea! We didn't talk. He had no idea what I was up to and . . ." She paused, shrugging her shoulders in despair. "Well, it works both ways, doesn't it?" She looked at her brother and welcomed his comforting embrace as she racked her brains. "We were strangers," she whimpered into his shoulder. "Oh God, please let him be okay!"

It was half an hour later before Detective Sergeant Maloney joined them. He sat at the far side of the table, laying a notebook in front of him.

"Okay, Esmée, here's what we're going to do." Although exuding an air of tremendous efficiency, of being a man in control, he lacked the pushiness of their previous conversations – he was softer, more human, so much so she almost forgot to be irritated by him.

She nodded, listening intently as he explained that they would need to put the facts together in order to build a picture of what might have happened. He told her that they should assume nothing until that picture was complete and asked permission to record their conversation, since shorthand wasn't his forte. They laughed together, politely, at his little joke. Very pleasant, very formal.

"Now," he said, clicking the mouse on the computer to commence their electronic recording and nodding to her when the microphone symbol on screen blinked to indicate that it was on. "I want you to tell me everything that has happened over the last few weeks."

Without hesitation she braced herself and told him her story. She felt removed from it, separated, like her story belonged to someone else. Leaving nothing out, she recounted it fully: her circumstances, her reasons, her strategy, its execution and final reaction. Throughout the rendition she remained calm and unemotional, allowing the story to tell itself methodically and without embellishment or exaggeration.

Once finished she was cold, trembling slightly while playing with the wedding band and solitaire-diamond engagement ring on her finger.

"Esmée?"

"Yes?"

"What did he do?"

She looked up from her hands. "What did he do?" she repeated, sure she'd missed something, "What do you mean? When?"

He took Philip's letter from the plastic sleeve at the back of his notepad and placing it in front of her continued, "He says in his letter 'I did it for us'." He paused, not taking his eyes off her for a second. "What did he mean, Esmée?"

She reached out her hand towards the note and, turning it on the table, dragged it towards her and read it again. "I have no idea." She had focused so hard on the first line, the remainder had missed her somewhat. "Really I don't know." She looked up again, annoyed with herself and ashamed that she knew so little and couldn't fill the dark abyss that was building before her.

"I think that's enough," Tom said, sitting forward in his chair while putting a protective arm about his now weeping sister.

Detective Sergeant Maloney nodded his assent to Tom, silently asking him to be patient for just one minute.

"I have one last question and then we'll call it a night, okay, Esmée?"

Wiping her eyes with the backs of her hands, she nodded her agreement.

"Esmée, what did . . . I mean does . . . what does Philip do?"

"He's a broker with Alliance Vie – they're a French Insurance company."

"Alliance Vie – what exactly does that mean?" Maloney probed purposefully.

This was an easy one. She grinned, wiping her streaming nose with a well-used and mangled tissue. "He's an insurance salesman."

Philip hated being called that. Like he was too good for it.

"And how was it going for him?"

"Great, I assume," she replied, shrugging her shoulders. "He was promoted about six months ago and bought the car as soon as he found out. He said they were going to offer him another grade promotion within the next six months. He's good with people.

They trust him." She let her words linger as the irony of the statement became clear.

Maloney pondered this last comment, scratching a few words on his pad before finally concluding, "It's late." Switching off the recorder, he stood up. "You need some rest."

He accompanied them through to the main office, telling them as they went that the search team would head out first thing, promising to call her with any news as it transpired.

It was a quarter past three by the time they were dropped home in the unmarked police car. The three girls, Penny, Lizzie and Fin, were alert and waiting for them when they walked through the door. There were lots of hidden gestures but no words as they made room for Esmée on the couch. She was so tired.

Tom handed her a brandy, but the smell of it turned her stomach.

"You know what?" she said, looking up at him. "I'd actually love some tea!"

"You're just like Mum," he said affectionately, taking a swig for himself from the glass before returning to the kitchen.

Lizzie and Penny followed him while Fin moved to sit beside her.

"Well?" she asked expectantly.

"It was his car all right," Esmée replied. "They think he threw himself off the cliff." It sounded funny to say the words no one had actually uttered all night. So funny, in fact, that she began to laugh quietly at first, but as the picture of her husband, leaping off the side of the cliff in his bare feet, formed in her head her laughter turned to a crescendo of hysterical screeches.

Fin, conscious of the sleeping children upstairs, tried to calm her, to reassure her with gentle words. With a rising sense of panic she realised that she wasn't getting through and Esmée continued her raucous roars of laughter. Ignoring the audience that had returned from the kitchen, Fin put strength in her tone and with a forthright sense of urgency commanded firmly: "Stop, Esmée, stop it!" to no avail until finally, seeing no other alternative, Fin raised her hand and slapped her friend hard across her left cheek.

Chapter 13

She awoke with a start. Disorientated, it took her a second to realise she was on the couch in her sitting room wrapped in a blanket with Fin snoring soundly on the sofa opposite. She had no idea where the others were. Pushing aside the cover, she sat upright and wiped the sleep from her eyes, the memory of the previous evening's events rushing to fill the vacuum inside her head. Unfortunately, it was a real-life nightmare and not a dream. Her feet padded softly on the tiled floor as she made her way from the sitting room to the kitchen and straight to the fridge to pour herself some ice-cold water. Her parched mouth was refreshed by the cool liquid and she consumed every last drop without stopping for air. Pouring a second glass, she leaned against the counter and brought the cold glass to her forehead, rocking it gently from side to side as if the steady motion could in some way dull the monotonous pounding in her head. What a week!

The silence of the house was refreshing. Looking up at the

clock on the wall she saw it was only just after five in the morning. Opening the back door, she sat at the small table outside, bringing her knees up against her chest to provide a little extra protection against the snappy morning air. It smelt of spring and clean laundry. Predictably, her thoughts were with Philip, wherever he was. She couldn't help but wonder about the car, about how it got to be there and in her mind's eye she traced his movements. It was chilling, the idea that he was out there, somewhere. Dead possibly. Or perhaps just running from her to teach her a lesson? A cruel, evil lesson. But something about the picture as it was building wasn't quite right. She could imagine him getting there, see him driving up the steep hill, picture him turning into the spot with the dramatic vista over the bay. She could see him pat both his trouser pockets for his phone like he always did when he got out of the car. But she just couldn't figure why he would have taken his shoes off. He was familiar with the path and it was sharp and rocky. Even knowing he was going to reach his final end, why would he go the proverbial last leg barefoot? While it might be that he was desperate, Philip wasn't stupid. She had to see it. Feel it like he did. She needed to be there to try to understand.

The irritation and frustration of her own ignorance drove her for the third time in less than a week to leave her children in the care of her sisters.

At that hour it wasn't surprising that, pulling into the Cliff Top car park, she saw hers was the only car there. Even the spot where Philip's was the night before was now glaringly vacant.

She turned off the ignition and let the smooth sound of the simmering wind entertain her.

She wondered if he had noticed this vast and beautiful bay before locking his car and wandering off. What was going through his head as he apparently removed his shoes and placed them so carefully on the floor? What time was it when he got there? Was it dark or was it light? Had anyone seen him as he supposedly strode off barefoot? Those bloody shoes. Didn't anyone see him and think "How strange!"? Did they not, perhaps, try to stop him, maybe report their unusual sighting to the police? Did no one, anyone, care? Obviously not. She measured up the lonely car park, watching as a few stray gulls pecked optimistically at the ground for food, crumbs dropped from the picnics of the many tourists this beauty spot attracted each and every day. People. Blind people. If he had stood at the top of a tall building, balanced himself precariously on its windy perch then perhaps they would have screamed and stopped to ask questions. They would have called for him not to be a damn fool, to come down and talk, to think of his family. Yes, then they would have taken notice.

The effervescence of the new day tempted her out of the confines of the car. The yellow gorse, shouting out with vibrant cheer, lured her into the bright brilliance of the unblemished morning. Contrasting perfectly against the purples, pinks and lavenders of the surrounding heather it spread like lava over the barren rocky track that led to the lower cliff path. She pulled her fleece tight to protect against the biting breeze that nipped deviously like a snappy dog, seeking out any small crevice into which it could creep. Instinctively she descended the path to the large boulder that protruded out of the ground, its grey top flattened and smooth, forming a natural seat where she and Philip had sat on so many occasions previously. Happier times, lovers holding hands, kissing lips, planning their future together, Christmases, summers, wet autumn days, this was their spot even though she couldn't exactly remember the last time they had walked this way. Regardless, there it was, present, solid, timeless and slightly overgrown. Evidence of previous less respectful visitors littered the thick green and wild grass at its base. She sat, unconsciously wiping her hand across its rough surface while reverently looking out to inspect the immeasurable expanse of the dark sea before her, its surface borrowing colour from the ominous clouds that hovered overhead: fast and full with the threat of rain. The translucent light on the horizon was dreamlike as the oncoming greyness battled and eventually swallowed the weaker iridescent blue sky way above. She could taste the salt in the air as the breeze whipped into a minor gale. Closing her tired and sore eyes, she drew that pure sea air deep into her lungs, felt it massage her face and hands, and steal her breath to make her light-headed and dizzy. She loved the sea, always had, invigorated by its powerful swell and enigmatic expanse. The sound of the waves thrilled her as they crashed on the rocks below, sending up salty spray to be carried by the wind up the cliff face before being sucked back, up to the skies, knowing eventually it would fall back to its unrelenting source. A hypnotic, never-ending cycle, powerful and majestic, a force to be respected, now more than ever as she pleaded with it, begged it, to tell her where he was. As her eyes scanned the endless undulating stretch before her, she wished for a sighting, a sign of his life.

It took a while for her to register the quiet hum in the distance, augmenting swiftly to a loud din, eventually blasting her from behind. Instinctively she ducked as the rescue helicopter flew frighteningly close over her head and back out to sea, the heavy chop of its propellers drowning out all other sounds as it tilted on its side to follow the curve of the cliffs.

They were looking for him.

She watched as it disappeared around the coastline followed shortly after by the signature orange and blue of the lifeboat crashing rhythmically on the waves, its crew scanning for a human form. Three times the helicopter flew by, each time a little further away than the last, but it didn't slow down, didn't circle or slow to hang over a spot twice. It just kept on flying back and forth, back and forth, weaving its way farther and farther out to sea.

Esmée watched its progress, willing it to slow down, to get closer to the waves, to signal a find to the cruising boats that had gathered and were now motoring around and around in coordinated formation. Today there were no sails up, no excited urgent shouts for the crew to tack left or right: this was neither a leisurely tour nor a playful challenge to the wind and waves. This was a search party made up of volunteers for whom seeking out lost souls was a vocation. And as she watched them, mesmerised by the trail they carved through the now choppy swell, she thought about the man they were searching for. She wondered if they would look harder if they didn't know he was a possible suicide, if they believed his presence in the distended waters to be a tragic accident? Would they be happy about selflessly risking their lives for someone who didn't respect his own? Accepting that he might have taken his own life was the hard part but it was harder still to ignore the tiny voice blabbering away in her head, the one that kept telling her no, how could he? Watching the rhythmic movement of the sea below, the niggling doubts continued to present themselves, each one seeming more reasonable than the last. Her heart was crying out to him, for him. The thought of his desperation tore at her conscience, the need to end his own life, his silence. Her pity and sorrow. But how was it possible for her to feel like this? Yesterday she hated him, the day before that she despised him, a week ago she had left him and before that had contemplated and hankered after the simpler life without him. Had she tempted fate with her ridiculous wanderings? And if he really was dead, what then? Was she responsible, had she killed him?

Shrouded in confusion, she tried to put some order on her destructive thoughts but the rough weather was really moving in now, making it hard to stay sitting and even harder to concentrate with the stinging wind bringing tears to her eyes. She couldn't watch any more and stood to let the lower cliff path lead her away from the focus of the search party. Leaving the activity behind, she thought about what he might have been thinking, she thought about the note. What exactly did he mean by "I did it for us"? What exactly had he done for them? Why? Maybe it wasn't a suicide note at all? A farewell note, perhaps, but not a terminal goodbye? Was it that he meant her to believe he was dead? It was possible. But if that were the case, then where was he? And if this was the fashion of her thoughts, then were the police investigating the possibility too? Would they start calling people? Start asking questions and begin looking for him alive and elsewhere? Anxious now, feeling like she was missing something, she deviated off the main track onto a lesser known uphill trail to make her way back to the car park.

For once her cliff-side memories from childhood took second place to thoughts of her husband. It used to drive Philip nuts every time they came this way, how she always, without fail, recounted the hide and seek games played amongst these ferns, as if he had never heard the stories before. Eventually the habit became a jest to get him going. Not today though. Today she was alone.

The dynamic combination of fear and adrenaline pumped through her veins as she manoeuvred her car back to the main road.

Driving back the way she came, Esmée considered the protocol of what to do next. There was no one to call really. He was an only child whose parents had passed away long before they met. She and the kids were the only family he had left.

There was work. She would have to tell them, she supposed, though presumably the police would get around to questioning them about Philip. But what should she tell them: Philip is dead? Gone? Missing?

Somewhere in the back of her mind she harboured the notion that perhaps, just maybe, this was nothing more than Philip's idea of cruel punishment: punishment for her subordinate defiance. Without a body he could be alive. And well. In her quest for answers where none existed, this seemed quite plausible. The more she thought about it, the more she could imagine him seeking out secret comfort in the arms of one of his many female conquests. She could hear him whine about his nasty wife and how she had left him, how she had taken his children when all he was trying to do was make a good home for his family. And as the seeds of her creative ramblings bore fictitious fruit, the image of him potentially in the embrace of another woman incensed her.

So strong was the emotion that by the time she got back to the house her sadness had been replaced once again by loathing.

The hum of the busy house was disconcerting after the solitude of her morning's ambling. The tempting smell of fresh coffee lured her into the kitchen and into the morning's circus that was breakfast time with the clan gathered tight around the small kitchen table.

"You okay?" Tom asked, handing her a steaming mug of milky coffee. "We were a bit worried when we found you gone."

"I'm good," she replied, returning his smile. "I walked around the cliffs."

There was a pause as they digested this information.

"Busy out there?" Lizzie asked then.

"You could say that," Esmée replied dryly. "Looks like every boat in the bay is out looking."

"Looking for what, Mummy?" Amy asked, licking the jam off her toast.

"Sharks!" Fin answered playfully, grabbing her niece by the waist from behind, provoking a thrilled shriek in response.

"Really?" Matthew asked with wide eyes.

"No, pet," Esmée replied, stroking his head. "Auntie Fin is only kidding."

"Well, we're off to town, aren't we?" Tom told her while seeking confirmation from the kids.

"Uncle Tom says we can feed the ducks in the park. Can we, Mummy?" said Matthew.

"Of course you can," Esmée agreed happily, the smiles on their faces warming up her chilled heart. "There's bread in the cupboard you can take."

"Fin's coming with us. Do you wanna come?" Tom asked.

"Do you mind if I don't? I need to think."

A tiny part of Esmèe took note of the glance Tom and Fin exchanged. Tom and Finn as a couple? Why not? Those two had always hit it off.

"Want some company?" Penny offered from across the table.

"Not really. I'd rather be on my own, just for bit."

"If you're sure you'll be all right?"

"I'll be fine, really."

"Well, I'll grab a lift with you then, Lizzie, if that's okay?" said Penny.

"Fine by me, but," she glanced at her watch, "I'm heading in five."

The house buzzed with activity until the plates were cleared, dishwasher filled, teeth brushed, coats, hats, scarves and shoes put on. Two sets of goodbyes later and the house was quiet again. Finally.

In the comfort of the silence Esmée made herself a fresh coffee, then sat back down at the table. A wave of guilt passed over her as she realised how little time she had spent with the kids over the last few days, having had to pass them off on their, albeit very willing, aunties and uncle. The novelty of the continuous stream of guests was bound to wear off soon and when that happened, no doubt, there would be the inevitable barrage of questions. Where was their dad? When were they going to see him? When was he coming back? As sure as the sun would rise again tomorrow, they were bound to ask after him, wonder about his absence and be curious about his return. She may have left him, may have wanted him out of her intimate life, but she never, ever, would have wished for his complete nonexistence. The day she discovered she was pregnant with Matthew was the day they had become inextricably unified. Children were the constant, not the love that they had promised would bind them together "till death do us part". How naïve! Love, in her case, appeared to be transient, the catalyst but not the glue.

With no family, few friends and only a small number of work colleagues, the number of calls she had to make wasn't huge. If he wasn't alive they needed to be told. And if he was? What then? Mortification? Humiliation? There was no one to ask, no one to check and see.

She leafed through her phone, scanning her contact list, not really knowing who it was she was looking for, hoping for inspiration in the names. He had cut himself off completely from their few mutual friends. How sad was that? He had no golf buddy or tennis partner, he didn't sail, didn't play pool and his football days were long behind him. Really it was just them. It had kind of always been that way.

The first person she called was Jack Ryan. Jack and Philip had worked together for the past few years managing the small team that was the Dublin office of Alliance Vie. They had, she supposed, become firm friends and nurtured a strong team bond. They were as close as work colleagues ever really become and together ran the business with integrity, or so Philip said. She and Philip had been invited to dinner with Jack and his wife, Grace, a few times and had returned the gesture at least twice. And while

Jack might not necessarily have been her cup of tea, Grace was a delight. Loquacious and vivacious with a wicked sense of humour, a sharp tongue and a thick Dublin accent, she made their evenings out thoroughly enjoyable, demonstrating that opposites really do attract. Searching out the number, Esmée could visualise their house: the colour of the walls, the pretty pictures of their three young girls set out neatly atop the lacquered upright piano and the dog that apparently wet the floor every time their doorbell rang.

His voice, when he answered, was suddenly familiar.

"Hi, Jack, it's Esmée, Esmée Myers."

"God, Esmée, how are you?"

"I'm good. And you?"

"Great, thank God, enjoying the fine weather. What can I do for you?"

With the pleasantries over, she paused only briefly to take a deep breath then got straight to the point.

"Jack, I'm ringing to see if Philip is with you?"

"With me? No, I thought you guys were heading off for a few days?"

"Where?"

"Where what?"

"Where were we supposed to be going?" Esmée replied curtly.

His nervous laugh was a sure indication that he wasn't quite sure where the conversation was heading.

"I don't know, Esmée. He never said."

When she didn't answer he filled the silence.

"I take it you guys didn't go away then?"

"Nope. When were we to come back?" She tried not to sound pissed off – it wasn't his fault – but it was easier said than done.

"I don't know exactly –"

"When did he leave?" she cut across him.

"Well, we had a pint last Wednesday – that was the last I saw of him." His tone suggested he wasn't going to remain this nice if she was going to keep going down this route.

"So the last time you spoke was last Wednesday?"

"Yes, Esmée! That's what I said. Look, what's going on?"

She couldn't bring herself to say the words. The phone began to shake in her hand. Beads of sweat bloomed under her arms as the nausea began to build.

"Esmée, is everything all right? Are you okay?"

"Well, no, not really. We can't find Philip."

"What do mean 'can't find' him?"

"He's gone. Missing. The police found his car on the cliffs yesterday but not him. Jack, they think he's killed himself."

"What? You're joking. But that's impossible – it's just crazy – sure why would he do a thing like that . . .?" His voice trailed off as he tried to make sense of what she was telling him.

"He's gone, Jack, and I have no idea where."

"Suicide? I don't think so." His words trembled as he spoke, but he was definite in his denial of the possibility. "Did he leave a note? Did he mention anything to you beforehand, any clue?"

Jack sounded just like Maloney with all his questions. But his seemed to have more sincerity.

"There was a note, but I don't really understand it. He said he did it for me."

"Did what?"

"Killed himself maybe? I have no idea. I wish I knew." She could feel the bile dangerously close to her mouth and bit her lip, focusing hard on diverting the possibility of tears. The last thing she wanted to do was break down on the phone to Philip's workmate.

"What do the police say? Are they doing anything?"

"They're searching for him now, at the cliffs."

"Oh my God, Esmée, I don't know what to say. It just doesn't make any sense!"

"You're all right, I wasn't really expecting you to say anything." The resignation in her tone was palpable. "But I have to ask, Jack, was there anything particular, anything at all going on at work that might make him . . ." Esmée didn't know which verb to use, "well, that might make him do this?"

"Jesus, Esmée!" Jack retorted. "No. God, no." He paused. "Things were hard, for sure, but nothing quite so bad as to make him . . ." Jack couldn't bring himself to say it. "He'd done a few deals recently that seemed to bring in the numbers . . . I don't know . . . God, Esmée, I'm sorry but I don't think so. I'd know if there was."

"But could you do me a favour?"

"Sure. Anything. What can I do?"

"Would you mind telling them at work?"

"Yes. Yes, of course I'll tell them."

"And, well, look, I'm not sure quite how to put this, but, well, things haven't been the best between Philip and me for a while now."

His swallow was just about audible.

He knew? She could feel it, could feel his mortification. Had she crossed the line? Too late to turn back now so she clenched her cheeks and continued. "The kids and I – we – we moved out last week."

She paused, offering him a chance to respond.

"Jesus, Esmée, I'm sorry, really I am."

"Don't be. It's been coming a while, you know that."

He didn't deny it. She kept going.

"Look, I know he was upset by it all, but to do this? I don't think so. He didn't love me enough to do this." She surprised even herself with her pragmatism, but it wasn't his sympathy she was after.

"Don't be ridiculous, Esmée –"

"Thanks, Jack, I appreciate your words, but genuinely, he didn't. But if you could just ask around, see if there was anything . . . anything else . . ." Esmée let the sentence finish itself. She had meant to say "anyone" but couldn't bring the word to her lips.

"As I said, Esmée, I don't think so, but of course I'll check. Let me ask."

"Thanks, Jack, I appreciate it." She let the silence connect them for a short while longer then, reluctantly, said, "I'd better go. Someone might be trying to get through."

"I'll give you a call in the next few days . . . after I've asked around . . ." he promised.

"Thanks, Jack."

"You might have news by then. He'll turn up. You'll see. Mind yourself, Esmée."

She called John Andrews next, Roger Burke after. Mick, Simone and Gerry. They were all the same. All friends who, it transpired, hadn't heard from Philip in months if not years. It fast turned into a futile exercise filled with empty promises to keep in touch.

Time tricked her. The mere moments she had thought wasted staring vacantly into space had actually been close to an hour. An hour of trying to put some kind of logic into this bizarre affair. What had he done? What was he running from? Was it her? Again, pointless thoughts.

The enormity of her situation was fermenting fast. How could he do this? How bloody selfish! What about the kids, his children? How was she supposed to explain this to Matthew and Amy – would they even understand? What if he never turned up? No body to mourn, no ceremony at which to grieve, no hope for life after death, no finale – nothing. At that moment she had nothing more ahead of her than an existence of doubt and futile hope, not to mention an abundance of unanswered questions.

Whether or not she believed he was dead, she felt certain that Philip had no intention of coming back.

By the end of the day there was no news from the search, and no news was, as they kept reminding her, good news. She had no alternative but to sit it out and wait for the police to contact her. It would, they told her, continue for one more day, maybe two, and after that . . . well, they'd just have to wait and see. But she couldn't just sit there. Waiting.

She needed distraction as much from her mental activity as from the anticipation of something, anything, happening. Like rows of spinning plates whirling furiously overhead her thoughts haunted her, each balanced precariously on needlepoint rods of reason. Mentally she raced from one to the other, constantly massaging, keeping them spinning in the air, spinning, spinning, avoiding any lull, any lapsed moment for her to falter and lose control. Missing one would be a break in the sequence that would have them come crashing down around her. And what then? Chaos! She wished for a pause button, a freeze frame where she could, just for a while, take herself away from the pressure of needing to think all the time and find the answer to why?

* * *

The Sunday papers gave his story no more than a few inches. Discreet and simple. Philip would have hated that. "*A tragedy for the young family*," they called it while the search, they said, "*continues*".

And for the first time ever, Sunday dinner at her mother's was torture. She and the children were met at the door with open arms, the instinctive contact teeming with a fusion of pity, despair, affection and tears.

"Mum," she whispered before her mother could speak, "I don't want to talk about it, okay? Not in front of the kids." She nodded towards the two trailing behind her.

And like a pro, composing herself, Sylvia bent down to their level as if nothing had happened.

"Well, just look at you two! And what exactly have you been up to?" she cooed adoringly at her grandchildren. The enthusiasm was a little overdone to the adult ear but, to the children, it was just the encouragement they needed and heeding the prompt they sat on each side of her to fill her in on the day's adventures.

A quiet, if tense affair, the afternoon was filled with the apprehension of unasked and unanswered questions. There would be plenty of time for them, but just now wasn't that time and, cutting the visit short, she took herself and the children home.

That bedtime she lay beside her son. They discussed the day's events and the meaning of life according to a curious six-year-old.

"Mummy, when is Daddy coming home?"

And there it was: quite out of nowhere, the question she had been dreading for days.

"Soon," she lied, not knowing what else to say. "You miss him, don't you?" she asked softly, his answer no more than a sleepy comfortable nod, his eyes weighed down as he snuggled closer to his mum. She stroked his head, thinking desperately of something positive to say without lying to him.

"Daddy won't be back for a while yet, Matthew, but I'm sure he's missing you too."

"Can we ring him? I want to tell him about . . . the dragon scales we found . . . in the woods today . . ."

His voice was beginning to slow and slur and his eyes were almost fully closed. She knew that she didn't have to answer because soon he'd be fast asleep. She stayed with him, lying beside him, stroking his soft hair and rubbing his smooth, round and rosy cheeks, her whole being bursting with love and the instinctive need to shelter and protect him and his sister. And once she was sure they were sound asleep she dragged herself up and secured their duvets in turn.

From the picture frame on the bedside locker, Philip's face stared up at her. If he were there, in front of her, she would have punched him hard.

"You idiot!" she whispered to it in the silence of the bedroom, her voice laced with contempt. How could he leave them behind? What kind of a man was he? And resisting the temptation to remove the picture from the room altogether, she settled instead on deliberately placing the image face down before turning out the light and tiptoeing out of the room. They deserved better and more.

Chapter 14

It was on days like this that she wished she still smoked. Even after nine years, every now and then she still got the nicotine urge and today was one of them. She sat in the car, looking out at the yellow double-panelled door that loomed ominously before her. Bathed in a feeling of anxious anticipation, like a student taking a test for which she hadn't studied, she opened the car door and got out.

It had been over a week since Philip's disappearance but she hadn't had the courage or the desire to come here. Till now. Even then it was prompted by Maloney who said he just wanted to look around. "Routine procedure," he'd called it when they had spoken that morning. He would meet her there.

The grass on the small front lawn was in desperate need of a cut while a few opportunistic weeds had begun to peep through the dark soil around the season's last remaining and tired-looking daffodils. She knew how they felt. Without waiting for Maloney, she put her key in the lock, reaching the moment she had been dreading: back at the house to which she swore she would never return. Turning the key slowly, she took a deep breath as she entered. Its familiar smell immediately seeped into her nostrils and, feeling like an intruder, she stood statue-still, not knowing where to start, or for that matter what exactly it was she was supposed to be starting. A small pile of post was gathered at the base of the door.

For show, if for nothing else, she called out in the silence, "Hello? Philip?"

As if this might, by magic, make him reveal himself from his really, really, good hiding place. There was no surprise when he didn't. The atmosphere felt empty and cold with the doors to the adjoining rooms closed tight, making the space feel slightly claustrophobic. She stood for a while, waiting, before picking up the post and going through to the kitchen. She didn't really know what to expect but one thing was for certain: it wasn't this. The place was spotless, immaculate even, just as she left it, except cleaner, if that were possible. There were no dishes in the sink, no bin overflowing underneath. The chairs were placed perfectly around the table and the curtains neatly tied up in deep swooshes – just the way she liked them. It was like she had never left, except it was tidier. Upstairs was just the same. The laundry basket was empty, not even a lone sock could be found in the bowels of the wicker container. Stepping cautiously, afraid of what she might find, she made her way into the room she had shared with him. She half expected to see the suitcase from his trip full and ransacked at the bottom of the bed where he would normally leave it for her to sort out. But no. It had been unpacked and placed squarely on the top of the wardrobe from where she had removed it almost two weeks ago. The clothes she had packed, the chinos, the shirts, all freshly laundered and hanging perfectly in the wardrobe along with all his other clothes. Nothing was out of place; everything was as it should be – on a normal day, that is. But today wasn't a normal day. Today she should be coming into a house that showed signs of life. She should see things missing, stuff out of place. She should have been able to imagine what Philip had done before he'd left, live his supposed last steps maybe. What he'd had for breakfast from the dishes in the sink, what he'd worn the night before by the laundry in the basket. What he'd put on that morning. Did she really care or was she just curious? She scanned the pristine rows and layers of monotone apparel laid bare in his closet.

As far as she could tell Philip must have left the house wearing nothing but those damn socks because everything else was right there in front of her with no gaps.

The bed was made with the bedspread creased neatly under the two firm pillows. The co-ordinated cushions sat upright, propped perfectly in position. The towels carefully folded over the rail in the en suite. Nothing, not a single item in their collection of remaining possessions, was out of place.

The door to his study was unlocked and ajar which in itself was unusual. This room was always locked. Philip insisted on it. She entered like a prowler, waiting for a second at the threshold with bated breath, waiting to be snared.

The room smelt of him, wafts of musky Gautier aftershave still clinging valiantly to the air. The room even looked like him, if that were possible: deep timber tones in contrast to the cream of the barley-coloured walls, oozing testosterone from every nook and every cranny, with the luxurious pile of the chocolate-brown carpet wrapping it up nicely in a quiet hush. This room was gifted by the sun in the mornings but there were no curtains on the windows overlooking the landscaped green outside – just wide timber Venetian laths bound together with an off-white fabric tape. She pulled them up tight to the lintel and let the golden morning sunlight change the atmosphere from dark and subdued to fresh and sophisticated, its rays bouncing off walls and glistening on the polished timber surfaces of his den. This room was originally supposed to be the nursery but Philip wouldn't hear of it, wouldn't switch his things into the smaller room, citing a lack of light and poor Feng Shui as his excuse. At the time she didn't really mind and let him be but now, as she continued her visual journey, touching each of his possessions, she felt nothing but bitterness. And curiosity. She was curious about what the hell he was thinking, about what he had done and why he had done it.

Philip could spend hours in this room, but what exactly he did in it she had no idea. Sometimes she would hear him batter away furiously for hours on the keyboard, other times there would be no sound at all. Sometimes she assumed he was sitting in his leather recliner reading the papers or perhaps listening to one of the hundreds of CDs in his cherished collection. He had an excellent cross-section of music, everything from rock to opera, and used to tease her in the early days about her own taste in music. Esmée tended to go for the melodic songs, ones you could sing to and get lost in the words, and so he labelled her taste as "mainstream" which, she supposed, was true. But it didn't preclude her from liking some of what he called "intellectual" or "experimental" sounds. He used to boast of eclectic rhythms and mention bands that she had never heard of or whose CDs she was ever likely to purchase for herself. But after a while, as if bored by his own little humiliating game, he stopped sampling his collection with her, preferring instead to lock himself away to explore alone. He, she thought, was a stereotypical music snob, with the notion that it was impossible for a Take That fan to like Beck too. The longer they were together the less he cared to know about her taste but she always kept an inquisitive eye on his.

Occasionally, secretly, she would use the spare key to go into the study and check out his latest purchase . . . and snoop around to see what else he might be up to in there. She never found anything suspicious – just confirmed that he was absolutely anal, with hundreds of CDs all stored neatly in upright holders, catalogued alphabetically according to category. Looking at it now, all neat and proper, she gave in to the juvenile urge and deviously took Oasis' "Wonderwall" from his rock and pop category and placed it purposely after Verdi's Aida in the classical section. Paul Weller trapezed over Cirque De Soleil, Bob Dylan found comfort next to Placido Domingo, Pink Floyd took pride of place atop Madame Butterfly, Michael Bublé courted Moby, while Shirley Bassey flirted with The Fratellis. It was guaranteed to drive him mental when he got back. A sobering thought: when he got back.

Running her hand across the smooth walnut surface of his desk, she asked herself if she really thought he was alive. For sure, she wasn't entirely convinced that he had taken his own life and the absence of any idea as to what exactly he was running from both scared and infuriated her immensely.

She sat into the oversized leather chair that squeaked for want of oil as she moved herself from side to side. Dwarfed by its vastness, she inspected his lair.

He has a great vantage point from behind his desk, she thought, surveying the entire room and out of the window from just that position. The black state-of-the-art flat LCD screen sat to the left of the desk, the keyboard to the right and the telephone more towards the front, leaving an open expanse in the middle for 'stuff'. But there was nothing on it except for the leatherbound blotting mat that hadn't so much as a scribble on it. She gently swept her hand across its top, checking her fingers for dust. If this were her desk, she thought as she rubbed non-existent particles from her fingers, she'd have bits and pieces everywhere – papers, pencils, books, pictures: stuff.

She had bought his last year's Christmas present, the antique chess set that now sat hardly touched on a top shelf, on eBay.

Her attention shifted to the computer. She pressed the silver power button on the hard drive perched underneath and listened as it whirred into action, powering up the slim display in front of her. As always strings of numbers and meaningless words flickered on and off the screen. She watched patiently as it went through its normal start-up procedure, waiting for the familiar blue-sky picture to pop up before her. Every now and then she would browse the Internet while she was in the study. If Philip knew she'd been dropping in to play with his equipment he'd have gone nuts! She went to meticulous lengths to conceal her presence, always careful not to touch anything but the computer and to delete the history of her electronic journey before she logged off.

But as she sat there, waiting for it to go through its normal motions, she was alarmed as the screen went through a new sequence, one she didn't recognise. She sat forward cautiously. If she were a dog her ears would have cocked, to listen more closely to its innards chug until the screen eventually took on its familiar vibrant blue colour but with a luminous white rectangle in its centre.

"*Password*," it said, its cursor blinking at her from the white box.

Stunned by the simple yet unexpected communication that flickered mindlessly she sat back into the chair, processing the consequences of this unforeseen request, too afraid to respond but equally afraid to turn it off. It had never asked her for a password before. Shit. Her immediate and instinctive reaction was panic: Philip will know I've been messing here.

It took only a few moments to remember his absence, which incredibly she remembered with relief. No need to panic. Then she felt guilt.

The ring of the doorbell broke the guilty spell. She couldn't turn the machine off quick enough so she unplugged it from the wall and, leaving the room she closed the door, leaving Philip's world behind her.

She was tired. She didn't have the energy to keep asking why? Why he left the door open. Why he encrypted his computer. Why he tidied up so well. Why he took off his shoes. Why he jumped off the cliff. Emotionally, she was shot.

She had wanted rid of him, wanted him out of her life, and now that her perverse fantasy had come true she had no place to turn for comfort.

The doorbell rang again. Maloney, she assumed. Coming down the stairs to answer the now-persistent ring, she noticed a box tucked into the alcove beside the empty coatstand. It was open and filled with some of her things: perfume, an old hairbrush, some odd ornaments, the pink pashmina Philip had bought her for one of their anniversaries. It sat inconspicuously, ready for her to fetch. She didn't remember filling it, but assumed nonetheless that she had and had forgotten it in her rush to leave.

She opened the door to greet her visitor, who was not alone.

Alarmed by the sight of two officers standing behind Maloney, she froze and stood there holding on to the door. Had they found a body?

"Don't panic," Maloney assured her. "This is just routine. We just need to take some prints that will help us identify Philip. Nothing more."

Relieved, she let the two men, on Maloney's instruction, go upstairs to the bedroom. Picking up the box at her feet, she led Maloney through to the kitchen and placed the box on the counter beside her car keys to make sure she didn't forget it again.

Then Maloney was offered tea and a stool at the breakfast bar.

They sat opposite each other, taking their first sips of the hot tea in silence.

"So. How have you been?" he asked finally, his words breaking the nervous tension that seemed to fill the otherwise sunny kitchen.

"Fine, I suppose," she replied, slightly distracted by the fresh-washed smell of him that filled the room. "Just trying to get on with things." She shrugged.

He nodded his approval.

She got up to stretch over the sink and open the window.

"This has been weird though," she added, indicating the house with a broad sweep of her hand.

"How so?"

"Well, coming back. The last time I was here wasn't that sweet." Her mocking tone was directed at him rather than herself.

"Sorry. I only meant . . ."

"I know. I'm just being facetious. It's hard, you know, since they stopped looking."

"Go on," he encouraged.

"It's like I'm caught in some strange state of limbo. I don't know what to do next. It's not like I have someone to bury. He's just gone. But not gone, if you know what I mean. He's still here really and I can't really get on with things. I can't actually visualise things without him."

The sudden rise of his eyebrow told her that he had misunderstood.

"No," she protested, blushing at the implied suggestion, "I don't mean like that. I'm not after some emotional reconciliation! I mean, he always figured in my imagining of how this new phase of my life might go. He'd be here. Not in a good way – he'd just be here."

She could feel the pressure of a week's worth of uncried tears gather force at the back of her throat. The last thing she wanted to do was cry now. Not with Maloney. He was fishing. Regardless of how decent he was being by listening, she could tell he was after something and, recognising the threat, she shifted focus back to him.

"Have you found anything helpful?" she asked.

There was a fleeting pause, but it was gone so quickly she thought she had imagined it.

"Not yet. But we're working on it. I wanted to see if there is anything here that could point us in a direction. Does he have a PC here?"

"Yep. Upstairs in his study." She blushed as she remembered her panic earlier.

"Is it okay for me to take a look? See if there is anything on it that can help?"

"Certainly."

"And is there a safe anywhere in the house?"

"Jesus!" she responded, slightly startled. "I don't think so – unless he has one concealed in his study. How very James Bond!"

His look in response suggested there was something more to the task than just "routine procedure".

"Are you looking for something in particular?" she asked.

"Okay, let's get this done," he responded, ignoring her question. He stood up and placed his mug in the sink. He gestured to the ceiling and unnecessarily asked her permission. "May I?"

She nodded her assent and left him to it. Her tour was done. But she followed his progress anyway from the safe distance of her kitchen, tracking the sound of his footsteps as he walked about the study and bedroom.

He took longer than she expected. Eventually he and the others came back downstairs. After a few quiet words in the hall, the other two left and Maloney joined Esmée in the kitchen.

"You have a lovely home," he remarked.

"This is not my home," she retorted firmly, standing up from the stool. "Are you done?"

"Yes."

"Find anything?"

"Nothing really. No safe anyway. I would like to take the computer with me though."

"You're welcome to it." She thought a minute before casually commenting, "It's tidy up there, isn't it?"

"I suppose," he shrugged.

"Odd, don't you think?" she questioned, testing to see how he was thinking

"Why so?"

"Well, is it not a bit too neat?"

"I can't answer that," he replied. "I don't know how you like to keep things."

"Not me. Him!" she barked, with a pointed finger directed upwards towards the absent person in the study. "I haven't been here, remember?" she stressed, her animosity towards him refreshed, negating the apparent friendliness of earlier. He really was such an asshole.

"Well, he did strike me as a bit anal when we met before."

"Oh, for God's sake! Forget I asked!" she said, feeling stupid as well as annoyed at how unhelpful and obtuse he was being. "I thought you were a detective or something."

"I am," he interjected calmly.

"Well, go do your job," she snapped back. "Go detect or whatever it is you do. This just isn't making any sense and you're not helping. Give me something. Anything that tells me you know what you're doing, because right now I can't see it."

"Look, Esmée," his tone was firm in response to her outburst, "you need to start thinking about the frame of mind he was in. People like him do funny things before –" He stopped dead.

"*People like him? People like him what?*" she shrieked. "People like him like to clean up dishes before they die? Freaks like him do their laundry and make beds? Losers like him run away without a trace? Assholes like him leave without so much as a 'seeya'? Is that what they do before they bugger off? Tell me, because I've not done this before. I don't know!" She was outraged by his lack of perception. "For all we know he could be out there. Somewhere. Laughing at us. At me. At you," she spat, her face souring with disgust.

"For God's sake, Esmée, calm down. Okay. Yes, I agree, it is a little odd. Yes, it does warrant further exploration. And, yes, we will look into it, I promise. We'll find out what happened – we always do . . . well, most of the time anyway," he clarified almost to himself.

The sudden twist of her head combined with her disgusted expression suggested he might have gone a little too far. All she wanted was answers, he understood that, but she had to see that there were still too many questions. "Oh, for God's sake, Esmée, we're looking at every possibility, possibilities that haven't even crossed your mind. We're doing our job, Esmée."

"Well, tell me," she pleaded. "Tell me what you think happened."

"I can't, because I don't know." He was trying to be firm without snapping at her. "You have to understand that I can't just jump to conclusions – it's my job not to. We need to find out everything we can, every bit of information and only then can we start to build a picture and then . . ." He watched with mixed emotion as she visibly shook, shrugging her shoulders in disappointed defeat. He felt pity for her ignorance, sadness for her loss, anger at her audacity and disappointment at her arrogance. But the trained professional took the higher ground and, despite his dwindling patience, assumed a softer calming tone.

"Look, Esmée, you know if he's alive we'll find him." He moved his head to search out her gaze. "You don't think we're that incompetent – not to explore every avenue – do you?"

Not wishing to insult him, she didn't answer.

"I know you think he couldn't have done himself any harm and we've checked the airlines and the ferries. If he's alive then he's probably still in Ireland because he didn't leave by any commercial route and he won't get into any other country without being noticed. His face will be all over the security network by now."

He stopped talking and studied her overwhelmed posture.

"Esmée?" he enquired slowly. "Have you heard from him? Has he made contact?"

"No!" she hotly denied, raising her face to look at him. "No, he hasn't!"

"Good, because if he does you need to tell me immediately."

She nodded.

He wanted to make her feel better, wanted her to know that she could trust him, rely on him even. Taking a step closer, he smiled a reassuring smile and reached out to place a soothing hand on her arm. But the spark that transferred on contact with her soft skin was electric, propelling him to disconnect instantly. She felt it too. He could tell. She blushed and her hand immediately replaced his on her arm.

"Right!" he announced unnecessarily, the colour in his face matching hers. "I'll take the computer and get out of your hair."

She heard him leave the room then bound up the stairs.

When he returned to the kitchen he placed the computer and a form on the counter.

"You'll need to sign this," he said. "I'll get the computer back to you as soon as we're done."

She signed it without caring if she ever saw the machine again.

Outside, the two officers were waiting, leaning against Maloney's car. One of them opened the boot and Maloney put the computer inside.

Esmée watched them drive away and around the corner, Maloney's parting words ringing in her ears: "You have my number, so if he does turn up . . ."

She put the box from the house into the boot of her car and set off for home.

It was only lunchtime but already she was exhausted and incensed, not to mention more than a little disconcerted by their brief but intimate encounter.

She was thankful when she returned after collecting the kids that they had the rented cottage to themselves. The last few days had been non-stop questions. She needed time to herself to think. Or not to think.

*   *   *

That evening she spent longer than usual putting Matthew and Amy to bed, reading and chatting with them until their lids were heavy and sleep was near. Comforted by their presence, she stayed with them long after they were asleep.

She hadn't watched telly in ages and for the first time in this house sat down to indulge in the wide screen and vibrant image on her own. She channel-hopped for a while, flicking through the soaps, current affairs programmes and documentaries, settling finally on an old war movie – but it wasn't enough to capture her full attention.

For all her wishing to be alone, now that she was she was lonely, and picking up the phone she dialled Fin's number. She just wanted to chat, see how she was getting on with her exhibition pieces, but it went straight to voicemail. It was too late to call her mum, Penny was on nights and Lizzie was away with work. Putting the phone back in its cradle, she had no option but to settle for her own company and, deciding on an early night, was just about to lock up when she remembered the box in the boot of her car.

She nipped outside in her stocking-feet to retrieve it and once back inside turned out the lights, put on the alarm and took the box up to her room. Perched on the edge of the bed, she opened it up and began unpacking its contents, trying to remember when and why she had packed them.

It quickly became apparent that although these were her things it wasn't her box. Well, she hadn't put the things in it. With most of its contents strewn over the bed she came to a layer over which lay a sheet of folded newsprint, its edges neatly tucked into the corners to make it fit. She removed it cautiously. Having been moulded so carefully to fit the shape of the box it had to be so for a purpose. With the paper discarded, curiosity along with her heart-rate was raised by the book-shaped packages placed in neat rows at the bottom of the box. Moving it to the floor to get a better vantage point, she knelt down and leaned in cautiously to examine the packages further. The bundles were hard to the touch but flexible all the same, each wrapped in plain white paper and tied with an elastic band. Taking one out, it was surprisingly light. She held it for a while, scared by what it might be. She had seen plenty of pictures on TV of the dark parcels of cannabis and heroin and this was just the right shape. Drugs, she thought, sitting back on her heels. He's a bloody drug dealer, that's what he's running from, she thought, her heart-beat beginning to race at the discovery. And he used her stuff to disguise it. The prick. How bloody dare he!

She breathed deep, hoping to steady her racing heart, and control the excitement mixed with fear at the thought of getting some kind of answers at last.

Ready to face the reality, she slowly unpeeled the wrapping from the corners, expecting to see a dark soil-like substance just like they showed on the news. But she was disappointed.

The white paper was now on the floor but in her hand she held thick stiff wads of purple paper. Wads of purple five-hundred-euro notes packed tightly together and bound with thin white strips of more paper.

There were fifteen bundles in total.

She opened the first and counted: one hundred five-hundred euro notes were now loose and burning in the palm of her hand. The fourteen remaining bundles, she guessed, were about the same size and probably held the same number of notes. There was now more money on her bedroom floor than she had ever seen in one place at any one time. Ever.

For some bizarre reason she lifted one of the thick piles to her nose. The notes weren't new and smelt as dirty as they felt. Filled with sudden contempt, disgust and disappointment, instinctively she cast it aside, as if it was diseased and contagious. The binding split as it hit the floor, scattering the notes all over the carpet.

Shock engulfed her. What on earth was she supposed to do with these? How had they got here?

Drugs? You fool! she chastised herself. You naïve idiot! It's not drugs, it's money!

Dirty money too by the looks of it, literally and figuratively speaking. But money from where? What was she supposed to do with it now? Philip had packed the box. He had left it for her to find. He had left her this money, probably thinking that she'd need it now that he was gone. His guilty conscience.

"Jesus Christ!" she swore in stunned disbelief. "Holy Mary

Mother of God and Holy Saint Joseph!" she cried out into the empty room, not caring that she sounded just like her mother, slowly enunciating each syllable as if her precise diction would make it all disappear. But it didn't.

Where would she put it? She couldn't keep it here. Quickly she set about gathering up the scattered notes, their filth stinging her flesh at every touch. Did he expect her to keep it? Did he expect her to be relieved by it? Did he want her to be reassured? Why did he think it was okay to keep her guessing?

Regardless, she knew this was bad, bad money, its presence already offensive to her and, by leaving it for her, Philip was implicating and tying her into whatever it was he was doing. What the hell was he up to? Whatever it was she wanted no part of it. Not one stinking euro of it. She checked the time. It was too late to do anything now – it would have to wait till morning.

She piled the money as best she could into the box. Taking it downstairs, she put the cumbersome lumps into two plastic shopping bags, one after the other, opened the back door and stepped out onto the deck. Scanning the small yard she searched for a place to put her foul fortune. She didn't want it in the house or anywhere near her. Lifting the lid on the coalbunker, as good a place as any, she buried it in amongst the black lumps and shut the lid tight.

There was no need to tell anyone except the police about it, she decided, as she scrubbed her hands over and over again, trying to rid them of the soiled feeling and grubby smell. Maloney would know what to do. He could figure out where it came from. For all she knew, maybe he already knew and was keeping it from her. God, maybe they thought she was part of it! What a frickin' mess.

Chapter 15

Esmée spotted him on the bright Wednesday morning. Maybe it was the long leather coat he wore on such an unusually warm late-spring day that made him stand out. More likely though it was his stance beneath the overhanging horse-chestnut trees opposite the school that made him conspicuous, apparently relaxed but with his eyes darting wildly, watching everything but focusing on nothing, lacking the intent and protective look of the parents who dashed through the finely tuned drop-off procedure.

There he was again on the Thursday and she was sure she'd seen him in the supermarket car park earlier that day and again in the shop itself, but when she went to investigate further, pushing her trolley from aisle to aisle, he seemed to disappear somewhere between the fresh fruit and the delicatessen. So when she spied him in exactly the same spot, opposite the school gates, on Friday morning, the morning after her illicit find, she made a point of tracking down the school headmistress, Mrs Jones.

"I don't mean to be an alarmist, but I've noticed a man the last few days watching the school from across the road."

Always a woman of action, Mrs Jones beckoned to Esmée, pushed up her ample schoolteacher bosom with folded arms and marched off with that scary kind of authority that only a headmistress on a mission could possess. Her Cuban-heeled shoes click-clacked furiously on the hard linoleum floor while her wide hips swung like a pendulum from left to right and back again.

"Where exactly did you see him, Mrs Myers?" she interrogated as together they arrived at the window of a front-facing classroom.

Despite the fact that Esmée and she would meet in the corridors every other day they still hadn't crossed, nor were ever likely to cross that line between formality and familiarity.

"Just over there," Esmée pointed across the street to the now vacant spot amongst the scattering of tiny white horse-chestnut blooms.

Even though the man had disappeared, not even the tiniest doubt crossed Mrs Jones' mind that Mrs Myers had actually seen this man. Of all the parents she had got to know over the years this was one lady who was reasonable and level-headed. Taking Esmée at her word, she thanked the observant parent, promised to be extra vigilant and immediately set about notifying the staff and the local garda station.

Satisfied and reassured by her responsible action, Esmée left the school and walked briskly back to her car which was parked only a little way down beyond the school gates. She checked her watch: it was almost ten past nine. The drag of her bag weighed heavily on her shoulder, laden down by the burden, both emotional and physical, of the sooty package.

She had called Maloney first thing, only for him to tell her he was in court all day and probably couldn't make it to the house till after six.

"Is that okay?" he asked.

"Not really."

"Why? What's up? Are you all right? Has Philip –"

"I'm grand," she interrupted. "I found something, that's all, and I need you to take it as soon as possible."

"What is it?" he asked, his interest aroused.

"It's . . ." She paused, paranoia setting in. "Look, I'd rather not say over the phone."

"Right. So could you drop it in to the station?"

"Yes, I could."

"Okay – well, Doug will be at the station from about eight – give it to him – he'll look after it for me."

She had wrapped the money up tight, binding it in sheets and sheets of the kid's coloured paper before putting it at the bottom of her bag.

Now, eager to get rid of it, feeling vulnerable with it in her possession, she quickened her pace, fishing the car keys from her pocket as she walked and beeping to open the car. She wasn't prepared for the tap on her shoulder and the deep voice that said her name.

He stood tall over her as she turned and raised her head, taller by about a foot, his broad bulk close, too close for comfort. Instinctively she took a step backwards, almost losing her balance as her foot missed the edge of the kerb, the car blocking her fall.

"Shit!" she exclaimed, one hand instinctively clutching her chest, startled by his close and intimidating presence. "You scared the life out of me!" She laughed uneasily, aware that she had just reported this man as a potential stalker. "I'm sorry, yes, I'm Esmée Myers. Can I help you?"

She tried to step around him and re-establish the comfort of her personal space. He took steps to regain intimacy and, again putting less than a pace between them, placed a disarming and forceful hand on her elbow.

"Get into the car," he instructed quietly and politely, steering her firmly by the elbow to the rear passenger door.

"I beg your pardon?" Her protest was ignored as she tugged hard to try and free her arm from his grip.

Thinking she was being mugged she called out, frantically glancing to her left and right, looking for someone, anyone who might help her, but the streets were empty with all the parents scattered in their various directions before the school bell had even rung. Panic pumped adrenaline through her veins and triggered the futile kicks that made contact with the ankles and calves of her assailant to no avail. He tightened his grip and pushed her backwards. She had nowhere to go, jammed tight between the cold metal of the car and the firm chest of her would-be assailant. From nowhere it seemed a second man appeared and jumped into the driver's seat as she struggled pointlessly.

"Don't make a fuss," the first man whispered close to her ear. "Just get into the car and you won't get hurt."

The force of his words was thick and menacing as he pulled open the rear door and pushed her towards it.

"Take the car!" she offered, scared and confused. "Go on, take it – my wallet too – there's money in it. Take it!" Her captured hands made a feeble push towards him, her eyes pleading with him, begging him to let her go.

Catching a look in her terrified stare, he too, if only for a split second, appeared confused, but it passed quickly as he registered what exactly Esmée thought was happening. His eyes sparked with the power her fear gave him and reflected venomously in his slow smile. Sensing her inhale deeply in preparation to scream, he leaned in tighter and pushed against her, closer this time, his laughter vibrating moistly on her earlobe while his fingers and thumb dug deep and sore into her flesh.

"If you want to collect little Mattie in one piece this afternoon then get into the fucking car!"

She felt his spittle slip warm and viscous down the side of her neck as he spat the command through his yellowing teeth, challenging her, willing her to disobey. With shaking knees and lurching stomach, she did as he asked and stumbled into the back of the car. He sat into the seat after her and, snatching the car keys from her grip, threw them to his companion who, with only a silent glance, started the car and pulled off quickly.

Cursing the child-lock that prevented her from escaping at the traffic lights, Esmée watched through the window as gradually they picked up speed.

"What do you want? It's the money, isn't it?" she demanded, her reasonable attempt at being masterful and in control utterly belied by the quake of her voice. "Who are you? Where are you taking me?"

But neither man spoke, her backseat companion staring straight ahead apparently oblivious, or at least deaf, to her frantic questions as they drove down the familiar streets of her village and out to the main road that fed into the city.

"Answer me!" she shrieked, hugging her bag protectively, cowering further into the corner of the seat, putting as much distance as she could between her and her captors. "Tell me, for God's sake! Please tell me where you're taking me!" Tears of sheer terror fell without shame down each of her flushed and shaking cheeks.

"Would you ever just shut the fuck up?" the man by her side bellowed, followed by a tired sigh and the casting of his eyes to heaven with a denigrating shake of his head, ostensibly bored by her, as if this was the most natural situation for him to find himself in.

The thud in her chest hurt as her stomach danced, threatening to throw up her morning coffee at her feet. She was scared, more scared than she had been in her entire life as familiar landmarks outside the window were soon replaced with places and buildings she didn't recognise.

They knew her, knew her children's names. Thoughts of rape and murder filled her head. Why her? Would she ever see her children again? What were they going to do with her? The pace of her sobbing intensified as thoughts of Matthew and Amy came rushing to the forefront of her mind and she thought of them totally parentless, orphans. What would become of them? She was all they had left. She imagined them waiting for her to come and pick them up, pictured Matthew taking his little sister's hand to wait anxiously for her in the school yard, watching the last of their friends go home. Esmée was never late to collect them. They never had to wait for her – she was always there to meet them, always on time, when they streamed out in single file from their classrooms to their designated and numbered white line drawn on the tarmac. Matthew would worry, would know something was wrong. Amy would probably sense it too and cry; she was still only a baby. She saw them in her mind's eye sitting on the miniature chairs against the wall outside Mrs Jones' office, clutching their schoolbags in their little arms. Waiting. Who would Mrs Jones call? Whose numbers were on the emergency form that she filled out? Her own first, then Philip's and after that . . .? Shit! She couldn't remember! It was so long ago since she'd completed it. She wept into her hands for her children and for herself and hardly noticed when they came to a standstill.

She looked out the window and into the dim light of a concrete car park but had no idea where they were. It looked like every other high-rise car park she'd ever been in. If she got out of this alive she would never be able to tell anyone where they'd taken her.

The man beside her took hold of her arm and yanked her roughly out of the car after him, almost pulling her arm out of its socket. He steered her towards a silver Mercedes with blacked-out windows in the next bay. This was surreal, she thought, close to hysteria, as the door opened smoothly and a hand emerged, motioning for her to join it. Reluctantly and with everything to lose, she did as she was bid, too afraid to run. Her nose snotty, her eyes runny and her chest puffing uncontrollably, she was in a state.

There were no lights on in the darkened car and it took a while for her vision to acclimatise and notice the grey-faced middle-aged and balding man beside her. He sat like royalty in the back of the luxurious cream-leather interior, an arm thrown casually across the seat, obviously anticipating her arrival.

"Mrs Myers, I hear they call ya," he greeted gallantly, his outstretched hand taking hers and shaking it slowly. "Is it all right if I call ya Esmée?"

She nodded, taken aback by his unexpected politeness, the thick Dublin drawl mirroring the style of his approach but definitely not the image of the car.

"Sorry if Tommo was a little rough with ya," he said, handing her a tissue, "but I really just wanted to meet ya."

All the words in her vocabulary left her. Unable to speak, she simply shook her head, too afraid to tell this man what she really felt. She sat sideways in the seat, on the edge and not quite facing him. She could tell even from his sitting position that he was a tall man, his large intimidating frame seeming to fill the rear of the car, the few strands of hair combed over the bald patch almost touching the fabric of the roof. This, combined with the dim light and the stench of his stale sweat and alcohol, took the warmth from her soul. She quivered, cowering and scared into the corner, holding on tight to the bag in her lap.

"Are ya cold?" he enquired politely, almost convincingly

worried, and without waiting for her to answer leaned forward in his expensive camel-coloured coat to adjust a control on the illuminated dial between the driver and passenger seat, his slicked hair-strands flopping comically forward on his brow as he did so. If she hadn't been in fear for her life she probably would have laughed.

"Tommo tells me," he said casually, fixing his mop and turning to face her full on, "that your hubby's been a bit of a naughty boy." He looked her up and down as he spoke, his eyes eventually stopping at her face, focusing on the faint bruise. He reached out his hand slowly to touch it, running his fingers over the receding pale-pink cut on her forehead.

She flinched at his touch. Her eyes closed as she tried to control the rising nausea. If he noticed her cringe he didn't show it but a tense and uneasy atmosphere seemed to seep into the car as he continued to explore her, persisted in invading her personal space with such intensity she felt she would pass out.

"Such a lovely face." His words were barely audible as his hand fell to her shoulder and passed leisurely over her breast, touching it with tentative reverence, his face filled with concentration as tiny beads of sweat formed on his brow, slowly sliding over his temples and into oblivion.

Her chest heaved while her lungs tried to compensate for the lack of oxygen and rush of blood around her body. Her arms clenched, holding the bag tight to her stomach, as if somehow it might protect her. Tighter and tighter she held on as his hand by-passed it to rest cruelly on her denim-clad thigh, just above her knee. Every muscle in her body seized as, moulding it in his palm, he travelled a slow journey towards its top. She held her breath, unable to look at the man for whom this touch was seductive while it repulsed, scared and sickened her. In normal circumstance she would have lashed out against such an intimidating, humiliating and blatant incursion of her person but fear of the consequences stopped her. He would enjoy punishing her, of that she was sure.

"Nothing permanent," he said finally, making idle nodding reference to her face, the seismic atmosphere shifting as soon as he extracted his hand from between her clenched upper thighs. His exercise was complete: he had achieved the desired effect, confirming that he was the master. Replacing his arm on the back of the seat he sat back to survey her face and reaction to his assault, silently mocking her, enjoying her discomfort, proud of the terror he instilled in her.

"Who are you? What do you want from me?" Esmée asked, her voice shaking as she looked defiantly at him.

"Don't you be worrin' about me just yet. I just wanna have a nice little chat, nothing else, that's all."

"This is about Philip, isn't it?"

"Ahhh, that it is. Me and Phil, we go back a looooong way," he crooned, placing peculiar emphasis on his name.

"Where is he?" she croaked, her voice struggling to escape from the scratchy dryness of her dry throat. Swallowing hard, she waited for an answer.

"Now," he said, settling further into the seat and looking up towards the upholstered roof as he replied, as if speaking to the gods, "ya see, that's the gazillion-euro question, isn't it?"

Cocking his head to one side he looked down to consider her, assess her, and pursing his lips together with due consideration he eventually presented his case.

"Your Phil, or my Bobby as I like to call him – seems he wants us both to think he's fish food somewhere at the bottom of the Irish fuckin' Sea," his arm motioned dramatically in waves through the space between them, "but we don't believe him. Do we?" He asked the question of her like she was a student and he the tutor.

She shook her head.

"And where do you think he is?" he asked.

Feeling like a brainless, stupid puppet she shook her head again. "I have no idea," she said, her eyes wide with fear at the unknown horror of what might come next.

His loud laugh ripped into her brain like a stiletto blade as he accepted her ignorance and exercised his power over her.

"You're lovely, do ya know that?" he complimented her, obviously distracted by her presence and proximity, slapping his hand on her thigh. "So, ya don't know where he is then?"

Esmée shook her head fast.

Sitting back into the seat, he seemed to relax a little.

"Well, let me tell you a few things about your fancy boy. Me and your hubby, we were . . ." He paused, scratching his unevenly shadowed chin as if searching for the appropriately intellectual words to describe their relationship.

"Hmmm, let's just say we were business associates. Yeah! Business associates," he affirmed, happy with his choice. "An' we've got some unfinished business to sort out. Some seriously fuckin' serious catchin' up to do . . . but now he's gone and done his little disappearing act and I can't sort him out." He was smiling at her now, as if this latest piece of information should give her great pleasure.

And it did in one respect, because now at least she knew why Philip was gone.

"What kind of business?" Finding her nerve, she asked the question, with genuine curiosity secreted somewhere behind the depths of her fear.

He considered her for a while before proceeding plainly. "Let's just say he's cost me time and money. A whole lotta time and a whole lotta money. Ya see, your precious partner liked the gee-gees. Loved them, he did. But he wasn't very good at it, now was he, and he lost shitloads." His tone was amicable and matter of fact.

"So this," Esmée dared, "this is about the money. It belongs to you?" and taking the sizable multi-coloured bundle from her bag cast it unceremoniously into his lap, glad to be rid of it. "Is this what you want?"

"Ah fair play to ya, Es. Can I call ya Es?" he asked as he ripped through the layers. "That's some bit of wrappin'! What the fuck is it? Pass the bleeding parcel?" he roared hysterically, amused by his own joke until finally he got to the last layer and flicked through the dirty notes, pile by pile, with an accomplished lick of his fingers, laughing as his count was complete. "No offence, love, but this isn't even close to settling up. We're beyond cash now." He placed the package down deliberately on the seat between them. He considered it for a second, as if debating whether or not to just take it, because he could, before pushing it back towards her.

"That's a lotta moola," he nodded, "but it ain't mine, love." He was almost apologetic as he announced, "Those notes ain't gonna give me back my time."

"Time, what do you mean 'time'?" Frustration was fast breeding panic. Esmée couldn't think. What the hell was he talking about? Pushing the thought aside, she focused back on the money: that she could understand. "There's no more apart from that." She pointed at it. "This is all I have. I don't know where he got it but there's no more."

"Don't be fuckin' stupid, woman! Keep the fuckin' money. I'm not after you or your money," he sneered. "I'm after your lesser half." He smirked at his own joke.

Adrenaline suddenly pumped through her veins, giving her an unwise and altogether false cocky confidence. "Look," she said, "I have no idea where he is and if I knew I'd kill him myself . . . so can I please go now?"

"Easy there, girl!" His voice rose abruptly. "Now don't go getting all smart-arsey with me." His eyes bored into hers menacingly. "I'm being nice here . . ."

Startled, she dropped her stare quickly, needing no more warning. "I don't know where Philip is, really I don't," she implored as calmly as she could, "and I want to go home. You're scaring me!" Her voice shook, courage deserting her, as she admitted the effect he was having on her.

"Well, he's one brave little bollix," he said, ignoring her plea, not quite ready to let her go. He hadn't finished his story yet. "That's what got him into trouble in the first place. A cocky selfish prick right down to his cold little pinkies," he mocked.

Esmée had no idea why he thought to share this information with her and wished he'd stop, but he kept going.

"Thought he could play with the big boys, thought he was smarter than the rest of us, thought he could shop me in an' get away with it. Did he think a fancy name an' a new hair cut'd keep him safe from me? Thick fuck!" Suddenly he bellowed: "I'm the scariest fucker in this fuckin' town! In this fuckin country!" He pulled himself together quickly, cracking his neck to relieve his tension. "But he didn't reckon on ol' Jimbo here having half a brain, did he? Didn't count on me mates helpin' out, bein' me eyes out here with me in there. No lying and hiding and begging forgiveness gets ya off the hook that easy, now does it?" He laughed raucously, eventually ending with a throat-tightening wheeze. "No wonder he's gone fuckin' missin' – I'd go missin' if I was after me!"

Esmée tried to keep track of what he was saying but the missing links in his oratory defeated her.

"I've got friends, I do. Every bleedin' where. All over the gaff. He didn't reckon on that now, did he? And here's me trying to help out. Sort out his problems. Even tried to teach him a thing or two, ungrateful fucker!" His words brought moisture with them as they were spat out. "But he fucked up good 'n' proper!" The rise and fall of his schizophrenic tone transformed again into a menacing growl. "And whatever scam he was running in that posh fuckin' job of his didn't come through and he comes runnin' to me like some selfish fuck. 'Oh help me, oh help me!'" he mimicked with a ridiculous squeak, "and I did and look where it got me. Last fuckin' time I'll do that I'll tell ya. Fourteen fuckin' years it cost me."

"Why are you telling me this?" she asked, willing him to stop. This was not something Philip would be involved in. He wasn't the person this rabid lunatic was describing.

"Because..." he returned resolutely, casting a knowing glance at her cheek before shifting slowly to the open pile of notes that lay ominously by his side, "you've earned the right to know what class of a bollix your husband really is, or ... possibly ..." he paused tilting his head and raising his eyes in mock respect, "was."

"And what makes you think I won't go to the police?" she asked.

He leaned in close. "You're not a stupid bird, are ya? Not like that last bitch he had. Jesus, she was some howler, I'll tell ya. Lovely bird but a stupid bitch. Not like you though. You're different." He moved in close, his face looming dangerously near. "An' anyway, you want those lovely curls on that boy's head to stay like that, don't ya?"

She pulled back, burying herself as far into the back seat as the fabric would allow, shaking her head vigorously, understanding perfectly what he meant.

"I just want a little favour. Teeney-weeney." He paused, lifting his hand once again to grasp her face in the palm of his hand. Turning it to him, he locked eyes with her.

It hurt, not his grasp or his fingers as they pressed on her skin but the intense brutal warning in his eyes as they bore into hers.

"I want you to tell him I'll be waiting for him."

Esmée nodded her assent furiously. "But what if he doesn't? Come back, I mean."

"Oh, he'll be back all right . . ." he said, his mouth close to hers. "You're a beaut."

She could almost feel the excitement vibrate through him, taste the testosterone as it oozed from his every pore on his disgusting lecherous body.

"And if there's one sure fuckin' bet, somethin' we can all fuckin' count on, it's his addiction to chance, one last stake – and you, my sexy lady," the pressure of his fingers clutching either side of her face intensified, "you'll be his biggest risk yet. And when he's there, right there in front of ya, you tell him I'm lookin' for him. You tell him Jim Brady has his number."

Chapter 16

Jim Brady. The name. It slammed through her like a careering juggernaut. He was there when her father was shot. He was the one they jailed. Her father died, killed in cold blood, on a Wednesday morning in June. Fourteen years ago. She was eighteen years old and Interrailing across Europe with Fin and the rest of the college crew. She would never forget the night she called home to tell her parents about the beauty of the Sistine Chapel that they had queued all day in the blistering Italian heat to see. But she never got to tell them any of it. To this day she had never described the beauty of her experience to anyone. How could she share the feelings of extreme passion and nerve-tingling happiness when possibly in those very same moments her father was breathing his last breath in a cold city hospital? He would have understood them. He was her kindred spirit. They were so alike, had so much in common. He would have felt that excitement too. She knew it. But she never got to share her feelings and she never got to say goodbye.

* * *

When they left her back to the same spot outside the school she was quiet and numb. Leaving the keys in the ignition and the engine running, both men got out of the car and walked calmly towards the main street, leaving Esmée bewildered and drained in the back seat with her bag still weighed down by the money by her side. And in her head the tireless mélange of accusations and questions and fears and answers and conclusions all mixed dangerously together, threatening to detonate if she didn't shut them down. She clutched each side of her head, hoping to stop the spinning, whimpering silently. How had she got here? This wasn't what she had ever intended to happen. Had she started this? Was this of her making? The rhetorical questions served only to feed her self-pity. She knew it. Even in his absence he made her feel inadequate. She couldn't let this happen, couldn't let her world unravel like this. It had to stop. She had to make it stop. If this was of her making, then the undoing was hers to administer also.

* * *

They sat in a triangle of silence. Although the story was told, Fin's mouth still hadn't closed. Flabbergasted. Dumbfounded. Aghast. Terrified.

"So go through that last bit one more time," Tom directed, getting up to pace the room.

"He said to tell him that Jim Brady has his number." Esmée was now tired and her head hurt like hell.

"That fucking bastard!"

"Tom!" Esmée pleaded and not for the first time, pointing meaningfully to the kids in the next room.

"Sorry, sis, but this is crazy shit," he excused himself, turning on his heel to work the rest of the room. "That asshole! What the fuck? What the fuck was he playing at?"

Esmée knew he was referring to Philip who had shifted in Tom's opinion to the aggressor, no longer the victim.

"Tom, I'm sorry but you're hurting my head," she pleaded.

"For God's sake, Tom!" said Fin. "Will you just sit down and stop shouting? It's not helping and frankly it's annoying!"

Her put-down struck hurt across his newly infatuated face, the chemistry between them undeniable.

Exhausted but focused, Esmée had hoped that between them Fin and Tom would help her make sense of the pieces she had been fed and deduce the bits she hadn't. But now, staring at the agitated faces in front of her, she wondered if she had made the right choice and wished she had called Lizzie instead.

"It was him? You're sure?"

"Oh Jesus Christ, Tom! Of course I'm sure. He told me his bloody name, for God's sake!" Exasperated, she let her head fall into her clasped hands.

"Maybe he's confusing him with this 'Bobby' bloke, whoever he is?" said Tom.

"I don't know. I don't bloody know!" She was reaching the end of her tether.

"You have to go to Maloney," said Fin.

At last. The voice of reason. Fin had mostly remained quiet, listening calmly as Esmée recounted the events of the morning.

"There's something else," Esmée admitted to her captive audience.

"Oh God . . ." Fin's head collapsed into her paint-covered hands.

Esmée shifted round to reach for her shoulder bag and upturned it onto the centre of the table. "This," she said, pointing to the notes covering her floral plastic tablecloth.

"Holy shite!" Fin exclaimed, her hand moving involuntarily to cover her mouth. "What the fuck? Where did you get this?"

Always so proper, foul language sounded odd coming from her best friend's mouth and for a split manic moment Esmée almost laughed out loud. Controlling herself, she recounted the story instead.

"Jesus Christ, Esmée, what on earth has Philip got himself into?"

"Do you think it has anything to do with Dad?" she asked, looking at her now noticeably quiet brother.

"It would want to be one hell of a coincidence if it didn't," he said. "Maybe it was meant for Brady – maybe this is why he grabbed you?"

"I don't think so," Esmée reasoned, "otherwise he would have taken it, wouldn't he?" Her mind was working overtime trying to understand what had just happened.

"I don't know, Es. It's bloody peculiar, isn't it?" Tom argued. "One day your husband disappears, then you find this heap of cash in a box and the next day you get nabbed by Ireland's answer to Don Corleone who just happens to be the guy they jailed for our dad's murder – seems like a bit of a no-brainer to me."

"I'm not getting you. Explain, Sherlock!" Fin challenged.

"They have to be connected . . . Jesus, I don't know . . . maybe Philip was trying to protect you. Maybe he was paying Brady to stay away, you know . . . Ah shit! I don't know!" He shrugged as his train of thought derailed.

Fin, still captivated by the money toyed with the bundles and asked, "How much do you think is in here?" Mirroring Esmée's action of the day before, she lifted one to her nose, only to put it down quickly with a grimace.

182

"There are one hundred five-hundred euro notes in each bundle," said Esmée. "And fifteen bundles."

"Hmmm . . ." Always the man for the numbers, Tom took a moment to calculate. "That's seven hundred and fifty grand."

Fin's eyes almost burst from their sockets. "You're kidding!"

"So what do we do?" asked Esmée.

Both women looked to Tom for an answer.

"Fin's right," he said. "We have to take this to the station and let the police do their job."

"Now?" asked Fin.

"Yes. Now."

"God, Tom, I'm not sure I can cope," Esmée sighed. The thought of going back to the egg-yolk interview room made her feel instantly nauseous. "This day has been . . ." But she couldn't finish her sentence. She had no words left.

"Don't be so ridiculous, Esmée," he said. "You really don't have a choice. This isn't some small-time anonymous petty thief. This is Jim Brady we're talking about and Philip. Look at us, like eejits trying to work out what happened. They need to see this and we need to let them do their job. Anyway, this isn't about coping, this is about doing what's right – and, besides, I'll be there all the way, so don't panic, okay?"

His words were weak assurance, but enough to get her going.

* * *

Maloney listened intently to the story as she told it. Esmée thought it odd that he didn't take notes or call anyone else in to listen.

He waited till she was finished then sat back in his seat, taking a moment to observe the two siblings before him: Esmée tense and exhausted, Tom enraged but outwardly calm. He could tell she'd had enough. Her eyes were cheerless and her shoulders slightly hunched. If it wasn't entirely inappropriate, he would love to take her hand, he thought, watching Tom's mouth move but without hearing his words. He wished she'd stop fiddling with her hair – it was too distracting watching her twist and curl the thick brown lock around her fingers.

Focus, Gregory, he told himself in a silent voice that in his head sounded remarkably like his father's.

Brady hadn't wasted much time in tracking her down. He needed to think carefully about the next steps, knowing that the potential for the situation to spiral out of control was considerable. But she had a right to know, he felt, they both did, although others didn't quite agree. Would this change their minds, he wondered as he sat forwards, bringing his hands to the table.

"Okay. Look, I need some time on this one," he said.

"You should have informed us that Brady was released," Tom accused him firmly.

"Yes, yes, we should have," Maloney agreed, "but we don't always get things right and this is one of those times." He took a deep breath, feeling a little cornered. "I can't explain right now what's going on but –"

"So you have something?" Tom cut across him.

There was no point in him denying it, but he could delay it.

"Yes, I have some information but I can't share it with you just yet."

"We have a right to know!" Esmée interjected. "I need to know!"

"I agree you do, but there is some sensitive information involved here and we need to make sure we have all the facts first."

"You'll need to do a little better than that, officer!" she snapped, her words meant to patronise, hoping to insult him, her patience exhausted.

"James Brady was released three days ago," he stated.

"I thought he got fifteen years!" said Tom.

Maloney shrugged nonchalantly. "Slightly early release, yes. He behaved."

"He behaved?" Esmée's words were woven with laughter. "He shot my dad!"

"Hold on there, Esmée, that's not the case. He wasn't the one who shot your father."

"But he knows who did."

"Maybe, maybe not. And if he knows he's not telling us, but that's not the point."

"You're defending him now?"

"No. For God's sake, no. But you have to remember the facts here. You're treading very sticky ground here so you need to be careful."

"And what about the money? And the things he was saying about Philip?" she demanded. "Was he right? Is that what was going on?"

Maloney shook his head, more out of frustration than ignorance.

"Well?" she growled. "Is there anyone here who knows what the hell is going on? I am completely in the dark, I've no idea what's going on and to be honest I'm not sure you guys are any wiser than me." She caught Maloney's glance and held it, mustering as much authority into her returning stare as was possible. "Do you have any idea what happened to me today? Are you actually putting all this together? The man who was in one way or another responsible for our father's death as good as kidnapped me today. I was threatened and – and – molested by this filthy disgusting creature, and you sit there telling me to be careful, to remember the facts?" She rose as her temper flared along with her voice. "You need to do better than this!" His silence was infuriating. Her fist slammed hard on the table. "How dare you sit there and tell me to be careful! You need to tell me what the bloody hell is going on or I'll find someone else who will!"

Both men watched, a little stunned, mute and powerless to intervene, as her temper boiled over and she did a circle of the small cubicle before coming back to the table to reclaim her seat, emotional and slightly embarrassed by her outburst. But she didn't apologise. She fixed her chair, pulled herself up to the edge of the table, took a breath and asked him calmly, if a little breathlessly, "So. What are you going to do?"

Tom put a reassuring hand on his sister's arm while Maloney shifted uncomfortably in his seat.

She was right and he was stuck. His hands temporarily tied. Raising his hands in acceptance, hoping to disarm her, he watched as her breath steadied and her composure returned.

"Esmée – Tom." He looked purposefully at each. "Let me assure you, I, we, are doing everything we can. But we can't share information with you until we know for sure that it is factually correct. And you're right –" he looked at Esmée, "it's unfair, but it's the right thing to do. You have to be patient just for a little longer."

"So what you're telling us," Esmée asserted, "is that you, contrary to what we see, are fully in control of this – you do know what this is all about but you're just not telling us?"

"That's about right."

"So, when do you think you will be able to tell us?" she asked.

"As soon as I can ascertain that the information I have is factually correct."

"And when do you think that might be?"

Maloney smiled, beguiled by her unrelenting, dogged persistence.

"Esmée, I promise that I will tell you everything I know as soon as I can. Is that okay?" he challenged, holding Esmée's glare without so much as a wavering blink.

She nodded her assent. There was nothing much else she could do but agree.

Happy he had the situation back in his control, Maloney used the piled-up cash as a way to get back on track. "I'm going to check the numbers on these notes to see if we can identify where they came from." And gathering up the piles, he got up and left the room.

"What do you think?" Tom asked, breaking the hot silence.

"It's bullshit. If he doesn't tell me what's going on by the end of the week I'm going to demand to see his superior whoever the hell that might be. And if I don't get answers then . . ." she paused to weigh up her options "well, then I'll go to the papers."

Maloney came back into the interview room and, placing a form in front of Esmée, told her she would need to sign for delivery of the money.

"One of my colleagues will be in shortly to count it with you. And as for your encounter with Brady, well, I need to speak to my Super but it doesn't sound like you're in any danger. If he wanted to do you harm he had ample chance this afternoon. That said, I'm going to arrange for a car to sit at the house to keep an eye out – and a visit to Brady is also in order, I think."

"No," Esmée protested firmly. "I'm fine with the car, but please don't go near him. I don't want him to know I've talked to you. I don't want him to come back." The idea that Maloney would provoke Brady further terrified her.

"Okay." Maloney nodded. "Leave it with me." He paused and added, not wanting to ignite the situation again, "Look, once you're done here, go home. I'll have a chat with my boss this afternoon and I'll call round myself later to make sure you're okay and give you whatever information I can."

By the time the money had been counted, three times, she was weary.

Tom took her hand. "Come on, sis, let's go."

And not a moment too soon.

"That place!" she remarked as they turned out of the narrow entrance. "How can anyone work there? It just saps every bit of cheer out of you."

Maloney watched them leave from the upstairs office. He wasn't happy about how this was turning out and wanted more than ever to mind this young woman, but for the moment all he could do was wait.

"I need to get something from Mum's," Esmée announced as they pulled away from the Garda Station. "It'll only take a sec," she promised her reluctant brother who was anxious to get her back to the house and neutral territory.

* * *

Her old bedroom still had the same wallpaper she remembered from the long and late nights preparing for her finals, the twin beds a reminder of the good and the bad times she shared in this room with Lizzie. Beneath the window sat a chest of drawers with lots of chips and peels, its colour more cream than white now, a telling sign of its vintage. The top drawers were Lizzie's while the bottom two were hers. She knelt down and pulled out the last drawer, almost empty apart from a faded purple manila folder. Taking it out, she pushed back the drawer and made her way back to the kitchen where she apologised to her mother again for her hasty visit.

* * *

Later, with Tom dropping Fin back to her studio and the children playing in the garden, Esmée set the folder on the kitchen table. She hadn't looked at it in years. In the early days, just after it happened, she would spend hours reading through the various reports, each saying the same thing but using different words. They were an assurance that someone cared, an expression of a sort of condolence for her loss. The cuttings themselves had long since faded, with their wrinkled corners evidence of many hours of reading and re-reading, but the words were all still there. Philip hated seeing her read them, hated having the folder in the house, calling it morose, and insisted she move on and let the dead man rest. But try as she might she couldn't discard his memory and, she thought rebelliously, if that wasn't moving on then so be it. So the folder moved sideways, back to her old bedroom where she hadn't touched it since. Until now.

Tears slipped quietly down her cheeks as once again the story came to life in her hands.

He had been escorting a Cash in Transit van, making deliveries in the county. They were on their first drop of the day. He wasn't supposed to be there, was only filling in for the day. That was her tragedy. If not Frank then it would have been someone else's dad. Or brother. Or uncle. Or son. On a normal day the job was fairly routine, boring even. They drove behind the blue reinforced van as it made its journey. Their job was to watch for anything suspicious. Keep a lookout. Which they did. On this Wednesday morning he was the passenger, Maurice Mahon the driver. Maurice described him as a great friend and valiant officer. He would never forget him, he had said in his emotional eulogy. That morning Frank Gill noticed a silver Golf GTI parked immediately outside the bank with the engine running and the driver alert and agitated. All he did was get out to take a closer casual look. Their car was unmarked and they were out of uniform. It shouldn't have caused alarm. He was also unarmed. They never found the weapon or established who pulled the trigger that fired the shot, but nevertheless Frank died only hours later from the bullet that punctured his body. The young manager's family, held in what was initially thought to be a tiger kidnapping, were released unharmed and Jim Brady was named as the mastermind, but not the murderer. As the investigation unfolded the news that it was an inside job was eventually reported and the manager who everyone felt so sorry for was in on the plan all along. Turning, as all snakes eventually do, it was he, this young Robert Toner, who would ultimately provide the evidence to put Brady away: his reward, witness protection and a new life in a location unknown.

The tragic victims in all this, the cuttings testified, were the young families affected by crime: Detective Gill's grieving widow and children and Robert Toner's distraught wife and young son.

She hadn't ever really given them a second thought: the Toners. She'd never wondered what became of them, was never curious about the little boy and his mother. Glancing now, however, at the yellowing picture in her hand, which showed them leaving their house, she did wonder. They were being hounded by journalists and photographers. The little boy's arm was being yanked by a frantic mother trying to get them both out of sight, his short legs trying to keep up and his little face scared and confused. With almost fifteen years' distance she could empathise. Julie and Harry. She narrowed the search by adding "robbery", "crime" and "prison". She wondered how they felt about Jim Brady. Did they know about his release? If she hadn't, why would they?

She took down her laptop, fired it up and launched straight into Google.

She typed 'James Brady' into the box and watched the long list of hits that quickly formed. She then narrowed the search by adding "robbery", "crime" and "prison". She scrolled through each item methodically. The news stories showed very little about his release, a small commentary about the return of a reprehensible crime lord to his lair the most interesting. Stepping into his world was like delving into the mouth of a savage animal, the particulars of his activities bringing with them an indescribable surge of anger and fear.

On the face of it, he had always been an upstanding citizen, paid his taxes and earned an honest living running a small taxi firm and a bar on the outskirts of the city. This obviously didn't account for his lavish lifestyle but he covered his tracks well and was always, frustratingly, one step ahead of the police. A well-respected neighbour, he lived "in harmony" in a small community on Dublin's west side, where people regularly had been "astounded" by the accusations made against such an apparently "lovely, caring man who helped so many people in the community."

But beneath the fortified surface, if the published reports were to be believed, were bountiful indictments of illicit deals, robberies and assaults, of punishment beatings and repugnant attacks on whosoever crossed his path. Despite being incarcerated, he still held the Gangland crown. An involuntary shiver washed through her as she remembered the touch of his fingers and the smell of his breath.

She typed 'Julie Toner' into the search box. Fewer results returned but she clicked on one of the familiar pictures from her cuttings. The image of Robert Toner himself filled the screen. His light brown hair falling in layered waves over hands that covered his face. Wrists tied together and shoulders hunched, he was being led away by a guard, flanked on either side by two suits who she assumed were his lawyers. But it was impossible to make a judgement about the man himself without seeing his eyes. Once again she wondered what might have made him do it. The unknown side to his story: the one that drove him to betray his family and friends.

The ring of the doorbell made her jump. She'd been waiting for him to call all afternoon. Maybe now he'd tell her what was going on.

* * *

On the other side of the door a nervous Maloney inhaled deeply, not looking forward to what he knew was coming. Rarely did he feel like this – dread his job – but there was something about Esmée that drew on his emotions. And while she was so anxious for information, he was sure what he had to tell her now wouldn't make her any happier.

The morning after Esmée was attacked by her husband he had sat at his computer and begun his research. If there was something to know he'd find it, of that he was sure. Initially Philip Myers turned up a complete blank. Sure, he was there in the database but only just. Apart from the registration of the car, the insurance and a driver's licence, Philip didn't exist. He had no parking tickets – ever. Had never been stopped or had his insurance checked. He'd never got a speeding ticket or a summons, which at his age was quite a feat. So he brought it to his regular partner Dougie for some inspiration.

"If he's clean, he's clean," Dougie offered. "Always the cynic, Maloney, eh?" he said, taking a playful swipe at his friend.

"There's just something about this one . . ." Maloney muttered.

"Yeah, big tits and long legs more like!" Dougie retorted, not so playful.

And a week later Philip was gone.

"You need prints," Dougie suggested. "Get his fingers and then we'll see who he is and what he's been up to."

The "routine procedure" line worked and allowed him to bring forensics into the house without protest from Esmée.

192

"Why not just tell her?" Dougie asked, intrigued by his partner's reticence and apparent new obsession.

"Because if she knows something she could wipe the place clean."

"Do you think she does?"

"No, but I want to be sure. Besides, if she hasn't a clue, I don't want to freak her out either."

"Don't go getting all soft on me, bud," Dougie warned, his double caution not lost on the wary Maloney. If Esmée knew what he was up to that morning in the house she would have had an even bigger meltdown. But he'd got his prints and answers with them.

At the weekly operations meeting they had planned on telling her along with the rest of the family about Brady's release but Brady was quicker off the mark.

"Snooze 'n' you lose," Maloney told his boss, with a told-you-so nonchalance, furious that this mistake had placed him so firmly in Esmée's line of fire and, boy, did she shoot! His ego still smarted at the memory of the insults hurled. The hardest part was that he had no option but to take it. They had missed their opportunity and were now uncomfortably on the back foot. This latest development placed them embarrassingly at an even further disadvantage and, it seemed, it was his task to catch up.

* * *

Maloney was nervous. Esmée Myers was making him so. Her long luxurious hair was falling simply about her shoulders, the waves resting against her shoulder blades. She was wearing tight-fitting jeans and a T-shirt. The unconscious sway of her behind as it moved was alluring and the outline of her breasts magnetic. He needed to focus, but his eyes were charged. This is crazy, he told himself, watching her as she checked on the kids.

Refusing both the tea and the seat, he rested himself against the kitchen counter, a folder in his hands. He then asked if there was anyone else in the house.

"Just me and the kids – Tom is on his way back here now," she replied cautiously. "Why?"

"We can wait until he gets here before we start," he proposed apprehensively.

His concern triggered alarm bells once more: Maloney was fast becoming the Messenger of Doom.

"No. I'm happy that we can get going without him. Frankly I just don't have the patience to wait any longer."

"Please, Esmée, trust me. Give your brother a call and see if he's close."

Complying, she called her brother, then reported: "He's just a minute away. Now please can we get on with this?"

"Let's wait."

"No. You need to tell me now what the bloody hell is going on!"

He locked eyes with her but was the first to drop his gaze.

"Believe me," he said. "It's best if we wait for your brother."

"Now. Tell me now or get out."

Well! She's asked for it, he thought as he cleared his throat. "Sorry, Esmée, there really is no easy way for me to tell you this . . ." He paused and braced himself.

"Oh God, just spit it out, will you?"

He drew a photograph from the file he had in his hand. Placing it on the table, he looked at her with apologetic eyes.

It was a photo of Philip.

"I'm sorry, Esmée, but Philip Myers, your Philip Myers, doesn't exist. That's not his real name."

And taking a large brown envelope from the folder, he extracted from it a photograph, placed it slowly on the table and pushed it towards her.

Tom arrived just in time to catch her as she fell.

Chapter 17

Esmée watched from the car. It was a familiar scene, one she had enacted herself almost every day. Fifteen years on and the little boy, it appeared, had become a man and a handsome one at that. Julie looked tired, she thought, observing the routine from the safe distance of the road. She wondered if he still lived at home, maybe got a girlfriend? Or was he in college and home for the weekend? He'd be about twenty-one now. And so handsome. His strong angular features so unusually striking: just like his father's. A young girl got out from the back seat of the car, her head firmly planted in a book, her long blonde hair tied back in two plaits. Dressed in jeans and a T-shirt, her slender delicate frame reflected that of her mother.

"Excuse me, young lady!" her mother called.

Esmée smiled to herself at the familiar tone.

"Don't go inside with one arm as long as the other – help, please!"

Reluctantly the girl complied and with her book in one hand and what Esmée guessed to be the smallest of the bags she huffed her way into the house.

They weren't what she had expected. They seemed normal enough, even happy as they went about their business, unaware of their observer only a short distance away. But then Esmée wasn't sure what she had expected. Someone like her perhaps? They, the kids, were so much older – as good as a whole generation older than her own. Nervous now, the hopeful abundance of courage having languished to almost nothing, she debated just staying in the car to watch. What exactly did she believe she could accomplish? Why was she here? But, getting out of the car, she knew she hadn't driven the two-hour journey to turn back.

She locked the car and made the short trek towards the pretty suburban semi-detached house, clutching her bag close.

Julie was just about to close the front door but paused cautiously on seeing Esmée approach.

"Can I help you?" she asked politely.

Esmée stopped in her tracks. She hadn't thought of what to say as an opener and now, faced with the dilemma, she was stumped.

"Ehh. I'm Esmée, Esmée Myers." Her name as it tripped from her mouth sounded absurd. "I wonder if I could have a moment of your time?" A moment of your time: where the hell did that come from she reproved herself silently, cringing from the inside out.

At five foot two to Esmée's five seven, Julie visibly grew: defensively her long slender neck craned upward and her chin extended outwards, her beautiful features belied by the scowl that washed over her face as her demeanour mutated from affable to hostile.

"I wondered how long it would take." Her disgust was

apparent from the venom held in her voice. "I told you people before: I have nothing to say to you. Have you no shame?"

Esmée held the door just as she was about to slam it, recognising her mistake immediately.

"I'm sorry, Julie, you misunderstand – I'm not a reporter. I promise . . ." the idea of a wasted journey having come this far made her breathless. "I just want to talk. My dad was Frank Gill." She paused, hoping the name would garner a different reaction.

For a split second Esmée thought she saw fear in the woman's eyes. But it seemed to disappear as she released her grip on the door and her face began to relax, a slight flush rising on her perfect cheeks.

"I'm sorry, Esmée, I didn't realise." She lowered her eyes for a minute as if to gather herself together. "We've had some unwanted 'guests' hanging around these last few days and I thought you were the first to venture to the door. What can I do for you?"

So Julie knew about Brady's release.

"Can I come in for a minute?" Esmée asked, reluctant to talk on the doorstep.

Assenting, Julie stepped aside and pulled open the door to let Esmée into her home.

And it was a beautiful home. She followed her down a narrow hall and into an extended open-plan living space. Esmée was blown away by the bright and beautiful room. Straight from a magazine, it was styled with strength and confidence. The oversized canvases and colourful furniture screamed sophistication to completely contradict the assumptions that Esmée had prematurely made about Julie: this was not the home of the quiet put-upon woman she remembered in the courtroom all those years ago. Julie had grown up.

Dressed in patent heels, a dark-grey pencil skirt and sparkling white shirt, with her naturally blonde hair pulled back tight in a ponytail, Julie was a reflection of her environment: sophisticated and elegant. She offered Esmée one of the comfy chairs in the lounge part of the room.

Slightly intimidated and feeling a little on the frumpy side, Esmée wished she'd made more of an effort beyond her jeans and striped cotton jumper.

"Tea? Coffee?" Julie offered, making her way to the granite-topped counter, her voice reverberating off the gleaming black surface.

"Tea, please," Esmée replied, self-consciously fixing her runaway hair and at the same time absorbing the incredible surroundings. "You have a beautiful home," she said, taking in the light that spilled from the Velux windows overhead, and the contrast it created on the surfaces it touched.

"Thanks. It's taken me years to get right, but I'm happy with it now. After it all happened," she gestured with her hands, waving back to what ever had gone before, "I went back to college to study interior architecture and this became my pet project. Therapy, if you will!" Her comfortable laugh advocated that her past was very much disconnected from her present.

"Well, it's truly amazing!" Esmée enthused, genuinely impressed with the result. "Probably cost you a lot less than the medical kind!" she joked foolishly.

But Julie didn't laugh in response.

"So!" she exclaimed, placing a tray on the coffee table and handing Esmée a mug before taking the seat opposite. "What did you want to ask about?"

Esmée fumbled for words in panicked response, unprepared for Julie's apparent willingness to talk. She had assumed at the very least that she would refuse to start and need some emotional persuasion.

The door to the kitchen opened and the tall young man appeared again, head first around its edge. Closer now, Esmée was eager to take him in: his long and thick brown hair, trendy with a heavy flick to the front, the breadth of his shoulders, the size of his hands and the long slender fingers that wrapped around the door.

"You okay, Mum?" he asked, looking pointedly at Esmée.

"Yes, Harry, I'm fine."

"I'm just in the study if you need me," he replied, his tone unmistakably spiked with warning, then he closed the door as he left.

"I'm sorry, Julie," Esmée apologised, indicating her now-absent son. "I didn't come here to cause any trouble."

"Don't worry about it – he takes his role as the head of the family very seriously – he remembers a lot," she said by way of an explanation, obviously proud but equally protective of him. "So, Esmée?" she prompted again.

But Esmée didn't quite know what to say. She felt an uneasy need to befriend this woman, but at the same time wanted to punish her for the ever-so-slight impatient tenor in her attitude. Did she think that she was the only one hurt by what happened all those years ago? What exactly gave her the right to patronise? Did she really think it was that easy to move on? How could she assume that the past would never catch them up? She couldn't possibly presume that knocking down a few walls and sticking up a few paintings would make everything all right. Impossible.

Looking at the striking and obviously strong woman in front of her, waiting with a smile for a response, Esmée knew she had the power to rock her world. Would she? Could she?

Originally the objective had been to come to the house and inspect this woman face to face: just to see who she was. Perhaps warn her about Brady if she didn't know already. Telling all wasn't part of the plan – after all, why would she wilfully refresh the pain? But now the pungent rancour welling inside her like infectious bile was threatening to consume her and blind her ability to reason.

The ring of a phone broke the malevolent progression of her thoughts.

Smiling apologetically, Julie got up to answer it.

What the hell are you like, Esmée? Cop on and relax. This isn't her fault. Pinching herself hard, Esmée fought the compunction to purposefully destroy this family further.

"Sorry about that," Julie said, sitting back down. "So, you were saying . . ."

"Well . . ." The inward battle raged as Esmée swallowed hard, ruing her decision to come here in the first place. Left with no option, she launched in. "We never met, you and I, but I've seen your pictures a hundred times. I suppose with Brady being released it brought everything back and I just wanted to . . . I don't know . . . speak to you, see how you were doing."

They sat in silence for what seemed like eons, each getting used to the other's presence, each trying to fathom silently what she should say next.

"So when did you hear he was out?" Esmée asked.

"They came and told me about it the day before yesterday."

More than I was afforded, Esmée thought to herself. "Do you mind me asking about Robert?" she asked, taking a lead from Julie's directness and getting straight to her point.

Julie shifted ever so slightly in her seat and thought for a moment. "Robert? Well, actually, I suppose I do. I haven't talked willingly about him to anyone in a long time and frankly I'm not sure I want to start now."

"Sorry. I know. I suppose I just wanted to know where he went. I know he went away under a witness protection programme but . . ."

"He could be anywhere: South Africa, Canada, the States . . . anywhere. I have no idea. We weren't told and I didn't ask."

"And you didn't go with him?"

"Us! God, no. After what happened? Are you insane?" She looked at Esmée, slightly perplexed. "You do know what happened, don't you?"

"I think so, but I . . ." She couldn't finish, feeling ridiculous and small.

"My goodness, you're really bringing it back today!"

"I'm sorry . . . I shouldn't have asked . . ."

"Don't be." Julie shrugged, taking a resigned breath. "Robert . . . was a prick. There is no other word for him."

The absurdity of hearing such a word come out of her proper mouth was a little surprising and Esmée felt her pulse quicken at the malice that packaged it. There and then Esmée knew she had opened the floodgates.

Julie leaned forward, her hands clasped as if in prayer on her lap. She took a deep bracing breath and retold her story.

"It was supposed to be a special evening. I had it all planned. I put Harry to bed a little earlier than usual and had an incredible dinner prepared. I remember thinking to myself at the time that this was going to fix everything." She paused for a moment and closed her eyes, taking herself back to the night before the kidnap. "He was late home and in a foul mood. I should have known something was up. He was so cross, so nasty. We almost didn't sit down to eat, but I had put so much effort into it and besides I knew if we didn't there would be more trouble. I refused to let him ruin it for me, for us both." Her eyes opened and she expelled an apologetic sigh. "Robert had a bit of a nasty streak. He'd lash out sometimes and, well, that night I just wanted everything to be perfect." She smiled tritely at Esmée, embarrassed by her own naïvety, in hindsight. "So we sat down and I told him." She took a reinforcing breath as she recalled. "I told him about Beth."

"Beth?"

"Yeah, I'd done a test that morning and it came out positive. I was pregnant. Just three weeks to be exact." She smiled tenderly at the thought. "It was a complete surprise, an accident even. So that night I told him. I genuinely thought he'd be delighted. He'd always said he wanted us to try again. But he didn't say a word. Nothing. Not even an expletive. He just got up and left. I was sure he'd woken Harry with the slam of the door but I just sat there, unable to move." Her breathing was steady but her tone subdued as she shrugged at the memory. "I was sure he'd be happy. I was sure it would change things. He'd been so distracted. I could do nothing right. And poor Harry . . ." She shook her head, her voice filled with regret and sadness, letting her sentence go rather than recall just how Robert vented his anger on Harry, the deficiency of words speaking volumes. "This was the side of Robert no one knew. It wasn't important to the case, they said, but it was, is, important to us. I think it helps explain him: how he was. I like to think that somewhere deep down," she held her gripped fist to her chest with a noble, hopeful smile, "that he did love us. I think . . . it was just that he was ill . . . Well, that's what I've said to the kids anyway. Gambling does that, they say." Her tone was matter of fact. "We never knew, of course, about the gambling . . . not until it came out in court."

Esmée's skin prickled as she listened, a perceptible sense of foreboding swelling as Julie, layer by layer, unwrapped her story.

"To be honest, I was actually relieved when it came out – I always thought it was me!" She nearly laughed. "I always thought that I'd done something wrong and I tried extraordinarily hard to make it right. But it wasn't me at all. It was just him. All along. Plain and simple." She stopped and shrugged, her hands open to Esmée, imploring her to understand.

And she did. Esmée knew full well, or was beginning to anyway: the parallel behaviour of inadequate feelings, unexplained outbursts and emotional torture . . . Jesus, this could have been her life Julie was describing.

They both brooded in silence for a while, acutely aware of the part of the tale still to come.

"He'd only been gone about half an hour – I was still sitting at the table – sobbing if memory serves me correctly," Julie continued. "Then they rammed into my house and came straight at me in the kitchen. I had no idea where Rob was, only that he wasn't there. For some reason I screamed for him, hoping he wasn't far away, but he never came. They had me by the hair and someone knocked me at the back of my knees. Jesus, it was sore!" She winced at the memory. "Pain like I have never experienced before. I actually thought they had cut into my skin it hurt so much. I was crying and crying and crying."

She didn't bother to hide the distress in her eyes, but swathed in an eerie sense of calm it spoke volumes about her anguish and what she had to do to conquer it and be able to talk about it this way.

She described how she fell to the floor and took kicks to her stomach, how they slapped her across her head as she struggled and cowered to escape them. They kicked her tummy: her unborn baby. They broke her down till she was silent.

"They wrapped this horrible tape around my mouth – it tasted like petrol – and put a cloth blindfold over my eyes. I must have looked a sight wriggling on the floor. I knew they were going upstairs . . . to Harry . . . I had to try . . . I tried to scream but my lips were stuck to the bloody tape. It tore layers off me . . . I couldn't see . . ." She heaved a breath to calm her emotions and quell her tears. "They tied Harry's legs and arms and wrapped a scarf around his little head to cover his eyes too. I could hear him cry. He called for me and his daddy . . ." She brought her hand unconsciously to her head and rubbed it slowly across her crown. "Then Rob shouted out for them to stop, but I couldn't see him. There was blood in my eyes and I couldn't see. I tried to scream, but sure that was a waste of effort. So I just cried."

Esmée didn't interrupt the silent interlude but let it rest between them, affording Julie the time to settle. She had no words adequate to offer even a small consolation for her ordeal.

"They kept us there for hours. They were so quiet. They didn't speak a word, not even to each other. I could hear them move, their clothes and footsteps, but not a word. I prayed for it all to be over, for sleep to come but it didn't. My eyes hurt and my belly, well . . . I thought she was dead." Instinctively she placed a hand on her tummy. "I lost track of time, but when it started to get bright I heard another man join them – clearly the boss – Brady. Immediately after that they left. Rob too. He tried to tell me later that they had taken him by the neck and forced him to drive to the bank and, well . . . I believed him. It never crossed my mind, not even for a moment that he could have been part of it. I didn't think he could ever be that cruel. But I was wrong and, well, you know what happened next." She looked apologetically towards Esmée. "I thought I was on my own but when I tried to pull the straps off my wrists I got a thump. Stay calm, I told myself, stay calm. Rob will be back any time now to get us. But after about an hour we were put into a car. They drove us about a half hour then we stopped. They left us there, Harry and me, on the side of the road."

"My God, Julie, I . . . I don't know what to say . . . I'm so sorry."

"Sorry? What are you sorry for? You did nothing."

She wasn't accepting any sympathy. It was as if her pain was propping her up and propelling her forwards. The pain was her saviour: it meant she never had to feel guilty about the hate she felt. Her pain was her medicine.

"Do you know, in all this . . ." she swept her arm in an all-encompassing gesture, "what the hard part was? Is?"

Esmée shook her head.

"It's knowing that he was there all along. He watched it all. In the house. Robert Toner," she stated powerfully, her anguish replaced by disgust, "had followed the thugs into our home and watched as we, his wife and unborn child were kicked to the groundfloor, bound and gagged. He stood and listened to his son cry out helplessly for him. Watched as our little boy struggled and whimpered in terror . . . And. He. Did. Nothing."

This was her closing statement for the prosecution. She was giving him the conviction he deserved but never got. He had been part of it all. Part of the whole deceitful scam. He played a part in both the planning and execution of the entire debacle and then offered up his own family as his alibi. To save his skin. The compulsive gambler in Robert Toner made him do things any good person wouldn't dream of, that's what they said in his defence. Robert Toner, they purported, was a sick man, a weak man. This along with misplaced compassion and a draw on his feeble scruples led them to morph him into a willing informant. They offered him protection and a new life, contending that giving up the gang and their leader was the smart thing to do. So easily convinced. So eager to save himself. So weak.

Brady had been the unfortunate winner of Robert's losing hand on a fateful night in the 8 of Clubs. That's, so the court was told, how they first became acquainted. Brady offered sympathetic terms while Robert tumbled deeper and deeper into Brady's debt. He was easy prey: a man with even less luck than talent and substantially less sense again. Robert was hooked and all Brady had to do was reel him in. The payback was The Job. It seemed so easy: a real wipe-the-slate opportunity.

"He used us," Julie uttered, quite matter of fact. "Risked his own family. He didn't give a monkey's about us, couldn't have cared less. Even when I told him we weren't going into the witness protection programme, he actually seemed relieved, didn't so much as try to change my mind. Yes. Robert Toner is a prick and if I never saw him again it would be too soon." She swiped imaginary filth from her palms in finality. Her job was done.

"So where is he now?" Esmée asked again, shutting down the guilt pangs that chastised her for asking the question she had come all this way for.

"I have no idea."

"Really? He just left after the verdict?"

"Yep."

"And he never made any contact, not even a phone call?"

"No. Not once. Anyway the programme won't allow it – either way. He left and we stayed and I haven't heard anything since. Why so interested in him anyway?"

"I don't know," Esmée shrugged. "A morbid curiosity, I suppose."

Harry returned to the kitchen and the conversation ended.

"Harry," Julie said, "this is Esmée. Her father was the garda who was murdered in the raid."

Her use of words intrigued Esmée further.

Harry took a firm grip of Esmée's extended hand and nodded politely in recognition.

"Good to meet you," Esmée said, feeling the ridiculous urge to comment on how much he'd grown.

Again he just nodded.

It was time to leave. Esmée made her excuses and left. She needed to be alone.

She got back into her car and sat, unable to gather herself together sufficiently to drive. She had known most but not all of the story – it had been fairly well reported at the time. But the parts that Julie had kept private and the bits that she didn't know at all were the parts Esmée was most interested in. That and the fact that while telling it Julie hadn't so much as shed a single tear. Was that acceptance or anger? Or both?

As she searched the depths of her own pain she concluded that what offended her most was the ignorance: how could Julie have been so blind, so naïve? How could she have been duped so easily? How could she, Esmée, also have been fooled so easily? How could she have allowed herself be manipulated like that?

Deep in thought, she removed the envelope that Maloney had given her the day before from her bag and took out one of three large prints. She hadn't believed him at first and if it hadn't been for Tom she'd have physically removed him from the house herself. But here, having seen the boy, now a handsome young man, for herself, having shook his hand and looked straight into those soulful green eyes there was no denying it. Harry was Philip's mirror image: he was his son. And Philip Myers was Robert Toner.

In fact Robert Toner became Colin Jakes before he was ever Philip Myers. That was the identity they gave him when they relocated him to South Africa thirteen years previously. He was set up in a bungalow with cash, a job and a whole new life: that was all part of the deal. As far as the authorities knew right up until they recovered the car at the cliff, Colin Jakes was still living in Pretoria so this discovery was a significant surprise to the security services. They too had questions unanswered, like how had he managed to change his name again? From where did he get his papers? When had he returned to Dublin and what had he been up to since then?

But for Esmée, with her connection to her husband established years before they had ever even met, the questions this revelation prompted were more of the emotional kind. Did Philip know who she was when they first met? Obviously, he must have. How did it not freak him out? Why had he never come clean to her? How did he never say? They were supposed to be soul mates. Did she even know who he was? Philip. Colin. Robert. Were they all the same? Impossible. They were all different: they had to be. In her head she imagined a wholly romantic version of circumstances and events that allowed their relationship to blossom without it being a weird and bizarre perversion of nature.

But sitting in the car, looking at the three pictures, the faces all looked the same, but they had three different stories. Her eyes were drawn to Philip. She let her fingers trace the outline of his face and the swell of his mouth. She didn't know him at all. And she felt exposed, like she was seeing him for the first time, but first impressions are inevitably deceptive and like dark mirrors they never reveal the truth.

Chapter 18

Day 62 and still no body. The initial suggestion by her mother that they should move back into Woodland Drive was quickly rejected. The house represented something obscene. Esmée felt violated. Like the last ten years of her life were nothing short of a lie. Had it not been for the existence of Matthew and Amy she would have been forgiven for branding them a horrible nightmare. Philip was not only a stranger but a psychological stalker: he had deceived her in such an intimate, convincing and fundamental way there was no way for her to even begin to understand or rationalise what had happened to her. What he had done to her.

"It's a kind of 'traumatic bonding'," the Garda counsellor attempted to reason, "It's connected to what's known as the Stockholm Syndrome where the victim develops strong feelings for the aggressor. It's a kind of defence mechanism . . ."

"But I'm the victim here!" Esmée protested.

"Yes, that's true, but with Robert –"

"Philip," Esmée corrected.

"Sorry. Yes, Philip," she replied, lowering her eyes in recognition of her blunder. "But here I'm assuming that Philip may have felt some manner of guilt towards you and your family and it's this apparent guilt that re-structures the argument slightly."

"What? That he's the victim?"

"Well, in a kind of roundabout way: in his own head, yes, he thought he was the victim. You held all the power. He probably felt like he was as much a victim as you."

"Are you for real? Do they actually pay you to say this crap? He's the victim? What, like I asked for this? Like I wanted him to do this to me. He found me. He chased me. I didn't know any of it so how dare you sit there with your little notebook and make me feel like this was my fault!"

"Mrs Myers –"

"Oh for God's sake, this is farcical!" Esmée snapped and standing up gathered her coat, bag and umbrella to leave. "There is no Mrs Myers. He wasn't real. It's not my name. I am Esmée Gill. Always was and still am. If you haven't managed to grasp that, then, well . . . I'm done here."

"Please, Esmée, you've misunderstood. Of course this isn't your doing. You can't be blamed. I'm only trying to explain from Rob's – eh, Philip's point of view – what he may have been thinking. I'm here to help you understand."

Esmée stopped in her tracks and turned back to the now standing counsellor. "Thanks but I don't think I need to hear this. I understand what has happened and no amount of 'psychological spin' can make this all right. I appreciate you're trying to help, just doing your job and all that, but this is too soon. I don't want to . . . I can't think of him as a victim."

She left the warm, mellow office standing tall, bolstered by her anger. She and Julie now had something else in common: they would both use rage as a mechanism to survive. Stepping into the grey wet day she didn't bother with her umbrella, liking the cold wet drops of rain and their cooling effect on her burning cheeks. What was happening to her? Why was this happening? She felt like such a fool. She had fallen in love with him and for years had given him everything: her whole self.

She shared with him everything she held dear. He had seen her at her best and her worst and she had been happy to share those vulnerable moments with him because she trusted him: loved him and thought he loved her. But really, how could he? How could he have made himself fall in love with her? Just like that? He sought her out. He made it happen. True love is supposed to be all about serendipity. Destiny. It's supposed to 'just happen'. You can't force it. Their love, if it even existed at all, was synthetic. Unnatural.

Lizzie was waiting for her when she got home. Recognising the dark mood, she allowed her sister to smoulder in silence, handing her a mug of tea. The two women sat in silence, each lost in the detail of the family woes.

The vibration of Esmée's phone ruptured the reverie. Jack's name flashed white on the screen. She sighed: did she really want to speak to her husband's colleague? She answered.

"Hi, Jack."

"Esmée . . ." He sounded uncomfortable.

In no mood for small talk Esmée pitched straight in. "What can I do for you?"

"I promised I'd look into things for you."

"You're very good," Esmée responded. She was tired and cross and sure this was just another wasted courtesy 'found nothing' call.

"Well, I thought I'd better give you the heads-up," he continued.

The resting demons of dread in the pit of Esmée's stomach woke instantly and lurched upwards: he had something. She sat upright in the chair.

"What, what is it? Do you know where he is?"

"No. Sorry. It's not that, but I may have a clue as to why he . . . well, why he went away."

"Go on," she encouraged cautiously.

"Well, I've had a look at everything – his files, his customers, the deals that were processed – just to see what he was working on before, before he . . ."

"It's okay, Jack, I know what you mean," she helped him along.

"Well, it appears that things aren't quite what they seem."

"No shit," she muttered quietly.

"There's a team here about to launch a full-blown investigation. I can't stall it any more. I wanted to be sure before I called. It's money, Esmée. We think he . . ." again a hesitant pause, "well, he may have lost some money."

"Do you mean stole?"

"God no, Esmée, I didn't mean that." Jack rushed on, mortified at being so transparent, ignorant of the litany of accusations facing the absent Philip. "There is probably a reasonable explanation – Philip wouldn't do anything like that."

"Yes, you did mean it and, yes, he would," Esmée stated apathetically.

"I'm so sorry, Esmée," he apologised, his words oozing pity.

"Thanks for letting me know."

"Look, if there is anything I can do . . ."

Conversation over, she cast the phone aside. "Christ, I need a drink!"

"What is it? What's happened?" Lizzie broached warily.

"Do you know what, it doesn't fucking matter. I don't have the energy to care any more." She dropped her heavy head into her hands and expelled a huge sigh.

Mentally she racked up each of the indictments and accusations, then reminded herself that he was gone. And for a moment she was glad. He had buggered off and left her, so she, in good faith, must act accordingly.

"Right!" she declared, jumping up, shocking Lizzie out of her chair. "That's it. If he wants to go, then let him. Come on! No time like the present."

And striding to the sink, she reached in under it and grabbed a roll of black refuse bags. Throwing on her coat, she grabbed her keys and marched toward the front door.

"Well?" she threw back to her sister. "What are you waiting for? Are you coming or not?"

Grabbing her things Lizzie, with no other option presented, submitted and tripped after her, if only out of curiosity to see what the hell was going on.

"Where are we going?"

"Back to the house."

"Why, what are we doing there?"

"What I should have done weeks ago," she replied, locking the front door behind her.

She had been avoiding this task, fearing latent feelings of regret that could distract her. But she was angry. There were no emotions of regret or shame or guilt or sadness, only biting rage that she needed to express. If he was around she would have barked savagely at him, probably swiped and whipped him hard. But he wasn't. The only part of him she could reach was his belongings.

"I'm not waiting for the bastard to turn up. He's gone. So let's get rid of him," she asserted, driving fast and steady through the streets.

"Jesus, Esmée, is it not a bit soon? He's only gone . . ." Lizzie questioned, keeping one eye on the parked cars they whizzed past and the other on the stony face of her sister.

"I know. But hey, this was his call. No time like the present. And once we're done, I'm getting drunk. Very drunk. If you'll take care of the children!"

They pulled up outside the house, the dust on the cobblelocked drive throwing up a plume as she pulled on the brake.

The air in the house was stale. A pile of mail jammed the door. Shoving it hard and pushing aside the paper mountain, she marched in. A quick rummage through the mail revealed that it was almost entirely junk mail. She shoved the few items of importance into her bag and checked her watch. She had a couple of hours before the kids needed collecting. With the decision already made that this was no longer their home, she had to deal with the problem presented by the house's vacancy. The subject bothered her: she hadn't the emotional fire to deal with it – until now. Now it was really clear and her prior reluctance slightly innocuous. The house couldn't be sold so it had to be rented. Simple. How difficult was that?

She walked the rooms, assessing the best place to start, focused and ready. The memories in this house were nebulous, with no basis in reality, all her happy days demoted to mere fiction. She had been an unwitting player in Philip's game and now it was over she was the one who had lost.

* * *

"Are you okay?" Lizzie asked as they tied up another bag, setting it aside in the hall.

They had spent the time in the house in near silence, with Esmée trapped in her thoughts.

"Not really, but I'll live," she smiled back at her sister.

"Wanna share?"

"Not really. I'll only cry if I do."

"Okay."

And so the silence resumed as, bag after bag, they packed up Philip till nothing but his smell remained.

* * *

They toasted her loss in Zac and Barney's bar in town, miles away from the sympathetic eyes of the village. She was glad of the anonymity. Fin took over as Lizzie and Penny left.

"So you've been sent to mind me?" Esmée asked bitterly.

"Don't be such a bitch," her friend replied gently. "They're so worried about you, and don't forget that they're all wrapped up in this too."

"I know, I know. And I should be grateful. I think they've had enough of me anyway." She emptied her glass.

"Need another?" Fin offered.

"You betcha."

Fin nodded to the barman, indicating a refill for her melancholy friend and a pint for herself.

"So how're you doing?" she asked. They hadn't seen each other in days with Fin occupied by her impending exhibition.

"Please, please, don't be nice to me," Esmée pleaded. "Can we talk about something else? How's your exhibition going?"

"Jesus! Frying pan and fire stuff there, honey!" Fin threw her eyes up to heaven. "It's a bloody disaster . . ."

The night wore on and the music got louder. Despite herself Esmée was enjoying herself, happy to be out and distracted by someone else's issues, Fin's hilarious tales an effective tonic that brought the absent smile back to her face.

"It's good to see you laugh again," said Fin.

"It's certainly been a while," Esmée said, feeling almost human.

"Seriously, though, are you okay?"

"Yeah, I think so. It's tough though."

Fin nodded. "But you're strong, Es. You'll come out the other side."

"I know. It just seems a long way off. You know, I'm actually beginning to think I've had a bit of a lucky escape."

"New beginnings!" Fin toasted, raising her glass and with it once again the mood. There was plenty of time for post-mortems, she thought, anxious to see her friend laugh some more before sending her back to reality.

Suddenly Fin's face dropped.

"What? What is it?" Esmée asked, alarmed.

"It's Lara."

"Lara who?"

"Lara Wilson."

"College Lara Wilson?"

Fin nodded.

"Where?" Esmée asked, turning on the spot.

"Are you sure you want to do this?"

"What? Oh that!" Esmée responded as reality bit. "Feck it, Fin. I can't hide for ever, and we don't have to tell her anything we don't want to . . . unless she already knows . . . ?"

"Not from me, she doesn't!"

"Well, then," she enthused, her prudence dulled by the alcohol consumed so far, "what the hell?" She shrugged. "Lara!" she called over the heads queuing at the bar.

Lara looked around, then seeing her old friend bounded towards her in amazement.

"Bloody hell, Esmée Gill, how the hell are you? If it weren't

for Fin we would have thought you'd been abducted by aliens."
She hugged her hard. "Wagon! You haven't changed one bit,
you're still as gorgeous as ever."

"Neither have you!" Esmée choked in between shrieks and
hugs.

"Yeah, right, have you seen the size of my ass? That's
changed!" she laughed, slapping her behind playfully.

Yep. Whatever about her backside, some things really hadn't
changed: Lara was still the gregarious whirlwind she always was,
whipping up a storm wherever she went.

"So what happened to you?" Lara asked above the din.

"I got distracted," Esmée replied dismissively.

"Well, I'm glad you're back. Now come and dance with me."

And her vivacity was infectious. Esmée hadn't danced in years,
she wasn't even sure she'd remember how, but it didn't take long
for her to get her mojo back and she was soon strutting
rhythmically across the dance floor with her dance partner of old
and loving every minute of it.

It was like history repeating itself. Lara and herself on the
dance floor with Fin holding court at the bar.

Fin realised it too and smiled smugly, acutely aware of Lara's
two escorts standing on either side of her.

"So, can I buy you a drink?"

She looked round to find a dapper young man in a sharp
pinstripe suit with a sparkle in his eye, beaming eagerly from ear
to ear.

"Why not?" she replied.

"Justin," he introduced, extending his hand, his perfect hair
shining under the down-lighters above the bar.

"Fin," she reciprocated with a smile. "So, are you Lara's
partner?"

"God, no. We're just workmates, that's all." He laughed. "I'm young, free and single, if that's what you're after."

Fin laughed. "I don't think so," she replied, trying to let him down gently, but liking his smile all the same. "I don't think I'm quite your type."

"I could be your Mr Grey," he smiled, raising his eyebrows seductively.

"Grey's not my colour, honeybunch," she countered "I'm more sixty shades of crimson, myself." She raised her glass to meet his.

"Touché!" he smiled, touching his glass to hers.

By the time Esmée and Lara got off the dance floor, puce and sweating, Fin and Justin were laughing raucously, a line of empty shot glasses decorating the bar in front of them.

"You've met Justin then?" Lara asked rhetorically, watching as the rambunctious pair slammed then dunked another shot.

"Me and Fionnuala, we're pals!"

"Really?"

"Yesh," he slurred. "She's my Mrs Crimson an' I'm her bit o' rough," he managed before sliding off the seat and passing out cold at her feet.

* * *

Esmée's fumbled for her house keys, still sniggering childishly at the memory of Fin and her new-found suitor.

"Bit of rough!" she repeated aloud, prompting a thump from her equally intoxicated friend.

"Ahh, stop!" Fin pleaded. "He didn't mean it like that!"

"Yes, he did and you know it! Christ, Fin, I'm not sure you quite know how good that felt!" Her face was still pulsing deep red. "I haven't felt that alive in years. And, I can still dance!" She sashayed across the kitchen, finishing with a not-so-graceful spin, knocking over the milk with a graceless swing of her arm.

"Easy, tiger!" Fin warned, catching the carton before it reached the floor.

"No, seriously, thanks, Fin, I wouldn't have done it without you."

"No problem – what are friends for?"

"God, I'm starving," Esmée declared with her head stuck in the fridge. "What do you fancy? There's a bit of trifle left."

"Just toast for me," Fin announced, popping two slices in the toaster. "Want some tea?"

"Yeah, go on then," Esmée replied, propping herself up against the kitchen counter, complete with spoon and trifle bowl. "Jesus, that Lara one hasn't changed a bit, has she?" She giggled between mouthfuls. "She's still great craic, isn't she?"

"Yep. She's off the wall," Fin concurred. "And you know, whenever I see her she always asks after you."

"She does?"

Fin nodded and smiled at her drunken pal, taking a seat at the table.

"Ahh, Fin," Esmée sighed with a pensive smirk. "You know, it felt almost normal tonight."

"Well, look at it as the way of the future," Fin munched, taking a ravenous bite of her hot buttered toast.

* * *

Her head hurt like hell the next morning – the morning-after downside of her antics the night before. Esmée couldn't remember the last time she'd felt this rotten. Her head still resonated with the pounding beat of the nightclub and her patience was seriously depleted. The kids sensed her weakness and like predatory animals they pounced, demanding her attention. When they were settled with toast smothered in

219

Nutella, anything for a quiet life, she slumped on the chair and nursed her throbbing head.

She felt rather than heard her phone vibrate in her bag beside her and dug in deep to retrieve it. A message from a number she didn't recognise.

EI605 09:20 12/6/27 ref HJ7895A

At first glance it appeared to be nothing more than gibberish, but on further examination it was patently clear.

This was a flight reference and, after everything that had happened during the last few weeks, she instinctively knew who it was from and why.

She went immediately to wake Fin.

"What do you mean he's sent you a message?" a very drowsy Fin asked, thick with the alcohol still very much evident in her body and none too pleased at being woken like this.

"Read it for yourself," Esmée instructed, passing her the phone.

"I need my glasses . . ." Fin fumbled, feeling the bedside table for her specs. "This isn't anything," she complained when she read it. "Now go away and let me sleep."

"Fin. Seriously!" But it was pointless: the girl was still drunk.

Returning to the kitchen she dialled directory enquires and got the number for the airline.

"I'd like to confirm a flight booking," she said.

"Sure!" came the politely trained, if a little overly cheerful, male voice at the other end of the telephone. "Do you have your reference number handy?"

"Yes. Yes, I do," she affirmed, fumbling with the mobile in her hand, and she called out the digits and letters as presented to her on the screen.

"And your name?"

"Esmée Myers," she stated clearly, adding, "Mrs Esmée Myers

– M. Y. E. R. S." for good measure and could hear, somewhere in the background, his fingertips zealously banging on a keyboard.

She pictured the cold sterile call centre where this man probably sat, in his symmetrical partitioned cubicle with his little earpiece extending over his mouth and instruction manuals for every possible eventuality close to hand.

"Yes, Mrs Myers, I can confirm your booking, leaving Dublin at 9.20 a.m., this Wednesday, twenty-seventh of June, arriving Málaga 11.30 a.m., local time."

"Is there a return journey with that?" she enquired quietly, trying to figure out what was going on, her Holmesian super-sleuth mind swinging into action.

"No, ma'am," he replied, "it's an open ticket. Would you like me to book a return journey for you now?"

"No. That's fine, thanks." And with that she hung up.

There was no doubt in her mind as to who had sent this text or, as the case might be, who had organised for it to be sent to her.

Spain! Bloody Hell! He had gone to Spain! What an unimaginative and clichéd place to hide out: there in the Spanish hills, with all the other fugitives that went before him, probably drinking sangria and eating paella. She could just see him fitting in with his hair slicked back, manicured feet and over-bronzed complexion. What a nasty little picture!

By the time Tom arrived, Esmée was pacing the floor, her hangover long since forgotten.

"What's up, sis?" he asked, throwing his coat over the back of a chair and sitting down.

"This," she said, handing him the phone.

"A ticket?" he asked, looking baffled. "Are you going somewhere?"

"No, well, I didn't plan to, but someone wants me to."

"Someone wants you to? Sorry, Es, but I'm not getting it. Who is 'someone'?" But she didn't need to answer, seeing the lights of realisation switch on in his head before he'd even finished the sentence.

"No – way," he whispered, shaking his head in disbelief at his own assumption. "You don't think . . ."

"I do."

"No way!" he repeated, staring back at the phone.

"Well, who else would anonymously book me on a flight to Spain? Of all places! It has to be him! Isn't that where they all go, these criminal types?"

"But that doesn't mean it's him and you're not getting on that plane to find out!"

"Of course I am, I have to," she shrugged, matter of factly.

"No. No, you don't," he reasoned emphatically. "You hand this one over to the police, let them sort it and if it is a joke or a hoax or whatever, then great – and if not, well, then they've got him."

"I can't do that!" she interjected, horrified and appalled at his suggestion. "They'll arrest him!"

"And? Isn't that what you want? Justice and all that? I know it's what I want." He handed her back the offending phone.

"Yes! Of course it is. And I will tell them, but not yet. I want to see him on my own first. I want to know why. Why he's done this to me."

"Well, let the cops go get him and then you can ask him."

"Oh for God's sake, Tom! Get real. Do you really think he'll tell me anything after I've got him arrested? No. I'll go to him. And then we'll see."

Collapsing heavily into a chair, she threw her head back and stared blankly at the ceiling. And here she was, thinking she had reached some glimmer of normality!

"It might not be him, you know," Tom said. "Maybe it's Brady? Maybe it's a trap of some kind? But . . . I have to say I think you're right."

"Christ, Tom, this is such a mess!"

"And assuming it is Philip, what then?"

"Feck sake, Tom! Don't ask me questions like that! I don't know!"

"Well, you'd better start thinking about it!"

"I know, I know," she replied, exasperated, running her hands through her hair for the millionth time. "You're supposed to be helping me out here, not complicating things even more!"

"I am helping, just not in the way you imagined."

She cast a sceptical sideways glance at her brother and laughed, shaking her head in disbelief. "How exactly do you figure that?" she asked sarcastically.

"All right then." He leaned forward in his chair. "What are you going to do when you get there?"

It was a reasonable question, he thought, intended to provoke further consideration, to make her think the whole thing through and, hopefully, change her mind or at least make her see how ludicrous her approach was.

"I'll just have to see when I get there, won't I?"

"Don't be ridiculous!" he shot at her.

"Tom, it's Málaga, not outer Mongolia! I'll book myself into a hotel and see what happens."

"Do you not think you're being just a little irresponsible?"

He sounded just like their mother – he even looked like her as he folded his arms and furrowed his brow.

"So!" she threw back. "What do you think I should do? Hand it over to Maloney and his cronies, let them bring him home? Sit back and do nothing? And what about yer man Brady? What if he gets him first?" She stopped as if waiting for him to reply but knew he wouldn't. "And yes, you're right," she conceded. "I probably am being a little reckless, and it could be something engineered by Brady, but I can't ignore it. I'm taking that flight and I'm going to see who booked me on it and why. I have to see if it is him, Tom," she implored, begging him to understand, "and if it is, then I need to see him by myself. I need to ask him why. There must be, has to be, an explanation for all this crap. But I'm not doing that in that horrible interview room because that's where we'd end up and you know it."

"Well, let me come with you!"

"No way! Absolutely not! And land you in the middle of this mess? No way! Besides," she continued with a smile, "someone will need to look after the kids for me." Her eyes were suppliant, pleading with him not to object further.

And he didn't. Shaking his head in silence, his face spoke volumes about his trepidation but inwardly acknowledged, knowing her as he did, that to protest would be a fruitless exercise.

"And please don't tell anyone. Promise?" she pleaded.

"Promise," he lied.

"Tell anyone what? What did I miss?" a dishevelled Fin asked, lolloping into the kitchen wearing Esmée's dressing-gown.

Chapter 19

The cottage had become stifling. Feeling increasingly claustrophobic, with too much time to think, she needed to get out, get some air and expunge her head of the tumultuous thoughts of Philip.

The sunny Sunday morning called for a trip to the park, a jaunt on the merry-go-round and ice cream served with fresh air and sprinkles. Gathering her little family together, she walked while the kids cycled the short distance, totally oblivious to the mélange of thoughts that were running amuck inside their mother's head.

Not an hour went by without his mental invasion. A passing Honda Prelude reminded her of when they first met. He was so grown-up. She remembered their first kiss in the hallway at Joan Hunter's twenty-first birthday party. Why he was there she never got to find out but he spent most of the night in the kitchen with Joan's older brother, mocking the hormonal college-going revellers. She remembered how he had picked her out of the crowd and offered to take her home in his beautiful white car. He was so much older than she, so sophisticated with his own apartment to boot, how could she resist?

"A big ride!" Joan had proclaimed the next day during the obligatory after-party post mortem.

And he swept her off her feet, wooed her with wine and whispers that touched her heart and when they made love for the first time he was gentle and giving. So different to her previous inept fumblings on the floor of a grotty student bed-sit. So grown up. She remembered the impetuous delight at his glance, the ecstatic ardour of his lips, the chaotic flutter at his touch and the overwhelming rapture of him, just him, that ultimately carried her on the heady wave to marriage. He made it that way, made it so easy for her to fall in love with him. He captured her with his smile, his kiss and his words. And that's all it was, until he said it to her: Love. She couldn't believe it was happening. It was too good to be true.

A hard day to bear the fact, walking the path to the park, that she was right all along. It was too good to be true.

Their habitual entry through the park gates without fail heralded the unleashing of the imaginary reins that kept her children close by and as she called pointlessly after them to "go easy" they escaped off into the distance in the general direction of the playground, leaving her to follow comfortably on their trail. They were doing all right, she acknowledged tenderly as she watched them go. Knowing that she would never fill the void left by their father she wished that she could, at the very least, make it less noticeable for them, less painful. She found it difficult to entertain the idea that they were part of a lie. She loved them to the moon and back and had always thought of them as the consequence of a tremendous love affair, but knowing it now not to be true she wondered how this would affect them. What would she say when they were older? Would they find out the truth? Did they even need to know? Would they resent her for being so gullible? Would they pity her or love her regardless?

Feeling maudlin and lonely and full of self-pity, she sat on the park bench and watched them play. Ordinarily she would join in, take them through the climbing frames and encourage them as they slid down the slide frontways, sideways, backwards, anyways, but not today. Today she needed time to think. Over and over she pondered the text on her phone and its implications. She had tried replying to it, had switched on the message-delivery notification, but it had yet to send her the customary 'delivered' message. It was an Irish number, probably one of those Pay As You Go networks. He must have bought it and taken it with him, she deduced.

The sun was hot on her face as she followed the frolics around the play area, thinking as they went of all the questions she had to ask him: all the hows and the whys . . .

"Mind if I sit down, Es?"

His voice dragged her from the mental purgatory. That voice! Her eyes fixed dead ahead and every muscle in her body went rigid. This couldn't be happening. Slowly she crooked her head around to look first at the familiar and unwelcome face of her uninvited companion and then automatically at the play area where frantically she sought out the familiar shapes of her two children. There they were with the man Brady had weeks before called Tommo. They were smiling innocently, captivated as he bent down to chat, handing them what looked like lollipops and then pointing, steering their line of sight, towards her. All three waved before strolling off comfortably together.

"Wave, Mummy!" Brady instructed lightly, giving her a nudge on the arm.

A massive surge of adrenaline spurred her into standing, her mouth opening to call to them, only to be grabbed roughly by the arm.

"Don't cause a scene," he said, smiling through gritted teeth, acknowledging the other mums who had turned to stare. "You don't want to scare them, do you?" His fingers tightened their grip on her arm as a means of belligerent encouragement. "Now!" he instructed firmly. "Smile and wave."

Her fear for her children was greater than for herself as she turned and spat at him. "You harm a hair on their heads and I swear . . ."

"Them's fightin' words. Ohhhh, I love a woman with a bit a spirit!"

"I mean it."

"I know you do, Es, darlin', I know you do!" He shook his head. "Relax!" His words were delivered pleasantly enough but with an undeniable threatening undertone. "Let's chat!"

This couldn't be a coincidence, she told herself in unqualified horror as reluctantly she sat back down beside him and watched her children walk over to the climbing frame with their new friend. They were in so much trouble. She had told them never to talk to strangers, Matthew should know better! Her head raced. First the text message and now this. Surely it couldn't be a coincidence? But how could Brady know Philip had, albeit abstractly and not conclusively, contacted her? Or was it Brady himself who had arranged the airline ticket?

"How's that hubby of yours?" he asked, smiling sweetly at her.

"I have no idea."

"Well now, that's a surprise!" he mocked. "It's been, what? A couple of months now and he hasn't come back for a bit o' you!" His eyebrows rose in disbelief as he trailed a slow leering look over her, and even though wisely enough he chose not to touch her, in her head she could feel his hands all over her.

"Jaysus!" he finished. "You must be gagging for it! Saw you out and about last week though . . ."

His loud throaty nicotine laugh penetrated the air around them, causing numerous unappreciative stares to fall upon its instigator, and instinctively Esmée wrapped her arms around herself.

"So," wiping the spittle from his mouth with the back of his hand, "no sign then?"

"I've already told you no!"

He studied her a while, his smile disappearing. She could almost hear the tiny cogs of his mind spinning as he considered his next move.

"Somethin' tells me you're not being honest with me."

"Why would I lie to you?" she asked, pointing to the climbing frame as she spoke. "Would I put those kids in danger for a man who has left me to fend for myself? I've got no money, no dignity and no father for my children." Brave and protective, she took a breath without pausing for more than a second and persisted in her pretence. "Do you not think I want to punish him as much as you do?" She didn't have to try too hard to sound passionate and credible in her defence because for a split second, for those exact same reasons, she actually considered turning him in to the bully who sat dangerously close beside her.

"You're a smart bird all right," Jim Brady finally replied, apparently satisfied and convinced by her performance. "Well," he said, pulling up the waistband of his trousers as he stood, "it's been nice chatting to ya." He turned and whistled in the direction of his human pet, flicking his head at the same time to indicate a swift return to his side, which Tommo did without question, leaving the two children safe and alone in the playground.

"I'll drop by again soon," he threatened while patting his overweight belly and scanning the area, and headed off in the general direction of the exit.

Her eyes stuck to the two men, watching them leave, and did not alter their focus until they were long out of sight. She thought she was going to be sick and leaned over herself to rest her elbows on her knees and her head in her shaking hands.

"Mum?" Matthew called as he ran to her from the other side of the playground, Amy in his wake.

"What did that man mean when he said he'd sort out Daddy for us?"

"Is he going to bring Daddy back soon?" Amy asked.

"Don't mind him," Esmée replied softly, trying her best to jest, as if she understood the joke and it was only they who didn't. "What he means is that he'll look out for Daddy and if he sees him he'll help him to make his way home." She hoped it sounded convincing.

"I miss Daddy!" Amy whined, climbing onto Esmée's knee and placing her thumb in her mouth as she snuggled into her chest.

"Don't be such a cry-baby!" Matthew protested, miffed by his little sister's almost acceptable display of emotion.

"Hey! Hey!" Esmée remonstrated, pulling her son to her. "It's okay to miss him, you know!"

"Do you miss him?" he asked, looking up to her, his eyes ardently searching her face for assurance.

"Of course I do." It was neither a lie nor a truth but a neutral statement where any other answer wouldn't have been acceptable or fair.

Kissing each of them affectionately on the head, she held them tight, taking strength from their innocence and unconditional love for her. As she looked out over the playground she was afraid, repeating the paranoid questions. Did Brady know about her planned excursion? Was it him? Did he arrange it to test her? To see if she would own up to a possible communication from her dearly, desperately, departed husband? Maybe. Well, it was too late now and she felt decidedly exposed to harm. Tom was right! She was being reckless and irresponsible. How could she put herself at risk like this with these two mites relying on her, who only had her? It wasn't too late to change her mind. She didn't have to take the flight, if she didn't want to.

Chapter 20

Like a junkie in Amsterdam, for Esmée airports were a real hit: an exotic cocktail of fear and excitement blended into one intoxicating rush. Yes, she loved airports – under normal circumstances, that is: like during the annual pilgrimage to the Canaries, usually Lanzarote or sometimes Fuertaventura, depending on how adventurous they felt. And at this point in her usual journey, corralled in the departure lounge along with her eager companions, she, would usually be just about able to contain her smouldering anticipation. But this time she was alone and was feeling about as adventurous as a minnow navigating shark-infested waters. This time there was no predictably fabulous package holiday somewhere predictably hot, predictably family-orientated and predictably well-organised to look forward to. For the first time in her life Esmée would be flying alone, and for the first time in her life she was dreading the flight.

Shifting on her feet, she looked again at her watch. With

departure time fast approaching she was beginning to worry. Her only instruction from the text was to take flight EI605 on June 27th – today's date. That was it. After that she was walking blind. She had assumed there would be further direction once she checked in but all she managed to glean was where she was going: Southern Spain's Málaga airport . . . and after that? Who knew? For Esmée, a marginal control freak, the ignorance was persecution.

From the shadows at the back of the departure lounge she studied the groups, which minded their belongings with protective caution, taking special interest in those who, like her, appeared to be traveling solo. Feeling conspicuous, sure she stood out from the multi-hued camouflage of fellow passengers, she extracted her book from the paper bag the shop assistant had placed it in only moments before and gave a poor impression of someone engrossed. Unused to paying this much attention to anyone else other than her children, she, like a sleuth on her virgin case, cast out furtive glances from behind the novel's pages. But the only thing her inexperienced eyes registered was a sea of dark glasses perched seasonally on the heads and on the odd pretentious nose. What should she be looking for? Trench coats and trilbies in this day and age, especially in this heat, were unlikely, never mind farfetched. How would she know if someone was looking for her? They, her fellow passengers, all looked harmless enough, with none standing out as a potential antagonist. Even the guy in the green bomber jacket and jeans ripped at the knees, carrying no hand luggage, seemed innocent enough. Clean-shaven and utterly absorbed in some fashionably acceptable male magazine, with no obvious scars or weapons, he didn't appear to qualify as the stereotypical criminal. Momentarily appeased, she forced her galloping breath to regain its natural rhythm. Ridiculous as it seemed to even wonder it, she was not, as far as she could tell, being followed.

It felt peculiar sitting unaccompanied amongst the families and couples with collectively more books, bags and buckets than your average pound shop. She could almost taste the cheap tanning lotion and she didn't know whether to be jealous or sympathetic to their cause. It was this irony along with the sudden surge towards the gate that put a rigid smile on her face. Seats around her emptied quicker than they had first been occupied as the sole and slightly dishevelled flight attendant took up position behind the desk. With her mismatched ensemble of fluorescent yellow jacket over snug blazer and fitted short skirt over pert buttocks she, in the absence of even a word, brought with her a blanket of anticipation provoking the flock to migrate mindlessly towards the desk.

Well, Esmée inhaled, silently priming for whatever was about to happen, here we go . . . won't be too much longer now. Sensing the underarm moisture begin to gather and further aggravate her discomfort, she reluctantly joined the congregating herd, feeling safer within their humming swell than exposed on the peripheries.

She hoped Tom would be all right with the kids. The mere thought of them brought tears to her eyes.

"Irresponsible" – that's what Tom had called her. And he was right. She was irresponsible, ridiculously so. What the hell was she doing? It was impossible to ignore the lurking sense of danger amplified by her lack of knowledge. Would she ever see the children again? With no idea of what she was heading for, she had no answer. "I'm going as much for them as for me," she had told Tom, silently convincing herself. "I have to go."

She knew instinctively that the sender of the text was him, and it had to end, this perpetual fear. Discreetly she wiped the tears from her eyes, throwing out a sideways glance, hoping no one had seen her stealthy move. The last thing she needed now was sympathy or attention. She had to be as inconspicuous as possible.

Taking a deep breath, she fused tighter into the crowd.

When eventually they boarded Esmée did so from the rear and took her seat quickly, keeping her head low as she slid into the hard-won window seat. Examining faces as they filed past she feared possible familiarity. What if she recognised someone? What would she do? She was well and truly trapped in this soon-to-be-apparently-weightless metal canister, so worrying about it now was pointless. In a perverse way she was kind of glad that the tedious wait was over, and acknowledged philosophically that she was about to embark on a new journey, literally.

Clicking her belt into position, she obediently watched the air steward perform the routine emergency instruction, checked under her seat to make sure they hadn't forgotten to stow her life jacket and then sat back to endure the ride. Beyond her little round-edged window the landscape rushed and blue replaced white which had already replaced the grey of the airstrip until eventually they glided easily over the cushion of patchy cotton-candy clouds. Resigning herself to the fact that there was literally no turning back, she let the thrust of the machine wash over her. A gentle stream of air seeped slowly from her lips as she tried not to let the relentless feeling of desperation take over. It was a bizarre sensation, ridiculous even, and she tried to remember how she felt when things were normal, when her life ticked over nicely, with her cosy house, her beautiful children and her husband. Her husband! What was it about her husband? Dizzied by the curious and confused thoughts of him, she gazed downwards towards the sea and, despite their distance, she couldn't help scanning the waves, knowing that they might hold the answers while she had none. But this trip would change all that, she prayed. That was the point. Whoever sent her that text probably knew by now she was on the flight. Was it a trick? Was he here with her too? Was he on the plane, enjoying the cardboard pretzels accompanied by a baby bottle of Chianti? She resisted the urge to stand up and sacrifice her anonymity; instead, she once again quizzed herself on how she managed to get caught up in this mess? What did she do to deserve it?

The hum of the engine and the sway of the titanium wings, like a gentle lullaby, provided a brief interval of calm, lulling her into a confused daydream. He was there. There beside her. She could smell him. Taste him. His face, his manicured hands. What was he saying? He was calling to her but she couldn't hear him, couldn't make out what he was saying.

"Speak up!" she called to him. But as she summonsed him, his image, slowly diminishing, eventually lost clarity, until he was nothing more than a wisp of vapour somewhere in the distance of her imagination.

"Are you all right, my dear?"

The hand on her wrist, like a red-hot iron, burnt her to the point of pain, extracting her rudely from her reverie. Esmée pulled back, instinctively bringing her arm up to her chest, and backed herself defensively against the wafer-thin walls of the plane.

The wizened fingers and manicured nails threw her. She was not as expected, this groomed old woman peering at her like a prim schoolteacher over bespectacled eyes.

"I'm sorry," she mumbled, "I. . . I . . ." But the words wouldn't come out.

"Don't worry, my dear," the woman said, polished nails reaching out to touch Esmée's arm, the maternal pat reassuring in a patronising kind of way. "You were miles away. Are you all right?"

"Not quite," she smiled uneasily. If only she knew! "More of a nightmare really," she qualified, smiling an insecure smile at the old lady. "A little scary. I'm sorry if I disturbed you."

"Not at all, my dear." Taking off her glasses, she turned

towards Esmée, her tone lowering as if imparting some secret divination. "You know, your dreams are nothing more than the expressions of yourself. Unlock your dreams, my dear, and you unlock the answers to your soul." With an air of finality she turned back in her seat, replaced her glasses on the end of her nose and returned to the idle page-flicking of her magazine, ignoring Esmée for the rest of the journey.

Mad as an American soap opera was the conclusion Esmée came to, finding it difficult not to sneak the occasional glance at the woman. But, even though the woman's statement bore the sentiment of mystical nonsense, there was something about it, something that actually rang true in a mad spiritual sense, if you were into that sort of thing.

She dreamt again and, in her dream, she saw him.

His body, floating face down, heaving with the rise and fall of the undulating waves. His arms stretched out, weightless, grasping at the dark viscous liquid – and his hands, his hands clenched and tight. Swollen and full, the roundness of his thighs apparent as the grey wool fabric of his trousers clung tight, strangling his legs while his shirt, turgid with water, meshed about his grossly engorged torso. And around his head a matted mess of thick brown hair spread out like a fan. And his feet, his bloody feet, thick, bloated and bare.

Chapter 21

Travelling light for a fast turnaround, Esmée easily wheeled her compact case through passport control, past customs and out into the long and dowdy arrivals hall. Keeping her head down, she tried as best she could to be alert to those behind her as well as in front. Ignoring the neatly uniformed and evenly tanned travel representatives who, smiling broadly, wafted branded name cards above their heads, she passed them swiftly to scan the small groups of people gathered along the main hall, obviously waiting on their travelling friends and families. Dressed in a light blue-and-white-striped cotton dress, blue cardigan and flip-flops, she moved through the arriving groups and eagerly sought out amongst the waiting crowds someone, anyone, who showed any interest in her. But none did, they all looked through her, seeking out their own familiar faces that, they hoped, were following close behind. Her inexperience made it next to impossible to be discreet as she walked the length of the barrier towards the exit and slowed, unsure as to what she should do or where she should go.

But there, right at the end of the concourse stood a man clad in shorts and a clean white polo shirt. She guessed him to be about forty and, with his head of thick black hair, dark-brown eyes, sallow skin and tanned feet he certainly wasn't Irish. She read the oblong card he held in his manly brown hands. In black block letters . . . was that her name?

ESMÉE MYERS

And so, like a cog slipping into its notch, the first part of the puzzle was coming together. They watched each other awkwardly as she approached and eventually came to a stop in front of him.

"Señora Myers?" he asked, raising his eyebrows while pointing to his placard.

Slowly she nodded, too afraid to speak.

"Come."

Stepping forward, he took hold of her small case and without introduction waved for her to follow him through the doors from the air-conditioned terminal to the dark and stiflingly hot enclosed car park. He moved so fast she had no option but to do as she was bid, almost running to keep in step beside him.

"Where are we going?" It took all she had within her to prevent the question from sounding like a screech. Be calm, be calm, she mentally instructed herself, quelling the nausea that threatened to spill her airline lunch all over the baking concrete.

"I take you to hotel," he replied while navigating expertly the many double-parked cars and the busy single lane of traffic, before stopping at a small white Fiat that had, long ago, seen much better days.

He opened the boot, threw her case in and slammed it shut before running around to her side. Opening the rear passenger door he indicated gallantly for her to get in. She looked first at the grimy leather back seat and then at his smiling Spanish face, quickly appraising both with equal scepticism and disbelief.

Despite herself, her head shook involuntarily. "You're joking, right?" she asked, mainly because the car didn't look like it would make it to the exit never mind a destination she assumed to be further away.

"Come!" he encouraged impatiently, ignoring her insult, once again gesturing towards his less-than-appealing chariot.

"Who sent you?" she asked, moving not an inch and looking to him for an answer.

"Eh?" A confused look crossed his face. "We go? Yes?" His eyebrows closed in on each other as he pointed to what Esmée assumed to be the general direction of their intended route.

"Who asked you to collect me?" she asked, keeping her tone calm and her diction clear and slow.

"I not understanding," he shrugged, shaking his head hopelessly and wiping sweat from his brow.

That left her with no option but to throw what little caution she had to the wind and just get into the car to find out for herself.

Smiling at his success and raising his eyes to the gods in relief, he slammed the door shut and scampered around to the driver's side. He started the engine and manoeuvred expertly through the steady stream of beeping cars and impatient drivers, all eager to lead the way out onto the motorway.

As they pulled out of the concourse, Esmée turned to note the cars behind. There were so many coming at them from all sides, but she tried to register as many as she could, paying real attention to the notion that one of them might be tailing her.

Her carriage was loud, bumpy and smelt like an ashtray – already she felt carsick. Picking up speed they cruised easily down the motorway. She opened the window as the heat and stench inside threatened to swallow her and closed her eyes to the warm wind, relieved by its cool rush on her flushed face and the feel of it blowing through the moist strands of her hair. How she knew it would be a long drive she wasn't sure – maybe it was the way he settled into his seat with his arm crooked comfortably out the window, or perhaps it was their fixed cruising speed in the fast lane as they rattled past, and ignored, the exits for one tourist resort after another.

She considered asking her courier again who had sent him but given his response at the airport knew it would be a waste of time and chose instead to cautiously monitor their progress out of the open window, watching the road signs and mentally calculating the distance from their starting point.

After what felt like hours the car slowed, moved into the inside lane and he indicated his intention to exit the motorway. The slip road circled up and around to the left until they joined a narrow minor road and began their ascent up a steep incline and into the mountains. Round and round the road weaved, snaking further up, ascending into the mountain like a shimmering black ribbon, knitting its way through the tiny hillside towns, each with more spectacular views than the last. Mile after mile the angst she felt bore down, increasing in sympathy with the augmenting altitude. The wait was killing her, the anticipation of what was coming at the end of the journey agonising.

She turned her attention to the transient view. Row after row of neat symmetrically placed trees and shrubs charmed her as they went by, their tended aspect a testament to the fertile landscape that despite the heat wasn't as scorched as the terrain below. And in the distance dark clouds rumbled, their load fermenting in broody readiness to overflow onto the parched land.

The winding road made their progress slow. They journeyed another half hour before, in the distance and stretching high above them, a castle exposed itself from around a corner. Perched on the edge of the emerging valley it seemed as if, with a gentle shove, it might just topple in at any moment. Its grey outline glowed against the background of the menacing sky.

The car struggled as the road narrowed and took a sharp angle skyward. Esmée hoped it was the final ascent to their destination. It took no more than a quarter of an hour to reach the fortified but picturesque and surprisingly busy town of Santa Alamosa, its name carved out of an enormous rock pitched proudly on the roadside on the way into the town.

Esmée couldn't silence her slow intake of breath as they crawled through the awesomely pretty streets and crossed the tiny squares. Lined with orange and lemon trees, their surrounding buildings were adorned with beautiful blooms which hung lavishly from shuttered windows overhead. And the people – perhaps it was the sun, but they all seemed so handsome, so vibrant, wearing the brightest of colours, busily going about their daily routine, chattering loudly, completely oblivious to the tired and emotionally confused woman passing them by in the beat-up car.

A firm believer in fate, that the behaviour and actions you bestow on others will come back to serve you, Esmée asked herself what it was she had done to deserve this? What had she done that had been so appalling, so immoral that its returning measure was to cast her into this nightmare? A nightmare that was confounded by the sheer beauty of this, the most romantic and idyllic setting she had ever experienced. Her heart was breaking. This was the kind of place you came to with a lover to hold hands and kiss, to dance, eat glorious food and laugh at sunset and fall asleep in each other's arms at sunrise. Yet here she was. Alone and scared and very, very angry.

When they eventually stopped it was at a door punched into a long amber stone wall. She stayed in the back of the Fiat, examining the exterior of the austere and unimpressive three-storey building, unsure if she should follow the driver and get out. He went to the boot and removed her case before opening her door and, extending his hand, invited her to join him.

"*Señora*," he said with a smile, "*este es vuestra hotel – vamos!*"

Taking his hand, she allowed him to help her out of the battered car, her legs and neck stiff from the journey. She found the air heavy and thick with not so much as a breeze to take the edge off the powerful heat that seemed to engulf her. She immediately felt beads of sweat form and trickle slowly earthward from between her breasts. Taking hold of the iron hoops attached to the imposing timber door, her escort pushed against its weight to reveal behind its bulk a wide-open space filled with sunlight, cool air and an array of lush green foliage. In its centre, a grand fountain released its water into a central reservoir that poured easily into a raised square pool.

"Wow!" Esmée exclaimed, turning on the spot to admire the beautifully tranquil interior, amazed by the cleverness of the walls round and above her which were punctured symmetrically by windows opening into the planted ecosystem. It smelt of sweet jasmine and honeysuckle and sounded like a heavenly paradise as from somewhere birds chirped in harmony with the calming cascade of the spilling water.

"Come," he said, holding open another door.

Taking a little time for her eyes to adjust to the dull light, she followed him down the chilly stone corridor which took them through an atrium and up a central mahogany staircase into a reception room. She had just enough time to scan the high walls and delicately frescoed ceilings before a deep mahogany panel opened on the opposite wall, through which came what must be her hostess.

"Señora Myers, welcome!" she greeted, pushing runaway

stands of her thick black hair back behind her ears.

She couldn't have been much older than herself, Esmée guessed, admiring the woman's slender figure as she extended her hand. Returning the smile, she took the presented hand.

"I am Isabella," the woman announced politely with a slight bow, her welcoming smile glowing from the deep pools of her dark eyes and the grip of her hand revealing a slender bone structure.

"I hope your journey was not too tiresome?" Her accent was heavy but seductive, and she was obviously well versed and trained in the English language.

"No, not at all," Esmée replied truthfully, disorientated and disarmed by the unexpected charm of her surroundings. "I'm a little stiff perhaps but it was a beautiful drive."

She turned with a smile to acknowledge her driver, to whom Isabella immediately spoke in Spanish. The pace of the exchange was mesmerising and, once complete, the man turned to Esmée and dipped his head.

"*Adiós, señora,*" he said and left the way they had arrived.

"Come," Isabella instructed, walking to the writing desk that sat in between the two windows, which had their shutters partially closed to protect from the blistering afternoon sun. From one of its drawers she extracted a thick ledger and, flicking through its well-worn pages, spread it open and invited Esmée to sign against her already inscribed name. There was no other detail on it apart from the day's date.

Esmée did as she was bid and returned the pen to its owner.

"Isabella?" she enquired anxiously. "Can you tell me who made this booking?" Then she added, "Who told you I was coming?" to make sure her question was understood.

But she needn't have worried. Isabella understood perfectly and offered her a shrug of her slender shoulders.

"We wonder also." Her smiling eyes were wide with curiosity.

"I receive a letter telling me of your arrival and with it a request to take you to the restaurant outside the fortification this night at seven o'clock."

Replacing the ledger, she then placed a guiding arm behind Esmée's back to lead her through the second door and exit the room.

"The letter did not say who it was from," she continued as they walked side by side through the cool corridors, their footsteps echoing against the hard stone floor to bounce back at them from the pale tiled walls. "So, a mystery!" she exclaimed gleefully, clapping her hands playfully. "How romantic! Maybe a boyfriend?" She smirked with raised eyebrows while Esmée smiled, as was expected, nodding her head politely. "Well, tonight we will know!"

At the end of the hallway they turned to ascend a second flight of stairs and then a third to the top of the house, stopping finally at the sole door on the landing.

Taking a key from the pocket of her skirt, Isabella inserted it into the lock, turned the handle and invited Esmée to enter the dim room before her. Following her in, she walked to the window to pull back the muslin drapes and push out the shutters, revealing the vast valley below.

"I hope you like your room – it is simple but comfortable. If you like to go walking I put some information cards here, but it is very hot today." She indicated the dresser which had a delicate lace covering. "The town is very hot but beautiful with many shops to stop and look. If you need anything please use this bell." She pointed to an old-fashioned porcelain button on the wall beside the bed. "My husband Pedro, he will come for you at six forty-five and take you to the restaurant."

Esmée was staring at the mahogany four-poster bed.

Isabella noticed her interest. "This bed," she said, unable to disguise the pride in her tone, "is the wedding bed of my grandmother's parents. It is very old. My great-grandfather made it."

It was indeed beautiful, Esmée agreed, admiring the delicate craftsmanship of the hand-carved headboard but hoping that the mattress wasn't an original part of the heirloom – she avoided the rude temptation to press down on it. Her hostess left the room, placing the key on the bedside table as she left.

Alone finally, catching her breath for the first time that day, Esmée walked to the window, feeling the threat of tears bite painfully behind her eyes. She was tired, utterly bewildered, and more than a little bit scared. With only a vague idea of where she was, she cursed herself for not listening to her brother. She sat into the window seat, pulled her knees to her chin and stared out at the beautiful but intimidating valley that stretched out shimmering in the afternoon sun.

If it was Philip who summonsed her here, he would probably know by now that she had arrived. And, it would appear, would be joining her for dinner.

It was hot and she was sticky, the impending storm adding to the tension.

She stepped into the shower and let the water wash away the salty remnants of the journey, cooling her down and freshening her up. Throwing her bag onto the bed, taking the opportunity then to test its age and constitution, she pulled out a skirt with matching top and flat sandals. That should see her through, the fabric comfortably light against her skin. She checked the time – it was still early and the jitters in her legs and uneasy thoughts chasing through her head were telling her that she couldn't sit there all afternoon, no matter how hot it was outside. She had to get out or she'd go nuts, and in search of real distraction decided to explore.

Isabella was right: it was blistering outside. The heat was arid, forming a sheath around her as she strolled through the rise and fall of the narrow undulating streets, doing her best to remain in the shade wherever possible. The place was buzzing; even mid-siesta it felt like a fiesta. She watched people scurry like late mad March hares while others ambled aimlessly, taking in the sights just like her. Some were laden down with bags of groceries, while others seemed happy to stand and chat despite the heat of the sun. The contrast was charming. It just seemed so alive, so upbeat. For a moment she wanted to be part of it, wanted to communicate demonstratively, laugh loudly and chatter wildly and belong to a place so beautiful perched high in the mountains. She wanted to forget her trepidation and melt into the surroundings, to forget the real reason why she was there and imagine another.

Every now and then she would stop to look. Using the chaotic shop windows as a pretext she would browse and then cast her eyes back the way she had come. But no one stood out, she saw no one person twice. Safe in the knowledge that she didn't appear to be followed, she wandered up to the old city to discover the ruined ramparts. In its time it had obviously been a grand castle, central to a rich and important rural community, and had stood, like a lion at the gate, protecting its subjects from harm. Much of its structure was still intact with a flurry of businesses supporting it. There were gift shops ablaze with a tussle of pleats and plumes, flamenco dresses and sombreros, donkeys and prettily painted pottery, ice-cream shops, flower stalls and cafés. She was enamoured of it all – the smells, the colours, the people, the place: it was electrifying.

She chose a spot in a small-canopied café to sit, watch and just think. Alcohol, although tempting, was dangerous so she selected instead a safe but equally satisfying alternative. Her *café con helado* arrived in an espresso cup accompanied by a tall glass filled with ice; the woody aroma of the coffee mixed with the warm smell of the street was intense. And as the heat of the dense liquid swallowed the ice, like a body into quicksand, she sank deeper with it. Gone. Suddenly the beauty of her surroundings served only to amplify her feelings of desolation and abandonment. She hadn't felt like this . . . well, not since her dad died. Self-pity took all flavour from the now tasteless coffee that she sipped, practising silently what she had to ask and say to Philip, if he showed up. She remained static, watching everything else move on without her.

Chapter 22

A church bell rang in the half hour with a single heavy chime. Her afternoon sheltering from the heat of the Spanish sun was over. It was time to go. A chill wind had begun to blow and the sun began to weaken as the clouds drew nearer. She settled her bill with the handsome waiter who smelt like lemon zest, claimed the last sip of her drink and took herself back to the streets. She was in no hurry with at least two hours before her rendezvous.

Making her way back to the hotel the afternoon heat seemed less oppressive, the breeze a welcome coolant. She planned as she walked, visualising what she would wear and what her first question would be. Somewhere in the back of her head the theory that it might not be Philip at all raised itself again and Brady's grinning features came to mind. But instinctively she knew that wasn't the case and spent the short journey back telling herself not to lose her head.

Thankfully there was no sign of her hostess when she opened the door of the hotel. She wasn't in the mood for idle chat and managed to find her way with great stealth to the top floor room uninterrupted. Under the spray of the shower she rinsed the salt from her body and let the refreshing jets cool her down. The pulse of the drops hit deep into her skin, opening up the channels to relieve her tension and stress.

You're here now, Esmée, she told herself. Now stand up and be strong.

She knew she couldn't let him manipulate her any more. She had to stand up to him. She had questions that needed answers so the attitude of an insecure weakling was not the one she needed to adopt.

She had thought long and hard about what to bring to wear and standing in her underwear surveying the outfit she was glad of her choice. Philip was supposed to be dead, and she was supposed to be his grieving widow and that is exactly who she needed to be.

She brushed her long hair till it was silky smooth, letting its natural shape create soft swirls at the ends. It fell heavy over her shoulders in layers like rich chocolate, its colour catching the light as she moved. Outside her open window the sky was dark and the rumblings of thunder created an empathetic air of anticipation: like something big was about to kick off.

A black lace shirt, tied demurely at the neck in a bow, her knee-length black skirt, black-patent stilettos and black lightweight mac together delivered a sombre but sophisticated look. She stared back at her alien reflection with butterflies in her stomach: this was it. The humidity was too high for make-up but she finished off with a scarlet lipstick – he hated that colour. She was ready to go.

Downstairs, she couldn't help but notice the curious look her outfit received from the ever-beautiful Isabella, but no matter.

She intended to play by her own rules.

Pedro had no English and communicated through smiles and exaggerated gestures along their fifteen-minute walk through the almost familiar narrow streets. The rain was beginning to fall and streetlights were already flickering in the unusually dark summer evening. Every now and then he pointed at something that he assumed should be of special interest to her, rattling on spontaneously in his native tongue, and even though she had no idea what he was saying Esmée returned his grins and impossible words with an encouraging nod and the occasional "Ahh!" and "Ohh" and "Yes, I see – beautiful!"

The restaurant revealed itself as they rounded a corner and entered a small flagstoned square. Framed on two sides by the high walls of buildings, there were cafés and shops buried deep in its arches, with tables diffusing into the square. Esmée's destination was marked on the opposite side by a bright red awning that stretched out into the square to protect the customers from the sun and now the rain. Waiters busily placed candles on the tables, creating a tempting ambience that shimmered in the descending moist evening light.

Pedro left her at the edge of the square and, waving her onwards, yapped a succession of indecipherable words, then left with a cheery "*Adiós!*" Quiet but impassioned guitar chords mixed with garlic aromas wafted persuasively across the square. She stood for a while just to look, bracing herself for whatever was about to come. Slowly she made her way towards the pretty tables, her footsteps echoing loudly in her ears. Was he already there? Was he watching her now? The butterflies in her stomach danced with nervous excitement and dread and her knees trembled slightly. There was no one sitting outside and, as she approached the door, she saw only a few groups at tables across the dark air-conditioned interior. A waiter approached her to offer her a table.

Her mind raced as she weighed up her options. Inside or out? Corner or mid-floor? Hide or be seen? Sensing her indecision, he took the lead and showed her to a corner table outside with a good vantage point of the square.

"The best table in the house!" he exclaimed proudly in perfect English, the sweet intimacy of the setting somewhat wasted in the context of her "meeting".

It was early to eat by Spanish standards but she was glad of the solitude and ordered a bottle of the house red. She watched the handsome waiter pour the ruby liquid into her glass, its aroma promising fruity delights as she inhaled deeply before sipping it. Dutch courage, she promised herself as she touched the glass to her lips again and this time took a generous sip, feeling its effect almost immediately: calming her nerves as she waited patiently for something to happen.

Chapter 23

She checked her watch. He was late. Had she come all this way for him not to even bother to turn up? Typically, her impatience prolonged the agony. Promising herself the limit of the time contained in a single glass of wine, she sat on, sipping her drink.

She was preparing to leave when she heard him, heard his familiar step, the slight drag of his left heel and heavy fall of his right as lazily he strolled towards the restaurant. She knew if she looked up she would see him but was frozen in fearful anticipation, unable to move, unable to breathe. By the sound of it he was in no hurry. She could feel his gaze burn into her as he approached. Her eyes closed in apprehension and behind the lids she could imagine his face, the same face that pushed her out of her house, the same face that sneered as she grappled with the ground. Her legs shook visibly when his footsteps came to a stop. He was standing in front of her. She placed a firm hand on her knee to halt its movement, unable to bring herself to look up, afraid of what was coming next. Without trying she could see his torso and legs. He wore sandals and no socks, with light linen trousers. His toes were tanned and manicured.

She waited for him to speak and when he didn't she took a hold of the stem of her glass and raised it to her mouth. Lifting her head she caught his gaze and took a grown-up taste of her wine.

For a dead man he looked remarkably good: tanned and lean.

"Hello, Esmée."

She forced herself to swallow without gagging on the tannic liquid then placed the glass deliberately on the table, hoping the shake in her hand wouldn't give her away. She didn't reply to his greeting but held his gaze dispassionately, she hoped. Controlled. In control.

He glistened from the raindrops that settled on his slicked-back hair. There was no denying he looked good in his longer-style haircut and open-collar shirt. It suited him, she thought as she observed him; it matched the look of his bronzed face and nonchalant stance. But he didn't look like a man who was hurting. He didn't appear to be uneasy at all. She had expected to see him somewhat agitated, edgy even. There were plenty of things he needed to be concerned about and Esmée wondered which should worry him most: the lies, manipulation, bigamy, fraud, theft? Or was it the truth that he should be most intimidated by? Funny how his spurious disappearance had fast become the least offensive of his misdemeanours.

But the man smiling seductively down at her was quite relaxed, showing no apparent signs of the stress or fatigue that guilt should bring. No! He was just fine, and actually seemed pleased to see her.

She prickled as he moved towards her, around the table and to her side. He knelt down beside her and took her face in his hands, exploring her like he was seeing her for the first time. His fingers trailed a path from her nose out across her cheeks to gently sweep across her mouth before he bent in and replaced his fingers with his lips. She didn't pull away, but sat impassively as he kissed her, his tongue viper-like invading her while his thumbs pressed gently on her cheeks.

"You look fantastic," he whispered in her ear, taking in deep breaths of her. Still she didn't speak, astounded by his audacity and sickened by his touch. She felt relief in his kiss: relief that she felt nothing for him. His kiss always had the ability to disarm her. He used it so often when it suited him to say sorry. But this evening, as the rain fell and the thunder rumbled, she felt no hunger to respond. Sensing her despondency he stood up and stepped back, adopting a childish look of rejection. A triumphant ray of sun broke through the clouds to momentarily fill the square in an opalescent glow of glorious golden light. His outline, darkened by the dazzling backdrop, became the silhouette of a man she had dreamt about, a man she had assumed to be dead, swallowed by the sea. Yet here he stood, very much alive, the silhouette of a stranger looking to be welcomed back into her life. This was the occasion she had been waiting for: her moment of interrogation. She had wished for this opportunity, dreamt about it, role-played and practised the conversation, but with it now in her grasp she was an empty vessel, but without the noise.

"Come on, Es," he nursed, his tone soft and encouraging, so different to their last conversation. "Speak to me. Say something!"

Sitting down opposite, he reached to take her hand across the divide of the table. But she pulled away abruptly, almost knocking the glass with her sharp recoil. She thrilled to see that he appeared visibly unnerved by her reaction, sitting back to shake his head. Was this real, she asked herself? Was he real? His reactions seeming almost delusional. Inside her head she counted to ten, hoping the steady rhythm would placate her jumbled thoughts.

"Come on, Es," he implored. "Please talk to me."

Baby steps, she cautioned inside, filtering the many wrongs and asking herself which should she address first? There were so many: her own, their children's, his job and work colleagues, not to mention Jim Brady's.

"How are you?" she asked, finishing off with his true name: "Robert."

"Ahhh," Philip smiled. "So you figured it out."

"Julie says hello. Harry too," she replied, choosing to ignore his patronising intention.

He nodded, smiling faintly, and looked away from her across the square.

"And your daughter is beautiful. Beth. She looks just like Julie."

Philip turned to her, his face a picture of his thoughts, but there was no regret there.

Infuriated, Esmée went on. "And as for Harry, my God, what a stunner! He's a young man now. Doing his finals, I hear."

"Before you judge me, Esmée, you need to understand what was happening at the time. I was in trouble. Real trouble. I had no option."

"Ahh, yes!" Esmée laughed, gaining confidence. "I know all about your trouble," she sneered. "He says to say hi too." The sarcastic smile dropped from her face. "Have you any idea what you've done?"

"I was sick. Out of control." He shrugged.

"And how do you know I haven't told him where you are. How do you know he's not here waiting for you to show up?"

"I know you, Es. It's not your style. You're not that cruel. I knew you'd want to see me alone. I'll bet you didn't even go to the police, did you?"

What a shit!

He smiled, knowing his assumption to be true.

"And Julie, what about her? You used her, just like you've used me. Why, Philip? Why?"

"I had to. There was no other way."

"There is always another way. Always."

The waiter's approach muted their conversation, but his swift departure after filling Philip's glass was a telling sign that while the words may have stopped, the cactus-like atmosphere remained.

Philip lifted the bulbous goblet to his nose, pompously swirling the liquid round to coat its inside. Like he knew what he was doing.

"You were different," he answered, savouring the flavours while drawing in their scent.

He'd known when he left she was bound to find out about his past. It was inevitable. She might not put it together herself, but others would, and she would be told. He wasn't quite sure if she knew the full story, but she knew enough. He was prepared for this encounter, he wouldn't have brought her here otherwise, and he assumed, if it sounded like the truth she'd be fine. This was Esmée after all: all she needed was a few tragically romantic scenarios and he'd win her over. He'd done it before; he could do it again.

He let the silent suspense build before repeating, "You were different," then looked up at her coyly. "From the first moment I saw you, I knew you were part of my future. We were meant to be together."

"Are you serious?" she choked. "How on earth could that be possible? You gave up your little boy and your unborn child, not to mention your wife. You gave up your entire family and you expect me to believe that I could replace that? You were there when my father died – you were there! How could that be right?"

"Fate," he justified simply. "Fate had in some bizarre way brought us together. I never meant it to happen that way. I thought I had lost everything and then there was you . . ." He let his sentence trail off.

"You are off your head!" she spat. "You ambushed me. You tracked me down and pursued me like some defenceless animal. You tricked me into loving you."

"It wasn't like that."

"Philip, you were living in South Africa. You had a new life. But you came back. You found me and then you married me knowing you were still married to Julie. Why? What the hell were you thinking? What part of our story seems right to you? It's wrong, Philip. All wrong!"

Philip studied his wife as she ranted, the way her eyes flared passionately, her wild gesticulations and heaving breast. She was so good, he thought, and wondered just how he could bring her round. He hadn't expected her to welcome him back with open arms – hadn't thought it would be easy to get her to forgive him – but she was here, wasn't she? And that was a start. How could he swing this, he calculated, detached from her emotions. And anyway, if he couldn't convince her to come of her own accord, he'd come and get her regardless. He was used to getting his own way, and this was no different. He wanted her back, whether she liked it or not.

"I can't explain it, Es. I just couldn't get you out of my mind. But none of that matters. I'm here. Now. And I want you." He leant in towards her, pleading.

She shook her head in abhorrence. He wasn't getting it. Not only that, he couldn't see that she was immune to his charm. He had passed his 'best before' date. Leaning back in her chair she observed him, calmly realising she wasn't going to get any credible answers off him here. He was incapable of the truth. He was delusional. He seemed to have convinced himself that he had done nothing terminally wrong.

"So this is where you've been living?" she asked awkwardly, changing the direction in order to buy herself some time and gather her thoughts.

"Yes, beautiful, isn't it?" he responded proudly, oblivious to the bite in her tone, and threw his arms open to the air as if to embrace his kingdom. "This sun!" he exclaimed, closing his eyes reverently, absorbing it as if for the first time. "The atmosphere! The people! Why," he asked whimsically, "did we never come here years ago, Es?"

She watched with disbelieving wonder as he then invited the hovering waiter to refill his glass and requested the menu in proficient Spanish. He smiled at her, raising his eyebrows as any good show-off would, but she wasn't an impressionable conquest any longer and didn't know whether to be fascinated or sickened by the arrogance of his display.

"So!" he said cheerfully, like the conversation of moments ago was a mere formality that was now done with, settling forward in his chair to rest his arms on the table, convinced he was making some headway. "How have you been? Really. How are things at home?"

"We thought you were dead!" she blurted out, amazed by his frivolous chatter and alarming disconnection from reality.

"Not you, Es!" he remarked shrewdly, folding his arms across his broad chest, "Not you. You knew I couldn't do that. Didn't you?"

The smug, self-righteous tone of his response irked her. How dare he! How dare he belittle the feelings of so many people about whom he was supposed to care.

"You're right, Philip," the words burst clear of her mouth. "I always knew it wasn't your style, but I never had you down for a coward, a thief, a liar or a bigamist!" She delivered her attack suddenly and forcibly, supported by a hard, intense and accusing glare, infuriated by his supercilious smile.

"I'm sorry, Esmée. I'm sorry I hurt you, sorry I hit you, but . . . but . . . you couldn't possibly understand . . ." He dropped his voice to a patronising whisper. "There were things . . ." He paused and looked down at the table as if searching for the right, simple, word that would adequately explain himself to this, his estranged wife. "Things that I don't expect you to identify with . . ."

"You've already said that and frankly I'm tired of your lame excuses. You need to credit me with some intelligence and just fucking tell me what the bloody hell went on! How about you start by telling me why you left your shoes and socks like that in the car? I'm baffled."

He smiled slowly, obviously reliving the moment. "No particular reason really. I just thought it was a nice touch, a small display of obsessive compulsiveness before I died – you know, get everything straight."

"Oh Philip, how very *you*!" she spat. "And the rest?" she prompted.

He observed her for a moment, taking stock of the spirited woman bristling in front of him, wondering what she would do, how she would react, if she knew the truth, the whole truth . . .

*   *   *

The security guard lay unconscious on the carpet with a bloody gash on his head. Robert didn't need to act shocked. He was. Things hadn't quite gone to plan. It was supposed to be easy. On paper and in theory it appeared effortless, foolproof even. He and Brady's team were to arrive at the bank just before 9 a.m. He would open up and wait for the time lock to release on the safe. Brady and his cohorts would lie in wait behind the screen. Amanda and Mike would arrive as they always did just after 9:15, Amanda armed as always with a coffee and muffin for Robert as well as herself. It was a running joke in the back office that she was besotted with him. On arrival, she and Mike were to be intercepted by Brady from behind the screens. They, thinking that Robert was being coerced, would co-operate and allow themselves be bound, gagged and locked in the office while Robert was 'forced' to empty the safe. Between them they assumed that the threat of danger upon Julie and the kids would be enough to guarantee compliance: there was no one brave or smart enough to play 'have-a-go hero' amongst Robert's workmates. Or so they thought. But it all went wrong when that gobshite Mike tried to cut loose. He always was an eejit. The son of a prolific developer who also happened to be their best local customer, how could Robert say no when asked for a reference? The reference that ultimately got him the job. In this bloody branch. He shouldn't have bothered. That fucking idiot cost him everything. Bill the security guard had no option but to intervene – it was his job – but got the butt of the gun at the back of his head from Tommo for his efforts. That's when Amanda made an attempt to trigger the alarm. Tommo and Brady lunged forward to stop her. In the ensuing confusion Robert had left the room. And saw the detective outside. Frank. Then the alarm went off. Blind panic reaped reflexive reactions. And then it was over. An apparently straightforward robbery had turned into murder.

Robert sat on the floor of the banking hall with a cup of sweet tea in his hand, watching the blinking blue lights of the ambulance outside and listening to the weeping testimony of Amanda as she recounted the event. He hated tea, let alone sweet tea, but he was drinking it anyway. It just wasn't supposed to happen like this. That wasn't meant to happen. What the hell was he going to do now? They got away, all of them, except him. But they left empty-handed.

"We're not done yet, Bobby, my son," Brady had whispered. "Open your fucking gob," he muttered venomously, taking a firm hold of Robert's balls, "and you're dead. Clear?" He tightened his grip.

Robert nodded furiously and then Brady was gone. Out the back door. Empty-bloody-handed.

Within minutes there were cops everywhere, closing off roads and securing the bank itself. The ambulance arrived after and word quickly came back to say they'd found Julie and Harry safe: scared but well. At first they were gentle with him: firm but gentle. But he knew the moment they suspected his complicity when the flavour of their questions changed. They became distinctly more hostile, their questions bullish and direct.

After a couple of weeks Robert was arrested. Turning against Brady was elementary. Despite the failure of the heist, he still owed Brady the money. There was no way he'd forgive that, on top of which Robert doubted Brady would believe he hadn't ratted them out: so why disappoint? He was a dead man walking. They offered them a new life, a new identity, a fresh start. And help for his addiction. The gambling had to end: that was a deal-breaker. But it was a sweet deal regardless: too good to refuse. Julie, however, was different. When the truth came out she went wild, savage even, and refused to find reason in his actions. He tried to explain his predicament and when that didn't work he lied. He told her Brady had forced him to do it, but that story unravelled as the court case progressed and, as always, the truth came out. What she just couldn't forgive, she declared with absolute finality, was how he could have even considered putting their children, both born and unborn, in such extreme danger. She threw him out that night, telling him to go and never come back. So he did just that. That simple.

Why she just couldn't accept that he had no other choice, he couldn't quite fathom. She left him and took his children from him. Estranged and in a foreign country, he found it difficult to divorce himself from what had happened. The death of Frank Gill affected him more than he could ever have imagined. At the time he was just there. Wrong place, wrong time. And, yes, it was sad. Horrible even, and he couldn't get the faces of Frank's family out of his head. At the time, still a free man, he attended the funeral and contemplated Frank's grieving children as they cried openly when the coffin was lowered into the ground. He was almost jealous of Frank Gill, whose wife wept with silent dignity as they filled his grave with soil. It was an accident. But it had become his accident.

South Africa was good to him. His house was beautiful, his job was great, the weather magnificent. The women, outstanding. But he couldn't settle. They told him that heading back home wasn't an option. If he came out of the programme, he did so at his own peril and cost. They couldn't and wouldn't protect him. And while Brady got fifteen years, he still had eyes and ears everywhere. Good sense failed Robert as he weighed up the odds. Distance numbed his reason and it seemed like a good idea at the time. He'd changed his name once before so he could just as easily do it again. It wasn't difficult – he still had the fake passport and birth certificate he'd bought to arrange for that safe-deposit box in Dublin before he left. He could use that. He'd liked the name, Philip Myers, there was something debonair about it, he thought, and so Philip Myers was officially born. Finding the impressionable young woman wasn't difficult either.

He picked her not only because she was the oldest of the girls, but also because out of all of them she seemed the most interesting, a real challenge. All he wanted to do was make it right. Make the pain go away. Her pain. He charmed, wooed her and promised to take care of her. It cost him nothing.

No sooner was he back than he found himself slipping into his old ways. Maybe it was the smell of the country or taste of the Guinness, but he just couldn't resist the draw of the cards. He was careful not to revisit his old haunts, but found new ones, better, more lucrative ones that had sprung up while he was gone. Promising himself that this was only a hobby, he managed well at the start, balancing small wins with small losses and exercising a control that his Gambling Anonymous mentor in Pretoria would have been proud of. That's what he told himself anyway. But as the years passed and boredom set in, self-control, like his first wife, left him to fend for himself. So he was right back to square one.

Then he heard Brady was to be released a little earlier than he was expecting. He had half-formed plans to disappear and relocate the following year to Spain, but Tommo's warning visit to his house meant he had to act fast, without perfecting his plans. As Tommo had gleefully revealed, his cover had been betrayed by himself of all people, in a bar one night after too many Jack Daniels, trying to impress a young lady, who by great misfortune happened to be employed by Brady's empire.

It was time to go.

* * *

Now, looking at Esmée across the table in the rainy Spanish square, it was time to reel her in. Again.

He splayed his palms flat out on the table in a self-righteous display of accepted defeat.

"All right," he began, making a deliberate show of preparing himself to bare all, "I am a gambling addict. I have an addiction: an illness. Cards are my thing, poker to be exact." He kept his eyes fixed firmly on the table. "I lost everything I had – Julie and I had – and more. I hadn't paid the mortgage in months and my credit cards were maxed out. I lost it all." He risked a quick glance upwards to gauge her reaction. She was blank. "Anyway," he continued, taking a deep breath, "I had the chance of one last game, a game that would change everything, if I won. The stakes were high, but I wasn't thinking straight. I was sure I could win. I'd played most of the guys before: they were amateurs. I was better than all of them. I was the player. Brady was there that night. We'd been up against each other before but he didn't really register. Anyway, that night he won and I lost. Simple as." He paused, eyes lowered, sighed and continued. "I had nothing else to sell, nothing of any great value anyway. That's when Brady came up with the plan." He stopped to swallow. "The robbery was meant to settle my debt to him. But, well, you know what happened there." He looked at her properly this time. He couldn't read her, her face, the wall of silence. "I was such a disappointment to Julie and Harry. I'd let them down. I was so ashamed. There was no way I could have made up for that. So I ran." He let out a repressed sigh, fixing a pained expression on his face. "But I was wrong. I shouldn't have run," he finished, sure his soliloquy had breached her defensive bastion. But when he looked up again he saw only disgust.

"Esmée!" he implored, trying again. "I paid the price. Please don't punish me again!"

He leant towards her, catching her stare, which she held on to, and leaning in to match his stance she whispered, "And what about me. What was I?"

"You? Well . . ." he searched, "you were . . ." He was lost for words and decided on a different approach: a kind of honesty. "At the start, yes, I admit, I was fascinated by you, by you all. And yes, I did track you. I wanted to help."

"Help! You wanted to help? Well, let me tell you, Philip or Robert or whatever the hell your name is, the only person who needed help was you!" She was revolted by him. She could see through his lies and barefaced excuses. Empowered by her animosity towards him and invigorated by her hurt, she wasn't willing to be held captive any more.

"Just let me explain, Esmée –"

"Explain? You must be kidding, right? I don't want your explanations."

"I need to tell you, I need you to believe me . . ."

"But I can't believe you, Philip, can I? I don't even know you. I don't know who you are."

"Oh for God's sake, Esmée!" he shouted. "It's not as bad as you think!" His booming voice resonated through the empty square, the pursuing silence deafening.

Esmée let the silence rest and his words sink in before replying. "Not as bad as I think? Are you mental? Philip, I've actually met Brady." She paused to let the implications of the admission sink in. "I've had his breath on my face and his hand on my tits. He accosted me in the park with the kids, so don't sit there and tell me it's not as bad as I think. It's *worse* than *you* think." Her breath came short and heavy, compromised by her fury. "I've been questioned, interrogated, searched, humiliated and threatened. After all I've heard about you these last few weeks, Philip, I wouldn't trust you with my spit!"

He was losing and he knew it. "I did it for you! I wanted to make it right." But his words were weak and lacking integrity – they were dying words, words from a man grasping at straws.

"For me?" she exclaimed incredulously, pushing herself further forward. "Don't you dare blame me for what you did. I never asked you to do anything for me." Her words were sharp and firm. She wanted to slap him, hard. "You really are a coward, d'you know that?" she hissed venomously, her eyes tight and oozing contempt. "And don't you dare lay your bullshit on me. You did this for no one but yourself."

They didn't notice the waiter until he coughed politely, looking over their heads uncomfortably.

"You wish to order now, yes?" he asked awkwardly in his cheerful English, mortified by the display he'd borne witness to.

Esmée picked up the menu only to throw it back down again immediately. "Actually, I'm not very hungry." She wasn't going to perform for anyone, no matter how embarrassing it would be.

Philip, without taking his eyes off her, spoke expertly in Spanish to the waiter. She had no idea what he was saying and couldn't have cared less but, whatever he said, their server retrieved the menus and swiftly retreated. He'd probably go in and tell his comrades about the arguing diners, but she didn't care.

She felt Philip's eyes bore into her as she took a long desperate drink.

He was judging her, assessing her, wondering where this new-found confidence had come from, wondering what to do next. She was different, very different and it felt more than a little uncomfortable, this new power she had over him.

"Why did you bring me here, Philip?" she asked, repositioning her glass on the table, tired now of the little man who sat before her, tired of the man she thought she knew. His game was over and she wanted to go home, the reunion nothing more than a pitiful anti-climactic farce. "What do you want?"

His mood in response to her tone was shifting. He wasn't enjoying this woman. He didn't care for the lack of respect and the nasty tone of her voice. There was no need for that. He did, after all, really do it for her. Her and her stupid family. When, he wondered, had she become so ungrateful? He was going to give this one more try. And then after that if she didn't comply he'd have to take up a different tack. He would give her one last chance, then his patience was used up.

"I miss you, Esmée," he gushed. "I want you to join me, come out here. We can start afresh just you, me and the kids." He held out his hand to her, willing her to take it, to see sense.

"You're kidding, right?" Was it possible that this man had the audacity to believe his offer was, never mind tempting, even possible?

"Es, please don't do this – the children need a father and you ..." He didn't need to expand any further.

"I need what? A man? A husband?" This time it was her turn to raise her voice.

"Keep your voice down!" he hissed as he looked around at the thankfully empty tables and shifted uncomfortably in his seat.

"You have no idea what I need – you haven't even the remotest clue!" she screeched, indifferent to the now-concerned waiters who had gathered to peer out from behind the safety of the tinted glass window. "Well, let me tell you something, Philip Myers," she continued savagely. "Whatever it is you're so sure I need it sure as hell isn't you!" She paused briefly to replenish her lungs. "You're a liar, a cheat and a thief and believe me those qualities don't figure high on my criteria for the ideal husband. And if I had a choice, if I were left to pick a husband without being steered and manipulated, it – wouldn't – be – you!" Her finger punctuated the last words, leaving no doubt that this time Philip had lost.

"Esmée! For God's sake, calm down!"

His plea went unheard as her tongue, loosened by the wine, drove unrelenting on its verbal rampage.

"You're not sorry, you're not even remotely ashamed of what you've done and you expect me to move here with our children, leave everything behind and live a life on the run funded by your ill-gotten gains?" She was bordering on hysteria, inflamed by his words.

"Es, I'm warning you!"

"You're mad, Philip, do you know that? And you can stop calling me 'Es'. I'm not your Es any more, and in case you forgot, I left you before you left me." Breathless and spent, she stood and yanked her bag from the back of the chair, knocking it over as she went, feeling remarkably lighter than when she arrived, a burden gone from her weight-laden shoulders. She was done. They were well and truly over. There was nothing to achieve by remaining. But she had one last message to give him.

"And the money that you took from the company, part of which I'm assuming you left for me to find – and what was that? Guilt money? – well, I want you to give what's left of it back." Looking down on him, she spoke with her eyes more than words. "And if you don't give it back, and I mean all of it, Philip, I'll tell your friend Brady exactly where to find you." She paused. "You've got one month."

With that threat she turned to leave but not before he lunged forward to take a firm hold of her wrist.

"Don't threaten me, Esmée," he cautioned malevolently, her words exposing the Philip she had last encountered.

She was almost relieved by this revelation and looked down carelessly at his hand.

"Let go of me!" she said calmly, holding his stare as his grip tightened dangerously. "I said," she repeated firmly, "let me go or I swear by God I'll scream so loud they'll hear me back in Dublin." Out of the corner of her eye she saw one of the waiters step forward onto the threshold of the restaurant, his presence prompting Philip to release his grip.

"Don't do this, Esmée!" he warned, watching her storm from the restaurant in her black high heels and black mac, the perfect attire for a grieving widow.

"Watch me!" she challenged without turning and marched with her head held high through the blustery town square.

Throwing euro notes nonchalantly from his pocket, Philip jogged after the marching woman who, technically, was never actually his wife.

"Esmée!" he implored, catching up to take hold of her arm, his tone reverting to the sorrowful pleading boy. "Look, come with me. Let me show you something. One last favour. Please?"

"No! I've had enough and I'm going home. Now, let go."

"Esmée, please!" He was begging now. "Come with me!"

"Philip, let go of me now!"

Philip dropped his grip in temporary defeat and watched her stride across the cobbled square, struggling to remain upright as the narrow spindles of her heels caught in the crevices of the rough street.

"I'll let you go this time, Esmée, but I'm not done yet!" he called after her, his voice echoing from all four corners of the square.

Hands on hips, he shook his head and smirked as she stumbled and cast a final defiant glare over her shoulder, her face a scripture of abhorrence and disgust. It was that passionate determination that first captivated him when they met. She was playing hard to get. Making him pay, and maybe he deserved it. He'd leave her a while, but it might, he admitted silently, just might take a trip to Dublin to change her mind. Maybe get the kids first. Then she'd see sense. He watched her round the corner then, taking a fresh pack of Marlboro Lights from his jacket pocket, he lit one and made his way to the bar on the corner.

"*Una cerveza!*" he called to the young bar tender, then turned to look out at the square, resting his elbows on the bar and pensively pulling on his cigarette before resting his greedy eyes on the two brunettes drinking chilled Prosecco under the protective cover of the canopy.

* * *

For a brief moment the man wearing the Barcelona FC hat pulled down over his brow had thought they'd been rumbled and their cover blown. Turned on by the shock assumption, his sweat glands had gone into overdrive to ooze an overwhelming quantity of liquid through the pores of his brow. Swallowing hard, he'd fixed the open neck of his aertex sports shirt and watched Philip approach the bar, immediately thinking of credible denials and explanations for such a coincidental encounter. His startled eyes had darted to meet Dougie's across the table. Thankfully Jorge, his Spanish counterpart, had missed the panic and had taken the swift reaction as both a warning and instruction. He immediately entered into an animated monologue, masquerading as conversation, in his native tongue. Maloney, seeming to listen intently, nodded occasionally, all the while keeping his malefactor captive in his periphery.

Now an involuntary sigh of relief helped neutralise the adrenaline that interfered with his heart rate as it became clear that Philip was merely stopping to smoke and unwind after his encounter with Esmée.

She had been easy to track. The information from her brother was brilliant. He could hardly contain his excitement as he thought of not just one but potentially two high-profile arrests. He just needed to nail this one. Philip was just a small part of a bigger deal. Like before, they said he couldn't have acted alone. There must, the bank's investigating fraud team told him, have been someone on the outside to fulfil the scam. And that was why they were there. They were to lay in wait and see who popped up. And they were bound to, so the fraud team said. Maloney had asked to be allowed to follow it through. The force, already on the back foot and humiliated at being hoodwinked by Robert aka Philip were happy for all the assistance they could get. So, although it wasn't their area, Maloney and his partner were on the job.

Dougie took some convincing.

"What the hell? Spain? You're havin' a laugh! I'm not going to Spain!" he scoffed, biting into his breakfast roll.

"Come on, Dougie, we've got a chance to nail this fucker."

"That's not all you want to nail, is it?" he jeered, wiping sauce from the sides of his mouth.

"Don't be an asshole!"

Dougie responded with a wink, a grin and a pursing of his lips.

"Come on, mate," Maloney pushed. "It'll look good for us. A great score. You've got your inspector's exams coming up soon. This could make a difference." He didn't need to say any more. Dougie was in.

The detail from Tom was specific and allowed them travel ahead and observe Esmée's arrival from the safety of the security zone on the top floor of the airport building. She looked so vulnerable, walking cautiously, watching behind as much as ahead, wary and alone, made conspicuous by her stealth. Even through the security screens he could feel the unease etched across her face as she scoured the awaiting crowds for her contact. Instinctively Maloney felt an urgent need to protect this woman, to watch over her and secure her safe return to her family.

I must be going soft, he chastised himself silently as he and a sweating Dougie followed Jorge, their appointed contact, to a waiting car that would discreetly shadow her as she exited the airport campus.

They hung back and waited while their newly adopted Spanish team put her under surveillance. They followed her through the day and later waited outside the hotel until she left with the man they quickly found out to be the proprietor's husband. An expert operation, they switched at every other street corner to secure their cover, keeping in constant touch with each other through discreet earpieces. She was never lost and certainly never alone. Whatever happened, the instruction was to keep her in sight at all times, find out whom she met and secure her safety.

Maloney, Dougie and the team had taken up position, but only after Philip had arrived. Curiously, he too had arrived early and watched Esmèe's entrance. He let her sit for almost half an hour before walking coolly up to her with, it appeared, not a care in the world. He too, Maloney assumed, was interested in seeing if anyone had followed her.

So, from the dark interior of the bar across the square, Maloney had watched the drama unfold. From the shadows he observed her. He watched her gesticulate, could almost follow the conversation by the vigorous movement of her hands and the visual contortions of her face – so confident – no, so attractive. There was something different about this indomitable woman across the square, something bullish. In her anger, the vulnerability and sadness of before was replaced by something, something almost powerful, and he liked it. He shifted uncomfortably in his seat, the stirring in his loins an inappropriate but not unwelcome reaction to his charge.

"What do we do now?" Jorge asked when Philip, taking his beer, with a charming smile joined the two laughing brunettes sitting at the opposite end of the bar.

Finishing their drinks, the detectives left the bar and strolled off in the direction of their jeep which was parked on an adjacent street. Once out of earshot, Maloney relayed instructions over the earpieces to the remaining agents.

"Tio, you stick to her like glue," he instructed and watched as a short-haired Spaniard nodded discreetly in his direction then picked up pace to follow Esmée. "Let us know the moment she leaves the hotel. Leon, go into the bar and watch him. If he leaves, follow him. We'll track you from the car." He turned to Jorge. "We have to keep an eye on this one. This guy is a small link in a big puzzle. Our job is to find the other pieces and make them fit."

They sat into the jeep and listened to the rain patter on the roof.

Maloney's pulse was racing. So he was alive. She was right all along.

"Well done, mate!" Dougie slapped him on the shoulder from the back seat. "You were right on the money with this one!"

They should be celebrating, Maloney thought, but something left him cold. He wasn't ready to cheer just yet. He thought about Esmée making her way to the hotel and wondered what was going through her head. What would she do next? She had no idea that they were there, watching her. The question now, he speculated, was whether or not she would, once back in Dublin, disclose her engagement with her assumed dead husband. Would she turn him in? Then he brooded over Philip back at the bar getting acquainted with his new female companions, flirting openly and enjoying himself according to Leon's report. He longed for the day when he could confront him, in a secure cell, get right under this git's skin to see for himself just what it was that made this asshole tick and wind him right down. He was close, so very close. All that remained was for him to bide his time.

Chapter 24

Esmée's very own war council met late on the morning of her return. Though ignorant of the presence of her inconspicuous travelling shadows, Esmée had suspected the consequences of her Spanish liaison would not move well in her favour. Unable to think clearly, the commotion of her thoughts creating pandemonium inside her head, she had called her brother for help. How she ended up with this 'family reunion' she wasn't quite sure.

"You never were good at secrets," she'd proclaimed in disgust, assuming that the inclusion of her sisters in this tryst was her brother's only treacherous indiscretion.

"Don't!" he'd warned with a raised finger. "This involves all of us and you know it. Anyway, they'd have killed me if they ever found out I'd kept this from them."

The meeting was headed at the top of the table by Tom, spinning a pen between his thumb and index finger, Lizzie on his right scribbling furiously, Penny on his left looking at Esmée like a lost bird, Fin next to her, solid and calm.

Esmée faced them all, numb and weary, and recounted the encounter with Philip.

"Right, so," Lizzie announced. "Let's just go through this one more time . . ."

"Oh, for Christ's sake, Lizzie, do we have to do this again? I'm tired, I've been up all night." Her head flopped heavily into her cupped and clasped palms.

"Yes, yes, we do. Whether you like it or not, you need to be prepared."

"For what?" she challenged. "What are they going to do, arrest me?"

"Don't be facetious, Esmée," Lizzie rebuked her. "You have to go to the police and, yes, they very well might."

"What for?" she argued. "I didn't know it was him."

"That may well be," said Lizzie, "but they may just as easily argue that while you weren't sure, you had a fair idea . . ." Her raised eyebrows begged a further retort.

Lizzie was only trying to help, Esmée knew that. It was her job as a lawyer to ascertain the facts. But going over and over the same details was mind-numbing and frustrating. She wasn't even sure she knew herself what had just happened. The lack of sleep and emotional energy was severely impairing her ability to think straight.

Having spent months wondering 'Alive? Dead? Dead? Alive?' the answer was troubling. She had spent so many hours living the moment in her head, the moment when she could face him, could ask him all the questions that had been stacking up. She had rehearsed her 'How dare you?' speech in the mirror because deep down she always knew she would see him again. Call it denial or defiance or just plain stubborn, she had never fully accepted that he had committed suicide. And now that the anxiously anticipated episode had passed, she couldn't tell if she'd done it justice. Reviewing the conversation didn't help much either as she only found fault with the bits she had said and the words that ultimately failed her. She should really have slapped him, kicked him hard where it hurt most, and was truly disappointed she hadn't. And now, here she was: stuck in the same time warp, right back where she started, at the kitchen table with a mug of tea in her hand, surrounded by Fin and her brother and sisters.

And now? What next?

Somewhere outside the realms of her consciousness they were discussing consequences – her actions, his actions, his probable return – because the authorities were bound to bring him back. And like a plague he was bound to spill his malodorous poison upon her children and sully their lives, just as they were beginning to be comforted by the warmth of a new life, a good life, a much better life than before. They were happier. Yes, they missed him, but freakishly the man they missed no longer existed. The night he left his car on the cliff the persona of Philip Myers really had drowned. Christ, how was she going to explain that one when they were old enough to be told? A wave of nausea engulfed her as the weight she had been carrying shifted from fear of his death to fear of his life.

"So we're agreed, that's what you'll need to do," Lizzie concluded, placing a professional hand on her sister's arm.

"What? Sorry. I was miles away."

Exasperated but sympathetic, Lizzie repeated the conclusions from the last twenty minutes of conversation which had apparently passed Esmée by unheard.

"You and I will go to see that garda fellow, what was his name again?" She turned to Tom.

He shifted uncomfortably in his seat. Now was a good time to come clean and tell them that Maloney already knew, but he daren't. He didn't have the nerve. Together his sisters were an indomitable force and he knew Esmée would kill him, so he kept his mouth shut.

"Maloney."

"Right – Maloney, that's the man."

"What, now?" Esmée interjected.

"No time like the present."

"Now?"

"Yes. Now."

"Ahhh, hang on! I-I'm not ready" she stuttered, stumbling over the words, feeling cornered by the decision she had no part in making.

"Ready for what? All you've got to do is tell him what happened and anyway I'm in court in the morning so it's either now or tomorrow night and I'm not sure waiting will do your case any good."

"Can Tom not go with me?"

"As your lawyer, for the moment anyway, I'd like to be with you. This is pretty serious stuff, Esmée, and I want to make sure you don't land yourself in it."

"I can't go now, Liz, I'm wrecked. I need time to think, get my head straight."

"I'm sorry, Es," Lizzie stated formally, "but in order to lessen the impact of what you have done you need to go as soon as possible."

Esmée took a deep breath and quickly flashed through what exactly it was she had done. In summary, all she had done was stand up for herself and, actually, she thought as she surveyed the four perturbed faces gazing back at her, she needed to do just that again, right now.

"Guys," she said firmly, "I know you all mean well but before

I tell them and they bring him home, which we are all agreed they will, I need to make sure we're protected and ready. So we'll go to the police when I'm ready. And not before. But I promise it will be soon."

Lizzie opened her mouth to object but was faced with the raised palm of her sister and the calming hand of Fin on her arm.

"Fin! Tell her! She really must do this, and do it now!"

"Lizzie, let it lie. Now isn't the time. She's exhausted."

With no other option, reluctantly Lizzie gave up. "Just don't do anything stupid," she warned and closed over her pad.

"I won't, I promise," Esmée smiled, hoping to reassure her younger sibling.

Waving them off, Esmée felt a chill down her spine and hugged her cardigan closer to combat the feeling of foreboding: there was a storm coming, of that she was sure, and she needed to batten down her hatches.

Although exhausted from the day's and yesterday's events, she wasn't able to sit still either. A tremendous sense of urgency motivated her to move and to act quickly. As far as she was aware, she and now her siblings and best friend were the only ones who knew that Philip was alive, so she needed to act before the truth came out. On top of that, there was also the as-yet-unconfirmed investigation into the missing cash that was still to come. And then there was Brady: the less she thought about him the better. Her solution was full separation. She had to distance herself from him in all senses of the word.

She had contacted a solicitor named Paul Collins some weeks back. He appeared to be a gentle, soft-spoken man but, Lizzie claimed, was a Rottweiler in negotiations. When they met first the conversation had been about Philip's assumed death. Now that he was alive, things needed to take a different turn. She was tired of being the victim, tired of the endless cups of tea, the war councils and family conferences that all centred round her and her issues. Enough. It was time to take control. She had the advantage of advance warning and needed to use it as a lever and be prepared for what was to come. She might not have been the architect of her past, but she would make damn sure she was the architect of her future.

Now she lifted the phone and told Paul Collins she needed to see him as a matter of urgency.

* * *

They met in his office and, once Paul confirmed that as her solicitor everything they discussed, outside of money laundering or criminal assets, would be protected by client confidentiality, Esmée told him everything: from Brady to Spain, she left nothing out. If he was surprised, he didn't show it but listened intently without interruption, every now and then lifting his pen to jot down some notes.

Finished, she sat back, tiredness beginning to consume her. Her lids were heavy and her head lightheaded.

"Well," he proclaimed, "this really changes things, doesn't it?" He smiled warmly. "Esmée, you have nothing to worry about. You will get through this in one piece and with your dignity intact."

She could have fallen asleep there and then, she was so relieved by her confession and comforted by his words. He, Paul Collins, was going to take care of her.

And Paul had been busy. He'd completed all his discreet enquiries, quietly gathering the facts but without giving his strategy away to anyone who cared to take an interest in what he was doing. Although the DPP had been naturally tightlipped about how they planned to run the case, a "reliable source" close to the case was able to advise a little on the allegations of fraud and based on that was able to speculate, hypothetically of course, what might be coming down the line.

Paul was also able to tell her that because Philip was Robert and Robert was still alive and by all accounts still married to Julie, Esmée wasn't his wife in the eyes of the law, so she had no responsibility regarding his actions or liabilities. He talked through Philip's properties, drawing little sketches and diagrams on his notepad to help explain and link all the pieces. He listed the bank accounts held in his name and the amounts in each. There were five in total and they were all more or less empty. Except for one: the only one in their joint name, which held the princely sum of seven thousand euro and which she could legitimately access. But Esmée wanted none of it. And even though she was absolutely entitled to at least a fifty percent beneficial interest in the house, the home, in which they had lived together as a couple, she just didn't want it. She had already moved out and now wanted out fully. And as for the money, well, she she'd cope. She would find a job and survive. She just wanted ties severed and a clean slate to start again. She knew Lizzie would have something to say and was likely to preach about what was rightfully hers, but Esmée wanted nothing more out of the relationship except separation. She didn't expect Lizzie to understand, but could deal with that eventuality in her own time.

"And there is also a safe-deposit box which is held in . . ." Paul checked his notes "the ABAW Bank."

"A safe-deposit box? I didn't think banks still used them?"

"Apparently so."

"Why did he have that?"

"That, Esmée," he replied sympathetically, "I cannot tell you."

"Well, how do I get into it?" she asked, curious about whatever it was Philip held so dear and so precious – or so incriminating – that it had to be kept in secret.

"You can't, well not immediately anyhow."

"Why not?"

"Because," he replied matter-of-factly, "you need either the body or the living person to do so."

"What the hell does that mean?" she asked, getting impatient with Paul's cryptic witticisms.

"It means Philip needs to be pronounced dead for you to have access, and even then you would need to apply to the court for permission. You are no longer," he reminded her, "his next of kin."

"But that's crazy, can we not just go into the bank and ask for it?"

"I practise the law, I don't write it," he smiled back in response.

"A safe-deposit box," she muttered to herself. "What was he up to?"

"Again, Esmée," Paul replied with a shrug of his shoulders, cupping his hands to the skies.

Esmée smirked at this. It wasn't his fault Philip was a devious bastard.

"Do you know how long he's had it?"

Paul lifted the sheet and scanned it.

"It appears he took it out in 1996."

Esmée did the quick sum in her head. "He can't have," she challenged. "He was still Robert then. Philip Myers only came to life by my guess around 1999."

"Well, that's what it says right here," he replied. "See for yourself." He handed her the page.

"Holy shit!" she whispered as she scanned it. "I'm now completely confused. Philip Myers, you have me stumped!" She handed it back to him, stating defiantly, "Well, I need to get into that box if only to find out what the hell he was involved in. He has taken me for a fool this long . . ."

"Well, then I suggest you go bring your non-husband back

because that's the only way you'll be able to do that," Paul offered, closing the file on his desk.

She left the office not so much in a daze as in a trance, over and over asking herself the same questions: What was he doing? What had he got that he wanted no one else to see? And how can I get into that box?

The beginnings of an idea flickered in her head as the doors opened into the foyer. Logic and reason tried to bat it back to the depths of her mind from where it was spawned, but stubbornly it refused to die. It gathered momentum as she walked down the street in the damp and blustery autumnal day.

It might work, it could work, she reasoned with her common sense and conscience. Risky but possible.

Teetering on the edge of conviction she quickened her pace, plucked her phone from her pocket, searched for the number then dialled Julie's mobile, determined to put an end to Philip's manipulation.

On the day she and Julie first met Esmée hadn't revealed her identity or relationship to Robert. She didn't think she had to, but that had now changed. Now she needed Julie. But whether Julie wanted to be part of it was a whole other question. They hadn't spoken since that day, so this call was likely to seem more than a little strange.

Julie answered after four long rings.

"Hello?"

"Hi, Julie, it's Esmée Myers."

"Oh. Hi, Esmée. How are you?"

"I'm good – you?" she responded, bursting with a need to just get on with it.

"Great, thanks. What can I do for you?"

"Are you around today? I need your help."

Esmée declined the initial suggestion of coffee around the

corner from where Julie worked – it wasn't an appropriate place to reveal herself completely.

"Why don't I call round to you this evening?" she suggested.

* * *

When they met that evening and had settled with mugs of tea in Julie's kitchen, Esmée introduced herself properly. She told her everything. How Philip and she had met, how they dated, then married and then how their life together had fallen apart. Telling her was as much therapeutic for Esmée as it was awkward. It helped that she and Julie were connected by their experience: they were both victims of Robert's manipulation, but likewise they were both survivors.

Julie's reaction was one of stunned but distant shock, like she had built up a Robert-proof blockade around her and was impervious to any pain either instigated or directly caused by him. Esmée both admired and doubted her resilience, not convinced that anyone could be that anaesthetised. But she drew encouragement from it and could see a glimmer of hope that she might indeed to able to persuade Julie to help her in cracking open the safe-deposit box.

* * *

A week later Esmée and her companion entered the old-style high-domed banking hall for the first time. Like something from Mary Poppins it hummed with the quiet hush of the daily activities.

"I can't believe Mom finally agreed to this," Harry whispered to Esmée as they approached the counter that circled its perimeter.

"Me neither," she whispered conspiratorially in return. Her legs shook, her stomach churned and her voice quivered. She couldn't believe she was doing this herself. Where was the cautious, risk-averse woman who only last week would have balked at an idea like this, never mind concoct it? "But what's the worst they can do? Arrest me?"

"Ehh, yeah!" Harry replied, his stomach jigging with nervous excitement. "But don't worry – we've got this covered. Trust me," he promised confidently.

"Are you sure you understand what happens if this goes pear-shaped?" she asked. "It's not too late to say no. We can always turn around and leave."

"We're here now," he said, as they reached the counter.

* * *

"I'm sorry, Esmée, but I can't agree to it. I hardly know you. And I'm not sure I appreciate you even suggesting it," Julie said from her stool at the breakfast bar.

"Suggesting what?" Harry asked suspiciously, entering the room.

Both women turned and looked at the young man, blessed with his father's good looks.

"Nothing," Julie said firmly, giving Esmée a look that told her the conversation was over.

"Mum," he asked again, this time with more purpose, "what's up? What's happened?"

Esmée was tempted to speak but decided against it. Julie had already decided and there was no point in pushing it. She was right anyway. It was a ridiculous idea, an irresponsible, reckless, risky and illegal act that if they were caught at could land them both in jail.

Julie was standing now and Esmée took it as a signal for her to leave.

"I'm sorry, Julie. I didn't mean to upset you. It was a stupid idea and I'm sorry."

"Mum?" Harry prompted.

"Just leave it, Harry, please!"

"If you don't tell me now I'll just follow her," he pointed towards Esmée who was ready to leave with her coat on and her bag slung over her shoulder, "and make her tell me!"

"Just go," Julie said, turning to Esmée, disappointment evident in her eyes.

True to his word, the key was hardly in the ignition when Harry knocked on the car window.

"Tell me," he said firmly.

"Sorry, Harry, it was a preposterous idea. I shouldn't have asked, shouldn't have even considered it in the first place. Your Mum is right. And I can't tell you without her permission." She put the car in gear. "You'll need to ask her," she said with finality, released the brake and drove away, feeling dense and humiliated.

What an idiot, she told herself, banging her fist on the steering wheel.

* * *

Just after she had put the children to bed, their story read and lights out, her phone rang.

It was Julie's number but Harry's voice.

"I'll do it."

Esmée smiled down the phone, his gesture warming her heart.

"Harry, you're a good man, really you are. But your mother is right. I had a remarkably dangerous notion that I have now dismissed. But thank you anyway." She could imagine Julie having a complete meltdown – she would if the roles were reversed. No matter how strong or how urgent the need to see whatever was in that box, was it really worth the risk to her and to Harry?

Julie came on the phone.

"He wants to help. He's sure he can do it."

"Thanks, Julie, but I can only imagine the fight he's put up. You're his mother. You trust your instinct. I appreciate his offer, but I shouldn't have even considered it in the first place."

"Yes, there was a . . . discussion, of sorts, this afternoon," Julie confirmed. "But he really wants to help you – he likes you," she said, giving an unconvincing chuckle down the phone. "But he said some things to me today that he has never expressed before. There are a lot of demons inside of him, all centered around his father. This may help him face a few of them. Make him feel like he's doing something, setting things to rights, finding justice." Her voice quivered on the last words and she paused for a minute, obviously overcome.

"But, Julie, we both know it's a crazy idea. If we get caught . . ."

"I know. And he knows. But it's his decision now. He's old enough, so he says, to make it."

Esmée felt nevertheless that she should make the right decision for all of them and refuse to go ahead. But then they would never know what was in that box . . . and it could be something that would make a significant change to all their lives.

"Okay. May I speak to Harry again, please?"

"Hi." Harry was back.

"Let's agree to make you up. But if both your mum and I aren't convinced you look the part, we back down and call the whole thing off. Okay?"

"Okay."

* * *

289

They dressed him in a beige cord blazer, polo shirt and chinos.

"I look like some kind of throwback to the eighties!" Harry objected.

"It makes you look comfortable," Julie argued, fixing his hair, recently styled to look like Philip's, with flecks of grey appearing now at each of his temples.

"I don't see what was wrong with the suit."

"It was trying too hard," she reasoned. "This has to be natural. Think George Clooney in *Ocean's Eleven*."

"I can do that," he grinned but then glanced back at himself in the mirror. "But not like this – I look like shit!" he moaned, poking at the bags under his eyes from an instructed sleepless night. "But I could live with this," he added, stroking the week's worth of facial hair that had been cultivated across his mouth, cheeks and chin. Neatly clipped and trimmed it gave him an all-important look, distinguished and mature.

Costume complete, he came down the stairs for a final inspection.

Neither Esmée or Julie said a word, as both were thinking the same thing: he was so like his father. Tears welled in Julie's eyes but never spilled. They were convinced.

The picture in Philip's passport that Maloney had only a fortnight ago returned to her was about seven years old so the age gap, visually, was not extreme. The biggest risk would be if the bank staff actually knew Philip – well, then they were stuffed. However, Esmée believed that risk was slight. The statement Paul had given her didn't show any transactions against the account connected to the box, and he had no other accounts with that bank, so the risk, they all agreed, was worth taking.

Esmée voiced what they were all thinking. "Only one way to find out!" She handed him the brown leather attaché case. "Don't forget this – it's a vital part of the operation."

* * *

"Can I help you?" the man standing tall behind the counter, dressed in a navy-blue suit, asked.

It wasn't too late, Esmée deliberated, her heart palpitating dangerously. She had to keep her hands clasped to stop them from shaking. They could just turn around and leave now, no harm done.

"Yes," Harry said quietly, expecting his voice to echo. "I'd like to access a deposit box. Please," he finished, minding his manners.

"Certainly, sir, and your name is?"

"Myers, Philip Myers," Harry said slowly and clearly.

"Thank you, Mr Myers. If you could bear with me, please, just one moment?" He again smiled and both Harry and Esmée smiled back, watching him slip behind a screen to a cluster of desks.

Harry took the opportunity to check on his accomplice.

"You doing okay?" he asked quietly.

He was remarkably calm, she thought, scarily so. Confident and charming, just like his dad . . . a compliment she chose to keep to herself.

"I'm good," she lied as the bank official returned, still smiling.

"That shouldn't be a problem, Mr Myers. Can I ask you to take the lift – just down that hallway there?" He pointed to a narrow corridor to their right. "If you go to the lower ground floor, Imelda at the desk will take care of you from there."

They thanked him in unison then turned and made their way to the lift.

It took a moment for their eyes to adjust from the brightness of the banking hall to the dull corridor and the even darker lift.

Harry pressed the button. The lift whirred loudly and stopped with a jerk.

291

"Just remember," he instructed quietly as the doors opened. "I'll take the lead."

The doors opened straight into a waiting area where a golden deep-pile carpet with dark-red walls and an oversized teak desk greeted them. A long comfortable sofa was positioned to the right matching timber side-tables at each end. Massive table lamps straight out of a five-star hotel lobby cast a warm hue over the discreet space.

A curly-haired young woman smiled expectantly at them from behind the extravagant bulk of the desk. She was well turned out, her shirt pristine and the bow in her bank-issue cravat-style scarf perfectly folded and sitting neatly just in the hollow of her neck.

"Mr Myers," she greeted. "Mrs Myers?" she asked as much with her eyes as her tone.

Esmée nodded.

"I'm Imelda. How can I help you?"

"I'd like to access my safe-deposit box," Harry stated confidently, placing his attaché case on the countertop.

"Well, you've come to the right place anyhow," Imelda returned with a professional well-groomed smile. "May I see your account number and your identification?"

"Certainly," Harry replied, opening both latches of the attaché case with an abrupt click. He took out the statement Paul had given Esmée and Philip's passport and handed them to the still beaming Imelda. Both he and Esmée tensed as they waited for her to inspect the documents.

Then, as practised back at the house the day before Harry turned to Esmée and asked her quietly, "So, Es, what time is our appointment with Dave?" His familiar tone and the use of Philip's pet name for her sent shivers down her spine. They hadn't practised that.

From the corner of her eye Esmée watched Imelda open the passport and glance up briefly at Harry.

"Eleven, we're meeting him at Luigi's," she replied to Harry, ignoring the sudden urge to vomit.

"Are you sure you want to do this? We don't have to buy it if you don't want to."

The meaningless words sounded casual enough, she thought. They were performing well. Harry launched into his rehearsed response while she watched and waited.

Imelda had pretty hands, Esmée thought, with beautifully manicured nails and long slender fingers. Weird the things that pass through your mind as you're waiting for the world to crash down around you. Her knees threatened to give way, the suspense killing her nerves. She steadied herself against the desk and watched. She could feel Harry beside her but couldn't hear a sound. Was he even breathing?

"You have your key, Mr Myers?" Imelda asked politely, bringing Esmée back to reality with a slight start.

"Yes, of course," Harry replied, immediately taking a set of keys from his pocket and selecting the smallest on the ring – the one Esmée had noticed on Philip's keyring that evening in the car. She didn't recognise it then, but knew instinctively on leaving Paul's office what it was for: the key to her very own Pandora's box.

"That's perfect," the lovely Imelda claimed, laying a document on the countertop. "If I could get your signature here – and here," she said, pointing to two 'x's.

Harry took the pen and signed Philip's name. Almost perfect, Esmée noted, seeing the familiar loop of letters.

"If I could ask you to be patient just a little while longer, we'll get your box ready for you. Please take a seat." She indicated the comfortable couch. "Can I get you anything? Tea? Coffee? Water?"

"No, thanks," Harry declined. "We're grand."

Careful not to give it all away, they shared a discreet gleeful glance to celebrate but no more. They were nearly there.

Intensely curious about the contents of the box and aware that the reason for its surreptitious concealment was not likely to be a good one, Esmée was nevertheless distracted by the thought of Philip and his likely return. Although happy that by the time they managed to find and repatriate him he wouldn't be her problem any longer, there was still a worry about how he would react when he realised she still didn't plan on having anything more to do with him. She doubted he would take it well and, if his behaviour in Spain was anything to go by, it wasn't going to be an easy journey. Part of her, a not so savoury part, wished that he'd stay right where he was, not come back at all, and found a bizarre irony in the fact that not so long ago she was willing him to turn up alive and well. But his presence now, given all she knew, was likely to cause her more grief than his absence. Maybe she wouldn't say a word at all: she could just leave him there. He'd never be able to come back here, not with Brady looking for him, whatever about the authorities. But they were fleeting thoughts, ridiculous notions arising from an even more ridiculous predicament.

A serious-looking young man, dressed in a pristine charcoal-grey suit, sky-blue shirt and a deep-blue tie decorated with a neat pattern of the bank's circular emblem, eventually emerged from behind a thick door clad with timber panels to conceal its secure fabrication. They matched, he and Imelda, their uniforms perfectly co-ordinated. He was hardly out of school, and with such a serious face Esmée wondered what made such a handsome young man look so surly.

"Mr Myers, Mrs Myers, I'm Andrew," he said without so much as a smile "Please follow me and I'll take you to your cubicle."

In a booth no bigger than a toilet she and Harry stood and

stared at the box laid in the centre of the table. A small thing, no bigger than a shoebox but stronger, formed out of some kind of grey metal.

The door gave a quiet thud as it closed and the room acquired a claustrophobic oppression. They both remained standing and stared at it for a while, Harry relieved he'd got away with the deception and Esmée nervous of what was contained in the box. Slowly she reached her hand forward and placed it on the metal lid. It was cold to touch but very smooth. She circled her fingers cautiously then taking its edge lifted it only inches at first to peek inside, afraid of what might jump out at her. When nothing moved and her nerve grew, she opened the hinged top fully.

There were two things inside: a notebook bound in black leather and an object wrapped in what looked like a white cotton tea towel. She put her hand in and lifted it slightly and, as soon as she touched it, felt its weight, recognised its shape beneath the rough cloth, she knew just what it was. Aware of Harry looking at her eagerly she cast him a glance to which he responded with a slow nod. She removed the bundle from the box and undressed it slowly, holding her breath as she removed the folds of cloth. The gun sat black, solid and menacing, dangerously alluring against the white cotton fabric. She knew what it was and exactly what it meant. The ramifications of the find and conclusion she reached about its association settled with repugnant certainty.

"Holy shit!" Harry exclaimed. "What the fuck?"

"Come on," she said, the air in the room beginning to thicken around her, the breath tightening in her chest. "I need to get out of here or I'm going to suffocate." Re-wrapping the gun, she placed it and the notebook in her bag.

Harry took her hand as they marched down the steps of the bank.

For a fleeting moment Esmée had almost felt sorry for the

lovely Imelda as she waved them to the lift. She would be in some mess when eventually it was discovered that someone other than Philip Myers had breached the bank's thankfully pretty-damn-lax security systems.

"Are you okay?" he asked, squeezing her hand gently.

"Not really."

"What are you going to do with it?" he asked.

"I have no idea. Just please don't tell your mother."

"Don't worry, Esmée. I understand the implications of our find. I'm not going to tell anyone. Especially not my mother – she'd have a breakdown. She says she's okay, but she's not. This might push her over the edge. I have to think about Beth too – she mustn't know. I'm not going to say anything. You have my word."

She had no option but to trust Harry. He was no threat, his focus being his mum and protecting her.

* * *

Julie was waiting for them when they arrived back.

"Thank God you're okay! You made it!" she cried, relieved they had returned alone and without a police escort.

"He was brilliant," Esmée enthused, following behind. "I literally couldn't have done it without you both! Thanks."

"Well?" Julie asked expectantly, looking at Esmée. "What was in it?"

"Not what I was expecting, that's for sure!" Removing only the notebook from her bag, she handed it to Julie. She and Harry had already examined it in the car and could make nothing of it. Inside the pages were filled with names and dates and a series of disjointed words.

"Yeah, a complete waste of time and effort!" said Harry.

"I was expecting so much more," Esmée said sadly.

"Like what?" Julie asked.

"I have no idea," she shrugged, "but just something more than this."

Julie was flicking through the pages of the notebook. "It doesn't make much sense, does it?"

"A code?" Harry offered.

"Absolutely no idea," Esmée replied, not caring one bit about the black book. She just wanted to get out of there. To be alone. To think.

"What do we do about this?" Julie asked, waving the book. "It must mean something to someone?"

"We can't do anything," Esmée said. "If we do they'll know we got into the box."

"Right," Julie signed. "Duhhh!" she laughed, relieved that the ordeal was over.

*   *   *

Robert watched the mayhem unfold as Tommo walloped the guard and Brady yelled at him.

"What the fuck did ya do that for?" he shouted, pointing at the unconscious guard and whimpering Mike, bloodied after the kick to his head.

"He was goin' for me," the aggrieved Tommo complained.

"For fuck sake! We agreed no shit would go down today! And you morons have already done damage to yer woman and maybe her kid." Brady whacked him hard across the face.

Tommo dropped the gun as he struggled to remain standing. He put a hand to his face and just as he turned his head to object he saw her reaching out. Amanda had freed her hand and was straining towards the panic button fixed to the underside of the table. Tommo yelled and lunged forward but Brady got to her first.

"You stupid cow!" he yelled, grabbing her wrist.

In the ensuing panic nobody noticed Robert pick up the gun and didn't heed when he left the room and closed the door. He hurried to the window and checked through the blades of the blinds if anyone had heard the shrieks.

Frank Gill was walking across the small asphalt car park. He'd done the cash run a few months back and Robert recognised immediately who and what he was. Why was he here? Could he hear the commotion inside?

Robert panicked as the undercover garda leaned down to the window of the silver Golf, their supposed getaway car, glistening in the glorious sunshine, and looked towards the bank.

He was coming over. He'd be at the door in minutes to investigate the delay with the delivery, to see where the helmeted men with the empty steel cases were. He'd see. He'd ruin it. Ruin it all. Silently he willed him to turn around and leave. He wished him away but he kept coming.

"Turn around – turn around," Robert whispered.

The alarm bells shattered the morning air.

Ironically it was Brady himself who had set them off. Having successfully stopped Amanda's attempted lunge for the panic button, he had stood upright and as he fixed his flopping hair looked down with contempt at the cowering woman. He didn't heed Mike sitting behind him, his back to the wall. He didn't notice as Mike raised his leg and foot, pulled back, aimed then pushed forward to reach the target of Brady's backside. Instinctively Brady's hand reached out to brace his fall and grasped the edge of the table, his thumb pressing against the discreet little white button underneath.

"Fuck," Brady whispered to himself.

The loud bellow of the alarm erupted into the early morning, causing everyone to jump, including Frank Gill who stopped for only a brief second before putting his hand to his hip. Robert mistook the reach for his phone as a reach for a gun. Adrenaline rushed to his head. Rushing to the door he unlocked and yanked it open it a crack, raised his arm, gun steady in hand, and pulled the trigger. No one was going to screw this up for him, especially some curious Pig. No way. There was still time, they could take what they needed. The gun fired and the projected bullet reached its target. Clean. Decisive. Deadly.

The banking hall was empty. All the activity was out the back. No one saw him do it. Firing from inside the door, he was out of the line of vision of Maurice Mahon, the driver of the undercover police car, who didn't even hear its loud recoil with the banging din of the bells. He watched him fall and cursed the silver Golf as it jerked into gear and accelerated away. The gun. What to do with it? Where would he hide it? He scanned the room quickly, looking for a spot. He knew they'd search the bank, then he'd be snared without doubt. An immediate calm, an almost psychotic moment of clarity, came over him: he was still the victim, he was his own cover. He quickly pulled up his trouser leg and pushed the gun into the leg of his sock, firmly wedging the nose into his shoe. He was still the victim. They'd not search him. And he was right. They didn't. His decision to keep the gun was a calculated one. He might need it again. It had both Brady's and Tommo's prints all over it: good security, if needs be.

*   *   *

Through the night she sat on the floor, her back to the wall, watching her children sleep soundly. She couldn't sleep. How could she? This was where she felt safest. She didn't want to be alone but couldn't call anyone. Philip had destroyed her and there was no way she could tell anyone that she had, albeit unintentionally, brought her father's murderer into their fold.

As soon as she'd left Harry and Julie, no longer buoyed up by their company and the excitement of their joint enterprise, her spirits had taken a plunge. Now, vulnerable and alone, she sat out the dark hours with tears streaming unrelenting down her face. She had reached the bottom of her endurance reservoir, with nothing left to give. She prayed for an epiphany, the moment where a solution would appear like an apparition to set everything right.

When it did come, there was no blinding flash of inspiration but rather a dispassionate logical reasoning that made perfect sense.

The sun was rising when she powered up her computer and Googled his name. She had come across a wealth of information about him before so she knew what she was looking for. He was a dangerous man, but Esmée knew that this was the best thing, the only thing to do. Terrified, but focused, she played out the morning as usual, taking the children to school, and then booked herself a cab, leaving a handwritten note on the kitchen table, in case she never came back.

"Where to?" her driver asked as she climbed into the back seat, his eyes meeting hers through the tinted rear-view mirror, dark but smiling.

She felt in her bag for the comforting bulk of her gym weight, foolish protection she knew, but reassuring all the same.

"Town, please."

"No problem, love. Grand day, isn't it?"

"Sure is, great to see the sun for a while." Deep breaths, she told herself, settle into the journey and when we're halfway in, then ask.

She could feel his eyes on her reflection and worked hard to combat the magnetic urge to look back. She needed to pee.

"Going anywhere nice?" he asked as they passed through the third set of lights.

"Eh . . . Nowhere special really, just a trip into the shops, that's all."

"My wife loves the shops, she does," he enthused. "She'd spend all me cash in those posh boutiques if she had her way. Does your hubby not mind ya visiting shops in the middle of the week?"

The mere mention of the word hubby and her heart skipped. A coincidence? Probably. Possibly not.

"Do ya not have a taxi company of your own out this way? It's a fierce journey all the way out here then back again. Gonna cost ya!" His head shook. He was laughing at her.

It was too soon, she knew, but she came out with it anyway.

"Actually, I like, I mean prefer, this company. A friend of mine owns it."

"A friend, you say?" This time she caught his eyes flicking at her. "Are ya sure 'bout that? You don't look like the sort to be hangin' out with my boss, and I've known Jimmy a few years now, I'll tell ya!" He held her stare for seconds that went on for hours.

"I haven't seen him in a while." The shake in her voice a dead giveaway. Her knees trembled and her heart ticked like a time bomb – any more and she, if not her bladder, would burst. "I wouldn't mind catching up with him again. Is he about?" She held her breath.

An electric silence prevailed for another three sets of lights. Red, Red, Amber. He didn't reply.

"Well, if you do see your boss, tell him I'll see him, today, same place as last time at twelve noon."

He dropped her, as requested, at the corner of O'Connell Street, taking her fare, and a considerable tip. She watched him drive down the quays then made her way to the station to catch the train home. She could hardly believe what she had just done. Her own audacity amazed her while the quake in her knees threatened to topple her altogether. Calm yet scared, she wondered what kind of a fall she was setting Philip up for, or herself if it all went wrong.

* * *

It felt odd to be in the park without the children. Rogue hollers of "Mum" triggering the instinctive reflex of her head while she sat on the same bench as last time, patiently, waiting. She had no idea if he would turn up, didn't know if she'd given him enough time. He was obviously a busy man. Her sudden empathy disturbed her.

She sat down on the bench in the middle of the playground and waited. Almost half an hour had passed when she spotted the taxi driver from her morning trip standing at a distance from her. Hands in his bomber pockets, he nodded to her and then walked in the direction of the exit. Assuming he expected her to follow him, she got up and followed him to his cab.

He was already sitting in the front seat with the engine idling – waiting for her, she supposed. This time she sat into the front seat. The door wasn't even fully closed when without a word he shifted the car into gear and hit the road towards the city centre.

The entire journey was travelled in silence. She sat still, with her hands clasped nervously in her lap. She kept him in her peripheral vision but he didn't so much as sneak even one curious glance at her.

Twenty minutes into the trip, he indicated and pulled into the car park of a pub on the outskirts of the city, in a landscape dominated by industrial units and vast open waste ground.

"Come on," he said, getting out of the car, and waited for her to join him before walking towards the entrance. "You've got some balls," he commented, shaking his head as they crossed the car park then walked ahead, not waiting for a response, and held the door open for her to pass through.

Her eyes took some time to adjust to the subdued light inside the bar which was a reverent throwback to the mid-seventies. Like an aging hooker, years beyond her libidinous glory, dressed in faded red-velvet embossed wallpaper and sporting crimson crimplene wall-lamps with dripping red-tasselled pleated shades, it cast a tone, a devilish hue, of what you might catch if you stayed too long.

The smell of stale beer, vomit and disinfectant turned her stomach as she ventured towards her host, perched on a high stool at the brown painted bar, highball in hand. Whiskey, she assumed. He drank long from his glass, putting it down, empty, on the bar as she approached. He didn't stand up.

"I'm not sure I like surprises, Mrs Myers." His eyes took their fill of her from top to bottom, predictably lingering momentarily on her chest. "Still lookin' good though." He intended to intimidate and reinforce his power.

But Esmée, quaking on the inside yet calm on the outside, stood tall in front of him, with her thumbs hooked into the back pockets of her jeans. She let him look. She'd known he would. She didn't care.

"So. What's the story? You're not missin' me, are ya, Es?" He let his laughter fill the vast but empty open-plan pub and watched her discomfort intensify.

He leaned over the bar and nodded to the shadows from where a skinny lad appeared, in jeans and a white T-shirt.

"Sorry about this, Es, but ya can't be too careful." Using his hand he swept the boy towards her.

Fleeting cold panic filtered through her like sand through a sieve as the boy swiped his hands across her body, under her arms, creeping between her legs and down her spine, leaving nowhere untouched. This was his job and he did it without so much as a smile.

"She's clean."

"Good man, Des. Now the bag." And as the heavy satchel was taken from her shoulder he got down from his stool and led her to one of the booths that wrapped the perimeter of the room.

"Drink?" he offered, releasing his grip on her elbow so she could slip into the leatherette seat, then sitting opposite her.

She wanted nothing, but her performance demanded that she accept. To get out intact she needed to display some strength of character and, despite the urgent desire to decline and run, she met his eyes and replied firmly, "Gin and tonic would be good," willing her voice not to give way to the coward fighting to escape inside. Leaning forward, she rested her folded arms on the chipped veneered table.

He snapped his fingers and a barman appeared who took his order and departed. Brady waited for the drinks to arrive, which they did almost instantly, before he spoke again.

"So. I'll ask ya again. What's the story?" His tone was firm but lacked the degree of menace she had experienced before. He eyed her curiously.

The relationship had changed. By searching him out, she had traversed the void from victim to informant and with that Esmée was rewarded with a fragile element of control. Her stomach and its contents tumbled like a cement-mixer. Conscious of her precarious position, she wanted to choose her words wisely and well. Now was not the time to be verbose.

"I've seen him. He contacted me."

"Ahhhha! Just like I knew he would!" Like a wicked wizard, his hands clapped loudly with glee. "So, where is he then?"

"Spain."

"You're fuckin' kiddin' me! Es-fuckin'-spana?"

Esmée nodded.

"What did he want, or need I ask?" His smutty smirk defied an answer. "Did you tell him I was askin' after him?"

Esmée nodded twice.

"And? What did he say?"

This was the point she had been dreading. The news that

Philip didn't seem to give a shit about Brady had the potential to incense the beast before her, to her detriment. Cringing inwardly, she gave it to him like it was.

"Nothing."

"Nothing? That fucker said nothing?"

She didn't know whether to shake or nod, but he wasn't after any further answer.

"The little bollox. Who the fuck does he think he is?" he said, his pitch increasing dramatically as the sentence progressed, punctuated by the slap of his fist on the table, so hard their drinks, and Esmée, hopped.

He saw her fear, noticed her cower. Incensed, he leaned over the table to shout into her face. "Does he really think he can fuck me over, play dead and get away with it?" His words were wet with disgust. "Not bleedin' likely!" He stood up and went to the bar. She watched him grip its rounded edge, lean towards it then push back to slap his palms down with a loud thunderous crack. Taking a moment to gather himself together he wiped the flyaway stands of hair back across his balding head and nodded to his right. As before, as if from nowhere, the lad appeared from the wings. Brady leant over and muttered something into his ear that made him move and disappear swiftly through the double doors between the optics.

Brady paused before turning back to retake his seat. Esmée watched with trepidation as his shoulders squared up and his chest broadened only to deflate slowly as he, chewing on the information, observed his guest quivering opposite him like a newborn lamb.

"And why are you telling me?" he asked.

There it was: the question she had been asking herself all afternoon. Why was she telling him? What did she hope to achieve? And what exactly did she want in return?

All through the night the mood of her thoughts had been one of rancid incredulity. How could she have let this happen? She had been the subject of such a gargantuan ruse: a sustained act of subterfuge that reeled her in and spat her out. How could she have let it happen? How could he have allowed their children become a heartbreaking consequence of that colossal sham? What kind of a twisted sick bastard was he? He was responsible, start to finish, conception to delivery, for the death of her father, for the lie they were living and now for tarnishing of their beautiful, innocent children's future.

She was and always had been nothing more than an extremely good cover for what he had done. It wasn't the guilt that drove him to find her, but fear of being found out: fear of being uncovered as the murderer of Frank Gill. If he had a conscience at all he wouldn't have allowed children become part of his lie. But he had. And they were. And that's why she was sitting in this dive with this particular character. It was an age-old cliché, but yes, she was doing it for the children. She would keep Philip's secret. She would maintain his charade. Not only that, she would guarantee that his violation would never, ever be uncovered. And after that all she could do was hope that, when the time came for Matthew and Amy to be told about their father and who he really was, they would understand and forgive her.

But that was none of Brady's business; he didn't need to know her reasons why, so instead she played to his ego.

"This evening my sister, as my lawyer, is taking me to report my evening with Philip to the Gardaí." She paused, lifting her head to make direct eye contact with him. "So I figured you'd find out about it pretty soon after."

"I'm flattered," he responded, accepting her unintentional compliment.

"With all due respect, Mr Brady, I took your threat –"

"Easy does it there now, tiger!" he interjected, raising an admonitory hand.

"Sorry, your advice, I took your advice seriously and, well, I'm not willing to put myself and my children in jeopardy, and frankly, you scare me more than my husband does."

"Again, I'm flattered." He paused with a short bow as he sat, judging her and her motive. "So, where exactly is he?"

"Before I give you this information I need you to promise to stay away from us. That we are done." If she was standing her knees would have given way. She was petrified but adamant that the parts she could fix she would.

He smiled, raising his eyebrows in a mix of admiration and respect. Nodding slowly he scrutinised her face, deciding whether or not to agree, deciding whether or not to slam her cheek. But she had guts. He liked that. And that prick Bobby was no friend of hers now either by the looks of things. So he took a little punt, lifted his hand, spat in it and offered her his word. She contemplated his extended hand with its now moist palm and measured the implications it presented: to take it meant she was in bed with the devil. To decline closed the door on any chance she and the kids had at a normal future. Better the devil you know, she mused and took a firm grasp of his hand and shook.

She took a piece of paper from the front pouch of her bag and handed it to him, holding on to it a little longer than she expected to, before finally letting it go.

"That's where I met him – he's around there somewhere." She took a gulp of her drink, the first and only, but she needed it. Putting it back on the table, she stood up. "I'd like to go now."

He watched her cross the faded and pockmarked carpet, calling her name when she reached the door. She stopped, turned and waited for him to speak.

"No message for the hubby then?" he called, his sharp smirk

307

betraying his intentions and for a fleeting instant she feared she'd made the wrong move. Eyeing Brady for the last time, she allowed the moment to pass.

Rather him than us, she justified to herself, then turned and left the building without uttering another word, wiping the palm of her hand off the leg of her jeans.

Chapter 25

Writing his name in urine before his supply expired was about the most exciting thing Dougie had accomplished in the last three weeks. Not even the sound of the crickets in the heat of the night sounded exotic any more. Proving his ability for the hundredth time, only this time adding his middle initial to demonstrate his prowess, he smiled, pulled up his fly then returned to his colleagues in the van, wiping his hands on the legs of his trousers as he walked.

Tio, having returned with coffee and pastries only minutes before, objected vociferously to Jorge's lack of hygiene as he selected but returned two cakes to the cardboard tray before settling on a temptingly flaky almond cookie. Dougie was no linguist, but even he didn't need a translator to interpret the foreign expletives uttered through flailing gestures. Smiling to himself, he concluded that the basic principles for stakeouts were the same worldwide regardless of rank. This was his twenty-fourth day in Spain: having drawn the short straw, literally, he had dropped Maloney back to the airport almost two weeks previously and been left to liaise with the team locally. If he never saw another jug of Sangria for the rest of his days he'd be happy. Inspector's exam or not, this wasn't what he'd worked his way up the ranks to do.

"Well, someone has to do it!" Maloney had teased just before he'd headed off, back to the reassuring chill and drizzle of Dublin.

Dougie had spent the majority of the twenty-four days sitting outside the villa shrouded in beautifully tended shrubbery on the east side of the town, just watching. In alternating shifts they observed and documented the movements of the suspect, Robert Toner, aka Philip Myers. They were monitoring his calls, photographing his encounters and tracking his every move. And it was as boring as hell. As far as Dougie was concerned there was no 'second man' or even an accomplice and this was just a massive waste of everyone's time and money.

Villa Mena was a prime piece of property. Rented in the name of an apparently fictitious Julio Martinez, with excellent, but also fictitious, credentials, the villa was perched high in the hills with a magnificent view of the valley and sea beyond. There was only one viable entrance route to the front of the house with a side entrance that led from the kitchens, wrapping itself around the property and back onto the street about fifty metres from the main gate, serving as easy access for the housemaid and waste disposal and collection. A twin garage with automatic doors faced onto the street, its roof doubling as a patio for the guest bedroom, which gave access to the teak balcony that cantilevered majestically over a lush, tiered and carefully tended landscape. But the foremost striking feature had to be a most inviting infinity pool carved into the ground with sweeps and curves, spilling over the edge as if down into the valley below. Toner aka Myers was a lucky man and, it transpired, a creature of habit: getting up at the same time, jogging for an hour before returning to shower, then Continental breakfast in Los Billares – like clockwork, every morning. During the day he toured the local resorts, ate in neighbouring towns or topped up his tan by the pool at the villa. By night he frequented a few of the local bars and restaurants – alone, to start, but often he would stumble home late with a companion or two. Each guest was photographed and scanned through the database for recognition, with no luck so far. For over three weeks now they watched him gallivant with little contact with either the "real" outside world or the underworld.

Munching on his cake, Dougie wondered just how long more of this he'd have to endure, deciding to make contact in the morning with Maloney to arrange for his return to Dublin pretty damn quick. For the moment, though, all he could do was watch the outside of the house and listen to the incessant bickering inside the van.

Tonight, it appeared, Philip, once again, had company. According to the roaming unit, he'd picked her up in La Palmera, a popular disco bar in town, consumed more than a few drinks with her, danced badly, then obviously invited her home. They fell intoxicated out of the taxi outside the villa, their drunken stumbling and laughing making it next to impossible to get a good picture of her. Under the cover of a blanket of long silky black hair and the fake-fur collar on her short jacket, her face was obscured. The image was crap and collectively they agreed they'd get a better one when she left. Like randy schoolboys they swapped fantasies, in poor English for Dougie's benefit, using hand gestures and mime, about the antics and acrobatics likely to be performed in the villa that night. Between sniggers and guffaws the monotony of the hours was endured, only interrupted by the heavy trudge of the refuse van and the calming whoosh of the road cleaner. When the morning shift team arrived, Dougie had had enough and was glad to go back to his meagre albergue to sleep and dream of his return home.

While he slept, the refreshed surveillance team waited outside the villa for the anticipated departure of Philip's guest. And they waited. But by ten thirty there was still no sign of either Philip or the girl. They called headquarters. At eleven fifteen a parcel was deployed for delivery. By eleven thirty the courier was banging on the door of an empty house.

*　*　*

Picking him up, she was told, would be easy. He preferred vivacious brunettes and liked to drink Bourbon, straight, with ice. She was given a recent photograph, a list of his favourite haunts, a heavy sedative powder and fifty per cent up front.

They were right. He was easy. Within an hour of spotting her mark she was sitting knee to knee with him at his table, having danced the Lambada and established a shared love of Jack Daniels. He was surprisingly good company. She didn't have to work too hard – in fact, she kind of enjoyed his company and kissing him was thrilling. If she could only enjoy all her nixers this much. Pity she had to put him out: she suspected he'd be great in bed.

Another life, she mused, dancing provocatively against his hips, disappointed by the idea that in this one she wouldn't get to follow through. So she was happy to gyrate a little longer, but when he suggested they leave, she didn't protest. They laughed the entire journey home and literally fell out of the taxi at the heavy gates that opened onto paved steps up to the villa door. Aware of the van, she manipulated her hair, arms and hand gestures so that her face was never in clear sight. Inside the door he was putty in her hands.

"A drink?" she suggested.

"Sure. Champagne?"

"Only the best!"

The powder effervesced to nothing almost immediately. Not a trace. Although she imagined she could taste it on his lips. Turning on the music, he invited her to dance and they sashayed over the short-pile rug, moving well in the beginning of the synchronised seduction, while he nibbled at her sweet-smelling neck only to, little by little, stagger and lurch clumsily as the drug took hold. His wandering hands missing their target, flopping limp by his side, as her neck morphed from nectar to night nurse. Sleep followed a blurred stupor and then he was cold. Stroking his face tenderly, she gave him one last kiss before turning on the TV, draining her own glass and waiting for her signal to leave.

The text came no more than an hour later and, as instructed, she left from the kitchen and followed the path that led past the pool to the bottom of the garden, where a faint track guided her towards the back wall of the garden next door. Taking a deep breath, she gingerly walked the narrow rough trail between it and the steep drop into the valley below. She felt rather than saw the track even out and, reaching out to her side, felt leaves instead of stone. Bending to her hands and knees, she tentatively felt out the discreet gap in the shrubbery she had been assured was there and, shimmying through it, found herself in a large garden and in no time was back onto the road, out of sight of the van she knew she had to avoid. Scanning left to right, she fixed her dishevelled skirt then walked the distance into the town centre to pick up a cab home. She was tired and had an early start in the morning.

Laying her head on her pillow before switching off her nightlight she wondered about poor Philip and what might become of him. She had learned not to ask. He didn't get another moment's thought and she was, in minutes, sleeping like a baby.

* * *

Like smoke they arrived, filtering without a sound, slowly spreading their deadly touch as they swept the house. Fully clad in black from head to toe, with soft soles and gloves, they moved through the villa, six in total. They crept through the house like ninjas, silently and methodically wiping every surface of all evidence of both its tenant and his guest. Without words they moved from room to room, communicating with their hands in a sharp military language learnt at a camp deep in the countryside.

When they were sure that all traces were eradicated they turned their attention to Philip, sleeping soundly now, on a plastic sheet in the centre of the living-room floor, naked except for his Armani boxer shorts. He was picked up and thrown over a shoulder and carried towards the back of the house, through the kitchen out to the rear yard, and placed carefully into the tall black-plastic waste bin. One of the intruders pushed the heavy container towards the side passage and down toward the service gate where he positioned it and then waited, deadly still but listening.

Inside the house the collected items were bundled into black rucksacks and positioned comfortably on the backs of the remaining ninja sweepers, leaving hands free, just in case. Then they walked to the service gate where they too waited.

They felt the truck first though their feet, then heard its trundle as it rode slowly over the uneven surface of the road, pausing every few minutes to pick up its next load. As the decibels increased and the vibrations intensified, one moved forwards and silently unlatched the gate, as another pushed the bin forward, then retreated around the corner and again, waited.

The refuse truck coasted slowly past the surveillance van,

coming to a stop at each villa gate to collect the bin. The occupants of the van did not heed the faces of the grimy council workers as they lugged the heavy vessels to the truck, hooked them to the mechanical arms and watched as they were hoisted and tumbled in mid-air, meeting the ground again with a heavy thud. Nor did they heed the bin that was lifted but never returned, nor the bins beyond Villa Mena that were never collected.

The shadowy figures left the way they had come, moving gracefully despite their heavy loads along the perimeter hedge, blending into the shrubbery and down the cliff face into the valley and the awaiting Land Rover.

Chapter 26

Not for the first time the security guard ran the kids off the land. These abandoned sites had become their playgrounds through the recession. Between them and the scavengers hunting for valuable trash, he had his work cut out for him. At one time there was money in these wastelands with long-since-forgotten machinery and equipment fetching hundreds, sometimes the odd thousand, euro. But these were nothing but material graveyards now, their wealth long since plundered. There was nothing left but relinquished dreams and unfinished grey and seamed concrete skeletons.

Wandering aimlessly, doing his rounds in the blistering heat, he lamented the good old days when opportunities were plentiful and dreams actually came true. In the far right corner, a wet patch, like an oasis in the desert, caught his eye. He couldn't explain to the authorities later what made him investigate – maybe it was his naturally curious spirit that instinctively told him something wasn't quite right – but whatever it was that lured him to it, he soon found himself digging away wet clay and loose rubble that filled a deep perimeter trench. The sun beat down on his sweating back as he cleared the hole to find, at its bottom, what looked like an old white chest, face down, its edge piercing an old water main. The trench had obviously started its life as a small hole, made bigger over time as the water seeping slowly out gradually eroded the disintegrating cast-iron pipe. The chest was heavy, but not so much that he couldn't move it, and heaving it slowly about he realised it was an old fridge. He let it drop back onto its proper base then stepped back for a breather. The force of its drop as it hit the ground and bounced a little broke the seal to let the old door open to a crack. Wiping the sweat from his brow, he put his foot to the door, fitting the steel toe of his boot between the door and the frame, pushing its rusted hinge with little difficulty. The stench that followed pressed hard into his chest, stealing his breath. Falling back, putting his hand against the dirt trench walls to steady himself, he couldn't have been less prepared for the contents that spilled out in lumps over his feet. The heat, combined with the moisture, obviously had been a pure breeding ground for the array of insects that poured like lava from the sarcophagus that had remained shut for months. His screams carried well in the still shimmering heat of the afternoon air, all the way to the village. Heads turned briefly in the direction of the echoing hills only to turn back again, disinterested, to the activity at hand.

The dismembered body tumbled from the box as he clambered from the hole, shrieking like a banshee. He had never experienced anything like it, not in his forty-five years, nor was he likely to see anything like it again. The image would haunt him: the sight of the decomposed body parts, putrid and decaying, and among them a band of rotting elastic bearing the name of Armani.

Chapter 27

One year later

Matthew stood like an angel on the altar of the church. His hands were held in prayer and his eyes were closed in semblance of deep concentration as he waited for his name to be called in the roll call of First Holy Communicants. He opened one eye, just a bit, to see if his mum was watching and seeing that she was smiled a big grin down at her. As his name was called he snapped shut the peeping eye and promised God to be a good boy. He looked so grown-up standing up there in his navy pinstripe suit – his choice, wanting to look just like James Bond – with his hair perfectly brushed and white rosette gleaming on his lapel. He was so handsome and such a great kid. Esmée felt so proud she could have burst. He had coped so well these last few months and had, through school and his First Holy Communion classes, appeared to have found solace in God, which, given his age and her own feelings on the Catholic Church, she found difficult to deal with. She supposed it was because through his innocent faith he still felt a connection to his father who was now, apparently, an angel in heaven, or so Matthew insisted. If only he knew. Matthew prayed to his angel father each night before bed and each morning as he rose. It repulsed Esmée to listen to his gentle mumbling but, despite her disquiet, she couldn't and didn't discourage this one comfort he had found.

"I wouldn't worry, sis – it's just a phase – he'll grow out of it," Penny had remarked when Esmée mentioned it to the girls. "It could be a boy thing too, you know – girls tend to be more open and talk about their feelings."

"I'm not worried, really, it's just an . . . observation more than anything else."

"Would you two ever leave the boy be?" her mother scolded, listening to them chatter. "There is absolutely nothing wrong with him – he just misses his dad who, you two need to remember, in his own little world was perfect."

Looking at him now beaming down at her, she agreed with her mum: she didn't need to worry. He was doing just fine. Thankfully Amy was just that little bit younger and more interested in her Barbie than what was going on around her.

She felt awkward sitting in the pew. The last time she sat in a church had been for Matthew's First Confession. How ironic, she thought to herself: confession! She felt uncomfortable then and even more so now. She could almost feel the crucifix vibrate overhead. But the shameful thing was that she felt no guilt. She wasn't sorry at all. Defiant in the face of her spiritual accuser, she was more than happy to justify her actions. Sitting there watching her son and seeing how like his father he was, both in looks and mannerisms, she thought about Philip. It used to be that she thought about him several times each and every day, mostly in anger. But that had passed and he had only recently stopped being her most frequent thought of the day. After her encounter with Brady she knew he'd turn up, one way or the other, but she didn't think it would take as long as it did. For three long months she had waited for news. Every knock on the door, every ring of her phone set her nerves on end. When word eventually came it was a relief.

* * *

As soon as she opened the door to him, she knew why he was there. Even though Maloney had become a regular visitor to the house, finding one excuse after another to call on her, this time his body language gave it away. Everything screamed 'sorry' from the get-go: from the stiff upright crane of his neck to the submissive lowering of his eyes. Before he'd even opened his mouth she could tell his first words were going to be "I'm sorry" and he didn't let her down.

"I'm sorry, Esmée, but it's not good news. Can I come in?"

Then it was over. Philip was dead. For real this time. Like she knew he would be. She didn't ask how but she knew why.

He mistook her tears as those of grief rather than relief, and instinctively went to wrap her in his arms, but her impulse was to jump and pull back. Maloney wasn't subtle, his intentions were becoming more than a little obvious . . . but she couldn't go blundering into any relationship just now . . . she needed time to find her bearings, to heal.

Humbled by her rebuff, Maloney faltered and offered only a brief description as to where they had found him, thinking she didn't need to know the gruesome details, but when she did eventually ask weeks later he told her what he knew. She felt nauseated at how he had ended up and disturbed by how little remorse she actually felt. She was responsible. But, she justified, Brady would have found him regardless sooner or later – she had just cut short the wait. Was she really that kind of person, the kind who could commit hideous acts but still sleep at night without feeling culpable in any way? If she was, then really she was no better than Brady, although her motives were far more noble, and she had two: Matthew and Amy. They were the antidotes to her remorse; she just needed to remind herself of that as often as she could.

"Does Julie know?" she had asked Maloney that evening as they waited for Tom and the girls to arrive to "comfort'" her.

"Dougie is on his way there now," he replied, still feeling foolish from her earlier rejection.

* * *

The day after receiving the news that Philip had been found dead she had gone to see Julie, who'd opened the door with a weak smile.

"I was thinking about you this morning," she greeted her. "I'm glad you're here."

They shared a brief hug, a small gesture to their token grief, which neither really felt but both were obliged to pretend.

"There isn't anyone else I can talk to about Robert," Julie said after they had settled down in the living room with coffee. "Do they know how it happened or who did it?"

"No," Esmée replied, afraid to look up. "But they think Brady may have had a hand in it."

Had Philip been a good man, an upstanding citizen, a pillar of the community there would have been outrage over his death. An Irish man murdered in the South of Spain and in such hideous circumstances? How could this have happened? But Philip wasn't any of those things. He had defined his path, so people weren't surprised it had come to a bad end.

And now, with his death, real this time, both Esmée and Julie had some bizarre decisions to make.

"I can't bury him twice," Julie told her with an apologetic but resolute expression. "As far as I'm concerned he died years ago and I'm happy with that. I'm happy now. What he did to us. What he did to you, your children . . . I'm glad the bastard is dead."

But Esmée wasn't ready to let him go that easily.

* * *

It was an unusually cold day, but then it wouldn't be Ireland if it wasn't unusual. Only Esmée stood in the chapel of the crematorium, looking tall and elegant in a black shift dress, heels and her black mac, the same one she wore the day she met him in Spain. She wore a cerise pink scarf around her neck, a splash of colour, a gesture to represent life after his death. She held her arms crossed in front of her with her hand resting clenched against her mouth.

The priest stood embarrassed before her. He'd never done this before: presided over a funeral with only a single mourner. He had to insist on even this small ceremony. "The dead deserve to be forgiven," he had told her, a final act of humanity before sending them on their journey to the next life. He coughed politely, ill at ease but determined to do his duty whatever this man's sins.

"Dearly Beloved," he began, looking at her, the only member of the congregation, but she wasn't listening.

Esmée couldn't take her eyes off the simple, unadorned timber coffin. He was gone. She remained standing throughout the short service, the words and readings merging into one long murmur that made no sense at all. And when it was finally over the haunting guitar and flute combination of Gabriel Fauré's Pavane accompanied the casket as it rolled slowly back and only when the two sumptuous scarlet curtains met did she take her seat. There were no tears and no prayers; she was numb. She let the evocative notes play out their elegant but humble finale then stood up and left the chapel. Outside in the cemetery in the half-hearted sunshine there was no ignoring the white outhouse adjacent to the main building, its chimney billowing a light grey smoke up to the skies. She sat on a bench intended for serene meditation and watched him burn.

Where had the Esmée of last year gone? When had she become so hard?

* * *

A firm squeeze from Fin on her leg yanked her back to reality where the Communion congregation was getting to their feet to celebrate in song. So happy. So optimistic, and thankfully infectious. The church burst into applause as the hymn came to an end and her handsome boy along with all the other children made their way back to their seats.

"You were fantastic," she told him as she bent down to cuddle him and kiss the top of his head.

"Mom!" he protested indignantly.

Outside in the courtyard there were photographs and smiles. The entire family had turned out to celebrate, including Julie and Beth. Harry wasn't quite ready to make that leap, but Beth was curious about her little half-brother and sister. And they were welcomed by Esmée's family with open hearts, minds and deep curiosity. Sylvia hugged first and spoke after.

At Matthew's request they were having "a barbeque feast" back at Granny's. And it was just that, with Tom at the helm wearing an apron and a grin. Rarely in control in a kitchen, barbequed spare ribs and marinated prawns were his culinary saving grace. Sitting in the heart of the gorgeous garden, they ate the delicious food, drank chilled beers and homemade lemonade and laughed. Lots. Conversation flowed freely and banter rolled as Julie was welcomed into the fold through hilarious tales and intimate confessions of a family growing up. Esmée took pleasure in watching the barriers come down as between them. Her siblings cajoled and encouraged Julie until she could see her shoulders relax and her smile reach her eyes. At that moment she herself was more relaxed than she had been in months. There was real joy in her life and although Philip, despite his true passing, would always feature in some part in her conscience, she had closure.

* * *

That closure had come on a cold and windy Monday morning. She had driven to the cliffs, parked and made her way down the shale slope to the dirt track that wound its way like a belt around the cliff face. She, just like Philip, knew this trail like the back of her hand and she had mentally picked out the best spot, where the drop was most sheer. Was this, she wondered, how Philip had planned his disappearing act, working out the time, the day, the detail in advance? Only he never actually got this far down. She met no one as she made her way along the undulating path, envious of the seagulls as they effortlessly rode the air currents. The wind picked up spray from the waves, which crashed against the rock face below, and carried it up to pepper salt on her face. She could taste it on her lips when she stopped. This was the spot. This wasn't a ritual, but she needed to take a moment to think. Admiring the wilds of nature around her, she committed Philip's memory finally to the depths he had pretended to go to.

Glancing around to make sure she was alone, she took from her bag a small but deadly bundle. Unwrapping it from its cloth bandage, she drew back her arm as far as she could, then putting all her energy into her swing cast her arm forward, letting go of the black weapon with a jolt. She watched it fly and followed its trajectory, happy that she had given it enough thrust to see it well over the edge to be swallowed by the sea below.

It was gone and with it any chance of Philip being exposed as her father's murderer. The enormity of what she had just done was patently clear to her, but if there was a chance that she could spare her family more humiliation and pain then she would take it. She didn't want her kids growing up with that stigma. For that she would do time herself. And if her brother or sisters were ever to find out what she had just done, not only would they not understand but they would never forgive her. But they would never find out. She would never tell and she trusted Harry would keep silent too, to protect his own family.

* * *

The ring of the doorbell interrupted the afternoon.

"I'll get it!" Penny sighed when no one else moved.

Tom looked at Esmée with a raised eyebrow as a casually dressed Maloney followed the grinning Penny through the French doors and out into the garden.

"Don't say a word!" she warned, handing Tom her plate, and went to greet her guest.

With a hand at her waist Maloney bent to kiss her on the cheek.

"Thanks for inviting me."

"You're welcome!" she responded with a smile.

"Where's Matthew?" he asked, waving the obligatory sealed envelope in his hand.

"Money Bags is under there," she replied, indicating the underside of the table where her son was quietly counting and re-counting his day's earnings.

"A true banker in the making!" He smiled wryly.

"Maloney!" Matthew erupted from under the table, his eyes fixed on the tell-tale envelope.

Laughing, Maloney handed it over and Matthew, rewarding him with a big grin, dived under the table again.

"I see I'm not the only guest," Maloney noted, looking towards Julie.

"I know," Esmée beamed. "She's great! And Mum loves her! Come on, I'll get you some food!" Leading him to the table, she offered him the spare seat opposite Julie before heading back to the smoking barbeque.

"You really need to sort that out," Fin warned her from beside Tom.

"God, I know," Esmée shrugged, filling a plate for him. "He's a good guy, but . . ."

"But what?"

"Oh, I don't know. We'll see . . ."

"Have you kissed him yet?" Tom asked devilishly.

"No!" Esmée said quietly, looking over her shoulder to make sure he hadn't heard.

"And why not?" he asked, and she replied with a look that warned 'don't push it!'

"Leave her be!" Fin retorted, digging him in the ribs with her elbow, only to repeat his question: "So, why not?" Then she and Tom broke into immature sniggers.

Grinning, Esmée grabbed a slightly incinerated burger, turned and walked away, her head held high.

The remainder of the afternoon came and went. Esmée sat and observed the characters around her, enjoying the mood and relishing the smiles. She had done the right thing, of that she was sure, and that is what made all of this possible. From behind she felt a hand squeeze tight on her shoulder.

"All right?" she asked as Fin threw herself into the empty chair.

"Jesus, I'm wrecked!" Fin moaned, kicking off her shoes. "And my hair stinks of smoke. It's hard work, this barbeque lark!"

"Thanks for helping out today – you two played a blinder!" Esmée responded while stroking her young son's hair as he snuggled into her lap, fast asleep.

"Anything for you, m'dear!"

"For me or for him?" Esmée grinned, nodding towards Tom who was munching away on the last of the prawns.

"Whatever!" Fin responded with a smirk. "He's all right, is your brother!"

"You're not so bad yourself!" Esmée said.

A blushing Fin swatted the compliment away with her hand. "Ah, stop now!"

"No, seriously, Fin, thanks for everything these last months – you've been so good to me."

"You don't need to thank me! I've only done what any friend would do. You'd have done the same for me."

"Yeah, except you wouldn't have been so thick as to end up in my situation!"

"Ah, for God's sake, Esmée, cut yourself some slack! You weren't to know. And you've done an incredible job, you know that, don't you?"

Esmée shrugged, but had to admit as she surveyed the scene in front of her that she'd done all right.

"Couldn't have done it without you," she replied gracefully.

Fin reached across, took hold of her hand and gave it a gentle squeeze. She didn't let go, but held onto it and they sat in silence letting the conversations around them filter in and out.

"Look at that," Fin said after a while, nodding towards the centre of the garden where Amy sat cross-legged on the blanket while Beth brushed her hair and was introduced to each of her twelve almost identical Barbie dolls.

"She doesn't know herself," Esmée mused, smiling affectionately at her chattering daughter. "She thinks Beth is just hers."

She sat and contemplated the two girls, Fin's hand still covering her own, and whispered, more to herself, than anyone else: "From darkness comes light."